Prime
Witness

Steve Martini

First published in Great Britain in 1993
by HEADLINE BOOK PUBLISHING

First published in paperback in 1993
by HEADLINE BOOK PUBLISHING

A HEADLINE FEATURE paperback

14

ISBN 978 0 7472 4164 5

Typeset by Avon Dataset Ltd, Bidford-on-Avon
Printed and bound in Great Britain by
CPI Antony Rowe, Chippenham, Wiltshire

HEADLINE BOOK PUBLISHING
A division of Hodder Headline PLC
338 Euston Road
London NW1 3BH

To the mothers, Rita and Betty,
for their interest, care and love.

Acknowledgments

In the writing of this book special thanks are due to California Deputy Attorney General Ward Campbell for his help and assistance relating to the law of international extradition; to George Williamson, Chief Deputy Attorney General for the State of California, Criminal Division; and to Deputy Attorney General Scott Thorp for their assistance in providing color and authenticity to the veiled processes of the grand jury in rural counties.

A special word of thanks is owed to the California Attorney General's Criminalistics Institute and its manager Victor C. Reeve for valuable assistance in the technical waters of forensic science.

To Jim Bissell, QC, Director of the Vancouver Regional Office, Canadian Department of Justice, and Mr John M. Loo, Crown Attorney of that office, I am indebted for their assistance and guidance in the nuances of the Canadian extradition process.

To Mark Berg, of Auburn, California, the consummate criminal trial lawyer, I owe unending gratitude for his encouragement and counsel on all things legal.

And I am grateful to all those writers and lawyers who during the course of my writing have provided kind words of encouragement or advice, including F. Lee Bailey, Edward J. Bellen, Melvin Belli, Vincent Bugliosi,

---

Dominick Dunne, Clifford Irving and Edward Stewart.

In particular, I would like to thank author and lawyer John Grisham, whose kindness in public print and whose words of encouragement in conversation reveal a generous spirit unaffected by the winds of fame.

And, finally, but not least of all, to Leah who has spent innumerable hours listening to my readings and rantings and who has stood by me with encouragement and interest through long years of struggle. To her and to Meggie I owe the deepest debt of all.

To all of these and others who by oversight I may have omitted to mention, I owe grateful thanks for their advice and insights that have allowed me to craft a work of seeming truth. For any failings that a reader may find in this regard, I am solely responsible.

Prologue

They are the birds of darkness and noiseless flight, fierce and savage. On the dead fly, the great horned owl can pick the eye from its head in the pitch black of a moonless night. On more than one occasion they are known to have attacked man.

It will take only three more nights to finish the job for which he's been paid nearly a year's salary. Though the risks are high, it is the easiest money he's ever made.

As in the previous four nights he parks his car in the trees a half-mile down the road. He takes Harvey from his cage, loosens the leather traces and removes the hood from the bird's massive beaked head. He holds his arm straight, gloved fist elevated a bit, and sweeps it forward, the signal for the bird to take to the air. In a fluid motion a broad canopy of feathers opens overhead and the massive bird lifts skyward. It is a vision of flight, an analogy of animation perfect in its silence. He watches as Harvey disappears into the shadows of the trees and the half-moon-lit sky above.

Named for the six-foot fictional rabbit in a vintage Jimmy Stewart movie, Harvey is sheer stealth, six pounds of streaking death on the wing.

He listens, and, after a few seconds, hears the telltale ruffle of folded wings, the only sound of flight Harvey ever makes. It is the sign that the bird has landed, ninety feet above, in the massive madrone on the makeshift perch. This place, high in the trees, will give the bird a better angle of attack.

He locks the car and checks to ensure that it is far enough off the main road so not to be seen by some passing pain-in-the-ass motorist, or worse a county sheriff on patrol. But it is nearly a mile to the county highway, and nobody ever comes down the old abandoned gravel road, at least not at night. He picked this place from an old plat map of the property got from the county recorder's office. It was best not to ask the owner for too much help. The less he knew the better, for both of them.

He makes his way through the brush, across the shallow creek, to the base of the tree and begins his own ascent. This is made easier by the climbing gear erected on his first night, rappelling ropes and a harness called a leg-strap saddle. He sets the pin in the foot-cam that is fastened to his shoe and starts his climb.

As he moves effortlessly through the branches of the blood-red madrone, ten feet up, twenty, the rope coils on the ground beneath him like some interminable serpent. For this he avoided the taller pines and stouter oaks, and picked the madrone. It has smooth bark that doesn't flake off in the eyes as you climb, and no sap to foul the ropes.

In four minutes, hardly winded, he is up on the platform next to Harvey. The bird is perched on a limb a few feet away.

He checks his watch. It is nearly midnight. Moving swiftly, he frees himself from the entangling ropes and prepares to begin. At most there are five hours of darkness left.

Quickly he gives Harvey the scent, this from a small sack he carries on a tethered line from his belt, a little leather satchel marked by shiny metal studs. It contains blood, bits of flesh, pieces of vital organs from the previous night's work. The body count now stands at four. With luck he will add to that tally tonight.

With Harvey the pattern of ritual is firmly established, first the scent, then the flight, then the kill. If it is true to form the bird will return in minutes, with blood on its talons.

With little ceremony he dispatches Harvey into the skies, then stands, stone silent and alert, facing the sheer basalt cliffs that rise a hundred feet from the valley floor to the west.

He is always uneasy when Harvey is on the wing. It is an anxiety born of the freedom of flight, the knowledge that, after all, this is a creature that in the fickle flicker of a thought can disappear over the horizon never to be seen again. Like good fortune to the lucky, and the affections of a beautiful mistress to her lover, this bird of prey returns to its owner for a single reason — because it approves of the company. It is a chastening relationship, one which is always open to the question, who is master, and who is servant?

As his eyes strain for vision to the west in the dense night air, an unearthly scream issues from behind him, high-pitched like a cornered cougar in agony. Though he knows this sound, it sends a chill down his spine that it should come from the wrong direction.

Struggling for balance on the platform he turns, his gaze cast down through the canopy of leaves to a spot two hundred feet below, across the winding creek. And for a fleeting instant his vision is fixed, the figures fused in his mind like the flash of a strobe in the moonlit night. Then Harvey is upon him, unwieldy wings, blood dripping from his talons, and in one claw the object of his frenzied flight.

With the bird balanced precariously on his gloved fist, he wrestles with the sharp talons of the closed claw. He coaxes the thing from Harvey's grip, and it rolls upon his gloved and open palm. A bloodied remnant barely recognizable in form and shape, it sends a quick shiver of fear through him. And without thinking, he drops it ninety feet into the flowing waters of the creek below.

Chapter One

This place has the undiscerning smell of death about it. Horse flies and other buzzing things are thick in the noonday sun along the Putah Creek. I would have been here an hour sooner, but for the chaos out on the county highway, drivers rubbernecking, tourists getting a little extra on their trek from the Sonoma Valley.

We are perhaps five miles below the dam where the river is choked to a trickling creek among boulders and gravel the size of golf balls. The heat off the rocks rises like some invading horde of vandals.

There are people here I recognize but cannot name, cops I have seen in the sheriff's office in Davenport in the last few weeks. Some of these are tripping through brush and weeds up to their armpits, what police call the strip method for searching terrain, three cops walking at arms length combing an area in quadrants for anything unusual.

Across the creek, in the distance, I can see soaring cliffs carved in the black lava rock by the river before it was tamed at the dam. Running up to these bluffs is a tangle of trees, oaks and a few tall poplars, their branches nipping at the promontories.

But the object of my interest is on this side of the creek, behind the yellow band of police tape wrapped around a group of small trees. Inside of this there is a single moving

5

figure, hunched and low, scanning the ground. In a navy-blue police jumper with bright white lettering high on the back, the initials 'DOJ'. It is a woman, short, a little stodgy, one of the criminologists from the State Department of Justice.

I walk from my car and move toward the taped area, stepping on strands of a broken barbed-wire fence, stretched to the ground from rickety and rotting split rail posts. A small trashed metal 'No Trespassing' sign is on the ground, rusted nearly beyond recognition, like perhaps it has been in the dirt and mud for a dozen years.

I circle, maintaining a good distance from the center of the search, until I have an opening, a clear line of sight through the trees and underbrush. There in a depression on the ground I see them lying on their backs, their arms stretched as if in crucifixion, faces to the blazing sun, two bleached and naked bodies, their midsections streaked in congealed blood, the color of rusted metal.

The flies and insects are thicker here, and the stench of death stronger in the midday air.

The body closest to me, a male, has tightly clenched fists. Tied firmly with cord, these have turned the black-blue of death. The victims' limbs are stretched to near dislocation at the joints, pulled taut by what appears to be a plastic-coated cord, similar to that used in the earlier murders. Metal tent-stakes have been used for this purpose, driven deeply into the ground so that only a small portion of the L-shaped tip remains above the surface. There is some blood, not much, congealed on the lower abdomen. From this I assume that, as in the earlier murders, there is a fifth stake, driven hard, transfixing the victim to the ground. If true to form, this is the cause of death.

I had read the reports of the earlier killings. This one it seems always takes his victims in tandem, a man and woman together, staked out in the same fashion. In each case, college students. The cops and their shrinks who study such things tell me there is ritual to this, a signature they have now linked to at least two other double murders, one in the southern part of the state, Orange County, and the other in Oregon.

My gaze is fixed on the two victims stretched out before me on the ground, ten yards away. More than feeling the revulsion this causes, I am struck by the indisputable fact that this time the killer has departed from his pattern. The woman a bit overweight, what the coroner will in his medical euphemism call 'well nourished'. There is an undeniable mane, disheveled and unkempt gray, atop the man's head. This time the killer has not taken the young, the college students, that before have been his only quarry.

My guess is the man is in his sixties. Considering the agony of death, it is difficult to tell. As for the woman, while her body reveals the wrinkles and sags of age, I can posit no guess. I cannot see her face. It seems this is another of the killer's trademarks. As I survey this sorry scene I marvel at the quirks of fate that have conspired to put me here.

Even as a kid, Mario Feretti was a crazy son-of-a-bitch, one of those people whose life was a candle burning from both ends. Increasingly, in the last week, I am wishing I had declined his request when he came asking. Now, with the third set of victims not yet cold on the ground, my regret is growing deeper with each passing moment.

Mario came to me three weeks ago with his tale of woe. At forty-three, he was a candidate for a triple bypass. He was married with three kids in grade school. Two members of the County Board of Supervisors now wanted to ease him from his position as the elected district attorney of Davenport County. These were people for whom opportunity knew no bounds, no sense of propriety. For my part, saying no to Mario was not in the cards. When he came to my office, he was still the kid I remembered from sand-lot ball and summer raft trips on the river. Mario had deep-set wild eyes, two large olives floating on egg whites and a continence that seemed, even with its impending medical problems, still filled with hell. When he asked me to take a temporary assignment as special county prosecutor – just to fill in, a few months, no more, until he was out of hospital, back on his feet – I could not say no. I now live with the consequences.

I turn away from the bodies on the ground.

Thirty feet away there's a man, a face like weathered leather, the most prominent features of which are a slender arching nose and forehead furrowed deep as crevasses. He is spry and slight of build. It is this man who has called me here.

Soaking wet, Claude Dusalt weighs perhaps one hundred and forty pounds. Of Basque ancestry, the son of a migrant sheep-herder, Claude chased wandering lambs through these hills for his father as a child. For the last thirty years he has trudged the same ground for the county of Davenport, the sheriff's chief of detectives.

As I watch, he speaks in hushed tones to a cadre of cops,

a small group now gleaning their instructions for the widening investigation. One of Claude's assistants is dispensing a few things to this gathering, little baggies and some clear plastic vials. These cops, who are not schooled in processing the scene, will gather the common elements found in the surrounding area, seed pods and other plant materials that might attach to clothing, soil samples and humus from the ground. If they are lucky they might later find a match to these elements on a suspect's clothing.

Claude sees me, but makes no move in my direction, nodding instead to acknowledge my presence. A study in animation, he is busy again, this time ushering one of his cops with a video camera toward the yellow-taped area and the bodies.

With his hands Claude is motioning for specific camera angles, close-ups, I think, of the bodies, articles of clothing laid out in a neat pattern by the head of each victim, pants and shirt folded as if freshly laundered, like some doting mother might lay them out for a child. Then the bizarre. Over the woman's head the killer has stretched her panties, waistband down around her chin and neck, obscuring her face. Through the leg holes and under the crotch-band, which is stretched tight over the crown of her head, he has threaded her brassiere, each cup protruding through a separate leg hole, like some grotesque set of mouse ears.

I stand there, frozen in time, thinking back to how I got into this, to my visit ten days ago with Mario in the hospital. His breathing was labored. 'You won't have to prosecute,' he assured me. 'Just hold their hands during the investigation. Bless the warrants, any searches. I've talked to the judges,' he said. 'They're all on board.'

He told me that he was on the mend. According to Mario he would be back in the office in ninety days, plenty of time to prep for a trial if it came to that.

I wondered whose pipe Mario had been smoking. He looked like death heated in a microwave. Only three days out from under the surgeon's knife, a triple bypass that had drawn every ounce of animation from his body, left him pale, a gray-green ghost against the white hospital sheets.

A thin, clear plastic tube framed his face and tousled hair, like the ear plugs from a Walkman, but in this case these carried only the muted sound of forced oxygen emitted from little twin nipples, one seated firmly under each nostril. Through this I watched as a procession of bloody little bubbles inched their way from his body to the bottle, like some fluid hourglass reminding me that my time there, with him, was limited.

We talked for a brief moment about the murders, the on-going investigation. His breathing turned hard, Mario was shaking his head, as much as conditions would allow. 'Sick,' he said. He was reaching for the nurses' call button. 'Sick.'

I thought for a moment he was talking about himself, then I realized he was not. Mario Feretti was describing the thing I am now appointed to pursue – what the newspapers around this state are now calling 'The Putah Creek Killer'.

'The shrinks will have fun with the profile on that.' The voice jerks me from my reverie. It comes from behind me, here, near the creek.

I turn. It is Denny Henderson, Dusalt's number two. He

is looking at the bodies stretched out on the ground. Henderson is sandy-haired, hapless and overweight. He wears a white polo shirt, stretched like a drum over his paunch, on which I can see the shadowed stains of some ancient meal, what the whip-end of a strand of spaghetti leaves when inhaled. His face is pock marked, a victim of early acne.

'Denny. How are you?' I ask.

He shakes my hand. We are on a first name basis now that I am on the side of the angels. It has not always been like this. In Davenport, where I have, over the years, occasionally crossed the river to defend a client, Denny Henderson has always kept his distance.

'Any leads?' I ask.

He shakes his head. 'Just like the others.' He fixes his gaze on the two bodies. 'Man doesn't make many mistakes,' he says.

The police photographer is now shooting the metal stake holding down the male victim's clenched right fist. He takes two of these, one up close with a small ruler in the shot for detail and another further back for perspective. He follows this routine on each of the stakes.

'Sooner or later the guy's gotta fuck up,' says Henderson. There is frustration in his tone, and his words have the ring of wishful thinking.

Dusalt sees us together and motions Henderson over, some details he wants taken care of. I think perhaps he doesn't want Denny talking to me too long. In his own way Henderson is Claude's go-for, though he doesn't seem to mind this role.

Dispatching Henderson in the other direction, Claude is

now making his way toward me.

'Mr Madriani,' he says. 'I thought you should be here. I hope it's not too much of an inconvenience.'

'No,' I say. 'I'm glad you called.' We put a face on it, the usual pleasantries, like what could be better than hovering over death on the ground on a bright Sunday.

He shakes my hand. In this he is formal and stiff. He is one of those skinny men of wiry sinew. Claude has the kind of thin, worried expression that makes you believe his chief maladies might be ulcers or hemorrhoids.

'Because you are new, I thought it best that you be kept informed.'

'I appreciate it,' I tell him.

He has been called here from a picnic with his family. He is not happy with this, but he says his family understands. If this is true they are more accepting than my own.

'Do we know who they are yet?' I ask. I am motioning toward the two bodies.

'No identities yet,' he says. 'We'll check their clothing for IDs after we have all the photos.' The cops are not disturbing anything, not until they have precise drawings and photographs chronicling the location of every item around the bodies.

'Kids walking along the creek found them this morning,' he tells me.

He points toward two teenagers, one of them being questioned and the other twenty feet away leaning against the trunk of a patrol car. The one being questioned is flushed with excitement, the other is a little green around the jowls. Investigators will keep these two apart until they are finished with their interrogation, to insure independent statements, stories that can later be checked against each other.

'They were quail hunting,' says Claude, 'trespassing on private property. Flushed a little more than they bargained for.'

I look toward the bodies. 'The MO,' I say. 'Like the others?'

Claude makes a face, something from the Old World, a lot of wrinkles and a screwed-up mouth, then nods. 'Pretty much,' he says, ignoring the obvious, that these two on the ground are no college students.

It is the third set of murders in less than two weeks for this rural county where big news is usually the column listing the drunk driving arrests on Monday after a heavy weekend.

'We're trying to get the cast of a tire track. Out there off the gravel road. A single vehicle parked behind some brush,' he says. 'It's a long shot,' he concedes, 'could have been made by the killer last night. Could have been made by a family on a picnic last week.' He shrugs his shoulders. 'Also we got a partial shoe-print inside the tape.'

My interest is piqued a little with this.

'Looks like a running shoe, pretty small,' he says. 'We think it probably belongs to one of the kids. They got scared.'

'Understandable,' I say.

'They left little tracks like chicken scratchings all over the place.'

Over by the patrol car an evidence tech is taking a cast of

one of the kid's shoes to compare it to the partial on the ground inside the tape.

There's commotion in the brush beyond the tape, across the shallow creek, a dozen reserve deputies, part of the local search and rescue team. They have drawn the poison oak duty. One of them crosses the creek, moving toward Claude.

'Lieutenant, you should take a look at this.' The cop is in mud to the ankles of his heavy boots. He's wearing the togs of search and rescue, an orange jump-suit with belts and metal rings for every occasion. In his hand he has a plastic bag. Claude takes this in his open palm and examines it. A small, twisted piece of metal. It appears to be broken off from something larger. Dusalt makes a face.

'What is it?' he says.

'Part of a foot cam,' says the cop.

Claude shrugs, like this means nothing to him.

'Used in climbing ropes. I think you'd better come across the creek and look for yourself,' he says.

Claude moves away from me now, shouldering me out, talking to the officer. Their voices drop and I cannot hear them.

Ignoring me, the two men start toward the creek. Unsure whether I should follow, I walk behind them, a little tentative. Claude turns to look at me. From the pained expression I wonder if he's going to chew my ass for following, too many footprints messing up the scene.

Then he says: 'Forgot my boots.' There's a stupid grin on his face. Claude has driven here, like me, in the family sedan. His field clothing and boots are locked in a patrol unit back at the county yard. He looks down at his white training shoes, one-hundred-and-twenty-dollar Nike Airs, then shrugs a little. With that he is mud halfway to his knees following the other cop across the creek. I look down at my two-hundred-dollar Boston loafers that were handy in the closet when the call came in, and I think to myself, 'He who waits also serves'. Curiosity has its limits. I am stranded high and dry on this side of the creek, left to contemplate my circumstances.

What had begun as a case of caretaking for a friend is now a burden that monopolizes every aspect of my life. My wife is furious — ready, I think, to leave me — my child neglected, my private practice in Capital City twenty miles away is a shambles, all because this favor for a friend now consumes every waking hour. Two days ago came the crushing blow, a phone call at three in the morning, a voice I did not recognize, a nurse at Good Shepherd's Hospital. Mario Feretti was dead. The judges of Davenport County now have me strapped and secured for the duration.

I watch as Claude and the other cop move through heavy brush to the base of a large tree. I can no longer hear what they're saying. But the big cop is pointing up into the tree. I look, but I can see nothing. Several of the search and rescue guys are moving around. For the first time I notice there's an evidence technician there with them. Like the reluctant bride, they are helping this guy with something, a heavy belt around his waist. There's a little argument now, from the technician. 'I don't get paid enough . . .' His voice trails off. They are girthing this belt down between his legs now. Claude is busy, holding the guy's evidence bag and talking to him like a Dutch uncle.

One of the search and rescue guys reaches out with one

hand, and as he moves I notice it, gossamer in the bright midday sun, floating down like a spider's web, a sheer strand of rope descending from the trees above. They are clipping this thing to the belt around the technician's waist.

Three of the bigger rescue guys take hold of the rope and begin pulling hard. The technician is off the ground, the little evidence bag dangling at his feet. The three guys pulling on the rope start singing, a slow mournful chant: 'Haul, haul away, we're bound for better we-a-ther . . .'

Before they can finish the first verse they're all laughing.

'Go slow,' says the tech. 'Take it easy.' The man sounds like some kid about to be pushed off the high dive.

'Hang on tight,' says Claude. Another chorus of giggles. The technician is now twenty feet off the ground and rising fast. In three seconds he disappears through a canopy of leaves, like the space shuttle through a deck of clouds. From my angle across the creek I can still see him. And for the first time I can understand why he was not anxious for this duty. The man is now fifty feet off the ground, suspended only by a thin rope.

Claude has the palm of one hand shading his eyes like a visor. But he's lost sight of the guy. Seconds later he's tripping through the creek toward me and a better line of sight.

He's laughing when he approaches me. At the scene of a gruesome double murder it is the kind of jocularity that only men who deal in pain on a regular basis could understand. I feel like an outsider. My sympathies are with the poor evidence tech who is now dangling a good seventy feet off the ground.

Then I see it, above his head in a direct line, a small

wooden platform laid in the crotch at the intersection of two large branches. But for the rope leading to this thing, it is masked perfectly in the trees.

Claude has now made his way across the creek. He is trying to shake mud and water from his shoes with each soggy step.

I'm looking up at the technician. 'What is it?' I say.

'Probably bird-watchers,' says Claude. 'The rope looks like it's been there for awhile. Some of those people are crazy,' he says, 'goofier than the birds they chase. But we'll check it out.'

The evidence tech has made it to the platform. Holding the rope with one hand for dear life, he tries to maneuver himself up onto this perch with the other. This doesn't work. Only as a last resort does he release the other hand from the rope, lunging for the platform. He bounces off the wood out into thin air suspended only from the harness at his waist. He flips upside down. He's clutching frantically at the rope again, finally righting himself.

Claude is chuckling to himself. 'Good move,' he shouts. 'You have a positive talent for clinging to high places. You should go far in the world.' There's laughter across the river. This is not having a good effect on the man in the trees.

Words echo down: 'You come up here and do it.'

'You're doing fine,' shouts Claude. He's laughing to himself again.

On the second try, the guy makes it onto the platform, belly down like a beached whale. He's motionless now, lying there on the edge. I think he's either resting, or else he's paralyzed by vertigo.

'What do you see?' shouts Claude.

There's heavy breathing from above, some muffled words, then the clear message: 'Some fucking asshole in muddy tennis shoes.' The man hasn't entirely lost his sense of humor. Still, he hasn't moved an inch since arriving on the platform. He's clinging to it like a stranded cat. I am thinking maybe they will have to go up and get him down. Given the sorry sense of humor, I am wondering if maybe they might not prefer to shoot him out of the tree.

'Tell us what you see,' says Claude. 'Let's process it and then you can get down.'

Several seconds pass, with nothing. But the man is now moving around a bit on the platform. He's gotten to his knees, though he still clings to the rope with one hand.

'Find anything?' asks Claude. 'Tell us what you see.' He's getting impatient now. Several seconds pass with silence, then the words filter back from the trees.

'Blood,' says the tech. 'There's blood up here.'

I look at Claude Dusalt. He is no longer smiling.

Chapter Two

I can see Harry hasn't shaved in two days. He seems a bit chastened but happy, at least for the moment, to see me. He should be. I have a release order signed by a Justice of the Court of Appeal to get Harry Hinds out of jail.

Harry's invited over to dinner tonight, to talk about how to parcel up my practice, until I can crawl out from under the Putah Creek prosecution. Nikki went to get the makings for dinner. I came to get Harry.

'Fucking Acosta,' he says. The Honorable Armando Acosta, the judge from hell, carries a torch for the two of us. A product of the bad blood spawned during Talia Potter's murder trial. It seems Harry has not been as fortunate as I. He has not escaped Acosta's wrath. Since Talia's trial, 'the Coconut' has been taking his revenge on Harry. Always the political tactician, Acosta would never undertake anything so obvious as a frontal assault on a lawyer with whom he has had personal differences. Instead he lies in ambush for Harry who had only a small part in Talia's case, baiting him at every turn. With Harry this is not difficult.

'The man's an asshole,' says Harry. 'Certifiable,' he adds. His voice has gone up a full octave in these five words.

Everyone in the little booking room, mostly cops and

their collars, can hear him. Harry was just slightly more tactful in court, the antics that landed him here. The jailer at the counter, a sheriff's deputy I have not seen before, is no doubt taking mental notes. Acosta will probably know of this latest slander within the hour. Fifteen years of criminal defense practice has not made Harry Hinds a favorite with the deputies who do jail duty. Harry takes the little envelope containing his personal effects from the property clerk. I nudge him by one arm toward the door, before he can do more damage.

I've managed to steer clear of Acosta's court for seven months, ever since the verdict in the Potter case. To do this I've had to affidavit him twice. This is the process used by lawyers in this state to remove a judge from a case without stating the reasons. I cannot challenge Acosta for cause, his obvious bias, the thinly veiled animus he harbors toward me. To do so would be to invite the fury of his brethren on the bench. Such are the unwritten rules of this 'Sanhedrin' we call the judicial branch.

The successful defense of Talia Potter has become the high-water mark in my career to date. She had been accused of murdering her husband, a prominent lawyer in this city and a rumored candidate for the nation's high court. It was the first time that Harry and I had worked together.

Harry is trying to tell me what happened in court, as if retrying his antics to a sympathetic ear will somehow make a difference.

'I know,' I tell him. I'm trying to keep him quiet, at least until we get outside. Things have been escalating between Acosta and Harry. Two earlier confrontations resulted only in stern warnings from the bench, a dressing down in public court, in front of Harry's clients.

Hinds, for reasons I do not understand, perhaps he is just too stubborn, refuses to affidavit the judge, and the Coconut loves it.

I ran into Acosta's bailiff in the courthouse lobby on my way over here. He couldn't resist giving me his version of the details in a crowded elevator. 'Hinds was back-talkin' the judge,' he tells me. 'Judge Acosta had no choice.' This according to a man who does everything for Acosta including occasional spit-shines on the judge's pointy little wing-tipped brogues.

What happened was chronicled by the court reporter in the record, the version I used in obtaining the release order from the Court of Appeal.

Acosta had set Harry up with some bullshit rulings on evidence. This is one of the Coconut's specialties. Harry's objections were each hammered down from the bench, rejected by the court. Hinds sprayed Acosta with a few well-chosen insults. Harry says these were expressed under his breath. 'Private thoughts,' he now calls them, like the Coconut somehow invaded his privacy by overhearing these.

Harry gets a little sympathy from me on this. Though some of his more descriptive terms for Acosta might be considered statements of fact by those who know the judge better.

Harry says Acosta has an acute sense of hearing. Unfortunately for Harry the court reporter also had good auditory senses. It seems some of the juicier excerpts from his secret musings ended up as part of the court's record.

In the end Harry was ordered to pay a $300 fine. There is no dispute about what happened after that. Hinds reached into his pocket, peeled off five crisp one-hundred-dollar bills from a gaudy money clip he carries. He approached the bench and plunked these up high on the wood by the judge's gavel.

Without being there, I know Acosta must have had fire in his eyes. He is no grocery clerk trained to cashier money. But the judge couldn't resist one last shot. Looking at the little pile of bills he told Harry: 'You must have learned to count at the same place they taught you your manners, Mr Hinds. I said three hundred.'

Harry looked up at the bench, then told Acosta: 'Credit it to my account, your honor. I'm not finished yet.'

Acosta ordered him to jail for thirty days. This was clearly excessive, an argument with which the Court of Appeal has now agreed. Even an insult to the Coconut's imperious pride does not warrant thirty days in the Capital County slammer.

'You owe me one,' I tell Harry.

'Tell you what, you shoot the prick and I'll defend you – free,' he says. Harry's talking about Acosta.

I'm glad that we've cleared the jail. Threats against judges, even those in jest, don't go down well with the local constabulary.

Harry is now checking his wallet, counting the cash that was there when he was booked, bill by bill. Such is his trust of the cops. Jail does not seem to have shaken him much. I think that like the Man of La Mancha, Harry sees this little episode as part of some noble quest.

The usual throng of humanity is gathered on the steps

outside the jail. These are mostly relatives, or significant others of those inside, deciding whether to spring for bail, or to pay next month's rent.

Harry and I make our way through this army of jail house regulars and onto the sidewalk in front of the building. We head toward my car a block away.

Hinds is grousing that he needs a shower. It seems he could not bring himself to use the communal ones offered in the jail.

'After all these years I'd like to remain a virgin,' he tells me. Like most defense attorneys, even Harry has his standards. Defending these people is one thing, showering with them is something else.

I tell him we'll pick up some clothes at his place on the way. He can shower and shave at the house before dinner. My wife Nikki will thank us for this thought.

Harry falls behind, finally stopping at the newsstand on the corner. He joins the little mob hustling the vendor for a paper. He hits me up for four bits. It seems the jail budget doesn't include a daily newspaper. Harry wants confirmation that the world has carried on without him for the past forty-eight hours.

'I've got to pick up Sarah at the baby-sitter's in ten minutes,' I tell him.

'It'll just take a minute,' he says. Harry burrows his way into the loosely formed line, not in the British fashion of properly queuing-up, but with head down, right shoulder used as a wedge. Harry in line is like a mole in rutting season. My guess is he's after the sporting green. He's probably placed bets on the pay-phone from the jail. He shoves the guy next to him in line a bit. The fellow gives

Harry a dirty look, then focuses on me like maybe I'm Hinds's trainer for this bout.

This face staring at me is something from the past. We each stand there. One of those awkward moments. He is older, but I suppose he would say the same of me.

After ugly seconds of silence, he says: 'Mr Madriani. A long time.'

There is nothing overtly hostile in this. But his tone tells me that if he had his way, he would nudge me off the curb, under one of the fast-moving buses now churning by in the rush hour.

We stand there, Harry lost in his paper. I'm not sure whether I should introduce them. The mixture of Adrian Chambers and Harry Hinds could be volatile.

'It's been a few years,' I say.

'Ten to be exact,' he says.

I've not seen Adrian Chambers since his conviction for suborning perjury, and his removal from the practice of law. In his late forties, he has aged well beyond those years. Of the hair that I remember, generous brown waves, he now has only a gray fringe ringing his head above the ears. This is cropped close to the head, military style. He is, after all, a former marine. Around his forehead there are the subtle shadows, a few age spots like amoeba creeping under the skin. In the handful of times that he has graced me with it, I have seen a tight-lipped thin smile. It always had the appearance of being forced. It is not that the man is without humor so much as that his chief amusement comes from denigrating others. Adrian is a bundle of scorn, tightly strung.

After all these years, if I were to pass him on the street I might not recognize him at all — except for two abiding features, his penetrating dark eyes, cold as steel, and a hard athletic body, the lean and mean obsession of a former gyrene. Studying him here as we each take the other's measure, I note that Adrian Chambers looks like nothing so much as Robert Duvall's incarnation of the Great Santini.

'They tell me you left the DA's Office.' He says this like he's been asking questions about me.

'Some time ago.' He's talking about the Capital County District Attorney's Office where I haven't worked in more than a decade.

'That's too bad. I was looking forward so, to seeing you in court again,' he says. 'I've waited a long time.'

'I still get there,' I tell him. 'I'm just on the other side now, at the defense table.'

'Oh, but it wouldn't be the same,' he says.

I am giving him puzzled looks, like what difference could it possibly make to a disbarred lawyer.

'The place is open to the public,' I tell him. 'Come, sit in the audience. Hiss if you like.' I give him a little grin like this unpleasant conversation is coming to an end.

Harry has found what he was looking for in the paper. From his look he could have saved himself the effort, and me fifty cents.

'Oh, they didn't tell you?' says Chambers.

He waits for me to say something, but I don't bite.

'I'm practicing law again. I thought they would have told you, of all people,' he says, 'being that you took such a personal interest in my case.'

I think my vacant gaze gives him some satisfaction. That

25

I am hearing this for the first time.

'Oh yes, several years now,' he says. 'Contrary to popular belief, there is life after disbarment. The state supreme court says I'm rehabilitated.'

'Ah.' I could congratulate him, say that I was glad to hear it, but it would be a lie. What's worse, he would know it. It is this suspension from the practice of law, more than anything else, even the time spent behind bars, that I think is the basis of his animus toward me. Chambers spent nine months in the county jail, courtesy of a indulgent judge at sentencing. Though his crime was a felony, the court took note of the fact that he was a lawyer, one of the fold, with no prior history of wrongdoing. Special rules for special folk. A non-lawyer for the same offense would have done hard time, I think.

'Practice isn't quite the same,' he says. 'A little smaller, less ambitious,' he says. What he means is not like the days of yore, pre-Henley, when he had a dozen associates in a high-toned office across from the courthouse, and a partner who walked off with everything when Chambers was jailed.

Harry has finally tuned into our conversation. Standing beside me, Chambers looks at him. Since Harry is in a wrinkled suit and has a stubbled face, I am sure Chambers takes him for one of my clients, and my practice for something seedy.

'Oh, no hard feelings,' he says. 'I want you to know that I don't harbor grudges. What happened, happened,' he says. 'Water under the bridge,' he says. 'Just one of those things,' he tells me.

'Sure,' I say.

'Let bygones be bygones,' says Harry. 'Forgive and forget.' Harry wrinkles his eyebrows, trying to think of a few more. 'Bear no malice,' he says. 'Bury the hatchet. Blessed are the meek,' he says.

Chambers looks at him, like who is this asshole butting in?

Not one to leave him in doubt, Harry sticks out his hand. 'Harry Hinds,' he says.

Chambers looks but doesn't touch.

'Forgiveness is good for the soul,' says Harry. 'Do hard time did you?' Hinds is cultivating him. I think he senses commercial opportunities, maybe a future client.

'No.' Chambers looks at him with an expression you might reserve for something run over on the road. 'And you?' he says.

Harry looks down at his suit coat, wrinkled and dirty, like something the homeless would wear. 'Oh no,' he says. 'Just trying to crack the Coconut.'

Chamber's expression is quizzical. He is wondering, I think, if maybe Harry's run afoul of a local ordinance designed to protect palm trees and their fruit.

'But I commend your attitude. It's the first step toward rehabilitation,' says Harry.

'And what's that?' says Chambers.

'Honest remorse,' says Hinds. 'It works good at sentencing too. It's what I tell all my clients.'

'That so?'

I'm sure that knowing Chambers, he can, just like Harry's clients, switch this on and off, his remorse, at will. It is no doubt how he regained his ticket to practice law.

Chambers smiles at me, lips tight as banjo strings. 'See

you around.' He says this, as if he means it, like perhaps I should pay more attention each time I walk past an alley.

'I doubt it,' I say. 'I'm a little busy, nursing an assignment elsewhere right now.' I try to quell any rising expectations of revenge.

He looks at me, a steely-eyed smile. 'We'll be seeing each other,' he says. One last contemptuous look at Harry and Chambers is gone, down the street.

In his day, Chambers had handled some heady cases, mostly white-collar stuff, though he had seen the seamier side of crime as well. He defended to a standstill the prosecution of the White Angels a decade ago, a group of Aryan thugs charged with the murder of a black man on the fringes of Oak Park. In his abrasive courtroom style he drew the wrath of the cops and the city's prosecutors. He also won, which, in Adrian Chambers's book, is all that counts.

'Delightful guy,' says Harry. 'A little like Hitler, but without the charm.'

'Yeah,' I say, 'with Adrian Chambers, his mouth's a dead give away.'

Harry looks at me.

'You know he's lying when you see his lips move.'

By the time we reach the house Nikki is so angry she is not talking to me. We were late getting to the baby-sitter, and Nikki was called from work to pick up Sarah. I know my wife well enough to recognize her look when I get to the house, a gaze that seems to see right through me as if I am nothing more than a hole in space.

'How are you, Harry?' She takes his coat.

'Fine,' he says. 'I'm doing fine.'

She turns her back on me leaving me on the stoop outside. Harry gives me a sideways glance, something that says maybe he'd be more comfortable in jail tonight.

'Mmm, smells good.' He puts a face on it. Odors from the kitchen are wafting out toward the front door.

'Sure does,' I say.

Nikki gives me one of her 'drop dead' looks, turns and heads back toward the kitchen. At least she has acknowledged my presence. The first step in the long road to redemption.

In the last weeks the stress here at home has been palpable, ever since I took on the Davenport assignment. I have tried to assuage Nikki, offering to boost the housekeeper to once a week. I even tried to take part of the load, some household chores, from her. The laundry became my province, washing, drying and folding. But the art of bleach put an end to this. Nikki took this task back after a few weeks when our underwear began to take on the gray-cast of the Confederacy.

These days Nikki is haggard, trying to handle a job and home, being both mother and father to Sarah, worn to a fine edge because I have taken on too much at my own job.

'Daddy, Daddy.' Sarah bounds down the hall and into my arms. 'Guess what I did in school today.' She has dark hair kept short in a Dutch cut, and oval brown eyes the color of rich coffee. A few transparent fawn-like freckles dot the bridge of her nose, and wonder dances in her every expression. Kindergarten is a new and daring adventure each day for my daughter. In the afternoon she rides the bus with the high-school girl down the street, the coolest thing since Barbie. As a result she talks constantly about all the homework she has to do and puts on a fatalistic expression that is comic in its efforts to look grown-up. Then she's off to the playroom for hours of self-important scribbling on reams of binder paper.

It is the first night this week that I have arrived home at a sufficiently early hour to see her still awake.

She is pulling me like a little tugboat down the hall with her whole hand around my forefinger. 'Look at what I did, Daddy. Look what I did at school.'

'Just a minute,' I tell her. 'I'll look at it in a second.'

Nikki asks Harry if he'd like something to drink. Beer, wine, a soda.

'A beer would be great,' he says.

'Let me get that, honey. You're busy.' I try to press past my wife to give her some help, a mild effort at amends.

In a move that would rival the queens of roller-derby, she gives me a hip in the side sending me past the refrigerator door and halfway into the hall, the leverage of the female center of gravity. She grabs a single bottle of Coors from the rack on the door and slams it closed. Two seconds later she is handing this to Harry, the head frothing up in a tall, frosted Pilsner glass. It is her way of telling me that, as far as she is concerned, I can die of thirst. I begin to wonder if I'm eating tonight.

Finding myself in the hallway in the semi-darkness by the phone, I stand there for a moment to collect my thoughts. This day is not turning out well — first a reunion with Adrian Chambers and now this. I pull the phone book from the little shelf under the phone and look in the Yellow Pages under 'Attorneys'. I am curious as to where

Chambers is hanging his shingle these days. There is no listing. I look at the date on the book. No doubt it was published before Chambers was reinstated.

I turn to the white pages and look under his name – a single entry in bold type for a commercial listing:

Adrian Chambers
A.C. Associates
Limited Partnerships – Business Consultants

I suspect that it was during the time when he was high and dry, without a ticket to practice law, that formed the genesis of A.C. Associates – any way to turn a dollar.

I close the phone book and drift back into the kitchen. Nikki looks at me with a gaze that could stop a charging water buffalo.

'Why don't you take some time with your daughter,' she says. 'Look at her school work?' she says to me.

I match her look for look. My own hostility is starting to build. I move toward the couch and Sarah.

Harry, sensing the onset of domestic discord, has lost himself in the din of the television set, channel surfing with the remote.

I sit on the couch in the family room while Sarah pulls wrinkled and folded pieces of construction paper from her plastic backpack, the one with spots like a dalmatian. I unfold these and begin to decipher letters and numbers, in no apparent order, printed large, block-style in various colored crayon. The numbers appear fine. The letters look like they have been copied from images in a mirror, they are nearly all backwards.

We read these together. She struggles and guesses at a few.

'Very good,' I tell her. 'Good job.'

She smiles at me, big and broad as if to burst with satisfaction, little tip-toeing jumps unable to control herself, overflowing with energy.

'She's coming along,' I tell Nikki.

My wife turns to look at me, a cold expression.

She has been on the rampage for more than a month, ever since my decision to help Mario Feretti, to immerse myself in the Putah Creek cases.

After the trial in the Potter case and our earlier separation, Nikki and I sparred over the revelation of my affair with Talia while we were apart. We spent long months talking about our marriage, a succession of trips to a counselor. In his presence we negotiated a contract, more wheeling and dealing than a leveraged buyout.

For her part, Nikki agreed that she would no longer keep her frustrations bottled up inside, expect me to develop the prophetic skills of a seer, her idealized version of male sensitivity.

I promised that I would make strides to confine my practice, compartmentalize my life so as to stake out more time for Nikki, and Sarah.

For a while this even worked. We took a few weekend trips, spent four days in the mountains camping. It was a new life. The stress melted from me like snow on a summer day. This lasted nearly three months. Then the lawyer inside my soul, like the genie in the magician's lamp, escaped – two back-to-back trials. My best intentions went to hell.

This was followed by Feretti's phone call. I found myself in material breach of our contract.

Nikki followed through on her part, gnawing on my ass at every opportunity. What angered her most was my failure to discuss the Davenport business with her before making my commitments to Mario. It is a point well taken.

Since then her ire has been steadily escalating. I tried to mollify her with assurances that my role was only temporary, until Feretti was back on his feet. Ninety days at most. I used Mario's line.

But Nikki can see through bullshit like a sniper through a starlight scope. She asked me if I'd gotten this prognosis from Feretti's doctor. I had to admit that I hadn't talked to Mario's physician. We were back into it, Nikki shouting, stomping around the house, pretending like she was straightening up, picking up Sarah's toys, throwing them haplessly in my direction.

Then Mario died. Since then life has been hell. We are no longer sleeping in the same room.

She is dishing up dinner, only three plates on the dining room table, a heaped one for Harry. He eyeballs me. Maybe it is true, that I am fasting tonight. Then Nikki tells us that Sarah has already eaten, watching a tape of Mr Rodgers on the tube.

We pull up chairs. I open the wine.

'Are you going through with this thing?' says Harry.

He's talking about the temporary assignment as prosecutor in Davenport County.

'Right now I'm on the hook,' I say. The fact is, I have signed a contract with an indefinite term on the assumption that Feretti would soon be back.

I make a face. 'Circumstances have now changed,' I tell Harry. 'I'm hoping that the county will understand. I've got a meeting with Judge Ingel tomorrow morning, to talk about it.' Derek Ingel is presiding judge of the Davenport County Superior Court. To those who know him, and behind his back, he is called 'the Prussian'. But I have not as yet figured out why. Right now he holds the balance of my practice in his hands.

Nikki gives me a look, a quick flash of anger. 'He's hoping *they* will understand?' says Nikki. 'I like that,' she says. 'How about telling them your wife doesn't understand? How about telling them to go away and leave us alone? I love it,' she says, 'my husband the lawyer. He has balls the size of brass doorknobs when it comes to pitching the cause of some sleaze-ball client. But for his family, when it comes to his ability to earn a living, well,' she says, 'then he's all meekness, hat in hand, kiss the ass of the judge. Your honor this, your honor that . . .' Nikki is up from the table getting something from the kitchen, her indignant mantra trailing behind her like some billowing train of wrath as she walks from the dining room.

Harry looks at me from under wrinkled eyebrows, like maybe I should take Nikki along to do the talking. We can hear her in the other room grumbling to herself now.

I explain to him the difficulties, the fact that the board of supervisors who will ultimately fill Feretti's job by appointment is deadlocked on a long list of candidates. Each supervisor is now backing his own horse. Naming a prosecutor in a rural county is, it seems, its own form of king-making.

'Why not just tell him that you aren't going to do it?' Nikki's back. 'That it was a favor for a friend. The friend is now dead, and that's it, it's over.' She tosses the dish towel on the table, like maybe I could take this thing with me and drop it in the middle of Ingel's desk.

I laugh a little, like such an approach would be ridiculous. This makes her more angry.

'We've been over this,' I say. 'The court signed off on the appointment,' I say. 'And I applied for the assignment.'

'At Feretti's request,' she reminds me.

'I will talk to Ingel tomorrow,' I say. 'I will do everything I can to get out.'

'Sure,' she says.

Harry I think senses blood about to be spilled. From Nikki's look, I think he suspects it may be mine. He steps in. 'The sheriff, what's his name?'

'Emil Johnson,' I say.

'He seemed like a decent sort — for a cop.' From Hinds this is a ringing endorsement. 'Maybe he'd help you get out from under. Talk to his friends on the board, maybe some of the judges. After all, he's an elected official.'

'I don't think he would help,' I say.

'There you go,' says Nikki. 'He won't even try.' She throws her napkin on the table, gets up and walks out again.

Harry had met Emil at Feretti's funeral. He came with me for a little moral support. Nikki was too angry with Mario for dying.

There at the funeral, hovering over the casket with friends and family, I'd felt a sharp slap on the back. I

35

turned, and it was Emil Johnson. Johnson is a fifth-degree redneck in this rural county, and has the beer gut and broad beam to prove it. Voters have returned him to office five terms running. This undoubtedly says more about the place than it does about Emil. He has been warding off growing opposition from more liberal elements at the university for years. If he is lucky he will retire in another term, unless alcohol takes him out sooner.

'Sad day, counselor.' He'd looked at me with soulful eyes, a face like a heavy-set basset hound. 'A man with young children.' Emil shook his head at the unfairness of it all.

I introduced Harry, who at the sound of the word 'sheriff' wiped the sweat from his forehead with his hand before giving it to Emil in a firm shake. Johnson didn't seem to notice.

'Makes one feel one's own mortality.' Emil was waxing eloquent, looking at the casket, patting his gut which hung over a brass buckle as big as a gladiator's shield, the letters 'Winchester' tooled across it. 'Mary-o was a good man,' he said. 'He'll be missed.'

For all of five minutes by the politicians of Davenport County, I thought. I hadn't noticed Emil throwing his own political weight, which is considerable, behind Feretti when Mario was hospitalized. Instead the good sheriff waited in the weeds to see if the supervisors would devour Mario, if they would seek to replace Feretti with one of their own hand-picked cronies.

'You got a problem,' says Harry, still eating. 'This is not a good thing.'

I think he means my crossing over to the prosecution.

Then he motions toward the kitchen. 'It isn't worth it,' he says. What Harry means is this case is jeopardizing my marriage, threatening my family.

'What can I do?' I say.

He makes a face, like he has no answers.

From the beginning Harry has made no secret of his view. He has not wanted me to get involved in this thing in Davenport.

When I first told him that I was only caretaking he looked at me wistfully. 'That's what Adam told the snake,' he said.

It is as if by crossing over to the other side, even on a short term appointment, only for purposes of the investigation, I have — at least in Harry's eyes — violated some sacred part of the defender's credo and placed some curse on my family life.

Chapter Three

Two years ago Derek Ingel was working in the bowels of the Attorney General's Office, shagging criminal appeals for the state. He found the fountain of political patronage in a GOP club with people who believe the only good Republicans speak in tongues and who foster the social ideals of Beaver Cleaver.

Since then Ingel has ascended to the judicial heavens faster than Elijah and his fiery chariot. He now sits as the legal pooh bah in this county, in the PJ's chambers of the Superior Court. These are not opulent, and I am offered a hard wooden chair on the other side of Ingel's desk for this audience.

He tells me how busy he is. This to let me know my time here is short. He is down one judge, a vacancy on the court, he says.

Talk among local lawyers is that Ingel is now pulling strings to put one of his cronies from the AG's Office in this spot. He has made statements in private, which he now denies, that only former deputy AGs are qualified to be judges in this state. Such are his views of social and professional diversity. If narrow-mindedness is a virtue, Derek Ingel is its patron saint.

We quickly run out of pleasant things to say to each other.

He leans back in his chair.

'So what is it that you want?' he says. The man has the animation of Calvin Coolidge, a human droid whose maker forgot to program a smile. I am beginning to understand how Derek Ingel earned his moniker – the Prussian.

'It's the nature of our arrangement,' I say. 'My agreement with the county.'

He gives me a long slow nod, takes off his wristwatch and sets it on the desk face up like he's timing some event. I am wondering if the floor will open up and swallow me at some point.

'Feretti's death,' I tell him, 'circumstances that none of us anticipated.'

'Ahh, yes,' he says. 'Tragic.' Then nothing more. He makes some noises like he's not sure exactly how this affects me. Stuck in the morass of Mario's job, one foot in private practice and the other here, forty miles away, and I have to get out my crayons and draw the man a picture.

But Ingel is not as dense as he makes out. What he really wants, I think, is for me to grovel. From his satisfied expression I think this is the part he likes best about his job. Attorneys, in three-piece suits, on their hands and knees.

I start making a case, the lawyer at work, the fact that circumstances were different when I signed the contract with the county; that the parties all understood that I was merely filling in for Mario, who is now dead. How long can it take to name a successor?

He sits listening to all of this, a few facial calisthenics to show that judgment is at work.

'It would be good,' I tell him, 'if we could settle the matter of my temporary assignment.' I put a lot of emphasis on the 'T' word. 'Put some closing time-frame on it.

'The county would be ill served by a change of prosecutors in the middle of some high profile case,' I say. I would wink at him and add 'like the Putah Creek stuff', but I think he gets it. Still he says nothing, a lot of dead in the eyes. Ingel is a torpid sponge. I'm beginning to wonder why I have bothered, when I could have stayed home and talked to myself.

After several minutes working up calluses on my tongue, he finally cuts me off.

'What's the bottom line?' he says. 'What is it specifically you want?'

'I thought I made that clear. A closing time-frame on my duties here.'

He looks at me, like be real.

I climb back in the saddle. 'With a vacancy in the office, it would serve us all well if a permanent replacement is found quickly,' I tell him.

He makes a face, seesawing his head like maybe this is so and maybe it isn't. Then he swivels in his chair a quarter turn so that he is now looking at the degrees and honors hanging on his wall.

'You put me in a difficult position,' he says.

'How's that?'

He turns to me, square on again. 'I'm going to be honest with you,' he says. 'You were not my pick for this job.'

Great, so let me go, I think.

'None the less,' he says, 'you signed a contract with the

county. This contract, I believe, is open-ended.'

He means that it has no specific term of months or years at which time it will expire.

'That's true. But at the time it was signed, the circumstances were clear,' I say. 'It was understood by both parties that I was merely filling in for Mr Feretti. During what was believed to be his period of recuperation. After surgery,' I say.

'But the contract didn't say this?' he says.

'Not expressly.'

'Don't hedge with me,' he snaps. 'It either did or it didn't.'

'It didn't,' I say.

'Fine.' He rolls back in his chair a little, looks at the ceiling. 'And so now you want out?'

I could say yes, but from his tone and manner I opt for a fall-back.

'I would like a reasonable time frame, for the county to find a permanent replacement. Support from the court for this position. Something to motivate the supervisors to move quickly instead of taking their time.'

'And what do you consider a reasonable time-frame?'

'A month, six weeks.' I make it sound generous, like the Creator built the universe in six days.

'And that's it?'

Maybe I'm getting somewhere.

'Yes, that's it.'

'Is there something,' he says, 'that makes you think the county's not proceeding in a timely manner? To replace Feretti that is?'

I make a face, like I'm not sure we should get into this.

'Oh, go ahead,' he says. The first smile I've seen this afternoon. Now I am wary.

'You can be candid here,' he says. 'In the confines of this office,' he says, 'confidences are sacred.'

I could test this by telling him I do abortions on the side. Instead I hedge.

'I hear rumors,' I say, 'scuttlebutt that there are budgetary considerations.'

'What have you heard?'

'Nothing specific.'

He looks at me like maybe he doesn't believe this.

The fact is I know more. The county is drawing down a block grant from the state for a large share of my salary, a condition that will end when they appoint a permanent DA. Local funding being what it is, the county grandees intend to nuzzle up and suckle at the tit of state as long as possible.

'It couldn't have anything to do with the Putah Creek things?' he says.

'I won't deny that I've considered those cases.' I make a face, the obvious.

'A prosecution would involve protracted criminal litigation,' I tell him. 'It could go on for a year. Longer. The county would be smart to get a permanent prosecutor on board before anything is too far along.'

'Maybe you don't think you're up to the task?' A little simper on his lips, imperious. Maybe he is wondering if I have the sand for the job. Or more likely he is questioning my commitment, a switch-hitting lawyer who has been prosecutor and defense attorney and now is back on the side of the angels. For a judge he packs a lot of prosecutorial baggage to the bench. I think Ingel is one of those judges who believes in putting a beveled edge on justice for the criminally accused.

'No. That's not it. I'm up to the task,' I say. 'But I have other commitments.' I wonder if this sounds as bad as I think, a lawyer on the dodge.

'Sure,' he says. Then a look that is a naked attempt to work over my pride, little jabs around the belt in the clinch.

I swallow hard. A piece of my dignity goes down with the saliva. But I think maybe he's about to let me go.

'I have a private practice,' I say. 'My arrangement was intended to be short-term. A few months. I would not have taken the position otherwise.'

He doesn't say anything. He knows as well as I that, once started, the Putah Creek cases will be like an Asian land war, much easier to get in than to get out.

'Some people have told me you're a good lawyer,' he says.

I make a face, like compliments are nice.

'In coming here your reputation precedes you,' he says.

Now he's sugar coating it. From Hyde to Jekyll in a heartbeat. The man is mercurial, more faces to his character than Lon Chaney.

'But I for one don't think much of lawyers who bed their clients,' he says.

Like the wind's been knocked out of me, a sucker punch. My face goes cold. He talks about dirt in my past, allusions to my earlier affair with Talia Potter before her case, when Nikki and I were separated, ancient history. This is not news, I think. It was in all the local papers, my cross to bear during the Potter trial. And I'd thought it was over, killed by the heat and bright lights of public exposure. Now Ingel is dredging it all up.

I say nothing, but sit there and take his shellacking.

'As a courtesy Judge Acosta called from Capital City,' he says, 'when he read that you'd been appointed as special prosecutor here. You will learn,' he says, 'that judges talk.'

Apparently like fishmongers. Ingel's been holding forth with the Coconut, Armando Acosta, Mexico's answer to the Lord of the Flies. I should have seen it coming.

Acosta presided over the trial of Talia Potter whom I defended in Capital City on charges of murdering her husband. This was seven months ago. Before that, during a period that I was separated from my wife Nikki, and long before the Potter trial, Talia and I had had an affair. This was to my eternal discredit, because Talia's husband, Ben Potter, had been a friend and benefactor. I had not disclosed my earlier relationship with the defendant to the court when I took the case. By that time the affair was long over. It was ancient history. But to my chagrin, the papers and the Coconut found out, during the trial. Acosta had threatened to draw and quarter me during the case. And to this day he has not forgiven me for this deception.

'He was not pleased that we took you on,' says Ingel. 'He has particular reasons for this.' He's talking about Acosta.

'I can imagine.'

Right now the Coconut's pleasure is not my concern. I am seething out to the tips of my ears. That Acosta should pack his arrogance across the river to poison my well on this side has me wondering if I have grounds to lay complaint to the Commission on Judicial Performance, the agency that dogs judges for misconduct in this state. No doubt my temporary role as public official swathes his slander in the protections of the First Amendment.

When I protest, Ingel tells me there's a reason for all of this. He means the Coconut's involvement in a case outside his own county.

'One of the victims,' he says, 'the co-ed Sharon Collins, was his niece.'

I sit slack-jawed.

'His younger sister's daughter,' says Ingel. He's giving me a lecture on the Coconut's family tree. Poor Mexican immigrants who made good, though his sister is not so well connected as the judge, so he is taking the lead on her behalf, according to Ingel, looking for a little extra justice no doubt.

Son-of-a-bitch, I think, of all the people on this planet.

'From what I understand Judge Acosta was like a father to the girl. Mother was divorced,' he says. 'He is pretty broken up over the whole thing.'

Ingel looks at me like I'm supposed to do something about all this.

'Sorry to hear it,' I say. 'He probably has a lot of company.'

Ingel stares at me.

'The parents of the other victims, the other kids,' I tell him. The message is clear. Tell the judge to get in line.

He gives me steely eyes.

'We need to get something straight,' he says. 'While you may have slipped through the cracks in getting here, you have a contract, and you will fulfil it, or I will see to it that you answer to the State Bar.'

'On what charge?' I say.

'Abandoning a client,' he says. 'Unless I am wrong, that is still grounds for legal discipline. And don't think about dumping the Putah Creek cases, rolling over on some early motions, allowing the cases to be dismissed so somebody else can refile them later. If I smell any collusion or negligence, I will have your ticket. You'll be writing briefs by mail order for lawyers in other states. Do I make myself clear?'

'Perfectly. I take it the county has no intention of retaining a permanent prosecutor for these cases?'

He makes a face, like if he knows he's not saying. He picks up his watch. 'If I can ever do anything more for you,' he says, 'feel free to ask.' He looks at me stone cold, something from Rushmore. I get up, out of the chair.

'One last word of advice,' he says. 'There will be a lot of people watching you.'

'Because of Judge Acosta?' I say.

'He does have a personal stake in all this.'

Sure he does, and he's driving it into my ass.

Chapter Four

The state crime lab is an immense, low-lying block of a building, a modern concrete fortress. It is set back the length of a football field from the street, behind a verdant lawn bisected by a ten-foot-high iron fence that surrounds the entire facility.

The largest of its kind outside of the FBI's lab in Quantico, Virginia, this place is the province of the State Attorney General.

Claude Dusalt has set up this meeting. He wants to familiarize me with the evidence early, in case his investigators need a quick search warrant. The Putah Creek killer is drawing increased press attention and Claude wants to be ready to move at a moment's notice, with the first break.

Derek Ingel, Davenport's answer to Roy Bean, has been looking over my shoulder on every move, wanting to know the state of our evidence. No doubt so that he can pass it back to the Coconut. So far I've been able to keep him in the dark, because that is where I am. Ignorance is bliss.

I fill out a form and get a security badge from a guard in a kiosk inside the main entrance to the crime lab.

A few minutes later I hear the click of heels on concrete. A woman is approaching down a long corridor. I can see her through the slotted glass of the security door. From a distance she has the look of a secretary. Her eyes reading me as she walks tell me this is my escort. She is short and a little dowdy, to the fair side of middle age. There's something familiar about her, but I can't place it.

'Mr Madriani.'

She is stone-faced, seemingly preoccupied. But in her tone I sense this is no receptionist.

'Kay Sellig,' she says. 'The director has asked me to brief you.' Brown eyes, caught between a few wrinkles and crow's-feet, look at me from under a salt-and-pepper wedgecut, something easy to care for. She doesn't offer her hand, but instead reads my mind.

'Not what you expected?' she says. She is a quick study.

'I don't know.' I lie.

Finally there's a smile, not amiability, but satisfaction at having read my thoughts.

In the limited universe of criminal forensics the name Kay Sellig conjures legend, a reputation that belies the image standing before me now.

We make small talk as she leads me through the labyrinth, the maze of little chambers inside this building.

Then, as I watch her walking from behind, it settles on me, this sense that we have met before.

'You were there,' I say. 'On the creek.'

She nods. 'I processed the scene.'

I have heard the name Kay Sellig for a dozen years, mostly banter in courthouse corridors, the war stories of lawyers, embellished with each telling. But I have always accepted as fact my good fortune that I have never had to cross this woman in court. In her time she has buried more than her share of criminal defendants behind the concertina-wired walls of Folsom and San Quentin.

Three more turns, down a short hallway, we enter a larger room and she slows to half speed. I sense that we have arrived.

The place is not unlike a high school chemistry lab in one of the upscale suburbs. Bathed in fluorescent light are a dozen large stainless steel tables bolted to the floor.

'Has Lieutenant Dusalt given you much detail so far?' she asks.

'We've had one meeting,' I tell her. 'What I know so far is what I read in the papers, and the few files that Mario – Mr Feretti – compiled before his death.'

'You want to ask questions, or should I do a narrative?' she asks.

Not having read the file, I'd rather listen. I tell her so.

'Fine.' Not looking at any notes she wings it, impromptu. 'The killer usually doesn't leave IDs, wallets and purses, he takes them. Except for the last murders, we've never found any of them. He probably has a shrine somewhere, someplace where they're all piled up. We've had to roll prints each time to identify the victims.'

She moves toward a big chalk board, one of those things supported on a rolling wooden easel. She flips the board to the other side. Here the surface is cork. Pinned to it is an array of glossy colored pictures. Faces, head-and-shoulder shots of death, taken against the stainless steel autopsy tables of the county morgue.

'The first one was nineteen – Jonathan Snider.' She points. Even in death this face has the artless countenance of youth.

'His girlfriend was eighteen. Her name was Julie Park.'

From her picture she was Asian, young and pretty. 'They were found on the Putah Creek twelve days ago. The killer made no attempt to conceal the bodies.'

She moves down with her pointer. 'The next two were found four days later. Sharon Collins, twenty-two, Acosta's niece, and Rodney Slate same age. Again no IDs. The bodies were left exposed on the ground.'

She points to the next faces of death, more aged this time, staring out at me from the cork board. 'The last two you saw at the scene, Abbott and Karen Scofield.'

The woman's head reveals a dark forlorn cavern on one side of her face, the grotesque image of an empty eye socket, several sharp cuts on the cheek and brow around the vacant cavity.

It is the first time Sellig has given any indication of having seen me at the last killing site. This woman does not miss much.

'For some reason he left his wallet and her purse. Maybe something disturbed him, we don't know. Scofield and his wife were divorced. He was a member of the faculty at the university, a scientist. Ornithology, I believe.' For the first time she is looking at notes.

I make a face, like this is Greek to me.

'Study of birds,' she says.

She approaches one of the tables, this one heaped with clothing. It might be anyone's laundry, except for the large blotches of dried blood on the white shirt and trousers in one of the piles. These are sorted on separate areas of the table, ready for placement in large paper bags numbered and marked for identification, part of the budding chain of evidence.

I notice that all the buttons are missing from the dress shirt. She tells me she cut these off at the crime scene and bagged them for evidence. They have gone down to latent prints, to be smoked in a chamber of heated superglue. It's a long shot but maybe the killer got careless and touched one of the buttons without gloves.

If the local politicos are worried about a botched crime scene, in Kay Sellig they have been smiled on by the gods of good fortune.

Sellig tells me that the stains on the victims' clothes were caused by gravity, blood flowing along the ground to the neatly folded articles of clothing placed around the bodies. There are no cuts or tears in any of these items, no evidence of any physical altercation.

'The pattern is always the same,' she says. 'The victims are always naked when killed.'

They have found one other piece of evidence. At the first murder scene police believe the killer may have inadvertently left a large plastic trash bag, the kind used to line trash containers. It was found near the creek, probably carried by the wind. It was empty, but a hole had been poked in the bottom. Sellig thinks this may have been used by the killer to carry the stakes and cord to the scene, the implements of death. One of the stakes may be responsible for the hole.

She has not had time to examine the stakes and the cord from the Scofield killings. The cord appears to be similar to that used in the other murders. The stakes are downstairs in latent prints.

'Any evidence of sexual assault?' I ask.

'Not that we can find,' she says. 'Medical examiner

found sperm in the vaginal vault of the Park girl, but whoever left it there was a secretor, and the blood type matches her boyfriend. Pubic combings turned up some foreign hair on the boy that matches the girl's.' She pauses for a second to let the obvious settle on me.

'Kids on the campus say the two were an item. We're thinking the victims got it on together, maybe an hour or two before they were killed.'

'How does he do couples?' I ask. 'A little risky isn't it?'

'He's probably armed, he may have help, we're not sure yet. The victims were all taken from deserted areas, abandoned parking lots late at night. In every case they were the last ones to leave some social function, or a work place. The killings were done in remote areas, except for the last one. The last one, the Scofield thing, was gutsy,' she says. 'He got a little close to the road.' She speculates that this may be part of his growing MO, an unmet desire for added chance. 'But he was also lucky,' she tells me. 'We're looking for motorists who might have passed that spot late at night, people who might have seen something. So far we've come up with nothing.'

She tells me that the profile experts, psychologists who make their life's work the study of demented minds, have, despite the lack of any evidence of sexual assault, not ruled out the possibility that the crimes might be driven by a sexual psychosis.

'Some of them think the metal tent stakes are phallic,' she says. 'According to this theory, what he does with them may be his own sick form of intercourse.'

They already have a psychological profile of the killer. There was a time when I would have given this all the credence of tarot cards. But I have become a believer.

'Except for the last two, he doesn't know his victims,' she says. They have deduced this from the fact that the faces of the victims were untouched, not battered or mutilated. Psychologists have determined that it is usually only in cases where the killer knows his victim that the face is battered. The closer the relationship, the more severe is the facial disfigurement.

'You say except for the last two. What's different there?'

'I'll get to that,' she says.

'He's probably white,' she says. Statistics show that in mutilation murders the victim is most often of the same race as the killer.

They gauge the age at between twenty-five and forty. Teenagers who kill are usually violent and impulsive, not the measured ritual of the Putah Creek killer. And anyone too old would have had his hands full with the male victims.

According to the profile, the killer probably lives alone. This is almost a 'touchy-feely' surmise, I think. But the shrinks reason that the killings' evidence shows signs of alienation – the murderer sees himself as an outsider, not part of any family group or close social setting. This may account for the fact that he always takes couples; his way of lashing back.

'We think he's spent a lot of time around the creek, he might live near there, or maybe he worked there in the past,' she says.

They have come to this conclusion based on the ritual nature of the crimes, the meticulous arrangement of the bodies on the ground, the careful array of clothing around the victims indicating that the killer was taking his time, confident that he would not be disturbed.

'He sees this area as his turf,' she says. 'He feels safe here.'

The cops are now keying on this last one, canvassing the area for anyone who might have worked or been seen living in the area, a field hand on one of the ranches, maybe a transient who camped there for a while.

One aspect of the psychological profile is most troubling.

'Killers who rely on ritual,' she says, 'don't usually stop until they're caught.' It is a sobering thought, but it gets worse.

'We don't know if he's becoming more violent,' she says, 'or if maybe he might have known the Scofield woman.'

I look at her, a question mark.

'He appears to have gouged the eye from her head,' she says. 'We're still trying to figure out why.'

With the panties drawn tight over her head, I could not see the mutilation at the scene.

We talk in more general terms about the investigation. Except for the profile, the cops are dabbling in the dark. According to Sellig, police can find nothing that connects any of the couples killed.

'The last ones, the Scofields, present a real problem,' she says.

I look at her, my interest piqued.

'Their age,' she says. 'He's broadened the boundaries. He's not confining himself to the college-age crowd anymore.'

'Maybe it's not age,' I tell her. 'Maybe the common link is the academic set, the university.'

She makes a face like this is a possibility. But she is still troubled. It is an axiom of serial crime, that when killers depart from the usual order of things, those pursuing them have even more reason to worry. The fact that the Putah Creek killer has now taken victims in their fifties injects a random element into the equation of pursuit. We talk about this, but she is stymied. Until Sellig gets the autopsy report on the Scofields she can form no real conclusions.

'What about the thing in the trees?' I ask. 'The platform.'

She's taking her shoes off now, moving toward a locker against the wall. It appears that even the half-heels were a concession to the company dress code, something used only for greeting the public. She is warming to me now, a little more casual. I take this as a sign of trust.

I ask her whether this perch in the trees is connected with the murders.

'We're still looking into it,' she says.

I probe her on what they found up there.

She makes a face. 'Some feathers, and blood,' she says.

'Animal or human?'

'Mostly animal, but there were traces of human blood as well. And some small bones, avian, we think.' There are more puzzled looks from Sellig on this. Like the loose ends just keep piling up.

'We've sent the bones and feathers off to the National Wildlife Forensics Lab, up in Oregon,' she says, 'for analysis.'

It seems there are only two people in the country who

have any background in such things. One of them is eighty-seven years old, a woman on the east coast. The other is a younger woman, her protégée, who has now been enticed away from the Smithsonian to the wildlife facility in Ashland, a kind of criminalistics lab for offenses against nature and the environment.

'They should have some answers for us in a few days,' she says.

'Your best guess?' I ask her.

'Based on the little bit we have?' she asks.

I nod.

'I'd say our guy,' she's talking about the Putah Creek killer, 'had nothing to do with the blind in the trees.'

'Then who did?'

'It's only a hunch right now. I'd rather wait until we get something back from the lab up in Oregon.'

I accept this, and back off.

'Did they find anything like this at the other two sites, down in Orange County and up in Oregon, a platform in the trees, feathers, bones?' I ask.

She shakes her head. 'No. And we've gone back to check the area again at the other two sites here in Davenport. We thought maybe we missed something. But there was nothing there either. No platform or ropes.'

She is pulling on a pair of white running shoes, the kind secretaries around the Capital use for fast walks at lunch, their answer to midday aerobics.

'You didn't happen to go up there?' I ask. 'On the platform?'

She nods. Suddenly she's all cryptic gestures.

Looking at her, somehow I knew that after the platform

was processed by the evidence tech, she could not resist going up and looking.

'Pretty good view?' I ask her.

'An understatement,' she says. There's a sly smile. She moves toward the locker against the wall and opens the door again. I think she's putting the half-heels away. But when she turns to face me again she's holding a long cylindrical object wrapped in a terry cloth towel. As she unwraps this I can see metal and glass and on the side, some lettering, and the words 'Mirador TTB'.

'It was found on the platform,' she says. 'The owner appears to have left in a hurry.' She hands this to me, to inspect.

'It's a spotting scope. This is a good one. It would cost about a thousand dollars. Shooters use them for long-range shots, to zero their weapons, to find the strikes on a target without walking two hundred yards.'

I'm turning it over in my hands, looking at it.

'It's been dusted for prints,' she says. 'We got one smudged latent, unusable, and found some traces of blood on it.'

'It makes no sense,' I say. There's an instant of dead silence between us as I look at the scope.

'You think whoever was up in the tree had nothing to do with the murders.'

She makes a face like this is a definite possibility.

'But they may have seen the killer?' I say.

She smiles. 'Take a look,' she says. She's motioning toward the scope in my hands.

I look through the thing, out one of the windows on the far side of the room. Across the broad verdant lawn like the gardens at Versailles, a secretary is taking lunch, seated on a bench with a brown bag. I turn the focus ring a fraction of an inch, a view like water through crystal. There is moisture on her cheek. She is reading, a little paperback cushioned in one hand — the title clear as the morning newspaper, Erich Segal's *Love Story*.

I consider for a moment in my mind's eye the elements presented; the magic of this little cylinder I hold in my hand, the scaffold high in the trees along the Putah Creek. I conjure the sum of this equation, the thought that perhaps somewhere out there is an aimless spectator to death, a prime witness to the murder of Abbott and Karen Scofield.

Chapter Five

The building that houses the Davenport County District Attorney's office is classic governmentesque. It dates back to the 1930s, something put up by the WPA, which at the time was viewed merely as functional, and built to last. It exhibits a kind of timeless grace, a classic architecture not seen in today's public buildings. The granite exterior and its broad stairway lead to a portico capped by three-story stone columns. These speak of authority in a populist democracy, though the facade is now a dingy brown, and inside the building is littered with over-crowded offices and marked by a neglect of maintenance.

It rests on high ground across from the courthouse, among a grove of tall oaks and walnut trees planted in the city center in the last century, a break against the oppressive heat of valley summers when temperatures routinely climb into the triple digits.

The prosecutor's office is small, only four deputies. Two of these are new, people out of law school less than two years, assigned only to misdemeanors.

And then there is Roland Overroy. Thirty years with the office, Overroy is part of the petrified forest of civil service; perennial dead wood. In this county motions to challenge the competence of counsel are called 'Roland motions', at least among lawyers who have dealt with

Overroy. He has never seen a court file he has read, or had a case he has not overcharged.

His special talent is a terminal lack of preparation, and a penchant for overlooking the obvious.

Ever since Feretti demoted him two years ago as chief deputy, banished him to the doldrums of juvenile court, Overroy has searched for petty problems in the office that he could amplify. He has played these like some maestro to anyone who would listen.

This morning the small staff is not a particularly cheerful group, camped as we are around the scarred metal table in the coffee room that doubles for conferences.

While I have met them all in passing, in the day-to-day chores of the office, this is our first formal staff meeting since taking on this assignment a month ago. I would like to make a good impression.

As I survey them the only faint smiles are from Gary Boudin and Karen Samuels, the two newest additions to the office.

Overroy is trying to size me up, wondering how much opportunity lies in the chaos caused by Feretti's sudden death. Lenore Goya's on the phone in her office. She will join us shortly.

Overroy has appropriated the only chair close to me at the table, as if my authority, as temporary as it may be, will somehow rub off.

On paper, the chief deputy's position has been empty for two years. Instead of firing him, which in civil service would take endless hearings and a forest of paper, Feretti with the stroke of his pen simply abolished Roland's supervisory position. While Roland remained on salary at his current pay, Mario figured pride would in time take its toll. It was an attempt to send a message that his career in the office was tapped out. But with Roland messages are best conveyed by *Western Union*, in plain English.

'A real tragedy,' says Overroy. He's talking about Mario's death. I suspect he did handstands when he read the obituary. Roland's middle name is duplicity. If he were a politician he would be the kind to cut down a redwood then mount the bleeding stump to make a speech about conservation.

'The guy was simply working too hard,' he says. Roland's way of offering condolences. 'He took too much on himself. Refused to share the load. I know.' Roland's shaking his head now, solemnly like some ultimate truism is about to follow. 'This job can be a killer.'

This is clearly not a fate that Overroy intends for himself. At sixty he is anything but burned out. He has a full head of silver gray hair, and a deep tan, not an ounce of fat on his body. I am told that Roland keeps a boat moored on the river at the marina, that in the summer he routinely checks out before three for afternoon cruises. He calls this ATO, (administrative time off), allegedly for all the long hours he puts in prepping at home for juvenile court. This had become a standing joke, but Mario had ignored it, finding Roland's absence easier to take than his interference and the constant poison he emits into the atmosphere of the office.

Overroy is clearly trying to take the lead in this gathering. He has made the introductions around the table, 'the junior staff', as he described them to me in a more private moment.

He has ordered Jane, Feretti's secretary, to furnish all of us with refreshments, coffee and, if I want it, Overroy offers to send her down three stories, to the basement, for a cold soft drink from the vending machine.

I waive off on this and ask Boudin and Samuels how things are going in the misdemeanor section, a little small talk to take the edge off.

'We manage,' Overroy answers for them. 'But I think we all agree that the office needs a little more structure,' he adds.

'Things worked a little more smoothly when there was more supervision.' What Roland means is when he was chief deputy.

'As for the office,' he says, 'you'll find that we all know our jobs. The place just needs a little continuity. Some-body who knows where things are, how they work.' He smiles at me, big and broad. 'Mr Continuity.'

I had been warned by Feretti that Roland prays at the altar of seniority. In Overroy' s world longevity would be the only measure for advancement.

Goya has just entered the room, she is standing behind Overroy in the doorway.

I give her a quick greeting.

Lenore Goya is a tall, slender woman. She wears a dark-grey suit, skirt to the knees, and a silk blouse. All very 'professional'. Except for her dark complexion, which in the leisure set might pass for a tan. She has the narrow nose and high cheek bones of a fashion model. If I hadn't seen her personnel file I might think she is part of Talia's country club set, all except for the eyes. These are deep set, piercing and dark, with an expression that belies little mirth.

She has been carrying the office since Mario was hospitalized. Between her personnel records and what Feretti had told me, I have pieced together a few bits of her life. She has worked for two other prosecutorial offices before coming here, both in Southern California where she racked up an impressive conviction record. A daughter of the barrio, she clawed her way out of East Los Angeles to graduate with top honors from USC and go on to take a law degree from that school, all on scholarship. She is a single mother with two small children. After spending her life in the inner reaches of LA she is looking for something better for her children, a quieter and safer life in a small town.

'I'm not here to shake things up,' I tell them. First impressions set fast and hard, like a dog's pawprint in concrete.

'If I have my way, you're looking at temporary help. I'm the county's answer to a Kelly Girl,' I say.

This draws a little laughter.

Roland is licking his lips, the taste of opportunity. Boudin and Samuels are nodding their understanding. But Goya is an enigma, her eyes searching me up and down, measuring my every word. I think the lady is a cynic. Perhaps we'll get along after all.

'There will be no change in assignments,' I tell them. 'I hope I won't be here long enough for that.'

Even this has no effect on Goya. She remains stone-faced, her left shoulder leaning into the frame of the door.

'Join us,' I tell her. 'I don't bite. Have a seat.'

'I'm comfortable,' she says.

We are doing a little spider-and-fly act.

Given her attitude, I skip the usual line of every civil service hack – 'assurances of an open-door policy'. Goya will see this for the bureau-babble it is. And as for Overroy, there aren't enough locks in the free world to keep him from my office.

'What does your schedule look like?' I'm looking at Goya.

'Why?'

'We need to talk about the felony calendar,' I tell her.

She looks at her little day-planner. Lawyers now carry these to every event and occasion like Baptist ministers with their Bibles.

'I've got time on Thursday morning,' she says, 'before court call, at nine. My office or yours?'

'Yours.' I will concede a little turf, an effort to bring her on board.

'Why don't I join you.' It's Roland trying to horn in. If he's going to climb back into the saddle of authority he knows it's now or never.

'I don't think we need to take Roland's time, do you?' I look to Goya.

Her answer is a flat, unaffected, 'no'. I think this woman does not suffer fools lightly.

Roland is crestfallen; little squints of acid at Lenore Goya. But this is only fleeting. He puts a face on it. 'It's true,' he says, 'I am pretty busy.'

People are getting out of their chairs, milling toward the door.

'Oh, one question.' It's Overroy. He is smiling again. 'If they catch him, who's gonna do "Shiska Bob"?'

I look at him, a question mark.

'The Putah Creek thing,' he says. 'Who's gonna get the case?'

I can't tell if he actually believes I would consider him for the assignment, or if he's just stirring dissension in the office, his way of getting the juices going in Goya.

'What did you call it?' I ask.

He's all smiles. 'Hmm?' A quizzical look. 'Oh, that. Shiska Bob,' he says.

I nod.

'One of the guys at sheriff's homicide,' he says. 'When you work there for a while you get a funny sense of humor.' He says this with familiarity, fostering an image. Roland, I think, would like us to conjure the picture, he and his red-neck buddies from homicide lapping up brew together, talking about the inside stuff, the hard core cases, the real dirt.

I shudder to think what Feretti might have thought of this headline 'Shiska Bob', blazing above the fold from the little local newspaper, the *Journal*, what Mario called the 'Davenport Urinal'.

'I don't care where it came from,' I tell him. 'I don't want to hear it again.' There's stone-deaf silence in the room.

'You might pass the word to the hot shot in homicide. I'll talk to the sheriff myself. We have families of the victims to deal with. We don't need to inflict any more pain. They will be angry enough if we don't come up with some answers soon.'

'I will,' he says. 'Sure.' The smile is gone from Roland's face.

For the moment I have side-stepped the question of who will get the nod on the Putah Creek cases, but Goya is looking at me. True to form, Overroy has opened the furrow and planted the seed of dissension.

My daughter is to be a rose petal, as distinguished from the shy violets, the seven- and eight-year-olds, in their hues of purple.

Sarah is dressed in a pink tutu, a rigid skirt that sticks out like the whirling rotors of a helicopter from her hipless little form. She wears this outfit over chartreuse tights, so petite I could not fit one forearm into them. Yet even these form wrinkles like the skin of an old apple on Sarah's spindly legs.

Nikki is busy with the camera, taking still shots of tripping pirouettes, poses by the fireplace in the living room, while I dress. Tonight is the capstone of a half-year of lessons and a month of rehearsals, a cast of hundreds. The children's dance workshop presents *Alice in Wonderland*. For this, the studio owner has rented the high school auditorium. It is the only place in town large enough to seat the legion of proud parents, and grandparents, siblings and cousins who will be on hand for this event.

As I look down the hall I see the litter of last night's gathering. We'd entertained, our guests had kids and these together with Sarah have trashed the better part of our house. The hallway is a scene of devastation. Ken and Barbie are on the floor, half naked. There is a littered trail of tiny clothes to the living-room door and beyond, left as if by some dying tribe of Lilliputians wandering in the desert.

'Do you have the tickets?' Nikki asks me.

I check my wallet. They're not there.

'I thought you had them,' I say.

'I gave them to you while you were shaving.'

I look in the bathroom. There they are on the countertop next to the sink.

'I have them.'

I hear Nikki sigh from the other room, something that says I would lose my head if it was not tethered to my body. Lately, she might be right. It seems that work is taking its toll, torn between two offices, living in the schizoid realm of half defense, half prosecution, commuting a million miles between each, daily.

'Did you get cash at the ATM?' she asks.

'Oh shit.' I say it to myself, under my breath, and still she hears it.

'I told you to get some money on your way home,' she says.

'I know, I forgot,' I say.

'Well, what are we going to do for cash?' she asks.

'We'll take it from grocery money,' I tell her.

'And forget to put it back,' she says.

While she talks I am raiding the system of little envelopes in the top drawer of our bedroom dresser; thirty dollars from the envelope marked 'Food'.

'Damn it, Paul.' Nikki is standing behind me in the doorway. 'I don't ask you to do much,' she says. 'I run the house, do the cooking, on top of a job,' she says. 'And you can't remember to go to the bank on the way home.'

'OK, I forgot,' I say. 'Give me a break.'

I pass her in the doorway, looking for my tie which I laid on a chair in the living room earlier. Sarah is watching television, the sound muted, CNN. It is the news I left on after dinner. Nikki is oblivious to television, so long as she does not have to listen to the noise. Increasingly of late, what little time I get, I watch in silent mode only hitting the volume for some seeming world crisis. It is part of the price for peace in our house.

I find my tie, stop for a moment, and watch my daughter. She is dark locks primped and combed, like a gossamer fairy princess in her costume. Her gaze, sparkling brown eyes like ripe olives, is anchored to the screen. Then I look. Pictures of starving little children in some far-off place, bodies emaciated, in pain, bloated bellies and round, wanting eyes. She fixes on these, intense, absorbed, a communion of the innocent.

The picture changes, a talking head. Sarah looks over at me. I am struggling with my tie.

'Daddy, what is wrong with those children?'

It's better, I think, to confront this, than to sugar-coat it.

'They don't have enough to eat,' I say.

'Why not? Why doesn't somebody feed them?'

'There isn't enough food where they live.'

'Why doesn't someone bring food to them?'

'There are bad men there with guns,' I say.

'Why doesn't somebody get rid of the bad men?'

In a nutshell, the circular debate of nations.

'That's complicated,' I say.

She looks at me, the first thing she has not understood. Like most little ones, Sarah has acquired selfishness only as a competitive instinct when confronted with the rivalry of other children at play. On a more native level she is an ocean of empathy. In the quiet and solitary play that she seems to enjoy, her dolls are nearly always sick, throwing-up. They suffer from a physician's desk reference of maladies. It is any excuse to mother them.

To Nikki and me, Sarah is a litany of little offerings, crushed petals and broken stems, the gatherings of the garden, scraps of paper colored and punched, certificates of devotion folded and rolled in every hue made by Crayola. Tonight, for Sarah, it is not so much her performance that matters, but that she offers this achievement, as a gift to us. At five, children it seems have no concept of a parent's unconditional love. In Sarah's limited view, I think, she feels the need to make some partial payment in the coin of acceptance, some compensation for our continued affections. She does not realize that she is compensation enough.

The phone rings in the kitchen. Nikki answers it.

'Just a moment,' she says.

'It's for you.' She looks at me, an expression that says, this better not be what I think it is. She hands me the receiver.

'Hello.'

'Mr Madriani. It's Claude Dusalt.'

'Yes.'

'Sorry to call you at home,' he says, 'at this hour, but it was important. We have a break in the case. Out near the university. Some evidence in a van. A lead on the Putah Creek killer. We need a warrant, tonight,' he says. 'Can you meet me at your office in half-an-hour?'

I swallow hard and look at Nikki. She is watching me through the practiced eyes of cynicism. On my face, in the cast of my expression, she reads the message of still another disappointment.

'I understand,' I say. 'I'll be there in half-an-hour,' I tell him.

Dusalt hangs up.

'I have to go,' I tell her. 'It's a major break in the case. They need a warrant.'

'What else?' she says, shrugging her shoulders.

She's already moving, grabbing her coat and purse.

With my wife I have learned over the years that it is not so much her words as her actions that convey true emotions. There is little hostility detected in her tone, more an expression of resignation. But Nikki is going about the routine of departure in stiff, measured movements, the sign of a deep, brooding fury.

'I'm sorry,' I say. 'These things happen.'

'Sure,' she says. She gathers up Sarah and heads for the door. 'You'd better hurry. It wouldn't do to be late,' she tells me.

'Daddy's not coming?' My daughter is looking at her mother with big oval eyes.

'Daddy has other more important things,' says Nikki.

Sarah's little saucers are now aimed at me.

I smile a little pained expression. I bend down to give her a hug to tell her that I am sorry.

Before I can, Nikki ushers her toward the car in the garage like some shepherded lamb. They are late, and in a hurry. My wife's words are the last thing I hear as the door slams closed behind them.

'Daddy has work to do tonight,' she says.

Another debit in the parental account of a father's love.

Chapter Six

'I want the van left where it is,' I say, 'under surveillance for now, until I can work up a warrant. Nobody's to touch it further without my approval. Understood?'

Claude has Denny Henderson taking notes as the three of us move at a quickstep across the commons and up the stairs of the county administration building. The lights out front have come on, though it is not yet completely dark.

'And I will need a good stenographer, somebody who can take dictation and who knows how to do a warrant.' I look at Henderson. 'Do we have anybody?' He looks at Claude who nods his assurance.

'Sheila Aikens,' he says, 'the older gal in your office. Feretti used her, said she was pretty good.'

'Find her. Get her here now. I want the van watched around the clock. And get the owner registration.'

'We've already got it,' says Claude, 'the vehicle registration.'

We push our way through the main door to the office.

Dusalt pulls a little notebook from his pocket. '1973 GMC. Guy's name is Andre Iganovich,' he says. He rattles off an address on the west side of town. 'We've had the apartment under surveillance for a couple of hours. DMV is sending us a photo from his driver's license for identification. Should we pick him up if he shows?'

'No. First we line up the legal ducks,' I say, 'a search warrant for the van. Then assuming what we've seen inside is golden, we get another warrant for the apartment. If he hasn't flown the coop we can detain him during the search. We'll take him down after we get an arrest warrant, based on the evidence.'

'What if he shows up at the van?' says Claude.

This is more perplexing. We can't let him drive off with the van and its contents. 'Detain him,' I say. 'Hold him for questioning. But no arrest.' I am adamant. I will not have some judge on review limiting our evidence, throwing out our case because we acted rashly.

Claude looks at Henderson. 'Pass the word,' he says. And like a shadow on a cloudy day, Henderson disappears into one of the empty offices to use a phone.

From down the hall I see a head, spindles of long dark hair back-lit by office light, and a pair of eyes peering around the jamb of one of the office doors. As I had guessed, it is Lenore Goya. Just as quickly as it appeared, the head vanishes back into its solitary sanctum.

Claude and I are now huddled in Feretti's old office.

He has not seen this side of me before. Up to now I have been passive, waiting in the wings to help only if called upon. But with Ingel and Acosta now kneeling on my throat, I am becoming, in the jargon of our time, more proactive.

I had noticed as we entered that Claude has assembled an entourage in the outer office, another cop in a uniform I don't recognize and a second man, heavyset, a gut like Babe Ruth, in a blue pin-striped work shirt. These are the percipient witnesses, the people who found the van, and its grizzly contents.

'We will need Sellig,' I say. 'Have Henderson call DOJ and get her out here.' I am taking no chances with one of the county crime techs. If the case against the Putah Creek killer starts here, I am determined that it will stand on a solid footing, evidence hard as concrete, nothing some slick defense attorney can suppress in a pretrial motion months from now.

'Now tell me what happened,' I say.

Claude's looking at his notebook again.

'Our guy,' he says, 'Iganovich appears to be a Russian immigrant, in the country four or five years now. We ran a rap sheet on him, came up clean, only thing we found is a license from the state, last October. Licensed security guard,' he says. 'No firearm permit.'

Claude's shaking his head. 'Can you beat it?' he says. 'Guy's probably not even in the country legally and he's working security.'

'We can worry about his immigration status later. How did you find this thing, the van?' I ask. I start looking for potential problems, the lawyer's mind at work.

'It's all real clean,' says Claude.

'Humor me.'

'Officer Dandrich, outside, is with the university police,' he says.

It's the uniform I didn't recognize.

'Two days ago he sees this van parked in one of the university lots. It's two a.m., the lot's reserved for day use only, the place is empty. He thinks maybe whoever owns it is working late. So he doesn't think anything more about it. He looks at the rear tire, it's been chalked by the meter maid. Yesterday he comes back on shift and the van's still there. There's a ticket on the windshield. He looks at the tires again, the vehicle hasn't moved. Traffic code for the university gives the guy twenty-four hours then it's towed. So he calls the tow truck company, a vendor down town.'

According to Claude this is a commercial garage under contract to the university.

I am following this unfolding drama, my feet propped on the leaf of the desk which I have pulled out for this purpose.

'That's where this guy Harold comes in,' he says. 'Mr Goodwrench?' He's referring to grease-and-pinstripes, outside in the hall.

'Mr Harold,' he says, 'is real careful. He's been sued before by the angry tow toads, so he makes it standard operating procedure whenever he takes a car from the university to inventory the personal property inside. He insists on doing this in front of one of the campus cops.'

'Trusting guy,' I say.

'Anyway,' he says, 'Harold and the campus cop,' he looks at his notes, 'Dandrich, they give the van a closer look. One of 'em discovers that the window, on the passenger side over the rear door, has been smashed in.'

'The cop didn't see this the day before?' I ask.

Claude shakes his head, shrugs his shoulders. 'I asked him. He says it was parked next to one of those cement columns in the garage. You couldn't see it unless you went around the column.'

'So we don't know when the window was broken?'

'No.'

'Anyway, Dandrich and Harold, when they see this thing, the glass gone, they're real curious. They reach inside, unlock and pop the doors.'

'The van was still locked?'

He nods. 'What do you think they found?' Claude's looking at me, a little pregnant pause.

I shake my head, like search me.

'A towel on the passenger seat, covered in what looks like dried blood. That's not all,' he says. 'In the back, in plain view . . .' He adds this latter with his hands outstretched, like he's protesting no foul, 'they find a pile of metal tent stakes, the little shiny ones, L-shaped — and bingo,' he says, 'coiled up on the floor next to them, nice plastic clothes-line cord, thirty feet of the stuff.'

I arch an eyebrow, like maybe we've hit pay dirt. 'Where are the stakes and the rope now?'

'Didn't touch a thing,' he says. 'Left them right where we found 'em.'

'Good. Get Sellig immediately. Tell her what you found and how you found it, all the details. I don't want anybody else to touch that van, understood? Tell her I'll need a report, a comparison to the rope and stakes found at the other murder scenes. And I would like it as fast as possible. Tell her we need it for a warrant to pick this guy up.' If we are to search the Russian's apartment, Sellig's report will be the lodestone in any application for a search warrant, and ultimately for his arrest.

Claude's fishing in his pockets. His hand comes out with a little vial of pills, some medication, then footsteps down the hall toward the water cooler. Several minutes pass. I get up, stretch my legs and wander out into the hall.

Claude is forty feet away at the cooler. He apparently has downed his pills, but now he's not alone. Lenore Goya is talking to him, the picture of animation. I can tell that Claude is having a tough time getting a word in. She sees me and stops. Two seconds later she disappears back into her office, and closes the door, hard.

Claude pockets the little vial of pills and heads back toward me.

'What was that all about?'

Dusalt makes a face and shrugs a little, like perhaps he'd rather not say. I persist.

'Just curious. She wants to know about Putah Creek. What's going on.'

'Did you tell her?'

'Sure. Why not?'

'Maybe I should invite her to join us?'

'I don't know.' Claude is a mask of indecision. I sense there was more hostility than inquisitiveness in their conversation.

'A little hurt pride,' he says.

'The fact that I was appointed to fill the gap?'

He nods. 'Sure. Feretti gets sick and the first thing they do is bring in an outsider. They don't even talk to her. She carried the load in the office even when Mario was here.'

I raise an eyebrow at this.

'He'd been going downhill for a long time,' says Claude. 'Goya covered for him. She paid some dues,' he says. 'She feels more than a little betrayed.'

There's a knock on the door.

'Come in,' I say.

It's opened by a woman, ringlets of straggly brown hair.

It's a familiar face. I think maybe the cleaning woman, lots of wrinkles, and bags bigger than Gucci's under each eye. Her dress is something from the Good Will. She is the defining element of frump.

'Can I help you?'

'You Madriani?' she says. A cigarette dangles from between painted lips as she talks.

'I am.'

'They called me at the rest home,' she says.

I take another look at her and think maybe she belongs there.

'I was visiting my mother.'

'And you are?'

'Sheila Aikens,' she says. 'They said you wanted me. You want me in here or outside?' Under one arm she has a large file folder, three inches thick, the kind that expands like an accordion, and a purse over the other shoulder. In her free hand is a Styrofoam coffee cup soiled by lipstick.

I look at Claude as if to ask, is this the best we can do? He smiles at me, a little sheepish.

'You can set up outside,' I tell her. 'I'll find you when I'm ready.'

She's dripping ash all over the carpet as she stands there.

'Yeah. Sure.' The grating tone of her voice has all the charm of a wood rasp dragged across a splintered board. Her lack of inflection says, sure — hurry up and wait.

She closes the door.

'Where the hell did she come from?' I look at Claude.

He makes a face, something from the old world. 'You'd have to ask Feretti.'

'It's a little late for that,' I say.

Dusalt gives me a shrug, like such matters are clearly outside of his realm.

Though it's not good to think ill of the dead, given Roland Overroy's sorry work ethic, and now the vision of Sheila Aikens lingering in my doorway like the odor of Pepé LePue, I am gaining a whole new perspective on Mario's management style.

'Where were we?' I say.

'Clothes-line cord and metal stakes.'

'Yes.'

I probe around the edges inquiring as to exactly where these things were inside the van when first observed.

'We didn't touch a thing,' says Claude. 'It was all there in plain view, in the back of the van.' On this, Claude is a little defensive.

'The vehicle was abandoned,' he says. 'The guy has no reasonable expectation of privacy. We didn't need a warrant to look inside.'

I look at him and smile. 'Two days in a parking lot?'

Claude blanches a little.

I don't want to have to shop for a sympathetic judge, someone who might buy this thin argument only to be slapped down later on appeal. In the judicial community, judges who issue warrants are like the rabbis of the ancient Talmud, each with his own relative reputation. Pick one who is not highly regarded and you will pay the price later, in spades.

'Have you talked personally to Mr Harold about the procedures he uses to inventory vehicles?'

Claude nods.

'Does he inventory personal property inside the vehicle

every time he takes one in tow?'

'Like clockwork.'

I make a face. 'Without exception?' I trust Claude, but I have seen too many cases in which the cops will fudge their facts to make them fit.

'Always. Invariably,' he says.

Claude knows what I'm asking; whether he feels confident in this information, whether he can sign an affidavit affirming these facts under penalty of perjury, for review by a superior court judge.

'Harold's outside,' he says. 'You wanna talk to him yourself?' Claude is testing me. Seeing whether I trust him, this hot-shot defense lawyer turned prosecutor.

'No.' I don't bite. 'We go on what you have.' A little investment in trust.

'We're OK, at least for the moment,' I tell him. 'A properly impounded vehicle subject to a routine inventory. Whatever we find should be fair game.'

It is one of the exceptions carved out by the law. A search warrant will not be required for the towel, rope and tent stakes found in the van. Assuming our judge knows the law, Sellig should be free to do her magic on them.

Claude smiles with this thought. The fickle gods of criminal process have blessed him.

'We still need to do hair and fibers on the van,' I tell him, 'and for that we'll need a warrant.'

He nods. So far so good.

We are getting hourly reports from Henderson and the group staking out Iganovich's apartment. He has not shown, either there or at the van. Claude is taking bets that the man is in Mexico drinking margaritas.

'The heat's on,' Claude says. 'Would *you* stick around?'

'No.' But it's a truism in the law that those who violate it, more often than not do dumb things.

I'm busy composing in my head, dictating to Aikens, who is bent over an old IBM Selectric that is covered by more ash than Mt Vesuvius. The woman is smoking like a chimney, keying out the affidavit for Claude's signature. Dusalt has firmed up his facts with the two witnesses and sent them home.

I have a single objective in mind; to convince an impartial magistrate that there is a reasonable probability that evidence of a crime is located in the Russian's van. With this, a warrant will be issued. We can then take prints and fibers, vacuum it for hair, check the tires for impressions, and hope that in all of this we will find some connection with the Putah Creek killings.

I am now dictating from hand-written notes, thoughts I have taken during Claude's earlier briefing, from his follow-up with the witnesses.

As I talk to her, I have one eye on the paper moving through Aikens' typewriter and the other on Claude, to ensure that I'm not departing from the straight and narrow as related by the university cop and Mr Harold.

Claude issues little nods every few seconds as I pass over critical bench marks in their scenario. He must be comfortable with this declaration. It is his ass in the flames if some judge thinks he lied.

I marvel a little at Aikens. Cigarette and all, her fingers move like a blur over the keyboard. She has used the correction key only once in two pages. I am forming a new opinion, regretting my rash assessment of Mario's leadership abilities. The lady knows her job.

'What about Lockyer?' says Claude, breaking into my thoughts. 'He's an easy touch. We get warrants from him all the time. A slam-dunk,' he says. Claude is dropping names in my suggestion box, the process of shopping for a judge who might issue a warrant.

I shake my head. 'Not on this one,' I say. Lockyer may be fine for an auto-theft ring, or a drug bust. But he's a former prosecutor. On this one the appellate courts will be taking a more critical look. I want a neutral, detached magistrate to review the affidavit.

I've already staked out my judge, placed my phone call while Claude was in the other room with his witnesses. Frances Kerney is a former presiding judge of the superior court in this county and known to be on a short list of candidates for elevation to the appellate court. By the time this case arrives on appeal, it is likely that she will be ensconced there. Whatever she touched while on the trial bench will no doubt receive the subtle benefit of any doubt from her brothers of the cloth. A cynical view, perhaps. But in a capital case you seize every edge.

I have Kerney on call. I possess her schedule for the afternoon and early evening, and her home phone number should we go late. I am prepared to grovel if I must.

I'm putting the wrap on the affidavit when I sense motion behind me, the swinging gate at the public counter. I turn. It is Kay Sellig and the patrolman I have assigned to chauffeur her — a courtesy intended to produce a quick turnaround. It has not failed. She has a preliminary analysis of the cord and metal stakes.

Sellig drops her briefcase, a slim leather affair, on Aikens' desk and turns a satisfied smile in my direction.

'Don't know who he is,' she says. 'But he's hung himself with his own rope.'

I'm all eyes. I tell Aikens to take a break. She reaches for the package of Camels in her purse and is out the door. In the next five minutes tobacco stocks will go up four points.

I turn to Sellig. 'What did you find?'

'He must have used whatever was handy. Or else he's a fool,' she says.

'The clothes-line cord,' she says.

'It's traceable?' I ask.

'Like a trail of bread crumbs in a cave.'

I am matching her own satisfied smile.

'It's composed of bundles of thread,' she says, 'tightly woven, and wrapped in a sheath of white plastic. No two manufacturers use the same number or composition of threads.'

She reaches into her briefcase and pulls out a single typed page.

'The cord found in the van has a hundred and twenty-one interior filaments, nine different plastic types and one metal filament.' She looks up at me. 'Identical in all respects with the cord used to tie down the first four Davenport victims.'

'The kids?' I say.

She nods.

I can see in her expression that this begs a question; the Scofields? Sellig ignores this for the moment. Half a loaf is better than nothing.

'It's good,' I say, 'but not conclusive. Might be strong

enough to secure a search warrant, certainly for the van, maybe for the Russian's apartment. How common is this stuff?'

'This particular cord is manufactured by only one company. But as to points of sale, it gets weaker. In this state, at least eight thousand stores sell the stuff, nationwide maybe forty thousand.'

My expression sags. A good defense lawyer would have a field day with this. A critical judge, asked to provide a warrant, weighing the odds, might say that these tent stakes and this cord are probative of nothing more than the fact that perhaps Mr Iganovich likes to camp.

But Sellig is still smiling. I sense in her demeanor that she's not finished.

'The white plastic sheathing around the cord is a different story,' she says. 'When it's applied around the filaments it's hot. The stuff shrinks to a tight fit when it cools.'

She's held the best for last.

'And?'

'The outer threads from the filaments leave their impression in the soft hot plastic on the inside of the sheath. The cutest little extrusion marks you ever saw,' she says. 'Just like fingerprints all over the inside of the plastic sheathing.'

There is a nanosecond of bare silence between us, Claude and I taking this in. Then, almost in a daze, Dusalt puts our mutual thoughts to words: 'Whoever possessed the rope in the van is dog meat.'

Sellig nods. 'Pure Alpo.'

She shows us a photograph, an eight-hundred per cent

blow-up of two pieces of plastic sheathing with its filaments removed. This looks like a giant straw, except for the little bumps and nodules on the inside of each tube. It is a magnified portion of the plastic sheathing with the filaments removed.

Even my untrained eye can see that the patterns on the two pieces are an exact match, nodules and bumps in all the same places.

'These are two matching ends of the same cord,' she says. 'The one on the left is the end piece from the coil of cord in the suspect's van. The one on the right was taken from the wrist of Sharon Collins, the last coed killed. The other piece is taken off the kids.' Sellig's referring to the student victims. 'It is conclusive,' she says. 'They all match. Sequential pieces cut from the same length of rope.'

I will not have to grovel before a judge for a search warrant.

Chapter Seven

By the time I follow Claude and Emil Johnson to the third floor, an evidence tech is already putting up yellow tape to block off one end of the hall close to Iganovich's apartment.

I grab Claude, whisper in his ear. 'We should get Sellig in here, now,' I tell him.

He nods and issues a quick instruction to one of the cops in the hall.

Two Special Enforcement officers packing M-16s, guys in black combat garb, with paramilitary training and hair triggers, come out of the apartment. One of them is unloading his weapon, soft-nosed cartridges in a clip, lead that will expand like putty when it hits a target.

The suspect is obviously not home. We wait outside the door. A few seconds later, Sellig is escorted up the stairs by a uniformed cop. She's carrying a small black case, like an undersized brief box. She goes in, and we follow. I have my hands in my pockets.

I feel a little ridiculous, trussed-up in a Kevlar flack jacket that reaches from belt to collar. Emil has asked that I be here, in case questions arise during the search. His effort I think to spread some accountability.

'An all-points bulletin has been issued for Iganovich,' he tells me. This based on the arrest warrant I secured.

'Be careful by the door.' Emil's command presence. Across the threshold there's a bowl of cat food, little white fuzz growing on its contents, and flies, flies are everywhere. The most overpowering sensation about the place is its odor. This is something between rancid meat and a leaking septic tank.

Claude has a handkerchief over his mouth. He is trying to make his way through the cluttered filth to a window on the other side of the room. He opens it and there's a slight cross ventilation. The full fury of this smell passes me on its way to the door where I am standing.

There are several days' newspapers piled up in the hall outside. They are rolled, wrapped in an outer cover of blank newsprint, but I can see dates on two of these. I make a mental note of this.

The place is sparse, what the fair landlord would have to advertise as a small studio apartment. There is a couch in the living room, a sleeper that looks like it hasn't been closed up in years, an event that may have coincided with the last time the bedding was changed. A small coffee table − it is difficult to imagine that this might have rested before a neatly closed couch at one time − has been pushed into a corner. It is now cluttered with old mail, newspapers and dirty dishes, remnants of food remaining on some of these.

I trip through this mess, careful not to disturb anything until Sellig is finished. She is opening the little case, putting on gloves.

She's co-opted two of the local evidence techs. They are taking pictures, pin-pointing the location of objects in the room. One of the deputies is wielding a video camera, doing a walk through and panning the rooms. This should take all of thirty seconds on his tape.

A few of the more curious neighbors are now wandering by the door, for a look inside. One of the uniforms is telling them to move on, back to their rooms or out of the building. He reaches for the door to close it, but Emil calls him off.

'What you wanna do, kill us?' he says. He's muttering to himself. 'Place smells like the foul end of my aunt Matilda.'

Sellig is busy carefully pulling clothes from the closet. This is not an extensive wardrobe, two pairs of pants, tattered chinos, and a light jacket. I think she is probably looking for blood stains. She comes up empty. She talks to one of the county technicians and two minutes later the guy is back with a small hand-held vacuum. This is made for police work, with a little box that holds a finely made filter. The technician is giving a pair of jeans the once over with this thing. When he's finished he pulls the filter and places it in a plastic bag. Another deputy then marks the bags for identification, and the process starts again on the next pair.

They are looking for trace evidence, a bit of sand, a piece of reed from the creek, something that might show up later under a microscope, that could place Iganovich on the Putah Creek, something to corroborate the clothes-line cord. They package the pants separately in bags, the jacket in another.

My hands are in my pockets, pushed all the way to the bottom, to keep from touching anything. I wish I could say the same for Emil. He is fingering little items in a half-open dresser drawer, personal trinkets that I assume belong to the suspect. He pulls a set of rosary beads from the drawer and looks at them, then at me.

'Fuckin' guy's probably an altar boy,' he says.

He drops the rosary on top of the dresser, laughing to himself. I hope they have already photographed this surface. If not the shrinks will soon be working on the theory that we have a religious freak here, a man who does the stations of the cross with each slaying. Johnson and his tripping little fingers will have the Archdiocese all over my ass.

'What do you think?' I'm talking to Claude, a little under my breath as I wander toward him in a corner of the room.

'I think our guy's on a trip, that he's not coming back,' he says.

I wrinkle an eyebrow.

'State Department informed us earlier today that he holds two passports, one Soviet,' he says, 'issued before the collapse, the other Russian, issued by the current government. First thing we looked for.' They've now gone through all the drawers, his closets, what clothing is left. The passports aren't here.

Except for trace evidence which they won't know until they examine the little filters under a microscope back at the lab, Sellig informs me that they haven't found much.

Henderson has caught up with us, huffing and puffing from the stairs. He wants to know what instructions to give the officers out on the perimeter, the people whose assignment it is to watch for the Russian.

'Keep 'em in place until o-six-hundred,' says Claude.

'Then cut 'em free. It's a long shot anyway,' he says.

'Do we know if he might be driving another vehicle?' Claude is asking the plain clothes detective beside him.

'I don't know.'

'Well, check DMV.' There's an edge to Claude's voice, like this is something somebody should have thought of earlier.

Emil picks up on this. 'Son-of-a-bitch,' he says. 'Why wasn't that done?'

'See if he has another vehicle registered besides the van,' says Claude. 'If he does, circulate the license numbers, especially to the guys on the perimeter.'

'I want that done now. Immediately,' says Emil. There's a lot of cheerleading going on here.

'I want us to see him before he sees us,' says Claude. 'If he wanders back home I want him picked up quickly and quietly.'

'Damn right,' says Emil. 'We don't need some fucking gun battle on the street with civilians in the middle or hostages taken.'

I don't say anything, but my senses tell me this is not likely to happen. Investigators who checked with Iganovich's employer, Ajax Security, have told us that he has not shown up for work in two days. Notwithstanding the prudent actions of Claude Dusalt to cover our presence here, I think Mr Iganovich is on the lam.

Henderson turns, sees a phone mounted on the wall behind me. 'Can I use this?' He is a big man, and out of shape. Anything to avoid one more jaunt up and down these stairs.

Claude has wandered off, in another direction. Emil

looks at one of the county evidence techs. Sellig is in the bathroom working through a mirrored cabinet over the sink. The tech shrugs his shoulders. 'We've already dusted it,' the guy says.

'Sure, go ahead,' says Emil.

I glance at it for an instant before Henderson can reach for the receiver on the wall, and something catches my eye.

'Hold on a second.'

Henderson looks at me.

'In a dive like this I would think he'd have a rotary dial,' I say.

Emil looks at the phone. 'You can buy that model at Costco for thirty-nine dollars ninety-five,' he says.

'You're right,' I tell him. But when Henderson reaches for it again I grab his wrist. I have a little micro-cassette recorder in my pocket, smaller than a pack of cigarettes, which I carry for quick dictation outside the office. I take this out.

'Let's keep the noise down please. Cool it with the little vacuum.' Suddenly the place has gone dead. Sellig is out of the bathroom to see what is happening.

Claude looks at me. I have a single finger to my lips like I'm hushing a child.

Emil is looking at me, wondering if I've slipped over the edge.

I click on the little recorder.

'Paul Madriani, July twenty-third. The time,' I look at my watch, 'is seven forty-three p.m. We are in the apartment of the suspect Andre Iganovich.'

I press the pause button on the recorder, pluck the receiver from the phone. But instead of dialing, I punch a single button, centered among others at the bottom of the phone. I hold the recorder to the ear piece. There's a series of little clicks as the forty-dollar wonder on the wall does the one thing that Andre Iganovich would most assuredly undo, if he could — it redials the last number called by the Russian before his hasty departure.

I am busy recording the little clicks that will give me the phone number if no one answers, or if whoever is on the other end hangs up once I speak. Instead, after three short rings the call is met by a recording of its own:

'You have reached Air Canada. At the moment all of our agents are busy. Please be patient and your call will be answered in the order it was received. Please stay on the line.'

Chapter Eight

Three days after the raid on the Russian's apartment I am working my way through the in-basket on the desk, sorting the stuff that cannot wait.

Claude is still busy checking passenger manifests at Air Canada; any lead on where Iganovich may have gone. On reflection, Claude says this makes sense. A Russian would not go south, to the warm climes of the Mexican Riviera. Canada makes eminent good sense according to Dusalt, easier to get back to the northern reaches of his homeland.

Suddenly there's a shadow, like some dark cloud on a summer's day. I look up. It's Lenore Goya, in the doorway.

She's tapping her wristwatch with her forefinger. 'Our meeting,' she says. 'Remember?' I can tell by her tone that she's a little miffed, a woman who likes to be punctual.

'Yes,' I say. 'I'm running a little late. Some administrative chores,' I tell her.

In fact, I've been going over disposition sheets for the office, monthly statistics on case loads for the various deputies. It is not a happy picture. It is becoming increasingly clear that I cannot afford to lose Goya. Without her, the office would be up a creek without the proverbial paddle.

I trail her down the hall to her office. It is where we had agreed to meet.

The place has the ambience of a coat closet, ten-by-ten with case files in folders stacked halfway up the walls.

'I hope this won't take too long,' she says. 'I've got a court call in forty minutes.'

'I thought it would be good if we broke the ice,' I tell her. 'General discussion about the office, ideas for improvement. Things you would change if you could.'

Her eyes open wide, a little mock amazement. She looks like the late Gilda Radner playing Emily Litella. 'You want to know what I think about the office?' she says. Like, come on.

I nod a little encouragement.

She laughs. 'In two words — It sucks.' She is grinning at me across the desk now, pearl white, even teeth, a dentist's dream.

I smile back. 'That's constructive,' I say. 'But maybe you could give me a little more detail.'

'Fine,' she says. She starts ticking off points on the fingers of one hand. 'We're understaffed. We're overworked. This year the felony case load went up twenty-six per cent. We haven't had a salary increase in three years. They're talking layoffs and a cut in health benefits.'

She tells me that every defense lawyer in the northern part of the state knows we can't try the cases we have.

'And on a personal note, I'd like a new office with a view, preferably something that looks out on the courthouse.' She thinks for a moment. 'I could do with an hour for lunch maybe once a week, that's optional,' she says. 'And, of course, I'd like your job.'

I look at her across the table. She looks back, still

smiling, her idea of a cerebral Mexican stand-off.

'You asked,' she says.

Mario Feretti was right. The woman is direct.

'Are you a candidate?' I ask.

'Get real,' she says. 'You've seen the people who run this county. Can you see them appointing an Hispanic woman as their DA?' She laughs at the image of this.

'Oh, and one more thing,' she says, 'as long as you're asking, you will either have to get rid of Roland, or immunize me for murder. Because if you don't dump him I intend to kill the son-of-a-bitch. He's running through secretaries like some snotty-nosed kid uses up Kleenex.'

It is true. In the last year, three seasoned steno's have left the office, something already brought to my attention by the other deputies.

I try to give Goya a few positive strokes. 'You hold the office together,' I tell her. 'Mario, Mr Feretti, spoke very highly of you.'

She smiles a little at this. 'Mario was a prince. I will miss him,' she says. 'We will all miss him.' It seems that her bitterness toward her situation did not extend to Feretti. There is something in her expression that tells me there was genuine affection here, that Mario's death has suddenly left some vast professional void in her life.

'He had a great deal of confidence in your abilities.' I am shameless. I play upon this.

She smiles. 'He had so much confidence that he asked *you* to take his place when he got sick.'

'He knew that you couldn't handle his job and the felony calendar too,' I tell her. 'Mario trusted you to get the job done.'

'Mario had no choice,' she says. 'He had a full plate and the county gave him nothing but kids out of law school for help — because they work cheap,' she says.

I remind her that Overroy is no kid out of law school. That he has been here for almost thirty years. But that even with his seniority it is she who is assigned the heavier cases.

'Spare me,' she says. 'Come back in thirty more and he'll still be here. You know as well as I do that around here "relief" is not spelled R-O-L-A-N-D.'

On the issue of Roland Overroy I have hit a raw nerve.

'I've been here seven years. I've been passed over for promotion twice. They say it's because they have no money.'

More likely it's because Roland won't retire. But I cannot say this to Goya. If word got out that this subject passed the lips of management, or if any move is made to seek his retirement, he could sue the county in the flash of an eye for age discrimination. For Roland this would be departing county service on a high note, something to augment his six-figure retirement check each year. It is little wonder that this state is going broke.

I encourage Goya to hang in there a little longer, to stick it out, that I will do what I can.

'Sure,' she says. 'But when a big case comes along, something making headlines across the state. Well . . .' Her voice trails off. Her facial expression tells me how this sentence will end.

The notoriety surrounding this case is eating on her. A few quiet conversations with neighbors in the building, and reporters had their story, and Iganovich's name. His picture was spread all over the front page of this morning's

Times. She knows that success in a high-profile prosecution like this is the stuff of which legendary legal careers are made.

'What hurts,' she says, 'is that they didn't even talk to me.'

I look at her, questioning this comment.

'When they filled behind Mario, the county supervisors didn't even come and talk to me. They just went to somebody on the outside.' She thumps the desk as if to make the point, steel in her eyes. 'I suppose that should tell me something.' She's shaking her head now. 'You know, I tried to leave last year. Gave Mario my resignation. He talked me out of it. I made a mistake,' she says. 'A big mistake.'

I had not heard this. Like a lot of things Mario never told me.

Then quickly she pulls herself together. She turns an agreeable smile my way, fighting back the bile. 'Then again,' she says, 'maybe it's just been a bad week.'

'It's only Monday,' I say.

'See what I mean?'

We both laugh a little, put a face on it. I see a lot of frustration here, masked by a quick wit. I sense no personal enmity, and I wonder if I would be so generous if the shoe were on the other foot.

'I will see what I can do,' I say.

She looks at her watch. 'I've got to go now. Court,' she says. She's gathering papers and a stack of files from off the desk.

'Lenore.'

She looks up at me.

'I will do whatever I can.'
'Sure.'

Chapter Nine

For a man who is inherently lazy, Roland Overroy exhibits an unusual vitality in the pursuit of political opportunity. Since Mario's death he has left no stone unturned in his efforts to cultivate people of influence in this county. He has in no uncertain way thrown his own hat in the ring of contenders for Feretti's old job.

While I have done all within my power to keep Roland out of the Putah Creek cases, I now discover that he has been busy, lobbying, back-dooring the sheriff on matters concerning these prosecutions. Overroy has convinced Emil that an encounter between law enforcement and the survivors of the Putah Creek victims would be a politic thing at this time.

'This is a major mistake.' I am talking to Johnson in the confines of his office. We are alone.

'It'll be a disaster,' I tell him, this proposed meeting with the Putah Creek survivors, a gathering of angry and dazed parents; families who are likely at this stage to blame anyone handy for their grief.

Overroy has demonstrated more cunning in this than I had credited to him. Rather than an overt play for Johnson's support before the board of supervisors, he has maneuvered himself into a position to advise the sheriff on the political fall-out of these killings. His bid for support will no doubt follow.

'They want a meeting,' says Emil. 'Whataya want me to do? I can't say no.'

The 'they', in Johnson's plaintiff capitulation, is the county's victim-witness program, a bureaucracy of its own making that has spawned a perpetual money machine for a horde of loosely wrapped psychic healers and self-described counselors. These people take referrals of crime victims and send the bill to the state for payment under the Crime Compensation Act.

'Roland met with Maggie Wilson yesterday,' Emil tells me. 'It's all arranged. The meeting is this afternoon.'

Wilson is the victim-witness coordinator in this county, the crime victim's answer to Don Corleone in drag. To defense attorneys trying to stave off a long term for their clients, she is known as 'Attila the Hen', a woman who missed her calling on the committee of vigilance. Alas, for Maggie Wilson, justice is blind reprisal.

I roll my eyes. 'Tell them I scotched it,' I say. 'You can blame it on me. Tell them we will meet with them privately at the appropriate time, when we have specific details to reveal. Right now there is nothing to tell.'

This slows him for only a second as he considers his options.

'Roland thinks it's a good idea,' he says.

'Roland would,' I tell him. Overroy has no concept of the dictates of a fair trial. It has not dawned on him that a public gathering of the victims will turn out the press like buffalo at a watering hole. He will poison the potential pool of jurors for a thousand miles.

Since the last set of killings, life in Davenport resembles nothing so much as festivities under the big top. One enterprising soul armed with the university's student mailing list is now marketing a stun gun packing sixty-thousand volts, packaged as a collapsible umbrella; no doubt his version of 'Singing in the Rain'.

Emil is sprawled in his overstuffed swivel chair, his cowboy-booted feet propped in the center of the desk, on top of a pile of police reports and booking sheets that have been sent up the chain for his review.

'Listen to me, Paul.' His voice is edging toward some southern homily. 'It's no big deal. We can hold their hands, pat 'em on the ass, tell 'em we're worken' around the clock to find the killer. It's the truth,' he tells me. 'Hell, all these folks want is some assurance, a little public recognition that they're in pain.'

I'm getting worried. Emil is beginning to talk like victim-witness with heavy jowls and a southern accent, the sensitive red-neck.

'The judges won't like it,' I tell him. 'It'll be a circus. Prejudicial pretrial publicity,' I say. Usually the judges don't get involved until later, but in a notorious case, they may make an exception. Such a meeting would be a spawning ground for new and additional arguments on appeal. I get a vision of Ingel's steely eyes, anticipate the phone call that will no doubt come when he hears of this.

He looks at me, an arched eyebrow. This has his attention. The wrath in the black robes. He thinks for a moment, weighs the anger of four superior court judges against the organized lynch mob that can be victim-witness and its followers.

'Well, you work it out with them. You talk to court and they'll understand,' he says. 'You've got their respect,' he tells me.

Now I'm getting my own haunches stroked by Emil, sunshine and southern bullshit.

'Listen, Emil.' I inject a little calm in my tone, my levelest attempt at sound reason. 'I've dealt with these people, victim-witness before,' I tell him. 'And they will not be satisfied. Give them a public forum and they will pillory both of us.'

'You worry too much,' he says. 'It's just a little private get together. Trust me,' he says. 'It'll be OK.'

From its opening gavel, Emil's meeting with victim-witness has the decorum of a mud-wrestling match.

As I expected, Maggie Wilson sand-bagged him, stacking the crowd with community activists and campus organizers, anybody looking for a cause, and an audience-share on the five o'clock news.

Claude and I stay in the back, not far from Roland Overroy, who I saw lurking in the shadows behind a pillar.

Maggie Wilson has arrogated a seat up close, in the front row, a pulpit for some cheerleading — a good place for roasting a southern hot dog. When Emil invited her to join him on the rostrum she smiled, then politely declined.

Then the press showed up. Wilson encouraged the guys with the boom-mikes to stick them in Emil's face. Reporters peppered him with questions about Iganovich and his whereabouts. The audience got personal about the investigation, demanding details on the method of death and other particulars at the crime scenes. This cut too close to the bone, questions Emil could not in good conscience answer. The crowd became abusive. After several minutes of this, Emil's southern pride is in full retreat. He has called a recess, time out to patch wounds in his corner.

'Son-of-a-bitch,' he says as he joins us in the back of the room. Emil is puffing hard. He has loops of perspiration the size of a draft-horse harness under each arm.

'Fucken' A,' he says. 'They're kicking my ass.'

I could say I told him so, but in his current mood he would probably deck me.

'Any ideas?' he says.

The crowd is busy getting coffee, taking a leak. For the moment Emil seems relieved that at least they are not doing the latter on him.

Claude makes a suggestion.

'We could get the families of the victims out of here, into a private room, strip the gathering of its legitimacy,' he says. 'Announce that they are now meeting privately with other officials.'

This would leave Emil to deal with the hangers-on, the wannabe grievers and those looking for a social cause. They will get twenty minutes of campaign oratory with periodic admonitions not to back-talk or question Johnny Law.

Emil dispatches Claude and two of his deputies to button-hole the families for a private gathering away from the press and public, his own form of latter-day segregation. Emil heads back to the rostrum and I turn to grab a drink from the fountain in the hall outside. People are still milling in as I push through the door. It's when I run into him, a swiping action, banging shoulders. We stop in mid-stride and he looks at me with deadly dark eyes, like something from the Spanish Inquisition.

'Mr Madriani,' he says, dusky and brooding. My name rolls off his tongue, the affectation of some early California Don Armando. Acosta's hair is slicked back, his suit an impeccable dark pinstripe, little kerchief in the pocket matching his maroon silk tie. I could retire on the metal in his cuff links to say nothing of the three-thousand-dollar gold watch on his wrist.

For an instant I am tongue-tied. It is awkward.

'Judge.' It's all that will come out of my mouth. I nod, forced deference.

The Coconut has a woman by the arm, dark complexion like his own, a fierce resemblance. I suspect this is his sister, the mother of the dead victim Sharon Collins. There are no introductions. It is not that friendly. Instead he whispers in the woman's ear, and a second later she walks off by herself toward the seats in the auditorium.

'I want to talk to you,' he says. This is no request. He wags a finger in my face, backs out through the stream of bodies jostling in the doorway. He finds a quiet area outside, on the steps in front of the building. Once there, he turns on me quickly, mincing no words.

'I don't know how you got here,' he says. He means my appointment as prosecutor. 'I had hoped for somebody,' he searches for the right word, 'more competent,' he says finally.

'Judge Ingel talked to you?' he asks.

I nod.

'Then you know why I'm here,' he says.

'I do. And you have my sympathies,' I say.

He looks at me, something halfway between meanness and a surly smirk.

'I don't want your fucking sympathies,' he tells me. He suddenly loses the clipped tones of affected English. 'You can shower all of that on the suckers inside,' he says. 'What I want is a look at the file, everything the cops have in the Collins case,' he says. He looks at me, stone faced. He knows I cannot give him this, confidential files on a pending murder investigation.

'Everything is being done that can be,' I tell him.

'Is that so?'

'It is,' I say.

'I can give you some help,' he tells me.

'In what way?'

'I have access to people in Capital County who have made offers of assistance.' He's talking about special treatment for a member of the bench. He tells me some cops, old friends, are willing to dog leads for him in their spare time. They will, no doubt, be given special treatment the next time they come looking for a search warrant or take the stand in his court. Such is the common currency in the halls of justice.

He tells me Davenport is a cow county. 'You know as well as I do that they have limited resources. I have no intentions of sitting back and watching as they close the books on my niece,' he says.

'No one's closing the books.'

'Then you won't mind if I look at the files.'

'You know I can't do that.'

'Can't or won't?' He's picking lint off the shoulder of my coat now, his message that I do nothing right, not to

109

his level of expectations, even to the point of my dress.

'Your honor.' I back away a full step. The lint on my shoulder belongs to me.

'I'm not looking for an argument or a difficult time. You know as well as I that the files in a pending case are not public,' I say. 'They are not available to anyone but the investigators working the case.'

Cold beady eyes, like some Aztec high priest about to do sacrifice on an altar of stone. In this moment he is, I am sure, measuring the myriad ways a judge can screw over a hapless lawyer. I suspect he has made promises to his sister that now, because of my intransigence, he cannot keep.

'What I would have expected,' he says, 'from someone like you.' Then his forefinger is in my face, manicured and long, and shaking with anger. 'Don't fuck up,' he says. His expression is cold and dead.

Then I hear the click of hard heels as he turns and leaves me standing alone on the steps.

Against my own better judgement I have drawn the private duty with family members, along with Claude in a smaller conference room off the main auditorium. I can hear table-pounding and loud voices outside, in the other room. Emil is having his own come-to-Jesus meeting with the press.

We are seated around a large table now, conference style, Julie Park's parents – her father Kim Park, a physician from Southern California – at one end of the table. The Sniders are next to him, then Mr and Mrs Collins and Acosta. Next to Acosta is Rodney Slate's mother. I am told that his father is hospitalized with a serious heart condition, no doubt worsened by the loss of his only son.

Acosta is silent in this meeting, his brooding eyes on me every second. He has always been one for the *appearance* of propriety. It is one thing to bend the rules, to slip a peak at official files, another to come here dripping saliva and demanding blood with the unwashed masses. That would be unseemly. He would rather back-door me with Ingel. So here he will sit, bide his time and listen to the others, ever the proper jurist, the soul of restraint.

There's a young kid, in his teens, seated next to Mrs Snider, a strong family resemblance. My guess is that this is a younger brother of the victim, Jonathan Snider. At the other end of the table is a man in a blue serge suit passing out business cards. He flips one down the table in my direction.

George Cayhill
Assistant Dean for Student Affairs

He has insinuated himself into this meeting, representing the interests of the university.

A woman next to Cayhill, in the dark glasses removes these to reveal high, prominent cheek bones, and wide-set hazel eyes, a bit reddened, I think, by recent tears. She is tall and slender, taller than I, with feminine and fetching moves. She has thick brunette hair, generous waves which cascade around her shoulders as she shakes it free. Her mouth matches the breadth of her other facial features, with generous pouting lips. It is the face, I think, of classic design, not the simpering beauty of a covergirl, but more unique. Her gaze is intense, like maybe there is something more than good looks behind these eyes. She wears little makeup. There is something wholesome in her looks, like the snapshot of a dressed-up farm girl in the 1940s. She reminds me of images I have seen recently on the silver screen, of Geena Davis in vintage flashbacks.

Without warning she fires a quick glance in my direction and catches me staring. She smiles, dimples forming in the recesses of her cheeks. She reaches across the table, long delicate fingers.

'I should introduce myself. Jeanette Scofield.' She says this matter of fact, like what you see is what you get, no pretensions here.

She is the widow of Abbott Scofield. He no doubt got the better bargain in this marriage. The woman sitting across the table from me could easily pass, in age, for his daughter.

She looks to the man beside her. 'My brother, Jess,' she says. I get all five fingers and a squeeze like an iron vice from the fellow sitting next to her. 'Jess Amara,' he tells me. I notice that Claude is eyeing the widow Scofield palpably. He exchanges nods with the man, like maybe the two already know each other.

'Ladies and gentlemen,' he says. 'I wish we were meeting under more pleasant circumstances.' Claude has no notes and is reaching a bit for a good opening in an awkward situation. I can tell he is a little pissed at Emil for putting him in this position.

'At the present time there are more than a hundred law enforcement officers working around the clock to catch this killer. The full resources of the state, through the

112

Office of the Attorney General, have been committed to this case and we are at present pursuing active leads.'

A dozen eyes are boring in on Dusalt, looking for something, more than a ration of statistics. Kim Park, Julie Park's father, is getting antsy at the end of the table. But the interruption is a deep baritone from another quarter.

'Lieutenant.' It is the man just introduced to me as Jess Amara.

'I think maybe we can cut through some of this,' he says. 'It's been in all the papers. This man, your suspect. What's his name?' he says, searching for the proper pronunciation.

'Iganovich,' says Claude.

'Yes. Iganovich,' says Amara. 'What can you tell us about him?'

Claude is looking at Amara, a picture of exasperation, as if somehow he's been outflanked.

'I should introduce you,' he says. 'For those of you who haven't met him, Sergeant Amara is a member of the Davenport City Police Department.' The reason for Claude's cool reception of Amara is clear. He knows that Amara, through scuttlebutt in his department, will have more information on the Russian as well as other aspects of the case, than has appeared in the local newspapers or on the tube.

All eyes around the table fix on Amara. Suddenly this group of grieving orphans has found a common resource, someone on the inside who like themselves has suffered a personal loss in this thing.

'Are you close to an arrest?' says Amara.

'We have leads,' says Claude. 'We've issued an all-points bulletin.'

'Then you think he's left the area?'

The others are watching and listening, leaving the inquiries to someone who knows what to ask.

'We have reason to believe that he has.'

'Then you know where he's gone?'

'We have leads.' Claude is back to safe ground.

Based on the Air Canada information, police now believe that Iganovich has fled north. The cops cannot confirm that he boarded a flight, as he no doubt used an alias to buy his ticket. There is an open border between the two countries not requiring passports. In his apartment the cops have found two credit cards issued in his name. Iganovich knows that to use these would be to leave a trail like irradiated bread crumbs. Authorities have frozen his small bank account to prevent any further ATM transfers. They believe this was the source of purchase for the airline ticket. When you're on the lam, cash is king. Broke, they believe he will be forced to the surface soon, driven to commit some foolish act for money.

'But you're focusing on a general area?' says Amara. He's back to geography.

'We have an idea,' says Claude. It's clear he's not going to give anything else away. If Amara knows more he will have to say so.

'Do *you* have any idea where they are looking?' This latter comes from Park, but it's not directed to Claude, instead to Amara.

The officer shrugs his shoulders, like this is not his party.

Park has a look of bewilderment about him, like a

favorite dog when its master moves a ball too quickly from one hand to the other. It is a dazed expression I have seen before, in the eyes of loved ones seeking answers in the days and hours immediately after a brutal murder.

'This man,' says Park. 'This Ivan Iganovich.'

'Andre,' says Claude. 'We believe his name is Andre Iganovich.'

Park absorbs this without much interest. 'According to the newspapers he was a security guard at the university? Is that true?' he says.

Claude makes a face of concession.

Park cannot seem to comprehend how the suspect in his daughter's murder could hold such a position of trust.

'Dr Park, the university didn't hire this man.' It is Cayhill from the far end of the table. 'We hired a licensed private security firm under a contract to provide some basic security for a number of buildings owned by the university.'

None of this seems to make much of a dint on Dr Park or his wife. The woman it seems is in another world, a cocoon of grief. She seems not yet to have come to grips with the notion that twenty years of tender love now lies on a coroner's cold steel slab two blocks from here.

'The important point,' says Cayhill, 'is that the suspect, Mr Iganovich, was not a university employee. He was an employee of the security firm.' Cayhill smiles likes some Fuller Brush salesman.

'No,' says Park. 'The important point is that my daughter is dead.'

'Oh, of course,' says Cayhill. 'I didn't mean . . . well you know what I mean.'

Cayhill is busy riding the wooden rocking-horse of civil liability, putting forth the theories of defense as laid out by the university's lawyers, trying to stem any early thought of a civil suit. This is the farthest thing from Park's mind at the moment.

He looks at his wife with a wrinkled expression, like who could care about such details at a time like this. From the look on their faces they still hold out hope that something said here perhaps will relieve a little of the pain of this loss. It is the perpetual quest of survivors in violent crime, the search for some explanation to a random death, the pursuit of an element of reason that at least in their minds gives some justification to a senseless act. The Parks have not yet reached the horn of cynicism. That will take hold as days and weeks turn to months, as the justice process moves through its slow grind.

Suddenly there is a loud clamor from the other room, Emil's little meeting with the press. It's one of the sheriff's deputies coming through the door behind us. He closes it again, locking out the din from the other room, leans over and passes a message slip to Claude, who reads it.

'Excuse me,' he says. 'Mr Madriani will handle the briefing for the moment. I will be right back.'

Suddenly eyes are on me.

'I have a question,' says Amara. 'Do we know how the suspect came into the country?'

This draws a blank expression from me. 'I don't,' I say.

'In order to get into the country an immigrant usually requires a sponsor,' he says, 'a relative, friend, maybe an employer.'

'I'm sure that investigators are looking into that.'

Actually I am not, but I make a mental note to talk to Claude about it in a private moment.

The gathering starts to digress, private conversations cropping up around the table as the survivors begin to communicate their common pain.

Park is talking to Amara, quietly about the immigration item, sponsors and the like. He is taking notes on a piece of paper he's taken from his pocket. As I watch him I wonder what the purpose of this missive can be. I had been warned by the shrinks that survivors of crime often react in predictable patterns. When the suspended disbelief of death finally dissolves it will first turn to rage, and then obsession.

Claude has come back. He settles into his chair and leans into my ear, the hissing of words. 'Go home,' he says, 'and pack. Enough for several days. We have a flight, ten tomorrow morning.'

I look at him. He says nothing more, but from the expression on his face the message is clear. Somewhere on this planet Andre Iganovich has come to ground.

Chapter Ten

After three days and four phone calls I have finally hooked up with Kay Sellig. I brace myself for bad news. It is written in her eyes.

'So much for special weapons and tactics,' she says. She is looking up at me, leaning on one of the metal tables in her stainless steel kingdom where we met this morning. Sellig is commenting on the curious circumstances surrounding the capture of Andre Iganovich.

I am anxious to hear what she has to say, but I am in a hurry. 'I'm on my way to the airport,' I tell her, 'with a flight in less than two hours.'

'Vancouver?' she says.

I nod.

I am booked with Dusalt to fly to British Columbia. It seems that Claude's strategy, the full court press on the Russian's finances, has spun gold. Iganovich was picked up by Canadian authorities yesterday afternoon, after an altercation with — of all things — two department store security guards. He was detained by the Royal Canadian Mounted Police after some suspicious conduct involving a pair of socks in a Hudson Bay Company store. While no shop-theft charges were brought, the officers discovered the outstanding American warrant for murder. He now sits in a detention facility in Vancouver.

'Then I guess we can say that at least we've got one of them.' Sellig deadpans this as she gives me the news.

'A copy-cat?' I say.

She nods.

I cannot say that I am surprised. It was something I had seen that day, outside Iganovich's apartment door, as police searched inside.

I'm wiping sleep from my eyes. I have been on the phone with the State Department in Washington since six this morning, being briefed on the US-Canadian Extradition Treaty. Iganovich is making noises of a legal battle to come. He is refusing to waive extradition.

'I wanted to break the news to you first,' she says. 'I haven't told any of the investigators yet. I can't stand crying.'

She is right. Emil and company have been busy for the last twenty-four hours, spreading the official line to every reporter who will listen, that citizens in Davenport, undergraduates at the university, are again safe, that from all appearances they have caught their killer. They are telling community leaders that they can now get back to what they do best, business.

'You're sure about this?' I say.

'No conclusive evidence,' she says, 'nothing I could give to a court. But the discrepancies . . . they keep piling up. If you're asking me my opinion, the answer is yes. Someone is mimicking our killer. And I'm not alone in this feeling. Have you talked to Lloyd Tolar, the medical examiner?'

I shake my head.

'You should,' she says.

'How could a copy-cat have the details; the folded clothes, the kind of rope, the stakes?' I ask. It is an axiom in the business of serial crime that police will withhold certain details from the press and public, a means of testing the compulsive confessors, the small and elite legion of crazies who plague every sensational case.

'In this case he could have gotten enough from news photos,' she says. 'God knows we've gotten the coverage.'

She is right. There have been a dozen pictures, two in national news magazines that showed the victims tied to the ground, a little editorial taste to blank-out the faces and genitals. There were close-up window shots of the stakes, and the rope, and the clothes folded in an arc like a halo over the victims' heads.

Sellig moves to one of the other stainless steel tables. The surface is divided into three separate sections each containing several pieces of cord and some metal tent stakes, shiny and new. The cord is the kind my mother used when I was a child to hang clothes on the line in our yard, bundled pieces of thread wrapped in a white plastic sheathing.

She picks out four of the stakes and moves these to another nearby table. They look like the others, except these have been taken down on a grinder to a needle-like sharpness. They resemble nothing so much as the point on a dagger.

'These,' she says, 'were used to kill the first four victims, the college kids.'

There are two remaining stakes in this group, like the others store-bought, but with more rounded points. These have not been modified.

'The two here,' she says, 'were used to kill the Scofield victims.' She raises an eyebrow and moves on, to the other end of the table where assorted pieces of rope are assembled in plastic trays.

'Garden variety clothes line,' she says. 'You can buy it in ten thousand stores across the country. Except that these pieces,' she's sweeping her hand over the first two trays, the rope from the student killings — 'these pieces each came from the same length of rope, each cut in sequence. They match the stuff found in Iganovich's van. They also match the rope used in Oregon and Orange County. From what I can see, Iganovich did 'em all.'

I remember her discourse on the subject, the affidavit used to search the Russian's apartment.

'The extrusion marks from the thread filaments on the inside of the plastic sheathing, they all match,' she says.

She moves to the last tray, the cord used to tie Abbott and Karen Scofield to the ground.

'Here we have a different kind of rope,' she says. 'A hundred and twenty-seven plastic filaments and different chemical composition. Produced by a different manufacturer.'

She waits for a moment, a pause for effect, to let this settle in.

'It was only what he couldn't see from the photos, the buried points on the stakes, and the composition of the cord, where he went wrong.'

I say nothing. I just listen. It is not what I want to hear. I am thinking maybe this guy just bought another rope, maybe his grinder broke down.

But she is dashing my hopes. 'There are other

discrepancies, too,' she says. 'The fact that victim identifications, driver's licenses, wallets or purses weren't found on any of the kids. Yet Karen Scofield's purse was left in plain view, with her wallet and complete ID inside. Abbott Scofield's wallet and driver's license were found in the pocket of his pants.'

Police haven't found any of the victims' personal effects in Iganovich's apartment. It was one of the first things they looked for, an evidentiary linchpin. They are checking now to see if he rented any other property, a storage facility, maybe the key to a bus locker.

'Nothing fits,' she says. 'The age of the Scofields, the location of their bodies close to a county road.' At first Sellig thought maybe it was a case of the man becoming more daring. Now she's not so sure.

And there is more. Sellig is troubled by the profile. 'It fits Iganovich to a tee,' she says. 'Every item. But, if it's consistent, the killer didn't know any of his victims. The pattern is he never took familiar game,' she says. She looks at me, a single index-finger to pursed lips. 'If this is true, why the mutilation of Karen Scofield? Why did he take her eye?' She has checked with the psychiatrists on this one. They are all in accord. They believe the killer mutilated the body, removed the eye because he knew this victim, and she knew him. It is the only explanation they have for this deviation.

'There's something more,' I tell her.

She looks at me.

'The newspapers outside of Iganovich's apartment door, the day the police searched.'

I had noticed them when I entered the apartment, the

123

rolled and unread pile of local papers against the door. Two of these daily editions had predated the Scofield killings. To me it seemed strange, that unless Iganovich was staying somewhere else in the Davenport area during this period, that he should leave these papers on the floor in the hallway. I tell Sellig this.

I have asked Claude to gather the Russian's telephone records for my review. There was something strange here. Again it is not conclusive, but it points in a definite direction. It seems the telephone call made from the phone in Iganovich's apartment to Air Canada was placed two days before Karen and Abbott Scofield were murdered.

'Either the man believes in long term planning,' she says, 'or he had already gone, before the last two victims were killed.'

'I'll need a copy of your report on this,' I tell her. 'As soon as possible.'

'I'll fax it to your office this afternoon,' she says.

'I will read it in detail when I get back from Canada. Until then we should keep this to ourselves.' We both agree on this point. The press would have a field day, and without leads on the second killer we would again find ourselves behind the eight ball.

There's a moment of cold silence in this room before she speaks again. She says it in a clear emphatic tone. 'I need your help, to convince the Sheriff and the local authorities. We should be looking for a second killer.'

Chapter Eleven

Vancouver is a city of bright-blue skies, vast inlets from the sea and stately old homes on winding tree-shaded streets. I had been here once before, with my parents, as a child, and I remembered the place for its broad green parkways like mowed velvet, and the patina-coppered roofs of some of its older, more imposing buildings.

It is a warm day and a brown haze, halfway between fog and something more sinister, drifts above the shimmering waters of the Burrard Inlet.

'How long could this take?' Claude says. We are in a taxi from the airport, caught in the thickening traffic of downtown.

'Extradition is not something I've done before,' I tell him. 'Maybe when reality sets in, Iganovich will waive extradition.'

Claude looks at me and smiles, the kind of grin adults reserve for a child's fairy-tale.

I have taken Claude into my confidence during our flight regarding the theory of a second killer, but have asked him not to discuss it with Emil, at least not yet. He has assured me that he will not. Given the sheriff's misplaced adventures in victim land, I think Claude will honor this.

The cab comes to a stop, double-parked in front of an

imposing building, a concrete obelisk that reaches forty stories into the sky.

Once in the building, we head for the twenty-fourth floor where there is a tiny woman seated behind the glass partition, her chin barely rising above the counter on her side.

'Mr Madriani and Mr Dusalt here to see Mr Jacoby. He's expecting us,' I say.

'One moment.' She reaches for the phone.

Jacoby is Queens Counsel and Director of the Regional Office of the Department of Justice in this province. Fortunately for them, our northern brothers do not get many multiple killers on the lam from the US. Because of the high profile of this case Jacoby has related to me by phone that he has standing instructions from Ottawa to handle this extradition himself.

'Mr Jacoby will be right with you,' she says. 'You can wait in here.' We kill a couple of minutes taking in the surroundings, then a voice from behind me.

'Gentlemen.'

I turn to see a tall, slender man, a head of balding gray, wheeling toward us at full pace from around a corner, his hand extended in greeting.

'Mr Jacoby. Paul Madriani,' I shake his hand.

'Oh please, call me Herb,' he says. It is an accent one might mistake for British, the words correct and clipped.

I introduce Claude. The three of us stand there exchanging a few pleasantries.

'You must be tired,' he says. 'Let's go to my office. We can talk and the two of you can sit down and relax.'

Jacoby leads us down a corridor flanked by little offices;

the Canadian version of good enough for government service. The furniture is classic institutional, mostly imitation wood. I see the craft of inmates' hands in this stuff.

But the views from these little cubicles are something Lenore Goya might kill for. A panorama of the busy harbor kaleidoscopes before me as I pass each open door.

A large corner office belongs to Jacoby, one of the perks of position.

'How's our man doing?' says Claude. 'Have you questioned him?'

'He's doing just fine. We've restrained ourselves with regard to questioning,' says Jacoby. 'But your suspect is very nervous. He blurted a few statements immediately after the arrest, some gibberish,' he says. 'Meant nothing to us. We made some notes.'

Jacoby has our undivided attention now.

'I'd have to look at the arrest report,' he says, 'to get the specifics.'

Claude gives me a look, like maybe we've hit some paydirt.

'He meets with his attorneys daily, and seems to be manageable,' Jacoby's talking about Iganovich. 'He's said nothing to us since his lawyers got hold of him.'

According to Jacoby, Iganovich blurted whatever was said to the security guards who held him immediately after his detention, before local police could be summoned and before he could be warned about loose talk.

'He has appointed counsel?' I ask.

'Legal aid,' he says.

I make a face. This does not fit my image of the people

who defend indigent renters in unlawful detainer actions back home.

Jacoby looks at me. 'Ours is a little different than your system,' he tells me. 'Though he does have an American lawyer as well.'

I look at him round-eyed, a question mark sitting across the table.

'Oh, yes. The fellow flew in this morning. Says he was hired by the family.'

Claude and I look at each other, searching expressions.

'Who is he?' I ask. 'The American lawyer?'

Jacoby shakes his head. 'I haven't met him yet. We may have that pleasure this afternoon. As long as you've come all this way, I would like you to meet my counterpart, Iganovich's Canadian barrister, Mr Lloyd Benson-Harrington. We'll go over to the jail later and you can talk to them there. They're meeting with their client. Maybe we can sneak a peak at the defendant as well.'

Claude likes this. His first look at the man in the flesh.

Jacoby paws through a few more pages in his file.

'Here it is,' he says. 'The police report.' He's reading, following the pencil-written lines, big hand-printed words for legibility, with one forefinger. 'It's not a confession,' he says. 'Don't know the facts of your case, but it could be an admission. Made no sense to us.'

'What did he say?' asks Claude.

'Immediately after being taken by store security, he resisted,' says Jacoby. 'It took two of them to wrestle him to the ground.' He's tracing with his fingers again. 'They picked him up, cuffed him and . . .' He's looking for it. 'Here it is. After they pick him up off the floor he says:

"You got my van. I haven't driven it in more than a week. I loaned it to somebody else. They used it, not me." That's it,' says Jacoby. 'As I told you it's pretty much gibberish.'

Claude gives me a broad smile. 'Not exactly,' he says.

Jacoby looks at us. We explain to him about Iganovich's vehicle found back in Davenport and, more importantly, its contents.

'Oh,' he says. 'Then it *is* significant.'

'I'd like to have Claude talk to the store security people, get their declarations under penalty of perjury,' I say. This will help tie down their perceptions of events, preserve the facts against fading memories. It will also put the lie to any defense allegations that the state was involved in extracting these statements or that they were the product of coercion.

I use Claude to gather these statements so I have a witness later if I need one. Otherwise I would have to recuse myself in the case, withdraw as the prosecutor, in order to testify as a witness. If there were no ethical constraints, it would be the perfect dodge out of my current dilemma. Nikki would love me for it.

'Of course,' says Jacoby. 'We'll make an appointment to get them in here.' He's talking about the two guards.

'One of them is in pretty bad shape,' he tells us. 'Your man did not want to go with them.'

'How serious?'

'I don't have the particulars. Leg injury or something. And some burns.'

'Burns?' I say.

'Uh huh. Electrical. One of those stun guns, like a little

cattle prod,' he says. 'He managed to touch one of the guards with it while they were wrestling him to the ground.'

'Did you get it?' I say.

'Umm?' He looks at me.

'The stun gun. Did the guards retrieve it?'

'Oh, yes. It's with his personal effects.'

'We'd like to look at it,' says Claude. 'Maybe take it with us?' His voice rises an octave, like maybe this is questionable.

'More evidence?' asks Jacoby.

'Could be.'

'Certainly. Anything we can do.'

'In that case,' says Claude, 'we'd also like some photographs of any marks left on the security guard by the device.'

'Sure. We can do that. I don't know what marks are there, but we can check.

'Now,' he says, 'I presume you've started the documentation? To complete the extradition application?' He shifts gears.

I assure him that this is in the works. I have talked to Goya about helping me when I get back, a bone to try to keep her content, until I can do something more.

'Good,' he says. He looks at me, a serious expression, to see that I have grasped the import of this.

'In extradition,' he says, 'the devil is in the details. The documents are king.'

He is right. This is black-letter law of the worst kind. The most rigid areas are those governed by printed statutes where strict adherence to law and procedure is the difference between success and failure, conviction and acquittal.

'There's an interesting issue,' says Jacoby. 'A little ticklish, but we may as well broach it now . . .'

'What's that?'

'The matter of capital punishment.'

I look at him.

'I don't know whether you're aware,' he says, 'that the death penalty is a highly charged subject up here. Canada abolished it some years ago. It complicates questions of extradition at times.'

I look back at him. Jacoby knows he now has my full attention.

'Surely, this is not a problem here?' I say. 'Not in this case?'

Jacoby makes a face.

'I wouldn't be so sure. It's all part of our treaty, the US-Canadian Extradition Treaty. Been in there for years,' he says. 'Either country can refuse to return a suspect if that person is subject to execution in the other nation. All perfectly above board. It's a question of political policy addressed outside of the formal extradition process.'

I look over at Claude, whose creased and thinning face has dropped nearly to the table top. The lawyers at the State Department in Washington have not told us that this could be a problem.

'Surely, I thought you were aware of this,' says Jacoby.

'I knew of the provision,' I say. 'I was not aware that it might be a problem in this case.'

'I would expect that the extradition hearing will go smoothly. We have talked about the evidence,' he says. 'It

131

appears to be solid. This can be provided by sworn declaration.

'But,' he says, pausing for a little effect, 'our Minister of Justice, while a tough woman, sadly sees little social benefit in capital punishment.' He arches an eyebrow as if to say that he himself does not understand this.

'You think there's a chance your Minister of Justice may decline to send Iganovich back south unless we agree to waive the death penalty?' I ask.

'There is that chance,' he says.

'You aren't serious?' says Claude. 'This man has murdered six people, and you want guarantees that we will not execute him if he's convicted. Not likely,' says Claude.

I nudge him with my knee below the table. Like most of his brothers of the badge, diplomacy is not one of Claude's polished charms.

'You must understand. There will be a great deal of controversy and press attention to this case as it wends its way through our courts.' He wrinkles an eyebrow, his way of telling me that politicians in this country are subject to the same forces of political gravity as those south of the border. They crumble under pressure. As I sit and stare at him I begin to wonder how I will break this news to Emil Johnson and the county fathers back in Davenport that, no matter how remote in the political seas in which they all swim, I may have to deal away the prospect of a death sentence for a stone-cold killer. If I know them, and I think I do, I sense that we are about to enter a game of international chicken with the only question: who will blink first?

* * *

The jail for the city of Vancouver is a block building five stories high, situated in the old city center. The surrounding buildings, many of them aging brick, are now run-down.

Jacoby leads the way. He has called ahead to let them know we are coming. Inside, he hooks up with a guard, a man in a neatly pressed uniform, light blue shirt with epaulets of rank, and dark pants.

He leads us through a series of three-inch-thick steel doors, like airlocks, all controlled from a room behind one-way mirrored glass. We pass through a visitors' area, a few inmates socializing with family, wives and kids.

'This is the main conference room,' says the guard. 'They are waiting for you in here.' He opens the door. There are two metal tables placed end-to-end, bolted to the floor, scarred wooden chairs around them. Iganovich's Canadian lawyer has stopped off on his way from court like a doctor on his rounds.

Jacoby makes the introductions.

Benson-Harrington is by all appearances an amiable man, professional in his approach, exuding no real venom.

Claude is busy sizing up the defendant. Andre Iganovich is seated at the head of the table. A surly look on his face, he is not interested in partaking of these social festivities. I am certain that this distance he maintains from us is something that sits well with his lawyer.

Iganovich is maybe thirty-five, brown hair in a crew cut, an unremarkable face, a little lop-sided, thin and narrow with deep-set, dark eyes, somewhat haunted as if he is still dazed by his capture and the events of the last week. The only exceptional feature are his teeth. They are stained a

dingy gray-brown, and spaced like broken pickets in a
fence. Like many from the impoverished places of Europe,
it is a countenance that most resembles pictures I have seen
from the last century, yellowed and aged daguerreotypes
of flatland farmers and back-hill country boys sent off to
fight and die in the Civil War.

He smiles at me, fleetingly. It is an expression that sends
a slight chill through my body, raises the tiny hairs on the
nape of my neck. His is a somewhat dense appearance, one
that conveys the same native predatory message as a
cruising shark, a look that makes me glad that we are not
alone in this room.

I hear the door open behind me.

'Ah!' Benson-Harrington is suddenly all animation.
'Your American counterpart,' he says. 'You two must
meet. Let me do the honors.'

I turn to look. The smile on my face fades like a dying
gas lamp. There before me, centered in the frame of the
door is the now familiar, if aged, face of Adrian
Chambers.

'We're already acquainted,' he says, then, like his client,
the lawyer offers me only a forbidding and humorless
smirk.

Chapter Twelve

The drone of the jet engines is lulling me to sleep. Claude and I are taking the red-eye south from Vancouver, and I am lost somewhere between slumberland and the snickering visage of Adrian Chambers.

Iganovich has now formally declined to waive extradition. On this, Chambers has counseled him, along with the more reserved Benson-Harrington. From their vantage point there is little to lose other than the good will of a state that wants to execute their client.

Claude scrunches down a little in his chair, the back reclining as far as it will go. He rolls his head in my direction and plants the question I have been waiting for.

'How did you two meet?' he says. 'You and Adrian Chambers?' Along with everyone else present at our meeting, Claude has sensed the obvious hostility between us.

'We go way back.'

'Bad blood usually does,' he tells me.

'A high-profile defense can be good for your practice,' I tell him. 'It can breed new clients. But in this case part of his motive is also a well-inspired vendetta.' I tell Claude. 'Something from Dante's inferno.'

'Tell me about it,' he says. From his tone I can tell that Claude now thinks he has a stake in this thing.

'You've got to understand Chambers,' I tell him. 'The man is obsessive, to the point of self-destruction. Maybe it's what gives him an edge on the rest of the world, his willingness to go to excess in pursuit of a cause.'

Claude looks at the middle-distance, like he doesn't understand this.

'There's a story,' I say. 'I don't know if it's true. But years ago, when Chambers was starting out, he represented some leather-vested bikers — people heavily into drugs, running the stuff from Mexico in the hollow tubes of their Harleys. It was early in his career, before the pricier clients sought him out. Anyway, Chambers represented them in a drug bust, took a small retainer and went to work.

'It's a classic equation in hard core criminal defense that if you lose, your client figures he could have done as well himself, and if you win, it's because he was innocent. Either way it is easy for them to justify the non-payment of an outstanding fee. In the case of the bikers, Chambers beat the charges in an early motion to suppress evidence. He sent them a bill for fees, they ignored it. He sent them another. It was like he didn't exist. As the story goes, he managed to entice these guys to his office, all three bikers, and I am told that there he collected his fee.'

Claude looks at me. 'How?'

I make a face. 'According to those who claim to know, he held two pistols: one semi-automatic, fully loaded to keep them at bay, and one revolver with a single round. He lined them up against the wall and proceeded to play Russian Roulette with their collective heads until they came up with the money.'

Claude swallows hard. 'It beats arbitration to get your

fee. How much did they owe him?'

'Four hundred dollars, I'm told.'

He looks at me wide-eyed.

'It was the principle of the thing.'

'And he got away with this, this collection of his fee?'

'The clients were not the kind to go running to the state bar, or the law.'

'With those kinds of clients you don't have to worry about the law,' says Claude.

'You're wondering why they didn't kill him?'

He arches an eyebrow, like this was more than a passing possibility.

'In Chambers, I think what they saw was a lot of rage, a man dancing on the edge of lunacy, like maybe the next time they showed up he might be holding a flame-thrower. It's why the early Indians didn't kill crazy people,' I say. 'They saw them as somehow closer to the gods. I think maybe the bikers looked into the eyes of Adrian Chambers that night, and saw their own mortality. It came down to the basics. Screwing with this guy simply wasn't worth the four hundred dollars.'

'After that, Chambers packed a loaded nine-millimeter everywhere he went,' I say. 'He got a permit from the sheriff, and let the world know it. Five months later, these same three guys showed up at his front door again. Like the Horsemen of the Apocalypse, they'd been trucking white powder all over the highway between Barstow and Bakersfield. Afflicted by the galloping dumbs, they'd been nailed again, and they were looking at doing some hard time. But when they arrived at Chambers's office this time they were packing a bankroll to choke a horse. They gave it, all of it, to Chambers up front.'

'Sounds like an American success story,' says Claude. 'How did you manage to get this Horatio Alger all over your ass?'

'Ten years ago he was a rising star in legal circles in Capital City. By then he'd cornered a good part of the upper-crust criminal defense practice in town. Lawmakers in trouble with over-zealous prosecutors, the lobbying set, a lot of politicians and their hangers-on. He made a lot of money. He also made a lot of enemies, mostly cops who were tired of taking his abuse in court.

'As is often the case in life, Chambers lost his focus in the details,' I say. 'One of his clients was Walter Henley, a bookkeeper and, by some accounts, principal bag-man for a group of lobbyists currying favor in the capitol.'

With this sign of high-level dirt, Claude is all ears.

'The DA's Office, where I was at the time, had Henley and two prominant lobbyists in its sights, hard evidence of bribery and extortion. We wanted to get Henley to roll over on the lobbyists.

'Chambers's theory of defense was not new, or original,' I tell him. 'He figured he could keep the lobbyists and Henley all back-to-back, inside under a common umbrella of defense, pissing out into the wind instead of all over each other. He had visions of holding out forever.'

'I offered Henley immunity and subpoenaed him to testify before the grand jury. He could no longer take the Fifth. He had to tell us what happened or go to jail.'

'So much for honor among thieves,' says Claude.

'Chambers fell into the net when he approached Henley

with a vast sum of money, cash from the other clients, to spin some yarn before the grand jury. What he didn't know was that Henley was wired for sound. The cops had set Chambers up. A little pay-back for all the grief he had caused over the years.'

'Chambers took your part in all this very personally?' says Claude.

'He had good reason. I tried for a five-year stretch on sentencing. He got nine months. And disbarment which he ultimately got reduced to five years actual suspension from the practice of law.'

'A slap on the wrist,' says Claude.

'He doesn't see it that way,' I say.

Claude is quiet for a moment, lost in contemplation as if he's fitting together the pieces of some puzzle.

'Son-of-a-bitch,' he says. 'We're supposed to be a team. Then I open the paper and find out you're keeping things from me.'

I'm in Emil's office with Claude. Johnson's holding a folded newspaper that he slaps on the desk in front of me.

'It makes me look like a fool when I have to read stuff like this in the newspaper. Reporters call me and I don't know what the hell they're talken' about.'

There on the front page of this morning's *Times* is a side-bar to the story about Iganovich's arrest in Canada, a two column headline:

Authorities Search For
Second Copy-Cat Killer

139

'Why the hell didn't you tell me about this?'

'I didn't learn about it myself until an hour before I flew to Canada, two days ago,' I tell him.

'Still, you coulda called me,' he says. 'There are telephones between here and Canada, or hadn't they told you?'

I read the first paragraph of the story, while Emil's chewing on my ass.

DAVENPORT – Sources close to the investigation of the Putah Creek killings disclosed today that they are now operating on the theory that a second killer, a copy-cat, is now at large and may be responsible for the murders of Abbott Scofield and his estranged wife Karen. Scofield, a professor at the State University, was found murdered along with his former wife early last week. Their nude bodies were discovered by two teenagers hunting along the Putah Creek, the scene of four earlier killings involving university students. According to highly placed sources police are now pursuing theories of a second killer due to discrepancies in the physical evidence found at the scene.

Fortunately for us, these 'highly placed sources' have drawn the line at divulging the specific evidence in question. As I read I cannot believe that Kay Sellig has had anything to do with this. I wonder who else in her shop may have known about our conversation. Then I think. True to her word Sellig had faxed a copy of her report to my office while I was away in Canada. It had lain face-up

140

on my desk with a pile of other papers for two days in my absence. Any of a dozen people could have seen it lying there, could have read its contents.

'Next time you have information,' he says, 'you tell me. Understand?'

I look at Emil, but do not even give him the satisfaction of a grudging nod. Johnson is, at heart, a bully. He is pressing the outer limits of his authority right now, testing to see if I will genuflect. I have not.

'And another thing,' he says, 'we won't sit still for any crap about waiving the death penalty.' Claude has told him about our conversation with Jacoby up north.

'What the hell are we supposed to tell the families? Some pinstriped ninny in Washington signed a treaty so we can't execute the murderer who butchered your kid? No,' says Emil. 'No deals.' His brow is twisted over one eye in anger. 'That son-of-a-bitch comes back here and he faces the death penalty.'

In actuality this decision rests with the chief prosecutor of this county, myself at this moment. But it is a weighty matter, one affecting the longevity of elected officials in this place.

Johnson is late for a meeting out of the office. He's looking for his little binder, a speech before the Rotary Club. 'Where the hell is it?' he says. Then he finds it.

'Tell them,' he says, 'tell them no deal. And find out who leaked this shit.' He's hitting the newspaper on the desk with his finger. 'It sure as hell wasn't any of my people.' In Emil's eyes this apparently is the only benefit of not knowing what was going on. His own skirts on this leak are clean.

He's heading for the door. 'We've already got problems with this son-of-a-bitch Park,' he says. 'Fill him in,' he tells Claude. 'Tell 'em what that slant-eyed prick has done.' Then he's out the door.

Claude looks at me, and shakes his head.

'Park made some derogatory comments about Emil in the press.'

'About now I'd like to concur.' I have little sympathy left for Johnson. 'The man will not take sound advice,' I tell Claude.

'Park has also hired a Canadian barrister,' he tells me.

'What?'

'We got a call this morning from the Canadian Department of Justice,' he says. 'Jacoby's had contact from a private barrister representing some of the victims. The guy wanted to know what was going on with Iganovich.'

'This is getting very messy,' I tell him.

'Could they cause any trouble in Canada, with the extradition?' he asks.

'They could piss off some people in high places.'

'Maggie Wilson's speciality,' says Claude.

'It could limit our chances to finesse Iganovich out of their country and back here. What did Jacoby tell their lawyer?'

'I don't know. We didn't get into details,' he says.

'Find out,' I say. I am worried that he might have told their barrister about the treaty provisions on the death penalty, or that the lawyer might stumble over them on his own. If so, all hell will break loose.

* * *

Eight-thirty in the morning, and I am greeted by the voice of the office receptionist over the com-line.

'Call for you,' she says. 'Judge Ingel.'

I pick up the receiver. It's a female voice on the other end, Ingel's clerk. She tells me the judge will be with me in a moment, that they are busy linking a conference call.

The voice, like gravel on a dusty road, comes a second later.

'Madriani, you there?' I can tell by his tone that Ingel is pissed about something.

'Your honor.'

'We'd like to know what the hell's going on.' I can hear breathing and background noise on the line.

'Excuse me,' I say, 'but who's on the line?'

'Judge Acosta,' he says. 'Who else?'

The Coconut can be a real case. Prevented from pawing through my files, he now uses Ingel to tap my phone.

'What is it you want?' I say.

'We're hearing rumors,' says the Prussian, 'that you're getting ready to cut a deal on the death penalty with the Canadians.'

'Who told you that?' I say.

'We have our sources.' This time it is Acosta's voice coming back over the line.

I can guess where this comes from. Emil has been talking to Ingel. His way of assuring that I hold the line on any deal for extradition.

'Well, you've heard wrong,' I say. 'And Emil knows better. I've already told him there will be no deals. Does he want it in blood?'

'Keep a civil tongue,' says Ingel. He's putting on a little

demonstration of authority for Acosta, telling me that there was no reason I should have barred the Coconut from my files. 'Judge Acosta was not asking to copy anything, just to look,' he says. 'After all, he has a legitimate interest in the case.'

'He does,' I say. 'The same as any other survivor. Maybe I should post all the investigative reports, all the contacts and leads the police have on a wall in the courthouse so they can all read them at the same time?'

'That's enough,' says Ingel.

'You see what I have to deal with?' Acosta tells him. For several seconds they cut me out of the loop of discussion, the general consensus being that I am an uncooperative asshole, all this while I listen.

It is a colloquy I might expect from two legislators, people who never see bounds to their perks of power and special privilege, but not from sitting judges.

'So how are you going to get him back?' Acosta is asking for my strategy on extraditing the Russian.

'The State Department is putting pressure on the Canadian authorities,' I say. 'In the end, we are confident they will return the suspect without any waiver of capital punishment.'

An audible 'humph' from the other end of the line, like he gives this little credence. I begin to believe that Acosta would prefer that I fail. I think that maybe his commitment to his sister and family is not as strong as his desire to tromp my ass.

'What about this copy-cat thing in the papers?' says Ingel.

'Right now just a theory,' I say. 'Discrepancies in some of the physical evidence.'

We go over this. Without divulging any details, I assure Acosta that this does not appear to affect his niece's case. Again a lot of mild scoffing on the other end of the line.

'You will keep us posted?' says Ingel.

'To the extent that I can,' I say.

'Yeah,' says Acosta. 'Sure. Like access to the files.'

Ingel consoles him a little, tells me good bye, like I can ring off now, while they defame me in private for a while.

I hang up. But for the next several minutes my ears are burning.

Days have passed and I am only now able to follow up on Kay Sellig's advice that I talk with the county's medical examiner, Dr Lloyd Tolar.

Tolar is a teaching physician with a full-time position at the university medical school. A trained pathologist, he is under contract to the county to provide coroner services — a position which he rolls neatly into his teaching assignment. I am told that he uses students to assist him in servicing the county contract, that the university receives the payment for this from the county. A cozy arrangement.

When I get to Tolar's office I am ushered to a chair in a reception area and told that the doctor is running late — a teaching assignment in another building. He is expected momentarily.

A second later I sense a presence behind me. When I turn I'm facing a kid, no more than twenty-five, in medical garb.

'You're Mr Madriani?'

'I am.

'Dr Jamison,' he says. He shakes my hand. 'I'm one of the interns assigned to assist Dr Tolar. He's not going to be able to meet with you today. Last minute conflict,' he says. 'He asked me to sit in, to talk to you, to answer any questions. We can use his office.'

Before I can say anything Jamison is heading toward a large glassed-in office on the other side of reception. I follow him through the door and he turns on the light.

'So, you're the acting DA,' he says. He eyes me up and down as if to pass a quick judgment. 'You're here on the Putah Creek thing,' he says.

'Yes. I haven't received a copy of the pathology report on the last two murders yet, Abbott and Karen Scofield.' I tell him that Sellig had advised me to come in and talk, that there was apparently some problem, questions before the report could be completed. I lift an eyebrow, 'And some information that perhaps we have a different perpetrator here.'

He projects poise beyond his years, self-assurance, more than a little arrogance.

'Some of our findings,' he says, 'we were not sure whether you would want them reduced to writing in the pathology report, or kept verbal at this point. A question of discretion.'

What he's talking about is the practice of finessing an expert report, in this case the autopsy, to keep certain critical information away from any adversary come trial. Normally such documents are disclosed during discovery.

'What are we talking about?' I say.

'Pretty clear medical evidence,' he says, 'that these victims were not killed where they were found, but moved there later.' He's talking about the Scofields.

'That the killer stabbed them with a knife first, and then tried to mask this with the metal stakes. It was well done,' he says. 'But not that well done.' A point of pride I think.

Jamison talks without notes, conversant with details. I suspect that perhaps he assisted Tolar in the autopsy.

I ask him to tell me more.

He says that they found a contusion on Abbott Scofield's head and evidence that he was unconscious when stabbed; the wife was not. Both were stabbed with a sharp single-edged knife about nine inches long. The stakes were inserted later into these wounds then driven through the bodies to make it look as if the same MO was used as in the earlier cases.

Sellig was right — this is dynamite stuff. 'Can you gloss it in the report?' I say.

'We can keep the facts broad, leave out the conclusions.' He says this like they have done it before.

I weigh the risks. Once in the report there is no way to take it out.

'For now,' I say, 'until we know who's going to be looking at the report, that might be best.'

Chapter Thirteen

This morning I make a mental note to immerse Lenore Goya in the particulars of the Putah Creek case when I get to the office. I will need some competent help on the affidavits and other documentation required for extradition. Before I head for the office I drive past the university soccer field and performing arts building.

A mile down the road I turn onto a tree-lined lane where the branches of giant oaks meet in the center of the street a hundred feet overhead. It is like a public park, but there are stately homes here, white columned Georgians and classic colonials set back a mile on manicured lawns. This is Davenport's version of faculty row, people with tenured job-security, something unknown to the average citizen in this country. Here live professors on public salaries who bought these mansions four decades ago for a song and who now live in cloistered comfort.

I pull to a stop in front of a mammoth Dutch Colonial with dormers larger than some homes I have seen. An old woman answers the door, her hair pulled back in a tight gray bun.

'Is Mrs Scofield in?'

'Who may I say is calling?'

'Attorney Paul Madriani.' I give her a business card with the county seal printed on it and she disappears, leaving me outside on the doorstep for the moment, behind the security-chained door which she has taken care to put on.

Several seconds pass and she is back. 'Please come in,' she says.

She leads me through a spacious entry way and into the living room. It is large and cluttered with the knick-knacks of a lifetime of work. If there is a theme to this place it is birds; carved wooden birds, books on birds, lithographs and an original oil, framed over the fireplace. Bald eagles and ravens, owls and humming birds. If it exists and has feathers I think it has probably found a place in this room.

The house has the signs of a grand structure, in its day. But it is dated, as if its owners have found other things to do with their time and money, besides remodeling and decorating.

'My daughter will be with you in a moment.' Before I can turn to look at her, the old lady is gone again.

I wander around the room, killing time, looking at the various mementoes. On an end table by the couch is a framed photo, black and white, a dark-haired man in pants that resemble riding jodhpurs. I pick it up to look more closely. He is handsome and young, standing in a field high with grass. I would hardly recognize him from the grim autopsy shots back in my office: Abbott Scofield in more youthful and happier times.

'It was taken right after his marriage to Karen.' I turn. Jeanette Scofield is standing in the doorway. 'The first Mrs Scofield. They were married in 1958,' she says.

'Sorry,' I say. 'Curiosity gets the better of me at times.' I put the photo back on the table.

150

'It's OK.' She waves a hand, like it's no big thing. 'He was a good-looking man, don't you think?'

'He was,' I say, 'good looking.'

'Everybody thought so.' She gives me a schoolgirl tilt of the head. 'My mom didn't want me to marry him. Said he was too old for me.' There's a moment of awkward silence as if by these comments she is forced to reassess the true measure of her loss.

Then shifting gears quickly, she makes amends for her appearance. She is dressed in a loose-fitting sweat shirt. There is mud on the front of this and a little on her chin. The running shoes are old and tattered, and the towel draped around her shoulders has smudges of dirt and mud. Her hair is pinned back on the sides and gathered in a loose pony tail at the back. She mops a little perspiration from her forehead.

'Gardening,' she says. 'One of my vices.' There's a giddy smile. 'Can I offer you something to drink?'

I beg off. She is tall, an inch taller than I, even in flat shoes.

'Mom,' she calls. The woman appears at the door as if she's been beamed down. I think maybe the old lady has an ear to our conversation. 'Would you mind getting me a glass of iced tea,' she says. 'You're sure I can't offer you something?'

'No. Thanks.'

She smiles.

'Please, sit down.' She gestures toward the couch, and takes a seat herself in one of two overstuffed club chairs, set at an angle in front of the fireplace.

'How do I rate a visit from the prosecuting attorney?'

she says. 'I've already talked to the police, your Lieutenant Dusalt?' She's questioning, as if maybe she has the name wrong.

'That's right. I've read his report,' I tell her. 'Just a few loose ends,' I say.

'Isn't that usually a detective's job?'

'I was in the neighborhood.'

'Is that like efficient government at work?' She smiles.

'Something like that.'

The flush of the outdoors is leaving her cheeks. She drapes one thigh over the other, a baggy pair of oversized men's pants, enough fabric for each pant-leg to wrap twice around each leg. She leans back in her chair. 'What would you like to know?'

'Just some general background information,' I say. 'I thought it might help us, as we move forward, if we know more about your husband's work. Can you tell me a little about it? What exactly did he do?'

'Ah.' She nods at this, then tepees the fingers of both hands, long and slender, under her chin.

'Abbott was an ornithologist,' she says. She smiles like maybe she might offer to spell this for me, but I'm not taking notes. 'His life — his passion — was the study of birds. As you can see,' she says, sweeping one arm across the room as if to take it all in. 'I sometimes wondered if he might have loved me more had I been born with feathers.'

I raise an eyebrow.

'No,' she says, anticipating my thoughts. 'We had a very happy marriage. He had his work and I had him. We each got what we wanted.'

Her mother returns with her tea, a tall slender glass,

sweating with ice. She puts it on the table next to Jeanette and looks to see if maybe she should sit down and join us.

'I'll be out in a minute, Mom.' The younger woman fixes her with a stare, and the old lady leaves. When she clears the room Jeanette looks at me, and in a lower voice behind the tall slender glass: 'She's been like a shadow,' she says. 'She's driving me crazy. I've told her it's OK, she can go home, back to Fresno. I can't get her to leave.'

I smile at this. She shrugs her shoulders, good naturedly. 'Where were we?'

'Your husband's job.'

'Oh, yes. Abbott was a tenured professor at the university. He taught several undergraduate courses, but his main duties were in the graduate school of zoology. He was on the tenure track committee for the faculty senate; very active,' she says.

All of this was in the investigator's report, details which Claude and his minions have reduced to writing.

'You told the police you can't think of anyone who might have wanted to kill your husband?'

'That's correct. I can't. But then,' she says, 'I suppose the parents of the four dead college students would say the same about their kids. My God,' she says, 'who could account for the actions of a demented mind like that?'

She talks a little about Iganovich, the reports in the papers, asks me if I've seen the man, talked to him.

'I saw him. We have not talked. His lawyers will not permit that.'

She apparently has not seen the article in the *Times* yet. I am not surprised. The papers from the southern part of the state do not circulate much, outside the capital, in this area. She will no doubt hear about it on the news. It is why I wanted to get here, to talk to her before she does.

'I'm curious, about the first Mrs Scofield,' I say. 'Their continuing relationship after the marriage broke-up.' This is something the cops did not tread on very hard the day after the murders.

'You're surprised that they would still see each other?'

I make a face, like this is part of my concern.

'You had to understand Abbott and Karen. It was mostly commercial,' she says. 'They worked together.' This was not in the report.

'On a personal level their divorce was a mutual parting of the ways. They remained friends even afterward.'

'You say they worked together?'

'Yes. Karen had no formal training, no real education, but she did have twenty years working with Abbott in the field. He had confidence in her, continued to rely on her for assistance, in some of his writings and his field work. She was an excellent photographer, took many of the photographs that appeared in Abbott's books. Some of the ones you see in this room,' she says.

'And you didn't object to this, their continuing working relationship?'

She smiles at me. 'Why should I?' There is an innocence here. I cannot tell if it is pure naîvety, or whether this is one of those secure souls for whom life's competitions offer no real threat.

'Do you know what your husband was working on at the time of his murder, what specific projects?'

'No,' she says. 'I haven't a clue. Why are you interested in all of this?' She's sitting forward in her chair now, curious about my little probes.

'As I said, it's just a few loose ends,' I tell her. 'We've been wondering,' I say, 'about the time immediately before their abduction that night. Whether there might have been something that put them in harm's way, maybe something they were working on that might have caused them to cross paths with the killer?'

'In answer to your question, I'm afraid I don't know what they were working on. Abbott's work was not something we shared.'

I hear a door slam, somewhere at the back of the house. Someone has come in. A few seconds later, I hear footfalls in the hallway and Jeanette looks up.

'Oh, Jess,' she says. 'I'm glad you're here. Mr Madriani has dropped by to ask me a few questions.'

Amara appears anything but affable as he enters the room. From the look on his face he is not terribly happy to see me here.

'I saw the county car out front and wondered if somebody might be visiting,' he says.

Sure, just a fortuitous pass on the street.

'Do you have any news for us, on who killed Abbott, or why?' he asks.

'Not that I can talk about,' I say. 'But then I'm sure you've been able to follow developments.'

'Has Jeanette been able to help you?'

'She's been able to clear up a few things.'

'They are mostly concerned with Abbott and Karen in the hours immediately before the murders,' says Jeanette. 'Mr Madriani wanted to know what they were working on at the time. I told him I didn't know.'

'You wouldn't know what they were working on?' I pose it to Amara.

'Abbott didn't talk to me about his work. As for Karen I never met her.' He looks at me. He does not sit down.

'Anything else?' he says.

'Not for the moment.'

'Then you have what you need?'

I nod.

'I'll walk you to the door,' he says. I am being dismissed.

I have discovered why Claude is so cool toward this man. Amara has something on the side, another business, an Asian trading company in which he dabbles in foreign investments in this country. It is the kind of thing that Claude would not like, a cop dealing in some sideline business, a potentially lucrative hedge against his years in retirement.

On the stoop of the door outside, I turn to shake Amara's hand. It isn't there.

'I don't want to seem uncooperative,' he says. 'But if you come back here again, call me before you do. I'd like to be present. I don't want my sister disturbed unnecessarily.'

'I understand,' I say.

With that he closes the door in my face.

It is nearly noon. On my way to the office I wonder why it is that Amara is so hostile, whether this is just his nature, or if there is something more. I am not allowed to dwell on this for long. As I drive past the courthouse toward the County Administration Building a block to the south, on the corner at the traffic light are three men that I know. One of them wears his hair long, to the shoulders and gathered in a pony-tail, Indian style. This is Benny Sanchez. With his brother Ernesto, he owns a bail bond agency. They have garnered a reputation and a working relationship with the cops on both sides of the river. I have seen them in town with their scabbarded rifles. They track down wayward clients with the relish of a good deer hunt. The two are fixtures around the local courthouses in this area.

Their presence here would be unremarkable except for the third man, who is talking to this posse comitatus. Short and stout, his back is to me as I swing through the intersection. But still I recognize him. I thought he had left town three days ago to return to his home down south. It is Kim Park.

Chapter Fourteen

I have pleaded with her and begged, but she seems adamant; Lenore Goya says she is leaving the office, resigning, though after much protestation she has agreed that we will discuss this one more time before her resignation is carved in stone, sent along to the county personnel department.

Today we are gathered for a little ritual, an annual event to honor the secretaries, an office luncheon that Roland Overroy insists is part of the protocol of the place. No one except Roland particularly wants to be here, the secretaries least of all. We are across the river, in Capital City. Overroy tells us there was nothing suitable to the occasion in Davenport. He has rich tastes.

Saudis is one of the priciest restaurants in town, and Roland makes the most of it. He has ordered little crêpes smothered in apricot sauce, and escargot, appetizers at eighteen dollars a hit, for a plate the size of a child's tea saucer. To this he has added three bottles of wine, imported French Bordeaux, of which he has now drunk two-thirds. His face flushed, he is getting more obnoxious by the moment.

His eyes go all round, as a hefty woman in a tight skirt ambles by our table. He slaps Boudin on the arm, gestures toward her backside, and in a voice that carries, says:

'Looks like two alley cats fighting in a bag.' For this we are all treated to a drunk's inane laugh. Boudin casts a quick glance in my direction, then humors Roland with a nervous grin.

It would be bad enough if Overroy were paying for this. But he has demanded that excess change in the office coffee fund be raided to subsidize this frolic, a sparse reserve approaching seventy dollars which he has now exhausted before lunch.

Goya has distanced herself, as far as she can get from Overroy, this I think to avoid killing him.

'Given the deal you got from the firm, Lenore, you otta be buyen' us lunch.' Overroy is loud, big gestures, out of place with his hands. His voice can be heard on the other side of the restaurant. He is talking to Goya about her proposed association with her new employer.

'Sure, Roland. When hell freezes,' Goya's reply to springing for lunch.

Overroy is laughing. She is not.

She is entertaining an offer from one of the big firms in Capital City. Though she is playing this close to the vest, I have heard rumors, probably the same ones that Roland has heard, that they have dangled a forty per cent pay hike in front of her, and a chance at a partnership. She would no doubt get an office with a view of something more than mortar and chipped red brick. I have little with which to tempt her back into the fold. I would offer her Overroy's fried testicles for lunch if I thought it would do any good.

'We'll have to talk about the Putah Creek stuff. I'm in a position to give you some help.' Roland is offering me his expertise. There's a little rivulet of wine dripping down his chin as he says this to me, a confident smile planted on his face. He is assuming that with Goya gone he will be getting heavier fare in the office, more noteworthy cases. I grit my teeth a little, unwilling to make a scene here.

Yesterday I caught him mucking in Iganovich's case, returning a phone call to the US Department of Justice through which all correspondence must flow on its way to Canada. The US Attorney General is the diplomatic conduit for all formal communications in the international law of extradition.

I chewed on Roland for five minutes and told him he was not to intervene in this matter again. He called it an emergency, something that could not wait. I kneeled on him one more time, and he appeared properly rebuked, said he understood. But with Roland I suspect that such assurances are only good until the next time.

The menus arrive. Overroy recommends the lobster to me. 'Delicious,' he says, kissing three fingers like a five-star chef. At market price it should be.

There are a few toasts around the table. Goya to the secretaries for their silent tribulations in making the office function.

Overroy not to be outdone, offers another.

I propose a quiet toast to Lenore Goya, a shameless attempt to pluck at the strings of guilt.

'To a great lawyer,' I say. 'Someone we respect and who we will miss greatly.' I nod toward her.

Lenore takes up her glass and smiles at me. With all that has happened she still harbors me no ill will.

'I can honestly say that, for the most part working with all of you has been a pleasure, a high point of my life,' she says. She is smiling. 'And there are others that if I lived two lifetimes, I will never forget.' I catch her glancing, slight sideways slits of hostility at Overroy, who is oblivious, working on one of the little snails with a thing that looks like a chrome cross between a nutcracker and pliers.

Harry Hinds has come over, across the river, in response to my call. He thinks maybe I'm getting ready to pack it in. Harry has come to encourage me to do the right thing, to cut and run. We are in my office with the door closed. I can hear Overroy outside at the public counter telling some off-color joke in a feigned Mexican accent.

'Got yourself in a little mess?' says Harry.

'What makes you think that?'

'With a hiring freeze, in a few months the place will look like a ghost town, you and an empty office.'

'Nonsense,' I tell him. 'Nobody would hire Overroy.' He laughs at this.

'I've got a plan,' I tell him.

'So did Hitler,' he says. 'It ended outside a bunker where they turned him into crêpes suzette. Why don't you tell 'em to jam their case where the sun don't shine and come back where you belong?'

What he means is on the right side of the law, with the honest perpetrators of crime. There have been times in the last weeks when this has looked appealing.

'The supervisors will authorize one more body under contract,' I tell him, 'part time, to help out with the Putah Creek case. They figure they can still save a little money, on the benefit package.'

'Good! Some fool's gonna buy bleeding ulcers with no health insurance,' he says.

I arch an eyebrow and look at him.

There's a moment of silence, mental telepathy, as my thought waves settle on him like ether.

'Wait a second,' he says. 'No way. Not a chance. I've got my own practice. Uh uh.' He says this with meaning.

I give him a look, like what are friends for?

'You're incredible,' he says. 'I'm shoveling shit against the tide trying to hold your practice together while you're over here, and now you want me to join you in this fool's paradise?' Harry is now overseeing two younger associates, lawyers he has brought in to handle some of my lighter cases.

'It pays three thousand a month − for half-time work,' I tell him.'

I can see a look in his eye, the glint of money. But he hesitates for only an instant.

'Not a chance,' he says.

Though I tempt him like a demon, it is what I expected from Harry. He has an abiding distrust of all things governmental. To Harry, signing on with the state would be to deal with the devil. He leaves me no choice. I will go and grovel with Goya.

I have no manhood left, but I have at least solved my problem. Two days have passed, and my knees still feel the psychic ache of having crawled on the hard linoleum of her office floor. Harry is back in my office, bringing papers for me to sign, some cases from my office that are being closed out.

There's a knock on my door.

'Come in.'

It's Overroy, his head and shoulders through the jamb of my door.

'Paul, you gotta come out here for a second,' he says. 'There's some screw-up over at county general services.'

It seems two guys are here with dollies to move furniture out of his office. He is all sunshine and smiles waiting for me to correct this little blunder. His office is palatial, bigger than my own. Feretti had not taken it from him when he struck Overroy's title, as chief deputy, from the rolls.

'No mistake, Roland, they're here to move you.'

He has the look of a letter delivered to the wrong address.

'What?' he says. It's a face unclouded by human thought, like a moose in the path of a high-speed train.

I'll say it slowly this time. Read my lips, I think. 'They're here to move you,' I say.

'Whataya talkin' about?'

'You're going down the hall,' I tell him, 'into Lenore's office.' I smile at him, a grin that says welcome to brick walls and bundles of files, asshole! In a more equitable world, Roland would be in a sealed coat closet with a naked light bulb.

'Aw-w-w-w.' He looks at me sideways like he smells a rat, like this is finally seeping in.

'Wait just a second,' he says. 'What the hell's goin' on here?'

Harry looks at me. 'Maybe I should leave,' he says.

'No.' I motion for him to stay.

'It's just an office move,' I tell Overroy. 'It happens all the time in corporate America.'

'Don't bullshit me,' he says. 'Tell me what's goin' on?'

'Like I said, just an office move.'

'Sure,' he says. 'You think I'm stupid?'

I give him a look that puts this question up for grabs.

Harry's drifted off to the side, out of the line of fire.

'What did I do to deserve this?' Softer now, Roland changes moods on me, the injured whelp, big brown eyes in my door.

'Nothing.' I tell him. 'This is not punitive.' I wrap this little package of insincerity with a bow and hand it to him.

'I've been in that office for sixteen years.'

'Then you should look forward to the change,' I say.

'Why didn't you come to me,' he says, 'and talk to me about this before you called the movers? This is highly unprofessional.' Now he's playing the injured bureaucrat.

'It was a management decision, Roland. Not something that required consultation.'

'Paul.' He is big and soulful. 'This just ain't right.' He's wobbling around in the doorway, stepping all over his tongue. He's working his way toward my office, trying to worm his way into my heart, the door half open behind him, his hands on the edge of my desk, trying to reason with me.

'You can't do this. I've got seniority,' he says. He looks around behind him like somebody might be in ear shot.

'Listen,' he says. 'You need another office, take Goya's. No. No. Better yet, take Boudin's, or Samuels's. Yeah, that's good. Take Samuels's. She's low on the seniority ladder.' His voice never gets above a hushed whisper,

Roland still looking around, over his shoulder as if the two of us are locked in the refined art of the deal. This is the Roland we all love, bargaining with someone else's possessions.

'No. I don't think so.' I mimic him, my reply in soothing low tones, as if it were the secret of the century. 'I need yours,' I whisper.

'Son-of-a-bitch.' He's bellowing at the top of his voice. His body jerks up off my desk. He's stomping around the office. 'Fucken' A. This is bullshit.' Roland is back on form.

'Not at all.' I give him genuine assurances. 'We need the space.'

'For what?'

'Oh, I forgot. I guess you haven't heard. Lenore's not leaving.'

He looks at me, dumbstruck.

'Yes,' I say. 'I thought you'd be happy. It's true. She's staying on with us. As soon as I can clear it with the board of supervisors she's gonna be our new chief deputy. She'll be working with me on the Putah Creek cases. She'll be taking your office.'

This is a lot of body blows for Roland to take all at once. It's a few seconds before he focuses. But then I see it, fire in Overroy's eyes, unseen flames, like the super-heated vapor of an alcohol-fueled roadster. He looks at me. 'This is bullshit.'

'One more thing,' I say. 'The files in Lenore's office. They belong to you now. You've got a nine o'clock court call Monday morning. Good luck. And don't let anything slip through the cracks.'

Harry stares at me, a mischievous look, the expression of opportunity, like maybe he could pick up one of the defendants on the Monday morning calendar and kick the other cheek of Roland Overroy.

Kay Sellig deposits a small suitcase behind the door in my office. She has just taken a cab here from the airport. She looks tired and drawn.

'How did it go in Ashland?' I say.

'They were helpful. Now ask me what it all means.' She shrugs her shoulders. 'A few more pieces to the puzzle,' she says, 'but who knows where they fit?

'First the blood,' she says. Sellig has spent the last two days in Southern Oregon, talking to experts at the National Fish and Wildlife Forensics Laboratory. They are working on the blood, bones and feathers found in the blind, high in the trees over the Scofield murder site.

'Most of it was animal, specifically avian. Bird blood,' she tells me.

'It's not a domestic bird,' she says. 'They've ruled that out.' This means it's not a chicken, or other beast of flight in the commercial food chain.

'That takes the edge off our theory that they might have been part of a ritual slaying,' she says. She's talking about the murders of Abbott and Karen Scofield. 'It's possible,' she tells me, 'but those who go in for such things usually use domestic animals, something easily obtained from a farm, or from somebody's back yard. Wild animals are too hard to come by.

'There's also a wrinkle. Some of the blood, small traces, was human. Common, type A. We think this belonged to

Karen Scofield. Abbott was type O.'

'Could it belong to the guy in the trees?'

She shakes her head. 'He was a secretor. Pretty rare, type B,' she says.

'Don't tell me,' I say. 'He peed for you in a corner of the blind.' I am wondering how they got their secretions to type our suspect.

'Close. He chewed tobacco. Spat the stuff in little black balls all over the platform. We were able to type the saliva,' she tells me.

'Remind me not to commit a crime in your jurisdiction.'

She smiles, a little satisfaction at this break. Sellig is unloading her briefcase on my desk, looking for her notes.

'The bones are mostly small, immature birds,' she says. 'Most of them still in the nest.' Besides the bones they have confirmed this from the preponderance of molting feathers sent to the lab. Mature feathers from the top and underwing, the kind that could have supported flight, were missing from the samples they observed.

'So we have a baby bird killer,' I say.

'Not just any bird,' she says. 'Birds of prey.'

I look at her.

'They examined the feathers. There's no question. These were peregrine falcons. Chicks maybe a month, possibly two, from flight. Endangered species,' she says. 'Protected by the federal government.' She tells me that the lab now has their own stake in this thing, that they are interested in whoever might have been involved in the killing of these birds.

'He could do some federal time if they catch him,' she says.

'They'll have to wait in line.'

'You think he killed the Scofields?' she asks.

'Do you?'

'It's possible. I suppose. They could have stumbled in on him. A federal crime. People have been known to kill for less.'

'But you've got to admit he was fast on his feet, pretty well prepared,' I say.

'The stakes and the rope?' she says.

I nod. If whoever was in the trees killed the Scofields he didn't lose a beat staking them off on the ground in copy-cat fashion. It is more likely, I think, that who-ever was in the trees was not the perpetrator, but a witness. For the moment there are too many unanswered questions.

I've been stalled for almost a week now on the preparation of the documents needed to return Iganovich to the state. Under the law of extradition, I must decide whether to charge him with the Scofield killings. If I fail to do this and he is returned, I may not try him for these murders later. The rule is you must know what you've got before you extradite.

'Maybe Iganovich did it after all,' I say.

She shakes her head. On this she is adamant. 'The discrepancies are too great,' she says. 'We think we now know how he was able to subdue couples.'

'How?'

'A stun gun,' she says. 'As an alien national, the law didn't allow him to carry a firearm on the job. So his employer tells us he used a stun gun.'

She sees my eyes go big and round. I've already told her

about the stun gun taken from Iganovich by the Canadian authorities.

'Exactly,' she says.

I ask her if she's received it yet.

'It's being shipped to us as soon as they finish processing it up there.'

The law in this state establishes only minimal requirements for the possession of an electronic stun gun. There is no licensing or permit required.

'How did he get it on the plane?'

'It only has a few metal parts. Detector probably didn't pick it up,' she says.

'Good to know we're in safe hands in the air,' I say.

'Anyway, the ME believes the victims were taken down with a stun gun.'

'How effective is it?'

She makes a face. 'Localized cramping of muscle groups, some intense pain. They'd be on the ground, pretty much out of it, anywhere from three to fifteen minutes, depending on the duration of the jolt.'

'Enough time to drag them into the van and tie them up.'

Sellig agrees with this.

'Would it make any noise?'

'About what you'd hear from a garden variety bug zapper.'

I mull this in my mind for a few seconds, then pop the question she knows I will ask. 'Did the ME find similar marks on the Scofields?'

She shakes her head. 'Not a sign.' Another reason for her growing conviction that Andre Iganovich did not murder Abbott and Karen Scofield.

'There's no sense waiting any longer to bring the Russian back.' I will complete the extradition package on Iganovich based solely on the murder of the four college students.

'I'll have to tell Emil,' I say, 'that we are no longer dealing with conjecture, that he'd better start looking for a second killer.' All hell will break loose.

Chapter Fifteen

Five weeks have passed since my sojourn to Canada. I'm finishing up a case at the Capital County Courthouse, finalizing a plea bargain with the DA, one item Harry will not have to worry about. We finish and I head for the men's room.

Inside I wash my hands over the sink, looking at my image in a mirror that is speckled by silver worn thin on the backside.

I hear voices outside in the hallway. There is something familiar to one side of this conversation, an aversion I cannot place. They are coming this way. I pick up the pace, rush to dry my hands.

The scarred wooden door behind me suddenly opens, and in the mirror I see a hulking kid in his twenties with pimples and spiked purple hair, more studs in his leather jacket than the average snow tire. As he moves through it, I notice that he is big enough to fill the entire frame of the door.

Following closely behind him is Adrian Chambers. He sees me and stops dead in his tracks. His mustached-lip ripples into a thin smile. In the spotted glass of the mirror this takes on a transparent, ethereal quality, a vision from the lower regions.

Chambers breaks off in mid-sentence the conversation

with his client, and from the doorway studies the back of my head. I feel bristles of hair standing up at the nape of my neck.

'Well, well, counselor, slumming are we? I'd have thought that with your pull, you'd be using the private johns back stage.' He means the ones with the gold fixtures and no graffiti on the walls, the lavatories used by the judges in the private corridors behind their chambers.

He finally moves a little, just a quarter-turn toward Pimples, who by now has made his way down the stalls.

'Excuse my social gaffe,' says Chambers. 'My client, Mr James Sloan, meet Paul Madriani,' he says.

I don't bother to look at the kid. 'Charmed,' I say. The spiked head is probably a pedophile caught hanging out in some grade-school john. At this point in his career, Chambers is no doubt busy working his way back up the criminal food chain.

'Mr Madriani here's *the* man,' he says. 'The District Attorney of Davenport County.'

The kid is now leaning into one of the urinals down the line. I get a look from him, all dead in the eyes, then a little quiver, like a shiver. I can't tell whether this has something to do with his bodily functions, or merely evidences an attitude toward the law. Chambers, I'm sure, would give this punk my home address and phone number if he had it.

'I've been meaning to call you,' he says. 'What's this I hear that you're not charging Iganovich with the last two murders, the professor and his wife?'

It was in all the papers this morning. Emil and I agreed that for the moment we would put a face on it, no public confirmation about the new stories of another killer, just vague references to insufficient evidence, and an on-going investigation.

'Well, Adrian, what can I say? If you read it in the paper, it must be true.' My back is still to him as I wad the paper towel and toss it in the can.

'What's the matter?' he says. 'Are we having a little trouble tying up all the loose ends? Or could it be that you're holding back, in case you botch the first ones, maybe you could fix it by charging him later with the last two?'

I turn and look him straight in the eye. 'Gee, Adrian, I wouldn't want to invade your turf. Fixing things has always been your speciality.'

Suddenly he's no longer smiling. His face is no more than a foot from my own. We're staring at each other, unwilling to blink, to look the other way.

Finally he speaks, 'Mr Sloan, I should tell you. Our friend here is a real straight arrow: Mr Ethics,' he says. He's talking to his client but without looking. The kid is having trouble getting Willie back in the barn. A dozen zippers on his jacket, and he can't work the one on his pants.

'A real do-gooder,' says Chambers. He looks down the row of urinals. He's lost his audience. The kid's gonna need a surgeon if he pulls up on the thing any harder.

Chambers snaps his head back toward me trying to get away from the porcelain comedy at the other end of the room.

He is a man who not only nurses a grudge. He fosters it, fertilizes it, cultivates it and watches it grow, until it dominates his life as thoroughly as an untreated cancer.

'You know,' he says. 'You ought to be a little concerned. You're bumping up against the statute for extradition. Getting a little close.'

He's talking about the sixty-day statute of limitations for an extradition hearing under the US-Canadian treaty. By law, if the hearing is not concluded within sixty days of Iganovich's arrest in Canada, the suspect must be released by the court.

'I don't think you have to worry about us blowing by the statute,' I tell him.

'Oh, I'm not worried.' He looks at me, an expression like he has something else with which to needle me.

'Tell me?' he says. 'Are you ready to dump the death penalty?'

'Don't hold your breath.'

He pushes past me, on down the row of stalls. 'Then it's all academic,' he says. 'You'll never get him back down here to stand trial.'

'I wouldn't be too sure,' I tell him.

'Funny thing about the Canucks,' he says. 'They're real sensitive people. Proud,' he says, 'and stubborn.'

He bounces a little more venom off his erstwhile client – from all appearances this is sailing well over the spikes on the kid's head. 'I think our friend here has a real problem. A case he can't fathom,' he says. 'But then I'm sure that's nothing new for him.' He moves toward the stall.

'I wouldn't push too hard if I were you, Adrian.'

He turns and fixes me with a stare, all the intensity he can muster in his mean eyes.

'Why not?'

'Because if you're not careful you'll flush the best part of yourself down that hole in there.'

The kid laughs, out loud, from the belly, the first thing he's understood.

I grab my briefcase from the top of the towel holder and walk out, leaving the pimply wonder standing there alone, chortling to himself, fighting with the zipper, and looking at the closed door of the stall which has now been slammed in his face.

But Chambers is right about one thing, though as yet he doesn't know the half of it. I do have a problem. With the looming discrepancies in the Scofield murders, even with hard evidence on the Russian, his defense will be able to play upon the thesis that somebody else committed these murders, that they did them all, and that the police are still looking for the real killer. Given time and his nimble mind, he will, I am sure, have handy explanations for the rope and stakes found in the Russian's van. With this as a growing backdrop, the Scofield murders are now poised, like a wrench waiting to be wedged into the cogs of my case.

They say that time cures all. My relationship with Nikki is not healed, a long way from it, but it seems that maybe we have passed over the rockiest part of my latest lapse in judgment, picking up the pieces of Mario Feretti's life. It has taken nearly two months to reach this point, but tonight she has even deigned to help me with one aspect of the Putah Creek cases. 'A family outing,' she calls this. More than a little sarcasm to her words.

I have offered to entertain Sarah in my office while

Nikki works on the computer. Sarah skipped through the door like she was entering Disneyland North.

'There it is,' I say.

Sitting forlorn in the center of one of the empty desks in the clerical pool is a small desktop computer from Karen Scofield's apartment.

Denny Henderson and Claude spent the better part of an afternoon searching her place for leads as to what she and Abbott were working on at the time of the murders. They came up empty, except for a few papers which Claude is studying, and the computer, which he delivered here.

Rather than screw with this little desktop machine, and risk the loss of vital information, I have called on Nikki. In her various jobs she has touched every computer known to mankind. She had been making plans to go for her master's degree in computer science, but this is on hold now, until I can find the time to take some of the load at home.

'Do you know what software she was using?' she asks. Nikki's talking about Karen Scofield and her little computer.

I shrug my shoulders and point to a pile of little cardboard boxes and books that Claude seized from the apartment when he took the machine.

She starts flipping pages, looking at the indexes to these books. I stand there for several minutes, feeling like a potted plant.

She looks over her shoulder at me. 'Go play with your daughter,' she says.

Sarah is at my desk, stapler and hole punch in hand, an assortment of pads and pencils at the ready. Every few minutes I am called in and handed important slips of paper covered in gibberish she claims she can read, numbers and a few letters, some of these are still written backwards. Tonight we are playing bank. She is the teller. This goes on for the better part of an hour until she bores with this game. Nikki is still fighting with the machine in the other room. Finally a few yawns from my daughter and she is pulling her shoes off, the sign that sleep is not far off. I put her on the couch in the reception area and cover her with my coat. In five minutes she is asleep.

I head for my office and settle into the chair behind the desk, pick up the phone and dial. On the second ring Claude answers.

'It's me,' I say. 'Did you find anything?'

'Not much,' he says. Claude is home poring through a stack of papers taken from Karen Scofield's apartment.

'Mostly personal correspondence. A few letters,' he says. 'There *was* something.'

'What's that?'

'Two letters to a laboratory supply company down south ordering live mice.'

'Mice?' I say.

'Yeah. The lady was into mice in a big way.'

'Probably experiments. Scofield was a scientist.' My deep, impenetrable knowledge of things scientific.

'Could be,' says Claude, 'but three thousand of 'em. In a four month period?'

'Three thousand? What could anybody do with three thousand mice?'

He makes a noise on the other end of the line, like search me. 'Maybe they were eating the things,' he says. 'Could be the latest hors d'oeuvre among the college crowd.'

'Did you find any sign of them at the university, in Scofield's office or his lab?'

'No. But it explains the pellets.'

'What pellets?'

'Grain, feed pellets for livestock. We found two one-hundred-pound sacks still stitched up, and a lot of grain dust, like there may have been more bags at one time, in the corner of the lab.'

'I don't get it.'

'Mice love the stuff,' he says. 'My dad used to use it to feed hogs. Had it by the ton. The mice always burrowed their way into the bags when he stored it in the barn. They feasted on it.'

'You think Scofield was feeding the grain to the mice?'

'I don't know. There's a couple of kids, undergraduates I'm told, who worked with him on projects from time to time. I'm gonna send Henderson over tomorrow to see if he can track 'em down. Maybe they can enlighten us.'

'Anything else?'

'That's it,' he says.

'Is that everything from her office?'

'Read it all, three times,' he says.

'Put the documents in the evidence locker for now,' I tell him. 'I'll see you in the morning. By then I should know whether we've got anything in the computer.'

We sign off. I hang up.

I can hear the clicking of keys outside as Nikki works away. I head out to see what she has. The little screen is all lit up with menus. I move in over her shoulder and get a quick glance, long lists of back-lit words as she flashes through screens.

'I assume you want data files, things she loaded in for storage or to be printed out?'

'Right.'

Halfway down the screen something sticks out, more than the standard three or four letter symbols – the word PEREGRINE.

'There,' I say. 'What's that?'

She punches some more keys and comes up with a clean screen. Up at the top is the name of the directory, PEREGRINE, with the hard disk drive designation, the little prompt letter c.

'Can we get into the directory?'

'This is the menu,' she says. 'We can go in, but it won't do us any good.'

'Why not?'

'Because it's empty,' she says.

'I don't understand?'

'If there were any files they'd be listed here, on the menu, by file name.'

She flashes back to the parent directory one more time. 'There it is, big as life, but no files,' she says. 'What about this?' She points to another entry. PEREGRINE.42

'What is it?'

'It's not a directory listing. No DIR designation. It looks like a data file that got misplaced,' she says. 'Maybe somebody hit the wrong key and dumped it into the root directory by mistake.'

'Can we call it up?'

Again she punches buttons and this time a letter appears

on the screen. There's no salutation other than the name, Bill, and no address as to whom it was sent.

I read it. The letter is like walking into a room in the middle of a conversation. It refers to subjects in past correspondence without any clue as to the substance of those items. I try to read between the lines as best I can.

> Dear Bill
> In reference to your letter of 9 Feb., three pairs
> are now in place. We are watching them closely for
> progress. An additional seven have been put out
> individually. If things continue to go well, we will
> be at full strength by early summer, and in a
> position to observe progress on an on-going basis.
> If you can ship four more pairs, before Spring, we
> believe we can place them before the snows fall.
> Will await your reply.
> Karen

'What do you make of it?' She's looking at me.

'I'm not sure,' I say. 'It would help if we had some way of determining what might have come before this letter? Other pieces in the chain of correspondence.'

'It's only a guess,' she says. 'But I think maybe the writer numbered everything under each topic sequentially, each file with a separate number.'

'Is there any way to find out what else was in the Peregrine directory? To retrieve the lost files?'

She makes a face like this is a long shot.

'Could you do it? Here in the office? I can't allow the computer to leave the office.'

She looks at me, like I don't even trust my wife.

'When am I supposed to come into the office to do this?' she asks.

'You can do it at night,' I say. 'I'll watch Sarah.' I can tell I am pressing the outer limits of Nikki's tolerance. She looks at me almost dazed that I would have the gall to ask this again. The audacity of the lawyer.

She gives me a major shrug. 'One more time,' she says, 'and then that's it. And you make an end of this case. Next quarter I go back to school, come hell or high water. Do you hear me?' she says.

I nod my agreement.

'I mean it,' she says. 'I don't care what your problem is. You get back to a single law office or we are history,' she says.

Five days later I am in Feretti's old office, cloistered with Lenore Goya, preparing for the eventual trial of Andre Iganovich. In Vancouver, they are now three days into an extradition hearing that was originally expected to take only two. We are getting hourly reports, color and play-by-play from Denny Henderson who Claude has sent north for this purpose.

Lenore and I are busy preparing for the preliminary hearing where we will test the evidence to date in front of an impartial magistrate, our quest for a holding order on the Russian to bind him over for trial on four counts of first-degree murder in the superior court.

In all probability that is at least four or five months off.

The phone rings on my desk, the hot line, direct from the outside.

'Hello.'

It's Henderson, breathless and excited.

'You're not gonna believe this.' He's sucking air like he's run the four-minute mile. 'He's on the street,' he says.

'Who's on the street? What are you talking about?'

'Iganovich. The court released him five minutes ago.'

'What?'

'A problem with the documents,' he says.

The blood in my veins runs cold. All documents sent to Canada originated in this office.

'Slow down,' I say. 'Tell me what happened?'

'Defense made a motion at the end of the hearing, what they called a "no evidence motion", based on a defect in the documents. It came out of the blue,' he says. 'Could have knocked Jacoby over with a feather. Iganovich's lawyers discovered that the certified copy of the charging statute was the wrong one.'

'What are you talking about?'

'The section of the penal code, the murder statute that we used to charge the Russian, it was an old statute that's been repealed and reenacted in another form. We sent the wrong one under certification up to Jacoby.'

Oh shit. I think this to myself, in that place reserved for all private panic. What Henderson is telling me is that someone has botched the uncomplicated job of copying the statute, and certifying it for use in the Canadian hearing.

'Hold on,' I say. I cup my hand over the mouthpiece of the phone.

'Who copied the statutes for the extradition package?' I'm asking Lenore.

She shakes his head, like she has no idea. 'It was done before you brought me into the case,' she says. 'What's goin' on?'

'The Russian's been released.'

Round eyes from Goya.

'Find out who assembled the documents. Get 'em in here,' I say.

She's out the door, to the steno pool.

I'm back on the line. 'Where is he now?' I'm talking about Iganovich.

'He left the court with his lawyers. I followed 'em downstairs. They didn't waste any time. Got in a taxi and left. Jacoby had two RCMP officers follow them. To try and keep tabs,' he says.

'I can't believe this,' I tell him. 'They couldn't hold him?'

'Jacoby says no. Says everything turned on the documents. Kept telling me the devil was in the detail, whatever the hell that means.' His voice fades a bit, like he's turned away from the mouthpiece. 'Here, you wanna talk to him.'

The next voice I hear on the phone is Herb Jacoby. 'Listen, my friend,' he says, 'I'm sorry, but there was nothing I could do. With the sixty-day statute running, the court had no choice but to release him. You should be happy you're not up here,' he tells me. 'His Lordship was rather pissed off.' Jacoby's talking about the Canadian judge. 'Three days of his time down the johnny flusher, and forced to release the man on a technicality,' he says. 'Not a good show. Not good at all.'

I apologize for the screw up. Tell him I'm getting to the bottom of it.

As I'm talking to Jacoby, my mind is wandering back in time, to Chambers's smug attitude in the washroom that day. Suddenly it hits me, he had been lying in the weeds for weeks aware of this deficiency in our filing, biding his time, waiting to spring this trap.

Jacoby wants to know how long before I can get another warrant up, to rearrest Iganovich. 'I trust you can understand, given the man's propensities we would rather not have him walking free up here too long,' he says.

'I'll have one in an hour,' I tell him. 'I'll fax it up there. It may take a little longer for the diplomatic note from the State Department.' This is a requirement to effect a provisional arrest in a foreign country, pending an extradition hearing.

Lenore's back in the office, followed by Irene Perez, one of the stenos.

I can tell by the look on her face that she is scared, primal senses tell her that she is on the carpet, but she doesn't know why.

I tell them to hold on a minute.

I hit the intercom button on my phone. I get Jane Rhodes.

'Get me the number for the State Department in Washington, the lawyers who did Iganovich. I'll wait.'

Irene Perez is beginning to shake all over my carpet. I think she may soil it if I don't relieve the tension. 'Sit down,' I tell her. 'Relax. I'll be with you in a minute.'

Rhodes is back to me. 'Do you want me to dial them?'

Thank God for a little efficiency. 'Yes. Ring me the

moment you have them. Tell 'em it's an emergency. If they're in a meeting, tell them we have to break in.'

Irene Perez is twenty-five years old, a single mother, with a little baby I have seen in the office on family occasions. She is pleasant and anxious to please. At this moment she is terrified, sitting in a chair across from my desk.

'I don't hold you responsible,' I say. 'It's my fault for not checking the documents,' I tell her. 'But I have to know how this happened.' I explain the mess up in Vancouver, the document in question.

'You shouldn't blame yourself,' she says.

I look at her, like thank you for this absolution, now tell me what happened?

'It wasn't among the papers you reviewed,' she says.

'Why not?'

'Because the code books were being up-dated. The annual pocket parts,' she says. She's talking about the little inserts that come out yearly, with the new laws, and are inserted into pockets in the back of each volume. 'We were replacing them. All the books were apart in the library.' She talks like she was on top of this project.

'What happened?' I ask.

'A lawyer from Washington called, I think it was the State Department. He said he needed the code section to complete the extradition package before he could send it on to Canada. He said he needed it by the next day. We Fed-Exed it to him.'

I look at her cross-eyed. 'Those kind of calls are supposed to be referred to a lawyer, Irene.'

'But it was referred to a lawyer. You weren't in.' She

looks at me with big, olive-eyed innocence. 'The only one here was Roland, Mr Overroy. He took care of it.'

I sit there, staring at her in stone-deaf silence, uttering a mantra in my mind's ear, cursing the cruel fates that lifted this thing from the able hands of Irene Perez.

Chapter Sixteen

The World Center for Birds of Prey. It is an unlikely name for an organization, but Nikki passes me a slip of paper with this moniker on it, a phone number, and a man's name. This is the information she's gleaned from the Peregrine directory, the files missing from Karen Scofield's computer.

'I think she was writing to this group,' she says.

We are meeting here in the cafeteria at the Capital County courthouse during a midday break. I am finishing up one of my old cases, a request from Harry, the first time I have been back across the river on business in over a month, and, strangely, it feels good.

'The place,' says Nikki, 'this center is located in Boise, Idaho. The phone number is from information. It's a current listing,' she says. 'I called it last night and got a message tape.'

'Enough,' I say. 'You were only supposed to search the computer.'

'No extra charge,' she says. She gives me a mischievous grin. 'Now do your part and finish the case.'

There's no address written on the slip of paper, just a post office box.

'How much of the correspondence were you able to retrieve?'

'Just bits and pieces,' she says. 'The back-up files were incomplete.'

'It would have been nice to know what was in those other letters,' I say.

'You're lucky you got this,' she tells me. She's spooning yogurt in little delicate tastes, turning the spoon over onto her tongue, this from a small plastic container that reads, Yoplait.

'How was *Fern Gully*?' She's laughing at me. Nikki took care to ensure that I honored my word to entertain Sarah while she worked on the computer last night. She brought along a dozen kids' books, the ones with letters the size of skywriting and a video tape that I played on the office equipment. I was camped in my office, Sarah curled up on my lap, reading and watching, until she fell asleep two hours later.

Nikki worked out the final missing pieces from the lost data this morning.

'I got his name, and the name of this center from an envelope she addressed using the computer, probably a label,' says Nikki. 'It said William. I figure it had to be this guy, Bill, in the letter. It's all part of the same directory.'

I look at her. 'A bit of a reach, isn't it?'

'Better than nothing.'

I concede the point. 'I'll put Dusalt on it this afternoon.'

Nikki's looking at the newspaper I have spread in front of me on the table, reading upside down.

'I hope you weren't planning on running for public office,' she says. A little dig. She's referring to the headline, halfway down the page.

* * *

DA Blunders
Suspect Freed

It's a big, bold two columns. It reads like a lead albatross around my neck.

'Farthest thing from my mind,' I say. I am rueing the day I crossed the river to Davenport, took on this thing from Feretti. Nikki and Harry were right. Only pride prevents me from giving them the satisfaction of admitting this.

'If this keeps up, I'm going back to my maiden name,' she tells me. Nikki hasn't seen the 'Davenport Urinal', which boiled me in oil this morning. The larger papers down south and the wires are treating the story straight-up, that Iganovich is under surveillance and is likely to be rearrested as soon as the documents can be prepared, a minor clerical glitch. It is the best spin we can put on the current state of affairs.

It's a different story here. I am being tarred and feathered in the local papers. The blame for release of Andre Iganovich has fallen squarely on the prosecutor's office, and more particularly on me. Emil Johnson is quoted in this morning's paper, stating in definitive terms that the release of Iganovich 'is a failure of our legal process', something that Emil sees as distinct and apart from the agencies of law enforcement, especially his own. Emil excels in the talents of politics. Voters will not see him standing around long near the scene of this car wreck.

Ingel has been all over my ass; an hour screaming at me on the phone. He tells me that this folly will track me back to Capital City, a black mark on my career, and that

Acosta is waiting for me there. As for Ingel, he is making noises about calling in the State Attorney General's Office for thorough-going investigation of the errors that led up to Iganovich's release, pointed questions for me to answer. 'It looks to me like gross negligence', his final farewell before he rings off.

I look over by the cash register, the stainless-steel conveyor of trays and customers. I see Lenore Goya. She would not be here, across the river, unless it was something important. She's scanning like a radar beacon, looking for me. I give her a high-sign with one arm. She sees us, works her way to the table.

'Have a seat,' I say.

She nods at Nikki, a warm smile, the strap of her purse slung on one shoulder, she throws her head to the side flinging dark tresses from the side of her face.

'No time,' she says. 'We've got problems.'

'It can't get much worse,' I say.

'Don't bet the farm on it,' she says. 'Jacoby just called. The Canadian cops have lost Iganovich. He slipped away from them. Last night.'

I'm at full tilt running for my car in the courthouse garage, heading for Davenport and whatever news I can get of the Russian's disappearance up in Canada. The court has given me a continuance on my afternoon session here.

I see my car, a figure standing by it in the dim overhead fluorescence of this concrete bunker. I draw up. In the shadows, the face turns. It is Armando Acosta.

'My bailiff told me you were headed here.'

'Word travels fast,' I say.

'I want to talk to you,' he says. 'I want to know what the hell is going on up in Canada. You're a goddamn incompetent,' he says.

I wonder for a moment if he's already heard, whether he knows that Iganovich has disappeared. Is it possible that his pipeline is better than my own?

'I'm in a hurry,' I say.

'You blew it,' he says. 'The extradition. They tell me you have to start the whole process over,' he says. 'How many months?

I look at him. He doesn't know. Not yet. He is thinking that the worst of it is more delay. Wait until he finds out the suspect is gone. My real troubles will start then.

'I warned them,' he says. He's talking about Ingel and the supervisors over in Davenport, where he tried to black-ball me on the assignment. I'm beginning to wish that maybe he'd succeeded.

'I have no time for this.' I push past him to the door of my car, unlock it with the key. He grabs my shoulder. I pull away from him. At this moment it comes as close to blows as we ever have. For an instant we stare at each other, intense and molten. Then he takes his hand from my shoulder, his eyes two burning coals. It is not the anxiety borne by his sister that troubles the Coconut.

'I warned you,' he says. He is back to finger gestures in my face, an inch away. 'If you fucked up, I'll have your ass.'

I'm in the seat, behind the wheel, the door closed, engine started. He's in my open window, which I have rolled down so I can see, to avoid crushing him against the car next to me, though the impulse at this moment is strong.

I begin to roll. His hands grip the top of my window.

'I'm going to the AG,' he says. 'A formal complaint. I'm demanding an investigation of your conduct. The attorney general should have had this case from the beginning. They will be all over your ass,' he says. 'Do you hear me? All over your ass.' He's beginning to shout as I pull back, out of the parking space. I ignore him through all of this, like he's not there.

As I drive away down the line of cars headed for the exit, I can hear his solitary voice, stripped of its feigned articulation, no longer elegant or precise, spitting venom at the back of my car, echoing off the concrete ceiling.

'The AG, you son-of-a-bitch. Do you hear me? You'll be hearing from the AG.'

Lenore, Claude and I are in Emil Johnson's office, on the speaker phone. I've gotten Harry to cover my afternoon court appearances. Emil is giving me stern looks from the other side of his desk, a prelude of worse things to come in the press, I think.

Johnson's got his feet planted in the middle of the desk, two gunboats, snake-hide cowboy boots with silver tips.

Denny Henderson is relaying, from Vancouver, the details of Iganovich's disappearance.

'It was early this morning,' he says. 'About four o'clock. He slipped away from the two cops staked out in front of his motel.' Coming over the line Henderson sounds like he talking through a hose.

'They think he had help,' says Henderson.

Emil is all eyes at this news.

'Help to escape?'

'Yeah.'

'What kinda help?'

'They think there were two of 'em. The cops up here have no idea who they were, but one of 'em caused a diversion, a fire in a dumpster down the street, a big blaze,' says Henderson. 'The cops thought it was a building. They left for two minutes to check it out. When they got back in position everything looked fine. In the morning they discovered that Iganovich was gone. The motel clerk says he saw him leave with two people, in a late-model sedan.'

'Great,' says Emil. 'Sounds like they oughta hire the clerk to do surveillance. At least he sees what's goin' down. Stay with it. And call us as soon as there's anything else.' Emil punches a button on the phone. The speaker goes dead.

'Hot damn,' he says. His feet are off the desk, his gut up against it. 'At least that explains the Scofield stuff.'

'Emm.' Claude is looking at him. 'How so?' he says.

'There were three of 'em. The Russian did the kids. These other two did the Scofields.' In Emil's mind, it's a nice neat little package. I think maybe he's planning to serve it up to press before the Canadians can reveal that Iganovich is gone.

'Why? What's the motive?' I ask.

'They're crazy,' he says. 'You saw the bodies. Tell me, are those the acts of sane people, logical minds?'

Lenore scoffs at this. 'If they were working together why didn't we find evidence at the Russian's apartment, or in the van? Forensics would have found hair, prints, something,', she says. 'And if they were working together, why the different rope on the Scofields, and failure to grind the stakes to a point?'

Emil gives her a sneer, as much as to say if she wants to join the club, play with the boys, she should at least humor his theories.

But Goya is a quick study. In one day, after coming on board, she digested all of the evidentiary reports. She can now spit the facts of the case at Johnson like a computer.

Emil looks as if he'd like to brush all this aside, troublesome little details. But Lenore is right. Something else is happening here.

'Well, what do we do now?' says Emil.

'We wait,' I say.

'For what?'

'Till we see what the Canadians come up with.'

'That's fine for you,' he says. 'Some of us have to run in this county, for re-election.' He emphasizes the end of this word.

'Not in the next two days,' I tell him.

'The public is fickle,' he says. 'They tend to remember things like this.' Helped along by one's opponent, he means. Emil would like to put a favorable spin on things before the pieces of this disaster become fixed like concrete in the public psyche.

'And what if we run to the papers, and the next day the Canadians take him again? You'd look a little foolish,' I say.

'Still, they fucked up,' he says. 'He got away on their watch. I'm not gonna wait for 'em to remind the papers that the only reason our guy was on the street was because of a mistake made in your office,' he says.

'I've got another what-if,' says Claude.

'Yeah?' Emil's waiting for this latest contribution.

'What if he kills again, up there?'

Emil's eyes get big and round. He hasn't considered this scenario. 'Son-of-a-bitch,' he says. 'We call a press conference right now and take the high ground.'

The arrest warrant and diplomatic note have arrived in Canada, and the political heat is getting severe. Claude and I have prevailed on Emil Johnson to hold off on any disclosures, his threatened news conference, at least for twenty-four hours. By then, if the Canadians have not found Iganovich, we will no longer be able to keep the lid on this thing.

For the moment, I am dealing with matters closer to home, Roland Overroy and his incompetence.

'Coulda happened to anybody,' he says.

This is Roland's excuse for the error that freed Andre Iganovich; Overroy's failure to check the pocket parts for the current law, the controlling murder statute in this case.

It is nearing six o'clock, the last business of the day. I have instructed Roland to stay after for this meeting. I have held off until most of the office staff have gone home. Overroy is in my office, called on the carpet to answer for his interference in the Putah Creek cases.

'What do you expect?' he says. 'In working conditions like this. I'm buried in cases. You put me in a closet down the hall and expect me to perform. You could at least have Lenore pick up some of her old cases.'

I remind him that the crucial error on the murder statute was made before he assumed Lenore's workload, back when he had time for afternoon cruises on the Delta.

He ignores this.

'You knew I was working on these cases. Why didn't you tell me about the phone call from Washington?' I ask this in measured tones, trying to curb my natural enmity toward this man.

'Because I already handled it,' he says. He is flip in his manner, dismissing the question. His idea of handling it was to deliver a statute repealed from the law nine years ago. I shake my head.

I have wondered whether this mishap was more a matter of design than negligence, Roland's way of doing me damage. But he is such a giftless bastard that in the past I have dismissed such notions.

Now I begin to wonder about the news stories, the disclosure to the press of our theories concerning a second, copy-cat, killer. Such revelations are not beyond Overroy, I think. His is a sacred crusade, recouping his pride and power.

I tell him there are people now making noises, demanding an inquiry by the state attorney general. This does not seem to bother him much, like maybe the buck in the office stops with me. I'm sure Roland could come up with a dozen artful answers to any probe, each one aimed at deflecting blame back on me.

I would fire him on the spot, but the Civil Service Commission would never allow it. They like graduated penalties, a million mistakes, each documented a dozen times in writing, with counseling sessions so that the culprit knows what he did wrong, and marathon warnings. So obsessive and time-consuming is the process that Roland

and hundreds like him have carved notches of incompetence, like badges of honor, on the arms of their desk chairs. Hawking each of his mistakes through the course of a single day would consume all of my time. And so he has survived through the better part of three decades, and five DAs.

'If you wanna blame somebody,' he says, 'blame that bimbo.'

I look at him questioningly.

'Perez,' he says. 'It was her job to get the pocket parts back in the books. She can't keep out of her own way. You ought to be riding her ass,' he says. One of the Roland's crowning traits; blaming others.

The phone on my desk rings — the back line. I pick it up. It's Claude, calling from the county jail.

I watch Overroy as I listen to Dusalt on the phone. Roland is beginning to muster signs of anger, working it into his face with effort. I have heard from others that he staged little screaming sessions with Feretti whenever required. And when it was over they would bury it and forget, and Overroy would go on as before.

I listen with interest to what Claude is telling me. Overroy is trying to read what is happening in my face, what tidbit may be on the phone. I make my face a bare stone tablet to keep it from him. 'I'll be over there in five minutes,' I tell him and hang up.

Roland doesn't miss a beat. Before the phone is in the cradle he is talking. 'Next time somebody calls for something in a rush, I'll ignore it,' he says. His opening shot.

'Is that a promise?'

This pushes him a notch higher.

'Since you arrived, you've been a son-of-a-bitch,' he says. A little name-calling to stoke the coals. 'You're worried I might get Feretti's job. You've been doing a number on me since you arrived. Constant harassment,' he calls it. 'Degrading assignments. You take a junior attorney in the office and give her the hot cases. It makes me wonder about you and her . . .' He bites his tongue before finishing this. The little gray cells are churning upstairs: false charges of advancement in return for erotic favors would constitute actionable sexual harassment by Goya against him. He knows this. She would have his ass in a federal court on a Title VII action before he could turn around. This whole thing is eating at him, that Goya is now in line for his old position. With Roland it is not merely that he himself must do well with virtually no effort, but that, by his terms, the only measure of true success is when the careers of those around him are in free-fall like plummeting drops of rain.

'What do you want me to say, Roland? You want my candid evaluation of your abilities. You won't like it,' I say. 'But if that's what you want,' I shrug, 'fine. You're not much of a lawyer. On a scale of one to ten I'd rate you a two. You're lazy, incompetent. You lack initiative.' I gaze toward the ceiling as if I'm running over some check list I have previously made. 'And I suppose I would have to say that on the whole, you're a major bore. Is that plain enough for you? Now that we're finished, I'll memorialize it in writing and we can put it in your personnel file. Now, are you happy?'

He looks at me, beady little crazed eyes. 'You're an

asshole,' he says, 'an absolute asshole.'

'Yes,' I say, 'and I'm all over you. So I'd advise you to open your eyes, light a match and take a good look, at yourself, and where you're headed.' My voice never rises above a conversational tone.

Before he can open his mouth I tell him, 'Get out. You'll have my memo in the morning.' It is the end of our session.

It's a dramatic exit, like an actor who's over-played his part. He slams my door, nearly breaking the glass.

I wait until I hear his footfalls diminish out the front door, then I grab my coat and prepare to meet Claude at the county jail. If Iganovich had killed in Canada because of this error, I would have haunted Overroy into an instant, early retirement. As it is, I think that the fates have lavished their entire cache of karma on Roland this day. Claude Dusalt's phone call was brief and to the point. Andre Iganovich was delivered, chained and cuffed, to the Davenport County Jail forty minutes ago.

They stand like Hawkeye and Chingachgook, more swarthy and not quite so lean. Benny Sanchez and his brother set bold profiles for the press photographers who are milling around them for an angle, that special shot to grace tomorrow morning's editions. The television crews are just arriving, setting up their lights.

I watch them through the one-way glass of an observation window in the jail, a little room that Claude has requisitioned. The brothers Sanchez pose in the reception area and tell reporters how they snatched Andre Iganovich from his motel room in Canada under the nose of the Canadian cops, and transported him across an international boundary while authorities on both sides girded themselves to find the fugitive. It is not an auspicious moment for law enforcement.

Claude tells me that Emil is in a quandary. He does not know quite what to do with these two men, whether to arrest them for kidnapping, or award each of them medals.

'Twenty-thousand dollars,' says Claude. He tells me that this is what Dr Park paid the two men to stalk the Russian through the extradition hearing, on the long-odds chance that they might have an opportunity to abduct Iganovich and bring him back.

'I've interviewed Park,' he says. 'Got him in a back room in case you wanna talk to him.' He tells me that Park is now a broken man. He is ready to do whatever time is required for this crime. According to Claude, Park was concerned that we were about to cut a deal on the death penalty.

'Said he didn't have any confidence that we would hang tough. So he took things into his own hands. Do you want to talk to him?'

'No. The damage is done,' I say.

'You wanna charge him with anything?'

'Not likely,' I say. On this I have the same problem Emil has. If charged and tried, any reasonable jury would award Park the Nobel Prize.

'Has anybody told Jacoby?' I ask.

'He damn near tore my head off,' says Claude. 'He says the authorities up in Ottawa are "outraged" − his word. I had to swear a blood oath that we had nothing to do with it. I think he's more than a little suspicious. He tells me they're getting ready to file a formal note of protest with Washington, demanding that we return the suspect for proper extradition. He wants to know if we'll agree to this.'

A few years ago such a note would have sealed our fate. Iganovich would have been returned to Canada for completion of extradition. A federal court would have blocked our prosecution until this was done. But the Supreme Court has changed all of that.

In a case involving a Mexican physician and the torture-murder of an agent of the Drug Enforcement Administration, the Supreme Court has thrown the gates open to abduction as an acceptable remedy for producing fugitives in US courts.

Claude's now looking over my shoulder, out through the one-way glass. 'Emil's arrived,' he says.

I turn. Johnson is in full dress-uniform, polished brass, a shiny chrome pistol on his hip, and shoes that haven't seen duty since the last parade.

He waltzes in like this is part of his regular evening rounds, just looking after the welfare of the drunks in the tank. Halfway through the main entrance he smiles with feigned surprise. What a coincidence, the press is here. This has all the guile of a silent motion picture. He's a beaming grin, from ear to ear, for the cameras. He's shaking hands with the Sanchez boys, a lot of back-slapping and congratulations. He maneuvers himself between the two brothers, and places an arm around each of their shoulders. In this pose there are toothy pictures of the three of them for the morning papers. The two brothers look as if they haven't slept in three days, wrinkled shirts and dirty pants, stubble on their faces like magnetized metal. Standing next to Emil they look like poor relations to Pancho Villa locked in a bear hug with George Patton.

I can't hear any sound, but I can see Emil warding off questions, the words 'no comment' forming on his lips through a forced smile.

Finally, he backs away from the crowd toward the door leading to our little room. Claude pushes a button and the latch buzzes open.

A burst of sound, voices, a fusillade of questions from the outer room. 'I'll have more to say tomorrow.' It's Emil's farewell. 'Tomorrow,' he says. He's through the door. It slams shut behind him with the authority of case-hardened steel, locking out the din in the other room. The smile fades from his face.

'Goddamn greasers,' he says. 'I oughta throw their worthless butts in the can, give 'em a good shower, and spray some DDT up their kazoos.' He's talking to Claude, still looking back at the closed door as if the Sanchez brothers were standing in front of him.

Then he turns and sees me.

'Hello, counselor.' He pauses for a few seconds mentally to regroup. He did not expect me to be here.

'Fine pickle they've got us in,' he says. 'Papers want to know whether we were in on this little escapade. Like asking if I still beat my wife. I'm damned if I do, damned if I don't,' he says. 'If I say we had nothing to do with it, we look like a bunch of boobs. If I say we blessed it, Park and Sanchez can call me a liar. Then we look even worse.'

He's shaking his head at his dilemma.

'What would you do, counselor?'

'I think you handled it well,' I say.

He perks up with this.

'A messy international situation,' I tell him. 'It's best that we say as little as possible for the present. No sense alienating our neighbors up north, or the State Department,' I tell him.

Though neither of these groups can vote for him in the next election, Emil seems to buy this, at least for the moment. He takes off his uniform cap and wipes the sweat out of the hat band with the palm of his hand.

'Will we be able to prosecute him?' he asks me.

I nod.

'For capital crimes?' He means can we invoke the death penalty.

'Yes.'

'Then maybe it's not all bad.'

'The Canadians will make a lot of noise,' I say. 'Big headlines.'

'Fuck 'em,' he says. Emil's version of the Truman Doctrine.

'God help us,' says Claude, 'when the next fugitive flees north.'

'As long as he doesn't come from this county,' says Emil.

Dusalt looks at me. 'You'll have to call Jacoby in the morning, and tell him we won't agree to return the suspect.'

'Damn right,' says Emil.

Chapter Seventeen

Lester Osgood is a judge of marginal abilities. He would have a tough time in any setting were he not king. But this morning Adrian Chambers and I are before him in Osgood's temporary realm, a dingy chamber in the basement of the county jail.

This place serves as the courtroom of last resort in high security cases in this county. We are here for the arraignment of Andre Iganovich.

The Russian is seated, chained to a metal chair that in turn is fastened to the floor. He wears an orange jail jumper, the word 'Prisoner' stenciled in letters eight inches high across his back. He is cuffed, and chained at the waist, his ankles shackled so that he sounds like Santa's reindeer when he walks. Two beefy jail guards, unarmed, stand behind him.

Chambers has another chair next to his client, at a small table. Between them is a court-appointed interpreter, a woman who will be chattering in undertones into the defendant's ear once we start.

There's a gaggle of press and television here, the cameras outside in the hall. They lend a certain circus atmosphere to the proceedings.

Osgood shuffles papers on the table. He is in a hurry, mention of an eight-thirty calendar back at the courthouse.

He slaps his gavel on the metal surface of the table and a hundred conversations die in mid-sentence.

'Mr Chambers, is your client ready?'

I'm standing alone off to the side, far enough away so as not to invade any whispered confidences between Chambers and the Russian.

'We are, your honor.'

Osgood looks at me.

'The people are ready,' I say.

'You have a copy of the information, Mr Chambers?'

Adrian holds it up, evidencing that he has received this, the charging document in these cases.

'Can we waive a formal reading?' says the judge.

Chambers is agreeable. This means Osgood can dispense with a voluminous and detailed reading of every word contained in the criminal information. Instead he hits the high points in laymen's terms. -

'Mr Iganovich.'

The Russian looks up at the judge. He does not appear overly disturbed by his circumstances. I would say less concerned than Chambers.

'You are Andre Iganovich?'

The interpreter is in his ear. A brief delay.

'Da.'

'Yes,' says the interpreter.

'Have you ever been called by any other name?'

Again an interpretation, then a dense look by the defendant. Suddenly, a twinkle in the eye.

'Sometimes call me some-of-bitch,' he says. A smile. Some laughing from a few of the reporters. Osgood looks at him sternly.

He tells Iganovich to speak his native tongue, to forget the butchered English and the comedy routine. 'It is better for the record,' he says.

'I will ask you one more time. Have you ever been known by any other name?'

Iganovich gives him a leering smile, then the eye, something which in certain countries might be read as an offer of seduction, one man to another. He does not seem terribly intimidated by Osgood's manner. I think perhaps he has seen more fearsome interrogation, maybe in the place from which he originates.

After interpretation: 'Nyet,' followed by the interpreter's, 'No.' He has no aliases, at least if he is to be believed.

'Andre Iganovich, you are charged with four counts of first-degree murder.' Osgood reads off the dates of the crimes and the names of the victims, the four college students, Julie Park and Jonathan Snider, Sharon Collins and Rodney Slate.

'Do you understand the charges against you?'

A brief conference as the interpreter works the middle ground between Chambers and Iganovich.

'Da,' says Iganovich. It is the last thing I can understand. Suddenly he's a staccato of unintelligible words, animated expressions, shaking his head, trying to bring up his shackled hands to ward off these slanders. During part of this, toward the end, he is looking at me, venomous little slits. When he is finished he spits on the floor in my direction.

'Enough of that,' says Osgood.

'Yes. Ah . . . ah.' The interpreter is playing for time

trying to pick through the exuberant language before she speaks.

'Yes, I understand,' she says. 'But it is no . . . ah . . . I did not do these things. I did not kill anyone. These are perverse lies.' She searches for the right word. 'Swill,' she finally calls them. I think perhaps he used something stronger; a little interpretive license. 'It is not true what they say, what that man says. He is a liar, a . . . ah . . .'

The term 'that man', I take to be me.

The interpreter searches the air for the proper adjective. 'A fucking liar.' So much for license. She omits the expectoration, only to look at the lugi, floating like some little green egg in its own juice on the concrete floor. There are limits it seems, even to verbatim translation.

'Mr Iganovich, I will not tolerate foul language in my court. We are here for a reason, to get to the truth of these matters. You need not worry, you will be given a fair trial,' says Osgood. He is a wellspring of calming tones, a picture of composed paternal authority draped in black.

Iganovich looks at him like he is lunch, then another seductive smile. I think the defendant has a penchant for men of power. He would like to get Osgood in this room alone, bent over the table with his gown raised from behind. At least half the members of the bar in this county would vote to give him the chance, if they could.

Osgood informs the defendant of the smorgasbord of pleas available under law: not guilty, guilty, not guilty by reason of insanity, nolo contendere. He asks Iganovich if he has discussed the matter of a plea with his lawyer.

It comes back from the interpreter that he has. Before she can finish: 'No guilty,' he says. He looks arrogantly off to the side, a smug expression as if this is his last word, an end of it, his final statement on the subject. Then he sees me, cracks a grin in my direction, something like a broken picket fence, a toothless map of the old world. But in his eyes is a look, like he is sizing me up for a coffin.

Nikki would love it. The arraignment, and I am already getting psychic death-threats. It is one of the reasons she insisted that I leave my job at the DA's Office in Capital City twelve years ago, the fear that one of my customers would ultimately get my home address, make overt moves on what to me, after a time, seemed like so many idle threats.

'Is your client ready to enter a plea, Mr Chambers?'

'He is, your honor.'

Very well. Osgood walks the defendant through each count. To each charge of murder in the first degree, the interpreter states, for the record, 'not guilty', after listening to Iganovich butcher the term in pigeon English. He has discarded Osgood's earlier admonition. The judge has given up.

'Mr Chambers, as to each and every count, do you join with your client in the entry of each plea?'

'I do, your honor.'

'Have you had a chance to discuss possible dates for a preliminary hearing?' Osgood addresses this to Chambers and me.

'We haven't, your honor,' I answer.

'Your honor, at this time, before we get to the issue of a preliminary hearing, the defendant would like to make a motion for bail,' Chambers says. He's crossing off items on a yellow legal pad as he talks. I can see several other notations below the one just eliminated.

Osgood looks over at me. He seems a little surprised, but not nearly so much as I. Chambers cannot be serious. A suspect who all but fled to Canada and sequestered himself behind the Chinese wall of extradition, and he wants us to put him on the street. I don't know who would be more dangerous at this point, Iganovich, who might kill again, or Kim Park, who would have a contract out on the defendant's life within the hour, were he to be released.

'Your honor, we would object to any thought of bail,' I say. My face is a full smile, like this is some kind of joke. I talk about the problems, the fact that the defendant is a public-safety risk, that he himself is a marked man in a community on the edge of hysteria.

'He is not a public-safety risk,' says Chambers, 'until and unless he is convicted. In this country there is a presumption of innocence. I would have thought Mr Madriani, so recently of the defense bar, would be the last to forget that.'

He sees me turn a little smirk his way.

'I'm glad Mr Madriani sees some humor in this motion,' he says. 'Perhaps it will be easier for him to find his way to some reasonable middle ground on the issue.'

'Isn't there some code section?' says Osgood. He's fumbling through his book on the table.

A state with a law for everything, and we have a judge who knows none of them. Like much of the bench in the rural counties of this state, Osgood was a borderline lawyer with better political instincts, one of three municipal court judges in the county. At local bar meetings he is the cock-of-the-walk, aloof to anyone not seen as his social peer, which includes all humans below the level of superior court. There is not the slightest chance that he would release this defendant on bail. He may not know the law, but he has mastered the theorems of politics in a small county. He will deny it, even if he has to ground his ruling on the school-boy doctrine of 'tough titty'.

I tell Osgood to look at section twelve-sixty-eight of the Penal Code.

He is all thumbs to the bench book, the judge's bible.

'In capital cases,' I say, 'where the proof is evident and the presumption great, the defendant cannot be released on bail. We would argue this is just such a case, your honor.'

'There,' says Osgood, 'I knew there was a statute.' Like he gets points for just seeing the issue. Osgood treats every day in court like a new bar exam with lawyers to kibitz him.

'But the proof is not evident,' says Chambers. 'And there is certainly no great presumption of guilt here.'

Osgood looks over at me, with a look that says, 'surely he doesn't expect me to apply the statute to the facts?' There're little hints of panic in his eyes, a look of what do we do now.

I try to calm him. 'It's not an overly high standard, your honor. The question of whether proof is evident or the presumption great, turns on whether there is *any* substantial evidence to sustain a capital verdict.'

I take him by the hand on a verbal tour of the stakes and the cord found in the defendant's vehicle, the bloody rag found on the front seat. The fact that forensics have tied these items to the four murders.

By the time I finish, Osgood is a full convert to my line of argument, confident, shaking his head, like certainly this has been clear from the beginning, a judge who's come to a decision.

'Mr Chambers, the District Attorney makes a persuasive argument,' he says. 'I think the section would apply in this case.'

Chambers is up out of his chair, trying to talk.

Osgood's hand is up cutting him off, like a good traffic cop. He doesn't want to hear anything that might turn his decision to mush. He would plug his ears and hum, if he could.

'Even if I were inclined to release your client,' he looks at the press out front, who are now getting writers cramp, 'which I am not,' he says this last sternly, with meaning, shaking his head now, jowls like Richard Nixon, swaying for emphasis, 'the law is clear. I cannot release your client on bail. The motion is denied.'

Chambers sits down, talks to his client, a few whispered exchanges, conversation through the interpreter. Iganovich trying to talk with his hands is hampered by more than a foreign tongue. The hand cuffs and waist chain are in his way.

'Where were we?' says Osgood.

'A date for the prelim,' I say.

'Oh yes.' He looks at Chambers.

'How long do you think for the defense?'

Chambers doesn't hear him. He's still talking to Iganovich.

'Excuse me, Mr Chambers, if you don't mind.'

Chambers finally looks at the judge.

'How long do you need for your case in the preliminary hearing. We're trying to fix a date.'

'It's academic,' says Chambers.

'Not if you want a date for prelim,' says Osgood.

'We have one,' says Chambers.

Osgood's getting pissed. He may not know the law, but he certainly knows proper etiquette in his own courtroom. Treatment like this from a lawyer does not cut it.

'Counsel,' he says. 'We are trying to fix a date for preliminary hearing. If you cannot help us, I will assume that your case will take no more than,' he thinks for a moment, 'two days.' The price of fucking with the judge. 'And we will set it for . . .'

'The preliminary hearing will have to be in ten days,' says Chambers. 'The defendant refuses to waive time.'

Osgood sits in his chair his body seeming to smoke, like he's been hit by lightning. He looks at Chambers, not certain that he's heard him correctly.

'Your honor,' I move toward the table, 'this case cannot possibly be ready in ten days. This is a capital case. A man's life is at stake. Does the defendant understand this?'

'He does,' says Chambers. 'If he's going to remain behind bars pending the preliminary hearing, he refuses to waive time.' He looks at me and smiles.

'Ridiculous,' I say.

Chambers shrugs this off. 'The district attorney has a choice, preliminary hearing in ten days or release my client and dismiss the charges.'

Chambers is citing the law. In this state, a defendant who refuses to waive time is entitled to a hearing or indictment within ten days. Otherwise he must be released.

'This is absurd,' I say.

Osgood's shrugging his shoulders, like what can I do?

'Talk to the defendant, your honor. Ask him if he understands the consequences,' I say. I am worried about appeal later, a trumpeted cause for incompetent counsel.

Osgood makes this point, like an echo with Iganovich through the interpreter. There's a little sorting out between Chambers and the translator. What is clear, what does not require translation is that Chambers is driving this decision. Iganovich sits passively and nods while his lawyer talks through the interpreter. His expression grows more sober as he contemplates. He utters something, a few words, his tone one of quiet resignation now.

'I understand,' says the translator. 'I follow my lawyer. I refuse to waive time.'

'Mr Chambers, I hope you know what you're doing,' says Osgood.

'I do,' Chambers smiles at him, a mocking little grin, 'know what I am doing, your honor.'

'Your guy's a real fucking hustle artist,' says Claude. This is how he describes Adrian Chambers.

I have asked Claude to make some subtle inquiries about Chambers, specifically how Adrian came to land the Iganovich defense. I an wondering how he will get paid. But there is no doubt as to *why* he wants this case. Besides a shot at my ass, he is getting advertising he could not buy, a case that regardless of outcome could go a long way toward restoring a ruined reputation.

'The Russian's got an aging aunt down in the valley,' says Claude. 'This was his contact to get into the country, and Chambers's key into the case. She's ninety-two,' he says, 'a few bricks shy of a full load, but still the closest relative.

'Seems her name was in the papers right after we searched the Russian's apartment. Some enterprising reporter dug it up out of employment records with the security company, Iganovich's employer. They interviewed her. She gave 'em a lot of babble in print, character references for her nephew.'

'Did you talk to her?'

He flips open his notebook. 'Seems Chambers landed on her doorstep with a briefcase full of contracts the morning the story appeared. This man lets no moss grow,' says Claude.

'She signed up?'

He nods. 'Didn't cost her a dime.'

'Generous man,' I say.

'A real prince.'

'What did he tell her?'

'That he could help her nephew. That he was convinced that Iganovich didn't commit the crimes. That her nephew had an honest face. Russian's picture was in the paper that morning,' says Dusalt, 'the one from his licensing file.' Claude's talking about the agency that licenses private security guards in this state. Photos are required for their application.

'The old lady signed on all the dotted lines,' he says, 'gave Chambers a full authorization to deal in the case with the only proviso that Iganovich accept him, ratify the contracts.'

'Which, of course, he did,' I say.

'Of course. Oh — and one other little piece of paper.' He takes a folded sheet of letter-size paper out of his pocket and hands it to me. I open it and read. It's a contract, signed by Chambers and the Russian's aunt, conferring on Adrian Chambers all film and literary rights pertaining to the Putah Creek murders and the trial of Andre Iganovich.

'Well, at least now we know how he's gonna get paid,' says Claude.

'Ten days?' she says. 'Get real. I figured we'd have at least ninety. I've got a full plate.'

Lenore Goya is in my office, through the open door. She's looking for some papers, something she laid down in the commotion on my return from the Russian's arraignment. She turns and is back out again, searching, mumbling to herself, under her breath. Lenore will bear much of the burden of preparation in the next nine days, this along with her other duties, some disorder already created by Roland Overroy who is now in over his head on several of Goya's old cases.

'So had I,' I say, 'figured we'd have more time.'

I humor her, tell her that, in refusing to waive time, Chambers shows all the signs of a man operating with less than a full deck.

'Wonderful,' she says. 'It'll give new meaning to the term incompetent counsel. Another grounds for the defendant to appeal.'

We both know this is garbage. Chambers is crazy like a fox.

'He knows exactly what he's doing,' she says. 'He's

jamming us. Balls to the wall.' Lenore is, of course, correct. There is method to his madness.

'Anybody who would do this in a death case.' She shakes her head. 'When they circumcised him they threw away the wrong part.' Her assessment of Chambers as a lawyer.

She settles into a chair on the other side of my desk, and begins to come down, out of the stratosphere. It is what saves her as a trial lawyer. While she has flashes of anger, she has learned to control these quickly, and to mask it in court.

She smiles finally, lightens up. 'Tell me,' she says, 'I'll bet Lester Osgood was a real help this morning.'

I roll my eyes as if to confirm her suspicions that the judge was worse than useless. 'I had to coach him,' I say, 'even to get it on the record that Iganovich understood the risks involved in shortening time. The judge was willing to walk away and leave it unstated.'

Now that Osgood has touched this case, he will no doubt draw the preliminary hearing. It will be his penance from the presiding judge for allowing Chambers to screw up the court's calendar.

We talk about this prospect, Lenore and I.

'If he gets it, he'll be in over his head,' she says. 'And the first sign of fear is hostility. He'll turn his wrath on us.'

She is right. I have visions of Osgood playing to the press, a judicial sonata designed to cover his ass, with an oft repeated theme — the prosecution served up this case, brought these charges, and now they are not ready. In the chorus he will sing the travails of the overworked and unsung judge.

'Every time he reaches for his gavel and it turns to shit,' she says, 'he will blame us.'

She looks at me cold and stark for a moment. 'Osgood might just cut him loose,' she says.

I disagree. 'It is the one thing he will not do. Even if he has to issue a grudging holding order to bind Iganovich over for trial, and blame us for the defects, he will do it. He will blame us for the plight that the court is in, pillory us at every turn, but he will without fail ship this case to the superior court for trial.'

What scares me is that it may be a defective holding order, based on marginal evidence we cannot defend on appeal, something that might be overturned two years from now after a costly trial, and conviction.

Lenore and I talk about the probable defenses that Chambers will raise in the preliminary hearing. We agree that he will not trot out his best horses for this show. Any surprises that might be fatal for our side, a potentially credible alibi witness, a notable forensic expert reading persuasive tea leaves, these he will save for the trial jury. The state's burden of proof in a preliminary hearing is not sufficient to risk everything at this level. If he shoots his wad and misses, he will have tipped his hand for trial, given us valuable information on his case. Instead, he will push us to reveal our own, to produce our best evidence, which given the shortness of time we may now be forced to do. With only nine days to prepare, finesse is not our first strategy.

'He'll kick us hard with Scofield,' she says.

I agree.

'It's a golden opportunity to confuse an already hapless

judge,' I say. If he is deft, Chambers will have Osgood asking more questions about these unsolved murders than we have answers. The press will have a field day.

'We will look like shit,' says Goya.

I raise my gaze, look directly at her. 'Unless,' I say.

She looks up. 'Unless what?'

'Unless we don't take him to a preliminary hearing,' I say.

Puzzlement on her face for a brief instant, then like sonar plumbing the depths, she reads my mind. 'A grand jury,' she says.

I smile and nod.

The grand jury has been an unused vestige of the criminal courts process in this state for the better part of two decades, ever since a liberal-leaning state supreme court ruled that every defendant was entitled to a hearing before an objective magistrate – a preliminary hearing – even those indicted by a grand jury. Two years ago, angry voters showed the liberals on the court the door, and their predecessors the light, when they voted by initiative to restore the criminal grand jury to its prior eminence.

As I look at her, I see a sparkle in Lenore's eye.

'It's perfect,' she says. 'We lock out Chambers, make him wait outside in the hall.'

Criminal defendants, while they have a right to testify before a grand jury, have no right to counsel there. Like the star chambers of yore, grand jury hearings are closed, secret, not only to defense attorneys, but to the press and the public as well.

'And,' she says, 'we dump Osgood.' There's a satisfied smile on her face with this thought. There is no judge to sit in hearings, to preside over a grand jury.

'Thank Providence for little favors,' I say.

Suddenly her mood is lighter, there is some cheer in her face, a way out of a tedious, and sure to be punishing, public hearing.

'I don't want to be greedy,' I say. 'But there's one more thing.'

She looks at me.

'At the moment you're closer to the evidence than I am,' I tell her.

I get a wary look, like she thinks maybe I'm on the verge of asking her to take on something more.

'Do you think there is any chance . . .' I study her for a short moment before going on, thinking. 'Do you think there is any way that we could get the Scofield evidence before a grand jury?'

She stares at me, a picture of puzzlement.

'You mean charge the Russian with those crimes?' she says.

I shake my head. 'No. I mean can you think of any argument, any theory that would permit us to play out the details, the physical evidence in the Scofield murders before this grand jury, without charging Iganovich with the actual murders.'

She looks perplexed, like she can't figure why I would want to do this.

'I don't know,' she says. 'Not off the top of my head. We control the proceedings, but that's a far reach. Some appellate panel looking at the transcript later might question the relevance,' she says. 'Might even find prejudice if they believe we used the stuff to further incriminate Iganovich without charging him with the murders.'

'You wouldn't recommend it then,' I say.

She shakes her heads, still a bit puzzled. 'Why do you ask?' she says.

'Nothing,' I say. 'Just a thought.'

We end. She leaves me musing in my office.

It's what professional prosecutors call 'a cop shop'. Buried two floors beneath the Davenport County Sheriff's Department, down a long corridor marked by outdated and faded civil defense signs, is a single door of solid wood, with no glass panels or windows, and no sign. We open it and step inside.

Lenore's behind me. I look at her. 'What do you think?'

She makes a face. 'For the kind of party we're throwing, it looks about right. How many cops upstairs?' she asks Claude.

'During the day shift in the office, maybe ten, twelve.'

It seems we have found our grand jury room. It's a problem in this state. With the high court decision fifteen years ago, grand jury rooms with their windowless façades, designed for secrecy, fell into disuse, and over the years were commandeered for courtrooms, or consumed by other burgeoning bureaucracies.

I have decided to convene the grand jury here in the basement of the Sheriff's office for reasons of security. Since Iganovich was delivered back to Davenport County we have received more than a dozen threats on his life.

We lock the doors and head back upstairs. Behind the public counter Emil Johnson is waiting for us.

'Counselor, you got a minute?' He wags at me with his finger, then turns and heads for his office.

I nudge Lenore to join us, and the two of us follow Emil's big haunches toward his office.

Inside he closes the door and asks us to take a seat.

'What's this I hear about a special grand jury?' he says. 'What's wrong with the one we got?'

'The key man system?'

He nods.

'Key man' is the selection process that permits a few powerful judges and elected politicians to put their friends and, in some cases, family members on the county grand jury.

'It won't work, Emil.'

'Why not?'

'Because the defendant has a right to a representative grand jury, a cross section of the population,' I tell him. 'Have you taken a look at your grand jury lately? It's whiter than snow. It has only two women.' I don't mention that one of these is the concubine of a county supervisor. 'There are no Hispanics or blacks.'

'Two thirds of that jury were appointed by the superior court judges. You're telling me that ain't good enough.'

'The white friends of white judges don't cut it,' I say.

This sets him back on his heels. By the look on his face I can tell that my words will be passed along, chewed on over stale sourdough rolls and wilted lettuce at the next meeting of the Lincoln Club with all the county pillars.

'Politics has nothing to do with it, Emil. Read *Smith v. Texas* and *Alexander v. Louisiana*,' I tell him. 'US Supreme Court decisions. They give the defendant the right to question the composition of the grand jury that indicts him. He can file a motion to discover the demographics of the jury as well as the method that was used to impanel it. If it's not representative, any indictment would be quashed. I assume you don't want to do this more than once?'

He shakes his head. 'We'll do it your way.' In the final analysis, Emil is a pragmatist.

Chapter Eighteen

'Let's see what we've got,' I say.

'Not much from my end. Like I told ya, a pack a tree-huggers.' This is how Claude describes his telephone inquiries into the World Center for Birds of Prey.

Lenore's back from the library, leaning against the edge of my desk. Claude's in one of the client chairs on the other side.

'I checked with the Boise police,' says Dusalt. 'It's a research outfit, and a sanctuary for birds. Cops don't know much about 'em. They pulled a few records for me, looked the place up on a map.'

'What do they do exactly?' I ask.

'According to the cops, they raise raptors.'

'You make it sound kinky.' Lenore winks at him.

'Birds of prey,' he says.

'I know.' She smiles.

'Hawks, falcons, birds of prey,' he says, 'they hatch 'em, raise 'em, and let 'em go in the wild. A labor of love,' says Claude. 'I'm told that the center is one of a kind. They take in birds from all over the world, breed them, and then do their thing to reorder the balance of nature.'

'Did you call the place, talk to anybody?'

'Yeah.' Claude looks at his notes again. 'I tried for this guy William Rattigan.' If Nikki is right, this is the 'Bill'

227

from Karen Scofield's computer files.

'He was away on business. I guess he runs the place. The Director, that's his title. The woman on the phone was cooperative, but she didn't know a lot. Abbott Scofield was a regional representative for the center in this area, sat on its board of directors with Rattigan. They were involved in a number of projects together.'

'Did she say where Rattigan had gone?'

'East coast for a seminar. I got the number of the hotel he's staying at. He was out so I left a message at the desk for him to call me back.'

'Anything else?' I ask.

He shakes his head and turns to a blank page on his note book.

I turn to Lenore. 'What did you find?'

She's been at the university library most of the afternoon.

'Guess how many listings?' she asks.

I shake my head like I have no idea.

'Five,' she says.

Goya's been playing with the computerized version of the *Guide to Periodical Literature*. Checking to see what she could find out about the Center in any magazines or other publications.

She reaches into her purse and pulls out a long narrow sheaf of paper folded down the center. She opens it up. It's several pages of letter-sized paper stapled together at the top left corner.

'This was the best of the lot,' she says, 'out of *Audubon*.'

I open the photocopied article and read.

She takes it from my hands and turns a few more pages

then flips it around and drops in on the desk in front of me again, tapping one of the photos with her finger.

I look at the picture, a wooden tower built at the edge of some rocky precipice, a silhouetted figure climbing a makeshift ladder to the top. I read the cut-line underneath.

On Idaho's Grouse Peak, university ornithologist Abbott Scofield climbs to a hack box to place extra food for young peregrines.

'If you want my guess,' she says, 'that's the project he was working on when they were killed.'

Lenore has wandered into my office. 'What are you doing for lunch?' she says.

I reach for my coat.

'My turn,' she says. She means to pay for lunch. The last two have been on me.

'I won't argue.'

'You know, the thing we talked about the other day? The Scofield evidence. There may be a way to get it in.' She means before the grand jury.

'Let's walk and talk,' I say. We head out the door.

'It's a little duplicitous,' she says. I wrinkle an eyebrow.

'We'd be setting up the other side, just a bit.' She explains that there would be no deception on the court.

'All's fair in that war,' I say. 'Within limits. What's your idea?'

'I've been doing a little research,' she says.

Neither of us are well versed in the aspects of a grand jury. To find the people best honed in this, you would have to go back through a generation of lawyers, most of whom are now retired.

'*People v. Johnson*,' she says. 'What's called a "Johnson letter".'

I've seen the case before, somewhere, but can't recall its rule.

She explains. It seems the courts have held that while the defendant has no right of representation before a grand jury, he has the right to insist that all exculpatory evidence, anything that could point to his innocence, be disclosed to the jury, who then can choose to look at it in detail, or not, as the jury chooses.

'What's the "Johnson letter"?' I ask.

'It's the mechanism the courts came up with to trigger the requirements of the case. If the defendant sends the prosecutor a letter,' she says, 'demanding that certain evidence, deemed to be exculpatory, be given to the grand jury, the prosecutor has no choice. He has to disclose that evidence. If he doesn't, it's automatic reversal. The indictment will be quashed.'

I whistle a high pitch. 'A real silver bullet.'

She nods.

We're out the front door, down the steps.

'Where do you want to go?' I ask.

'How about Quiche Alley,' she says. This is the salad and soup spot a block away, light fare. We head in that direction.

'What I don't understand,' she says, 'is why you want to do it? The Scofield stuff could be dynamite. Confuse a jury with it and Chambers will turn it into the best defense going.'

230

'Very likely,' I say.

'We don't charge his client with the Scofield murders, but instead admit that there's probably another killer out there someplace, still on the loose. If I were defending, I'd love it,' she says.

'Exactly. You don't think Chambers has already seen the possibilities in Scofield? He'd have to be a fool,' I say. 'But it's still an open question, how damaging the stuff would be.'

We walk a little further in silence. Then I speak.

'What are twelve innocent and objective souls going to say when they see the Scofield evidence at trial, when it's mixed and stirred in a courtroom with the other testimony, the physical evidence? Is it going to explode in our faces, or go inert.'

She shrugs like she has no idea.

'Precisely,' I say. I look at her, a sideways glance as we walk down the street. 'That's why I want to take it in front of the grand jury. To test drive the case.'

She stops in mid-stride and looks over at me, tracking on the strategy. She laughs a little. 'Interesting,' she says, nodding her head. I can tell the wheels are turning upstairs. 'And Chambers isn't there to see you do it.'

I smile. 'Just like a shadow jury,' I say.

We start to move again, down the street.

It is the latest fad among the civil sharks who try the megabuck tort cases. Hired, private focus groups, average citizens paid to be locked in a room for days with lawyers. There the attorneys sample their wares in advance of trial, their theories and evidence, to see what will sell and what won't; the best defenses. Mine is only a modest take-off on this latest tool of litigation.

'But we won't have to pay for it,' I say. 'All we have to do is figure a way to get Chambers to ask that the Scofield evidence be played out in the grand jury.'

'That won't be too hard,' she says.

I stop. I look at her.

'Simple,' she says. 'We send him a letter telling him that it is not our intention to put the Scofield evidence before the grand jury, on grounds that it is irrelevant and could confuse jurors. We give him a citation to *People v. Johnson* in the letter and let him read the law.'

I smile. Lenore Goya is becoming a quick study on the temperament and tactics of Adrian Chambers. Like a shark to the blood, her correspondence will, no doubt, draw the quickest Johnson letter ever crafted by human hands in this state.

I smile at her. 'My treat,' I say. Lenore has earned her lunch.

Chapter Nineteen

It has come like a hot rocket, Chambers's rendition of the so-called Johnson letter, produced so promptly that it is difficult to believe it was crafted by human hands.

Lenore is ecstatic. It is all she could have hoped for and, as I read it, perhaps a little bit more.

'He's probably waiting for us to file a motion by way of objection,' she says. Goya is certain that Chambers is girding himself for our pitch to the court, our anticipated argument to keep the Scofield stuff away from the grand jury.

'He'll grow a long white beard on that watch,' I tell her. His letter is unequivocal. He's thrown the door wide open for us. He won't be able to complain later that the Scofield evidence is irrelevant or prejudicial to his client.

'If we can get the jury to bite, we can run it up the pole and see how it flies.' I'm talking about the details, the discrepancies in the Scofield case. We are both wondering whether we will be able to convince a jury of the existence of another killer, a copy-cat. If we are lucky, we will have a dry run to find out.

Lenore has also given me some bad news in this meeting. It seems Kay Sellig, with her ear to the ground at the Department of Justice, has gotten wind that Acosta's formal letter of complaint has arrived there, questioning my handling of the Russian's extradition from Canada. She has no idea what the Attorney General will do with this thing, but for now it is ticking like a bomb in his 'in-basket'. All I need right now is the bad press of some government inquiry looking over my shoulder.

For the moment I'm holding Chambers's letter, studying its terms.

As if it were fired from a sawed-off barrel, Chambers has loaded his Johnson letter with a lot of scatter shot. He has reached into the hot ashes of defeat on his failed attempt for a quick preliminary hearing, and seeks to try his case before the grand jury by correspondence. This is, in my view, a mistake.

In addition to the physical evidence found in the Russian's van, Iganovich had made those damaging utterances at the point of his arrest in Canada, statements overheard by the two security guards who took him into custody. While it is debatable whether any of these statements could be viewed as wholesale admissions, a jury might see them as concessions of guilty knowledge. It would not be a far leap of faith for a jury to conclude that it was not the vehicle which concerned the defendant so much as its contents.

Chambers now uses his Johnson letter to put a favorable spin on these statements before the grand jury. He claims that his client was concerned by the thought of delinquent parking fees on the abandoned vehicle. According to the unlikely story, Iganovich thought this was the reason for his detention in Canada. He plays upon the fact that the man spoke only broken English, that he was in a foreign country and confused. He claims others had parked the car for Iganovich and failed to provide him with the parking stub, that the Russian thought this was a big item, that it played upon his fears, and bred anxieties. Hence his blurted statements about the van. It is a fanciful story. I can only credit Chambers with an inventive, if somewhat implausible, imagination.

True to form, he does not identify this convenient third party, the person who allegedly parked the van.

'It begs a question,' says Lenore.

I look at her.

'How does he intend to get this story before a jury,' she says, 'at trial?'

Goya is right. Without Iganovich as a witness on the stand to play out this unlikely scenario before a jury it may be a song with a single chorus, one that will be sung only here, before the grand jury.

'Maybe he has another witness,' I say. 'A friend who will testify that he parked the vehicle.'

She makes a face. 'And incriminate himself?' she says.

I shake my head like I have no other explanation.

'We'll have to wait for the disclosure of their witness list at trial,' she says.

'Maybe not,' I tell her. 'For evidence to come before the grand jury it must be admissible at the time of trial. We have a right to know the source of this testimony before we place it in front of the grand jury.'

'What are you saying? We force him to identify the alleged driver of the van now?'

'That's one way.'

'He has another option,' she says. 'He could strip the item from his letter, take it off the table for the time being.' Lenore guesses that, when pressed, this will be what Chambers does.

She is probably right. It is a notorious practice, and one that emanates from the darker side of the defense bar, the last-minute production of a convenient alibi witness. It is an invitation to perjury as old as the law.

The legislature of this state has sought to deal with it over the years, crafting laws which require the early posting of witness lists, to give the prosecution time to check out the credibility of witnesses before they take the stand. But even these are sometimes bent by judges in an effort at fairness, to give the defendant a final word.

'Let's make a demand on Chambers,' I say, 'invite an offer of proof as to which witnesses, if any, will verify his story on the parked van.'

'Flush him out?' she says.

I nod.

I can tell by the look on Lenore's face that she likes this approach.

For the moment, however, there is something about Adrian's letter that is, to me, more troubling. I have looked at it from every angle, so much so that its corners are now dog-eared. As I read it again, I get an uncomfortable, queasy feeling, that something is wrong.

'His letter is like a road map. And I'm troubled by the specifics.'

'How he knew the details,' she says. 'I was wondering that myself.' Lenore has seen it, too, though she mentions it only now.

'How could he know what was in the Scofield file?' I say. 'It's been sealed. We didn't charge his client with these murders,' I make a face. 'So Chambers has no access to the particulars involved in these crimes.'

'A good guess on his part,' she says. 'He knows, for example, that we've matched up ends of the cord used to tie the first four victims to the ground. It was in the police reports in those cases. The same with the metal stakes, that the ones used to kill the college kids were ground to a point.'

'Possible,' I say. 'Could be simple deduction. The fact that we didn't charge Iganovich with the Scofield killings tells him that we failed to get a match on the rope and the stakes in those cases.'

This is what she is thinking. It is plausible. Chambers would not be likely to miss such a thing.

'It's a smart move,' she says. 'You make a blind allegation in your letter that the rope and the stakes don't match and then wait to see what we do. In order to dispute it before the grand jury, we have to produce evidence in the record, a match. He reads the grand jury transcript and knows precisely what we have. Either way he can't lose. If we sit mute and don't counter any of this with hard evidence, he can safely assume we can't produce a match at trial.'

I am looking at her, tracking her line of thought. 'So when we get to court, he uses these unexplained crimes, the discrepancies in the evidence, as a lever to lift doubt in his defense.'

She nods. 'I think so. That's where he's going. He'll try to sell the jury on the theory that somebody else did 'em all. Chambers will argue that unless we can tell the jury who did the Scofields, there is a reasonable doubt, that his client is not guilty of any of them.'

She is right. This is clearly his line of attack. It might not be enough to acquit, but it could certainly hang the average jury, leave them hopelessly deadlocked. The county would be faced with the prospect of another costly trial. Chambers would take his revenge, laughing each inch of way. Confronted with the prospect of still another trial, Derek Ingel and Armando Acosta would make it their special mission in life to crush my career.

I look again at Chambers's letter lying open on my desk. There is something else that troubles me, something I do not mention to Lenore. It is the tenor of this writing. Chambers is far too sure of himself. His words are not the image of someone dealing in the dark, juggling details grounded on conjecture.

In one area he has slipped over the edge, revealed a bit too much. It is the tire tracks, the ones at the Scofield scene.

Imbedded in the letter, three paragraphs down is Chambers's assertion that vehicle tire-tracks found at the scene of the Scofield killings do not match the tires on his client's van. He is, of course, correct. The police have indeed found tracks and, moreover, come up with no match.

The problem is, there is no mention of any tire tracks in any of the reports on the earlier killings. It is something that is isolated, confined, mentioned only in the Scofield file. This information on the tire tracks, Chambers could not get from any serendipitous conjecture.

There is no way that Chambers could have known about this, I think, unless he has eyes and ears inside my case, unless he has been talking to someone close to the investigation.

Chapter Twenty

'We're going out,' says Nikki.

'Emm?' Saturday afternoon and I'm lost in the *Sporting Green*, at the kitchen table; the first time I've read anything unrelated to work in a week.

'Even when you're here, you're not here,' she says.

I drop the paper, a pained expression, and apologize.

When I look up, Nikki has her purse over her arm. It seems that this is the extent of my life of late with Nikki and Sarah, an endless train of amends for lost weekends and late nights in the office.

'Where are you going?' I ask.

'I've been talking to you for the last five minutes,' she tells me. 'You haven't heard a word I was saying.'

She's right. Nikki's been working at the sink while I huddled behind the paper. Her voice has been a constant din in the background, competing with the television, which Sarah is still watching in the other room. But I have seen and heard none of this, not even the box scores, which my eyes have traversed four times on the page in front of me. My mind is on Putah Creek; the choreography of my grand jury.

'I'm sorry,' I say. 'My mind is elsewhere.'

'Right.' Nikki gives me a look, like what else is new?

'I'm taking Sarah to the movies, and then we're having

dinner with Laura Benson and her girls.' Laura Benson is another 'lawyer's widow', married to a trial mogul, one of the local tort sharks, who at any time has more irons in the fire than the village smithy.

Nikki has joined the 'widows' web', a network of lawyers' wives, who in effect have given up all hope of weaning their husbands from their obsessive work-ethic. I have seen some of their literature, mimeographed sheets with the motto on top:

> Live with 'em or leave 'em –
> either way you lose 'em.

It is the latest in self-help for the lawyer's spouse.

'Your dinner's in the ice,' she says. 'The dish covered in foil. Five minutes in the microwave,' she tells me.

'What time will you be back?'

'Whenever we get back,' she says. This is another of their tenets: brazen independence, to the point of impudence.

'Some clue as to a time would be nice,' I say. 'Today? Tomorrow?'

She ignores me. 'Sarah. Turn off the TV. Let's go. We don't want to be late.

'Don't worry about us,' she says. 'Sarah and I are going to have fun.'

My conscience begins to ease a little with this thought.

'When you're finished with your trial you can join us,' she says. 'We'll still be here . . . Maybe.'

This is her exit line. She leaves me, with the knife still twisting in the open wound.

* * *

We are now three days in on the presentation of evidence to our grand jury. Straightforward and uncomplicated I have spoon-fed them Kay Sellig's testimony of the rope and metal stakes, the match that points to Andre Iganovich as the killer of the four college students, the manner in which that evidence was found and the details of his flight from Davenport.

Goya and Sellig have worked out the details on the Scofield evidence. Now they are lying in wait for an opportunity to put this before the jury.

We have decided that no matter what, we will not reveal the medical evidence from Dr Tolar's autopsy: the fact that the Scofields were killed elsewhere and moved to the Putah Creek. I do not want this in the grand jury transcript for Chambers to read. I will hold it like a trump card for trial.

My biggest fear is that they will let the Scofield evidence slide, read the Johnson letter and yawn. In our final strategy session, Goya and I had discussed a little farce, something she and I could play out if things went badly, a few questions and answers in front of the jury. This was intended as a way to drag the bait, to set the hook, to draw a motion to hear the Scofield evidence. But our hastily drawn parody was thin, shallow as a sandbar and nearly as dangerous. It was not likely to deceive the quick-witted, particularly a judge on appeal, or Chambers if he chose to test the indictment. An appellate panel might wonder what our colloquy is doing in the record.

Lenore said she had a better idea. I listened to this with some trepidation. But, in the end, I agreed.

Our enemy thus far has not been the facts or the law or, for that matter, the wily mind of Adrian Chambers who is present here only by his writings. Instead it is the small contrary factions on this jury that are causing the most grief. Little budding walls of animosity have cropped up between groups of jurors. These have nothing to do with the issues or the evidence before us.

From the perspective of a prosecutor, the best grand jury is a closed and intimate thing, like a family pulled together in crisis. The introduction of a single discordant member can cause considerable pain. And I have found mine.

William Geddes has short cropped hair and a thin angular face. He is a transplant from the big city, a retired cop. Off on a disability dive from the Los Angeles Police Department, he lives like the landed gentry, with his horses and his fourth wife, on a spread outside of town. From all appearances he is a fifth-degree loud mouth with a wandering libido.

Between belches over Diet Coke, he's been drooling all over the table, lecherous looks at Lenore Goya and another juror, a young school-teacher, a blonde, seated at the other table across from him.

On the first day of evidence, Geddes copped looks at the blonde's long legs under a short dress, until she showed up the next day in pants, and sat down the line where he could no longer leer without wrenching his neck.

Yesterday he crossed the line. He hit on Goya. It started with a few soft off-color jokes and guileless references to sexual trivia. Not to anyone in particular. Geddes uttered these just under his breath in the quasi-privacy of our afternoon break, as if it were all in good fun, an innocent quest for a few laughs. But always his eyes were on Lenore, like a radar dish searching for prurient shadows.

Then he made his breathless move. As she headed for the door on an errand, in passing traffic, he spoke in her ear just loud enough to be overheard by two of the other jurors and me.

'How about a drink, just you and me, after work?' he says. Novel, he is not.

As for Goya, she slowed only half-a-stride, turned and looked him in the eye. 'God already put one asshole in my pants,' she said. 'Why would I want another?'

One of the jurors doubled-up over at the table, laughing out loud.

Geddes shot them a mean look.

This did not faze the man, a farmer of Dutch stock, built like a snow plow. Geddes was relegated to a variation of his initial malignant gaze. He put a face on it, tried to pass it off.

'Jesus,' he shook his head and laughed. 'I'll bet she gives head like a barracuda.' It was a feeble search for sympathy from the male contingent, an appeal to the redneck brotherhood that did not fly.

Goya had cleared the door and didn't hear his last comment. The jurors I'm sure thought this was lucky for Geddes. Otherwise he would have been explaining to his wife, how it was that Mr Doodles, Geddes's one-eyed monster in the turtle-neck sweater, got his two cylinders crushed.

This morning Geddes is obstreperous, a seeming stream

of pointless questions, as if by this he is taking his revenge on the group.

The three farmers sit next to each other at the table like Larry, Moe and Curly Joe; with beefy, hairy forearms folded across their chests.

A college professor and two housewives sit on the other side, quiet, not disposed to ask questions or make comments, except under their breath to each other. I have no idea what they or others on this jury may be thinking.

Ravi Sahdalgi, a Pakistani graduate student, is closest to me, sitting near this end of the U-shaped tables.

'Rag-head.' It is what Geddes uttered under his breath the one time Sahdalgi sought to speak up. This thoughtful and introspective man has been silent ever since.

Next to Sahdalgi is Vernon Shupe, a law student. Young and well educated, I think Shupe sees himself a likely target for Geddes's venom.

Like a magnet laid over a compass, Geddes's insufferable behavior has stripped me of any sense of direction with this grand jury. His odious comments have driven them underground. In their silence, the roving eyes around this table tell me there is consensus on only a single point; that if this were a lifeboat adrift on the high seas, the vote to put William Geddes over the side would be without dissent.

We are now on a mid-morning break. I have finished the presentation of our evidence in chief, everything except Chambers's exculpatory evidence, the items in his Johnson letter.

Jurors are heading for the door, to stretch their legs, to get a smoke.

It's starting to get a little warm in this room, the problem of a dated building.

Lenore Goya, who is nearest the door, heads for the phone outside on the wall, to call maintenance to have the thermostat turned down.

Two minutes later she comes back in.

'Are you ready to do it?' she asks. She's talking about the Johnson letter.

I take a deep sigh.

'Yes. Call them in,' I say.

She gets three of the jurors, who are outside on the loading dock, and we go back on the record.

I bring them to order, tell them that they have heard all the evidence the state is prepared to produce at this time, that this is, in my view, more than sufficient to return indictments on four counts of first degree murder against Andre Iganovich.

I see a number of nodding heads around the table.

'I believe that the evidence you have seen and heard, is more than sufficient to charge the defendant with special circumstances,' I say, 'permitting the death penalty.'

There is considerable evidence of torture, and that Iganovich lay in wait for his victims before he killed them. A finding as to either of these could result in a verdict of death.

'However,' I say, 'there remains one item of business.' I explain the procedure regarding the Johnson letter, that I am not an advocate for the contents of this missive, that they are not required to take evidence on any item contained in it. But that I must reveal it to them as a matter of law, and that they may, if they wish, review the evidence

245

in the Scofield murders. I put a face on it for the record transcript. It wouldn't do to be too overt in pushing this thing.

It is now too warm for comfort in this room. I take off my coat.

I have Goya pass around copies of the letter, the evidentiary points and legal arguments raised by Chambers. Heads go down as they read.

Goya looks at the door. She would like to open it, get some fresh air in the place. But with a grand jury, secrecy takes precedence over comfort. The faint but growing odors of the country are coming to full blossom in this room. After a few seconds Goya looks at me. She, too, has picked up on this smell, something from the barnyard, brought to life by the heat now permeating this room.

Several minutes pass. A few of the jurors turn the letter over on the table or lay it down, signaling that they have read it, that they are waiting for me to move on.

The last few jurors put down the letter. I study them for any sign of curiosity, scanning for an inquisitive face, some leader among them who I might induce down into this pit with me.

'Are there any questions?' I say.

Blank gazes, not a single hand.

'Ladies and gentlemen, I know it's a long letter. Perhaps we need a little more time to digest it.'

They give me pained expressions, the grown-up version of pissed-off adolescents in a history lecture. The message is clear. They are ready to hang the Russian. They want to go home.

Finally a hand. It is Vernon Shupe, the law student. Good boy.

'Mr Shupe, yes.' I smile at him, all the ardor of a used-car salesman.

'You haven't indicted the defendant on these murders?'

'No, Mr Shupe, we haven't.' Please. Please. Ask me why.

'Why,' he says. 'I mean, why would we hear evidence on crimes that aren't charged?' he says.

Son-of-a-bitch, I think. Wasn't he listening. All the while I smile at him, hoping to cultivate our conversation.

'Good question,' I say.

He grins at me, proud of having asked it.

'Because defense counsel believes that these later crimes and the circumstances surrounding them may serve to exonerate his client. From that perspective it is important.' I add this last, a flourish to encourage more.

'Oh.' He settles back in his chair.

'Oh'. That's it? 'Oh'. There's an almost audible groan from Lenore at the table next to me. I bore a hole through Shupe with my eyes. Unless he sharpens his mind he will look like Swiss cheese after three years of law school.

'More questions?' I say. 'Someone, anyone?' I move my gaze quickly around the table, no movement except for William Geddes. His nostrils suddenly going crazy, persistent little flares, sniffing the air.

'Yeah, I got one,' he says. 'What in the — excuse me — fuck is that?'

He looks at me.

'Don't you smell it?' he says. 'Like somebody died.'

The woman sitting next to Geddes on one side looks at

him with an expression that tells the world 'it wasn't mine'.

Geddes looks down the line under the table across from him and starts to laugh.

'One of our farmer friends,' he says. He's pointing to a pair of cowboy boots, expensive snake's skin with silver tips. These are crossed under the table on the other side from Geddes.

'You outta at least scrape 'em a little bit before you come here,' he says. 'Let me guess – horses?' says Geddes. A cackling laugh.

He draws a disapproving glance from another juror, a member of the university faculty who would rather endure the odor than Geddes and his language.

I am afraid that what, up to this point, has been a silent brawl among this jury is about to spill over into a more public confrontation.

Sam Holland, the farmer on the other side, is one of the icons of agribusiness in the valley. In an ordinary setting I would think that he and Geddes might find something in common, a redneck heritage. But Geddes has killed any chance of this.

Holland gives us all the cowboy shrug. A gesture that can mean anything from an apology to the crudest obscenity, depending on how you want to take it.

Then he points his finger at Geddes. With Holland's close-cropped beard and flowing gray locks, cut at the collar, he is the buckaroo's image of Michelangelo's *Creation*; the accusing forefinger just the slightest crook at the end, pointed from a fully extended arm.

'And you,' he says to Geddes, 'you're flat-ass wrong.'

Geddes looks at him, stiffening his neck, ready to take up any challenge.

'It's bullshit,' says Holland. 'I woulda thought you, of all the people in this room, woulda recognized that.'

Geddes is out of his chair.

'Gentlemen, please.' I have both hands up, like a referee about to break a clinch between two fighters. 'Let's focus on the issues, the letter before us,' I say.

'I've had enough of him,' says Holland.

'Well kiss my patoot,' says Geddes.

Holland takes one step on his way around the table.

'Enough,' I say. I slam one of the heavy briefing books on the table. A thunderous thud.

They look at me, Geddes and Holland. Both men stop in their tracks.

'Now sitdown,' I make it a single word, for effect. 'Both of you. I've a mind to seek contempt, a visit with Judge Fisher,' I tell them.

Grudging, dragging each step, Holland backs off, neck bowed like one of his pedigree breeding bulls. He settles into his chair, and gives Geddes one final look, what a dog might get before being nailed by Holland's pointy gunboat boots.

Geddes gives him what could pass for a mock snarl, the look of some mangy cur safely outside the confines of the coral.

I look at Goya. She's rolling her eyes, like what next?

'This panel has a decision to make,' I say. 'The letter that is before us raises serious issues. The question is whether there is a motion to hear the evidence in the Scofield murders as requested by the defendant and his

249

attorney. We must focus on that,' I say.

Goya sensing her cue, chimes in. 'Should we analyze the issues point by . . .'

'What for?' Geddes cuts her off.

'We've seen and heard enough,' he says. 'Your guy's guilty as sin.' There we have it, from on high, as if with this proclamation and a seal I could take it to an executioner.

'What difference does it make whether they gas him for four murders or six?' says Geddes. 'I don't wanna waste any more time. I've got things to do. Business.'

I put Geddes down one more time, tell the panel there are procedures that must be followed.

'Procedures,' he says. 'A waste of time.' He looks around the table, at Holland, Shupe, and some of the others. Dead silence.

Then a quiet, retiring voice, behind me off to the right: 'Mr Madriani?' Ravi Sahdalgi has a question.

'Yes? Mr Sahdalgi.'

Geddes looks at the ceiling.

'This evidence in the Scofield murders. Is it material to the crimes charged, to the murder of the four college students?'

'It could be,' I say, 'depending how you read the evidence,' I tell him.

'And the defense attorney,' says Sahdalgi, 'he is arguing that whoever killed the Scofields also killed the others, but that this is not his client?'

'That seems to be his argument.'

'Then I think we should hear the evidence,' he says.

I look at him, full on. 'Is that a motion?' I say.

'Yes, it is. I move that we hear the evidence in the Scofield murders.' He looks quickly at Geddes. There is firm resolve in his eyes, like the look of a prophet once he's convinced his word is holy writ.

'Crying out loud,' says Geddes. He's moving like he wants to get up.

'Sit down, Mr Geddes. The matter is not open to debate, unless there is a second,' I say.

He slumps back into his seat, muttering to himself, a few profanities. I think I hear a quiet racial slur. He looks at Sahdalgi. Geddes's legs are splayed wide, his chair tilted back resting against the concrete wall behind him, the look of some surly adolescent.

'This is bullshit.' He says it under his breath looking now at Holland, little slits of meanness.

It is all that is needed.

'I second the motion,' says Holland. His look says it all: 'there take that'. 'And I call the question,' he adds. This latter shuts the door on any debate with Geddes only halfway out of his chair.

'All those in favor,' I say, 'of taking evidence in the murder of Abbott and Karen Scofield, please raise your hand.'

Like stooks of corn in a Kansas field, twenty-two arms reach upward, toward the ceiling.

Geddes makes a face, a deep groan. In his own way, he has done me an inestimable service. This jury, with a little help, has finally found its voice. It has also cut William Geddes adrift, leaving him alone on the high seas of human contempt.

I look over at Lenore. She is all smiles, the look of one

whose well-laid plans have paid off. We will drink later this evening, after session, at Tories, the bar around the corner, Lenore Goya, myself and, of course William Geddes, for Geddes has played his part to perfection. In this little episode I draw a singular lesson, that Lenore Goya is a quick study in the science of social dynamics. Hers indeed was a better idea.

It was a well-hatched plan, one that closely, but cautiously skirted the bounds of jury tampering. Geddes, while baiting the others to draw a motion, could not himself make the motion, second it or even vote for it. To that extent he had been compromised by Lenore's brief conversation with him. She had explained to him, outside the record, why we wanted to bring the evidence in. He cut her off, told her to say no more. The rest was pure Geddes. It is said that no actor plays any role so well as himself. In the case of William Geddes, I am now left to wonder.

Claude has been busy dogging William Rattigan, the elusive Director of the World Center for Birds of Prey, a man in perpetual motion. Claude finally nailed him yesterday in his office, only to discover that Rattigan was about to leave on another trip, this time to Southern California, a seminar at UCLA.

It took some talking by Claude, references to the broad subpoena powers of a grand jury in this state. Rattigan has agreed to a slight detour, to meet with us this morning at the Capital City Airport. Anything he can do, he says, to cooperate.

This morning, he sits across the table from Claude and

me, in the crowded airport restaurant, shaking his head solemnly.

'It was routine,' he says. Rattigan's talking about the work that Abbott and Karen Scofield were doing.

'He was contracted to perform some early research on diminishing peregrine populations in the eastern coastal range of your state,' he says. 'He was one of three regional research directors we had working on the project.

'There's nothing to hide,' he says. 'No mysteries. Peregrine populations in the US have been on the decline for years. They've been an endangered species now for more than a decade. But they are a resilient breed. It's why we keyed on them, as opposed to other species. We believed that there was a strong possibility that with work we could restore them. If not to their original numbers, at least we could bring them back from the brink of extinction.'

'So what was Scofield's part in this?'

'He did initial research for us out here. Mostly locating sites for natural habitat. Places where the birds would have a chance to gain a foot hold if released into the wild.'

'What kind of research?' I ask. I want to know if these activities might have caused him to cross paths with his killer.

'We had a protocol,' he says. 'We would check for a number of things; the absence of natural predators; pesticide use in the area; human foot traffic; projected growth and development; civilian aviation that might disturb breeding patterns.

'We worked from a list. The data was all fed into a computer and favorable target areas were identified, mostly public lands, where we could release the birds into the wild. Sometimes they would migrate short distances and resettle. Usually not too far.'

'Anything else besides research?' Claude is probing.

'Under the contract, Dr Scofield was also responsible for releasing the birds and monitoring them for a brief time afterward.'

'The falcons, where did he get them?' I ask.

'We bred the initial birds at the center. When they were able to fly and hunt, so they could feed off the land, we would ship them out to Dr Scofield. Part of his contract called for assisting us in the release of the birds into the wild. They were tagged. He would feed them for a while and monitor them for survival and adaptation to their surroundings, nesting, breeding of young.'

'That explains the feed pellets and the mice,' says Claude. He's talking about the items purchased by Scofield in large quantities but not found at his lab.

'These birds would eat mice?' says Claude.

'Live, if possible,' says Rattigan.

'Do you know where Dr Scofield released the birds?' he asks. 'Exactly where on the Putah Creek?'

'Where?' says Rattigan.

'The Putah Creek.'

'That doesn't sound familiar,' he says. 'Let me check.' He pulls his briefcase onto the table.

'I have copies of his working maps with me,' he tells us. 'But Putah Creek — that does not sound right. As I recall, from my discussions with Abbott, the areas of release called for the birds to be placed in the coastal range.'

Rattigan finds a large map in the flap inside the cover of

his attaché case. He opens it on the table and studies it for several seconds, tracing features with a forefinger.

'Here,' he says. 'This is the spot. In this area.'

He points to a location on the far side of the Napa Valley, a hundred miles from the site of the Scofield murders and the bird blind in the trees along the Putah Creek.

Claude gives me one of those looks, the kind reserved for strange phenomena. Then he reaches into his coat pocket and pulls out four clear plastic envelopes, little zip-lock bags, and lays them on the table.

'Could you look at these and tell us what they are?' he says.

Rattigan picks them up, one at a time and studies them, carefully. He lays three of them on the table.

'No question,' he says. 'Peregrine feathers. Chicks,' he says. This confirms the information from the Wildlife Lab in Oregon. The last pouch he's still holding in his hand, lifting it toward the light in the ceiling. It's a larger feather, broad and ruffled, striated in its coloration.

'Not this one,' he says.

It's one of the feathers we've not yet been able to identify. We are still waiting on the lab report from Oregon.

'Do you know what it is?' I say.

'Were all of these found in close proximity?' He answers a question with a question.

'Yes,' I say. 'They were virtually mixed together. On the ground,' I say. Actually they were found together in the blind, but I keep this to myself.

'I don't understand it,' he says.

255

'What don't you understand?'

'Abbott's surveys. They didn't show any trace of predators. We checked carefully. It's the first thing we always look for.'

'What are you talking about?'

'This feather,' he says. 'It belongs to a great horned owl. It's a bird that's not indigenous to this area.'

'You mean the area on the map. The coastal range?'

'I mean this state,' he says. 'The great horned owl is native to the northern forests, Canada and the Northern Rockies. Not down here.'

Claude and I look at him.

'So that I understand,' I say. 'This owl. It would kill the falcons if they were in the same area together?'

'In an instant.' He looks up from the table, and the feathers cased in plastic. 'It is a mortal predator of the peregrine falcon,' he says. 'But don't ask me how it got here.'

Chapter Twenty-One

Lately I have been drawing subtle pressure from the county grandees to make a package-deal of this prosecution, to charge all six of the murders to the Russian. It would be an easy thing to do. It would clean the plate, make a lot of friends for me in this county, among the city and university hierarchy.

But there is a problem. I harbor deep suspicions that Chambers is playing this hand with still one more trump card, something he is holding in reserve, until trial. I got a glimpse of it that day, outside the Russian's apartment as the police searched inside. It was in the news papers on the floor, outside in the hallway. Two of those were dated before the Scofield murders, a hint that the Russian was already gone.

It is something you develop in the practice of trial law, a sixth sense. Too often it comes as a prelude in the shadow of disaster, like a fly being swatted on glass.

We have not been able to establish on what date the Russian crossed over into Canada. But I suspect that Chambers can. If I am correct, he is waiting in the weeds to spring this on me. If I charge his client with these last two murders, he will present a gold-plated alibi, ringing down the curtain of doubt on all of the charges. It is why it is so important that I make a plausible wedge that I can drive between Abbott and Karen Scofield, and the other murders.

There's a knock on my office door, knuckles rapping on glass. It opens. It's Jane Rhodes, my secretary.

'Someone here to see you,' she says. She's holding a business card in her hand, looking down, reading.

'A Mr Golumbine,' she says. She steps in and drops the card on my desk.

> Dennis Golumbine
> Deputy Attorney General
> Government Law Section

'Show him in.' I have been waiting for this visit.

A second later, a guy whose age I could not guess, gaunt like some cadaver, thinning dark hair and wire-rimmed spectacles, is ushered into my office. He forces a smile, a thousand more creases in a face like a withered prune.

'Mr Madriani,' he says. He extends a hand. We shake.

I look at his card. 'Mr Golumbine.'

'Bean,' he says. Pursed lips for precision. 'It's pronounced Golum-bean.'

'Have a seat,' I say. I gesture toward one of the client chairs on the other side of the desk. I can guess why he's here. The seriousness of purpose is plastered on his countenance like a fresco on a Renaissance wall.

'What can I do for you?'

'We have a complaint,' he says, 'regarding your office, and I've been assigned to look into it.'

I give him a face, like is this so?

'Yes,' he says. He reaches down into a briefcase, a bell-shaped affair down by his feet and comes up with a yellow note pad. 'A complaint regarding the current prosecution of,' he looks at his notes, 'Andre Iganovich I think is the defendant's name.'

It has taken a while for the Coconut's correspondence to float to the top of all the effluent clogging the AG's in-basket.

'Excuse me for a moment,' I say. I pick up the receiver and press the com-line, then a couple of numbers.

'I wonder if you could come down here for minute?' I hang up.

I turn back to Golumbine. 'You were saying?'

'We have a complaint regarding the handling of this case, specifically errors made in the processing of a request for extradition. We would like your cooperation in gathering information so that we can respond to this, and determine what if any errors were made.'

I make a face, an invitation for him to go on.

'It's a rather serious matter,' he says.

'It's also ancient history,' I tell him. 'You're aware that Mr Iganovich now resides in the Davenport County Jail and is awaiting trial on multiple counts of murder?'

'We had read that,' he says. 'Still.'

'Tell me a little about this complaint,' I say. 'Who filed it?'

'That's confidential,' he says.

'By law?'

'Department policy,' he tells me.

'Surely you can tell me its contents?'

He shakes his head.

The door opens, and Lenore Goya comes in. Golumbine looks at her and is up out of his chair. I introduce them. He has the manner of a village lecher, leering looks as he takes her in, and a limp hand-shake.

'Ms Goya's been assisting me in the prosecution of this case.' Lenore has also been doing a little homework with Kay Sellig. She had warned us that somebody would be coming over from Justice. She didn't know who. She also told us that Acosta's letter did not get a receptive hearing from the Attorney General. The man is an astute politician. Why get drawn into parochial battles. He shuffled it down the line to others with no direction or clear mandate.

'You say "Department policy" prevents you from sharing the contents of your complaint with us?'

'That's correct,' he says.

I look at his card again. 'What's the Government Law Section got to do with extradition?' I say. 'I thought extradition was a special section over there?'

He coughs, a little hack, and straightens his tie. He shoots a glance at Lenore whose skirt has ridden up a few inches on her crossed thigh. 'We help out where we can,' he says.

I nod and smile. 'Just helping out.'

'Yes,' he says.

'So what is it you want?' I ask him.

'Access to your working papers, your files,' he says.

I raise an eyebrow. 'Everything?'

'Yes.'

He may look like warmed-over milk toast, but the man has balls of brass.

'Can I ask you,' says Lenore, 'what's your authority?'

'Excuse me?'

'Your statutory authority,' she says, 'to intervene in a pending prosecution?'

'Oh, we're not intervening,' he says. 'Merely making an inquiry in response to a complaint.'

'Fine,' she says, 'what's your authority for such an inquiry?'

He's no longer looking at her legs. Instead he's now fumbling through his briefcase, which rests in his lap, going through this like Fibber McGee in his cluttered closet. After assorted papers and a day-runner, he comes up with a blue-bound paperback volume, an abridged *Penal Code*. Several seconds thumbing with a wet finger and he cites her a section.

'Can I see it?' she says.

'Certainly.' He hands her the book.

'This pertains to the attorney general's right to review requests and orders for extradition, *before and while they are pending*,' she says. 'I see nothing here about requests for extradition which have been dismissed or otherwise terminated.'

'I think it's not clear,' he says. 'We believe we have broader authority.'

'We?' she says. 'You're talking about the Attorney General? Has he specifically ordered this inquiry?'

'Well, my superiors,' he says.

'And who might they be?' I ask him.

Golumbine's beginning to sweat.

He gives me a couple of names, mid-level functionaries in the Government Law Section.

I take him in another direction, over the falls.

'I understand you know Judge Ingel?' I say.

He looks at me, wariness crowding into his eyes now.

'He's an acquaintance,' he says.

'Oh, I understand you guys used to work together, in the AG's office, that you were pretty close, I understand.'

'We know each other,' he says. A little color, the flush of discovery coming into his cheeks.

'He didn't call you, by any chance, in connection with this, did he?'

A lot of coughing, his hand covering his mouth. A handkerchief comes out, but instead of wiping his mouth he uses this to sweep the sweat from his forehead.

'We can't discuss the particulars of an official inquiry,' he says.

'Ah. Official inquiry.' I nod, like I understand this.

'Do you have a formal opinion interpreting this section?' says Lenore.

Golumbine is beginning to feel like he's caught in a vise, between Goya and me.

'Emm?' He looks at her.

'An AG's opinion setting forth your office's authority relative to this section?' She pointing at the provision of the *Penal Code* that Golumbine would try to ride into the confines of our files.

'I don't know,' he says.

'Well maybe you can look.' She dumps the volume back in his lap. 'And a letter signed by your boss.'

'What are you talking about?'

'Ms Goya makes a good point,' I say. 'It would be nice just to cover all our bases, if we could have a letter of request signed by the attorney general before we open our files. You understand.' I'm up out of my chair, hand extended, like this meeting is over.

'It was good meeting you,' I say.

Golumbine's scrambling, one hand filled with assorted papers and his note pad, the other holding the *Penal Code* from his lap. He is trying to juggle his briefcase clinging to the handle with one pinky finger. He will need a brace on this tomorrow.

Lenore opens the door for him and points the way out. Stooped at the waist, he shuffles out the door with all of his shit. For the moment we've dodged the Coconut's latest bullet.

William Geddes has withdrawn from the grand jury, pleading undefined personal hardship. Alienated from his colleagues on the panel, the price of his little performance, an early departure was Geddes's idea. And I did not discourage it.

Given his ex parte conversation with Goya, brief as it was, the fact that he will not now vote on any of the counts completely dispels even the slightest hint that she might have tampered with this jury. Geddes has been replaced by one of the alternates, a woman who has heard all of the evidence.

She, along with the others, is now two days in on our dry run of the Scofield case, my test drive of the theory that there are two separate murders.

Yesterday, Goya and Kay Sellig took the jurors on a forensic tour of the rope and tent stakes, the differences between those at the first two murder scenes and the ones used to tie down and kill the Scofields. Sellig went as far as she dared, right to the cusp of actually testifying that a copy-cat did the Scofields.

That is something we have reserved for today's witness.

In another life, Harold Thornton has taught, but never tenured, at several prestigious university campuses. These appear large on his curriculum vitae. A former instructor in psychology, he is now on call to a handful of law enforcement agencies in this part of the state, their resident expert on criminal profiling.

A good expert witness will advance your cause without appearing to be an advocate. To the jury he will come across as a good teacher: objective, dispassionate, never tending toward overstatement or extremes of position, the very soul of academic integrity. In short, the dreamboat expert is every hustler's vision of the ultimate flim-flam man. This goes double if you are delving, as I am today, into the dark crevices of the human mind.

'Would you state your name for the record?'

He gives it, spelling his surname for the court reporter.

'Do you hold any academic degrees?'

'A doctor of philosophy,' he says, 'in psychology.'

'And your specialty?'

'Clinical psychology,' he says.

He gives the jury an overview of his academic background, training, teaching assignments, scholarly papers published, all the items that would qualify him in court as an expert witness, someone allowed to offer opinions on matters within the area of his expertise.

'In your professional capacity have you ever assisted law enforcement agencies in constructing personality profiles, what has become known as criminal profiling?' I ask.

'I have,' he says.

'How many times have you done this?'

He thinks for a moment. 'Actual construction, or collaboration?' he says.

'Construction,' I say.

'Six. No. No. Five times,' he says.

I wince a little with this, deep inside where the jurors can't see. I had hoped for more, a longer train of experience. Thornton was supplied by Kay Sellig for a single reason; on short notice he was the only expert available in the area.

'Can you explain to the jury the science of criminal profiling, how it works?' I ask.

'It's quite simple,' he tells me, 'straightforward.'

A small psychic signal erupts in my head. I get queasy when academics tell me anything is simple.

Thornton kicks into overdrive. 'Profiling is predicated on certain psychobiologic presumptions,' he says.

Just what I thought. I cut him off.

'Dr Thornton. We're all a few units shy of our medical degrees here,' I say. 'In layman's terms would be nice.' I smile at him, pleasant and warm.

He gives me a pained expression, then wades in. 'Profiling,' he says, 'is based on a singular observation that the way any activity is carried out, the way that it's performed, will tell you a great deal about the person who performs it.'

Good, I think. To the point, unadorned.

'Applied to criminal acts,' he says, 'if we know the habits and personality traits of people who have committed certain types of crimes, we can then use these to generate behavioral descriptions of the classic perpetrator of that particular crime.'

I turn to get some papers from the table. By the time I come back Thornton is narrating, hip-deep in the bogs of abstraction again. I see heads nodding off at the table, like it's time for a mid-morning nap.

'Sex,' I cut him off in mid-sentence. 'Let's talk about sex crimes, Dr Thornton.'

Two of the farmers who were dozing, come out of their chairs, like it's milking time, reaching for the udders.

'Do you use profiling in sex crimes?'

'Oh, sure. Serial rape is a classic example.'

Thank God for little favors.

'But you can't use it on every kind of crime?' I say.

'No, no,' he says. 'There are entire categories of crime, in fact most crimes, where profiling would not work at all.'

'Can you give us a few examples?' I say.

'Sure.' He thinks for a moment. 'Any crime where there is limited contact with the crime scene. Simple robbery, most thefts. These are crimes that don't usually evidence any particular psychologic disorder. In these cases, little of the personality of the offender can be determined from a study of the crime scene. If somebody reaches into a register and takes money at the point of a pistol, you're not likely to be left with much but fingerprints,' he says.

Like a slow-burning briquette, this jury is beginning to catch. I can see little embers of interest from the jury around the edges. Thornton is taking on the mantle of teacher, the best cover for a good expert.

'Because greed is too common a human vice to make

profiling useful in those cases?'

'Exactly,' he says.

'So what kinds of crime lend themselves best to personality profiling?'

'Usually these are cases with considerable physical activity at the scene, in which the victim is subjected to substantial violence by the perpetrator. Rape, as I said, is a good example,' he tells us. 'Sexual homicide, any crime of violence on a person involving some ritual, severe torture, cases involving mayhem, disfigurement or mutilation of the victim, either before or after death. These are the classic cases for useful personality profiling,' he tells us.

'Why is that?'

'Because these acts would, by their very nature involve some serious psychological disorder,' he says. 'The physical manifestations of the crime scene, the act itself is often patterned by the subconscious in predictable ways. We know this from past similar criminal acts perpetrated by others suffering from some of the same mental disorders. This sets the perpetrator apart from the norm, causes him to stand out, not to the casual observer perhaps, but to the trained investigator who looks at a suspect's background.'

I take him on a little digression. We talk about the traits and markers, the building blocks that make up the personality of the typical offender for the various categories of crime.

These have been developed in hundreds of interviews by experts, talking with the twisted minds incarcerated in prisons and mental hospitals, in some cases pacing the executioner in a foot race to the death chamber in a quest for knowledge.

'Can you tell the jury how these markers, these individual traits, are applied in the usual case to apprehend a specific offender?'

'What we've found is that by the time an individual reaches an age,' says Thornton, 'at which he . . .' He explains that the perpetrator in these cases is usually male. 'By the time they commit such a crime or a series of similar crimes, major felonies that would lend themselves to profiling, these people have already established certain patterns of behavior in their lives.'

Direct examination of an expert is like a song, a form of litigious poetry. There is a proper rhythm. It moves from the general, broad theories, to the specific case studies. If done well, it leaves the jury with a hard concrete view of things, a sense that your man's views are part of the real world, not some ethereal vapor bubbling over a bunsen burner.

'Can you give us a real example of how you've applied a criminal profile, a true case?' I ask.

Thornton muses for a moment, the intense look of painful experience.

'A case in another county,' he says. 'A series of ritual slayings. One of the markers, a common pattern of behavior for this particular brand of sado-masochism, based on the earlier case studies,' he says, 'told us that the perpetrator quite likely had an early history, a childhood fetish for mistreatment of animals, torture of pets. That sort of thing. We had four principal suspects. So we searched the record on each, juvenile authorities, schools, family members, friends from years past.'

Thornton tells us how investigators learned to probe for the sick underbelly, to slip the subtle questions without asking; 'did your friend ever pull the wings off some living bird? Fricassée the neighbor's dog on the run with flaming gasoline for a frolic?'

'The sharp investigator, the best cop for this sort of work,' says Thornton, 'is the good-old-buddy just indulging in confidences about youthful pranks.'

I look at the jury as they study each other. The message: beware of Joe-six-pack with a badge.

'After two days of questioning by nine different officers, a miniature census, one suspect drew a crowd of investigators. Nine hours later he confessed to all five murders,' he tells us. 'When done right, and if you are lucky, that's how it works.'

I look over at the jury. Thornton has achieved critical mass for an expert, he has laid the ground work, established the practice of profiling as something higher on the plane of science than astrology, more credible than reading tea leaves.

I round the last curve and chase for home, the core issue.

'Dr Thornton, have you had occasion at our request to study those crimes, those series of murders commonly known in the area as the Putah Creek killings?'

'I have,' he says.

'So as to avoid any confusion among the jury, would you tell us which crimes you have studied in this regard? The names of the victims?'

Thornton wants to look at his records and notes to refresh his recollection. He identifies three separate sets of murders as having been referred to him by the Davenport County Sheriff's Department, the two sets of student killings and the later murders of Abbott and Karen Scofield.

'And with regard to these murders, were you asked to prepare personality profiles regarding the perpetrator or perpetrators of those crimes?'

'I was.'

I make clear that in doing this Thornton has not had access to Andre Iganovich, no interviews, opportunities for observation, something Chambers would no doubt pursue if he were here on cross-examination. It is the principal weakness of this test run, that no adversary is present. So I play devil's advocate.

'And applying your expertise, as a licensed and trained psychologist, your experience in years of personality profiling, have you formed any opinion regarding a personality profile of the perpetrator in these cases?'

'I have,' he says.

'Could you share that opinion with us?'

He's looking at his notes. 'With regard to the murders of Julie Park and Jonathan Snider, the first of the student victims, and Sharon Collins and Rodney Slate, last two college victims, it is my opinion that they were killed by the same person.

'With regard to the murders of Abbott and Karen Scofield, it is my opinion, based on scientific evidence, that these victims were killed by a different person or persons, not the murderer of the four earlier college students.'

I wait for a moment, allow this to settle on the jury. It is the zenith of my case on this point. All that is left now is to back-fill with the rationale, the reasoning that supports the good doctor's views.

'And how did you come to this conclusion?' I ask him.

'While there are a number of factors,' he says, 'the one overriding and principal element would be the facial mutilation of the victim Karen Scofield. From the pathology report, her left eye was removed from her head after death.

'Studies tell us,' says Thornton, 'that facial disfigurement is performed in these cases for a single reason; because the killer and the victim were personally acquainted. In the usual case the closer the relationship, the more severe the facial mutilation. Here, with the removal of an eye, I would venture that the murderer knew the victim well.'

He tells us that the symbolic message in all of this is unavoidable, remove the organ of sight, and in the subconscious mind the killer remains hidden from, undisclosed to, his victim.

To demonstrate this fact to the jury he uses one of the photographs, a color picture of Karen Scofield's head as it lay on the coroner's slab.

'The killer used some violence to remove this eye,' he says. He points to three deep slashes, one nearly cutting through the brow on the top, and two more deep into the cheek under the eye. 'Not exactly surgical precision,' he says. 'He was probably in a panic, a frenzy when he did this.'

'And your opinion regarding the earlier victims, the students?'

'That the killer and these victims were strangers. There was no facial mutilation as to any of the earlier victims.'

'Is it not possible,' I say, 'that the same killer might have murdered all of them, that he didn't know the students, but did know Karen Scofield?' A little counter-advocacy here. A show of fairness, exposing a potential softness to our case.

'From case studies, I would say only the most remote of possibilities,' he says, 'highly unlikely.' The true scientist, Thornton abhors the notion of absolutes. It is one of the things that breeds believability.

'There is a general pattern to serial murders,' he says. 'There are killers who know their victims, who select them from a pool of acquaintances. There are pattern killers, who murder only strangers, victims of opportunity. As a general rule the two types or categories of killers do not cross over. We know from studying past cases that generally they will not kill some acquaintances, and some strangers.'

This apparently is the linchpin, the keystone of his opinion that there were two killers − Karen Scofield's missing eye. While there are other factors, this one element is so persuasive in Thornton's mind that it tends to override everything else.

'Were there other factors, doctor? Any other reasons to suspect a separate murderer in the Scofield cases?'

'Yes,' he says. 'The age discrepancy between the Scofields and the students. While not unheard of, this is unusual in pattern murders,' says Thornton.

'Also, the tools of death,' he says. 'The killer would usually not change rope or stakes if he had an ample supply, which according to the police report the suspect Iganovich had in his vehicle. These are generally part of the ritual,' says Thornton. 'And these murders are ritual slayings,' he says, 'make no mistake about that. The arrangement of the articles of clothing in an arc about the head of each victim, the use of undergarments to cover the face of the female victims, all point to a liturgical crime,' he says.

I look at him, a question mark.

'Ritual murder,' he says for clarity.

'No,' he says. 'In my opinion, there is no question. The Scofields were not killed by the same perpetrator who murdered the four college students.'

'Can you explain the similarities in the crimes, the use of stakes and similar cord?'

'A crude attempt to mimic.' He looks straight at the jury with this, the polished performance of one who is no novice on the stand. 'What you would commonly call a copy-cat.'

'And your conclusions as stated here,' I say, 'these are based on your review of the evidence, your considered professional opinion as an expert in personality profiling?'

'Absolutely,' he says.

I look at my shadow jury, wondering whether I have made my case, whether I have driven a factual wedge between these crimes. Based on theory and conjecture, the food of academic opinion, there is nothing more I can give them. All that would remain, the only recourse if this fails, is to dredge up the killer of Abbott and Karen Scofield, and to lay bare his motive before them.

Chapter Twenty-Two

'Good to see you again, and congratulations,' he says. Don Esterhauss is chairman of the Davenport County Board of Supervisors.

His words of cheer are for the indictments returned yesterday against Andre Iganovich, four counts of first degree murder with special circumstances, the killings of the college students. This is front page news around the state this morning. Iganovich is now bound over for trial in the superior court.

Esterhauss is all smiles as we shake hands over fluted linen napkins at Sibble's, a block from the Capitol on the other side of the river. He has asked for this meeting, a social gathering according to Emil Johnson who set it up, so that Esterhauss and a few others can get to know me a little better.

As I scan the players here, I begin to suspect that I've been ambushed, that there is something bigger on their agenda.

Emil is already seated on the other side, land-locked behind the large round table of the built-in booth.

He's munching on a bread stick loaded with enough butter to fill a farmer's churn. His napkin, tucked in at the top of his shirt, fans out over the meandering foothills of his sunken chest and expanding gut, which is pressed against the table. Emil is fighting a one-man war against anorexia, and he is winning hands down.

'Counselor.' He nods but does not offer his hand or try to get up.

There's a woman sliding out from behind the booth to join Esterhauss. She looks vaguely familiar, all smiles and pearl-white teeth.

'Have you met Davenport's mayor?' Esterhauss is doing the honors. 'Janice Shaw, Paul Madriani.'

She is the familiar face. To date, I've not met her. My dealings have all been with the county, but I have seen her at functions, the last time at Feretti's funeral.

Blonde, in her early thirties, not unattractive, she has the features and build of a pixy gone solemn, little freckles around a turned-up nose. Her hair is clipped at the shoulders, curled at the ends and flipped under. Today she is wearing a power suit, blue pin stripes with enough padding in the shoulders to stop a bullet.

She is all smiles, felicitations on the results from the grand jury.

'I've heard so much about you,' she says. 'The county's fortunate to have your services. A major coup for the board.'

Esterhauss shines.

Her idea of good fortune, it seems, is my subsidizing the county budget, holding at bay Nikki, who may lynch me if she does not leave me.

Seated at the other end of the curve is George Cayhill, the assistant dean for Student Affairs from the university. Cayhill and I met at the victims' meeting weeks earlier. He extends a hand, a cordial welcome, then he returns to his menu like a man who knows business is about to be done here.

The timing of this meeting seems a bit fortuitous. I had tried to beg off, to postpone it for a few days. But Emil was insistent. I suspect it has something to do with the fact that tomorrow I am planning to make a clean breast of it, finally going public with information on the Scofield case, official confirmation that we are in fact looking for another killer. Since the first revelation in the papers it has been no secret. The papers are black with headlines, the tube ablaze with speculation. There is little sense in attempting to stonewall it longer. I have told Claude to schedule an early morning press conference for the announcement. And I suspect he has told Emil.

Shaw possesses the charm of a good politician. She is talking in my ear, a flowing river of sincerity, broader than the Mississippi – and about a deep as Sarah's wading pool. For the moment she's grasping my hand like a coveted prize, smiling, with a gaze that has locked on me like some radar-guided weapons system.

'Please sit down,' she says. She slides back behind the table and motions me to follow. I am now trapped around the curve of the table, caught between Shaw and Esterhauss.

'A drink?' she says. The waiter sensing commotion, an opportunity for new commerce, has made his way to our table. They already have cocktails lined up in front of them. I've been invited to this party a half-hour late, maybe so the other guests could get their signals straight.

'A glass of white wine,' I say. The waiter starts to hand me the wine list. 'Your house label,' I tell him.

'And fill this.' Emil hands the guy the empty linen-draped basket. Bread crumbs, a neat little column, like the bodies at Gettysburg, litter the table all the way to Emil's place setting. If he keeps this up, we will need the jaws-of-life to extract him from behind the table when we're done.

'Things seem to be moving very quickly,' says Esterhauss. He's talking about the indictments. 'The board is very pleased.'

'Glad to hear it,' I tell him. 'Now if we can only satisfy a jury.'

'Indeed,' he says. Esterhauss is toying with his drink, something in a short tumbler. He is a tall, lean man, in his mid-forties. Long wisps of hair, brown-turning-gray, are carefully combed to cover the thinning retreat on his crown, something that is growing like the polar hole in the ozone, and, from all appearances, dreaded nearly as much by its owner.

Esterhauss operates the local hardware store. He is well spoken, and proper in his demeanor; a product of the university. A graduate with a degree in history he lowered his expectations after school, the price of living in a quixotic college community with its limited horizons for those beyond academia. Like many of the aging hippies-turned-merchants, in places like Berkeley, he is now commercially dug-in for the duration, selling shovels and rakes in Davenport. But he has made the most of it, living the vicarious life of the statesman through local politics.

'How long before the actual trial starts?' he asks me.

'It's always hard to say,' I tell him. 'The art of any good defense is the stall.'

'I hope he can't delay too long.'

'I wish you were the judge hearing his motions,' I say. He laughs.

'You know the defense attorney, this man Chambers?' he asks.

'I do.'

'Is he good?'

I nod. 'He's aggressive. Unpredictable. Knows his way around a courtroom.'

'Once it gets started, I suppose what — a few weeks?' It is a dozen questions. This guy should do depositions. Esterhauss is trying to find out how long the actual trial will take. Pretty soon he'll have his abacus out on the table, sliding little beads, calculating the cost to the county.

'Adrian Chambers knows all the organ stops of delay,' I tell him. 'It is a tune he plays without much effort.' I tell him that it's not possible for me to make a reasonable guess on the length of the trial until we are closer, until I know how many witnesses he is likely to call, the various theories of defense.

I could make him gag on lunch, tell him the truth, that it is likely that we will all be off enjoying the fruits of an ill-gotten retirement before this thing is cleanly in the can, before all of the criminal appeals are exhausted.

'They say he may be incompetent to stand trial,' says Cayhill.

'They'll try to ride that horse,' I tell him. 'The first move Chambers is likely to try will be to have his man sent to a state mental hospital for a long stretch of treatment or, failing that, psychiatric evaluation.'

I hear a heavy sigh from Esterhauss, like he sees this

thing dragging out, somewhere over the horizon, more little beads on the deficit-side of the county's ledger.

'Come on, fellas, give the man a break. Let him look at his menu, order some lunch.' Shaw is playing the maternal guardian. In what is quickly shaping up as a routine of 'good cop-bad cop', I get the clear impression she is not destined to be the one who will hit me with the sand-loaded sap. I'm still trying to figure who at this table is her equal, to play the heavy.

We order. I search for the Australian lobster – market price. As I am the guest, this will put a little stress on their government per diem. It is part of my cost for what I sense is shaping up as an in-house mugging.

We sip our drinks and munch on. We are halfway between the salad and the entrée.

'How long do you think it will be before the rest of the indictments are brought?' says Esterhauss.

I look over at him, a question mark.

'Before they indict this fellow on the Scofield murders?' he says. He's talking about Andre Iganovich.

I am jarred. I study them for a moment, Cayhill and Shaw. They are pictures of innocence. But I think it is all a little too pat.

I look at Emil. He's busy ladling soup over the void as if he hasn't heard this.

I am supposed to think that he has not told them we have no intention of charging the Russian with the Scofield killings. I begin to smile. They are playing this little farce for shock value, making me out as the heavy, the carrier of bad tidings, so that when they hear the facts, faced with their fury I will back-pedal, consider the options, which I am sure they have by now well honed.

'You haven't been following the papers,' I tell him. 'There are problems with the evidence, major inconsistencies. I'm surprised you missed this.'

'We saw the stories,' says Esterhauss, 'but I didn't give it much credence.'

'So, I guess this is gonna slow you down a little,' says Cayhill, 'before you can indict him on the later crimes?'

'No,' I say. 'It's gonna stop me.'

He looks at me, big round eyes. 'What do you mean?'

'I mean I'm not going to indict Andre Iganovich for the murders of Abbott and Karen Scofield.'

'My God, why not?' he says. His tone conveys volumes, the point being that if only I could massage this evidence a little, all the rough edges would drop off. Surely there must be some way I can make the facts fit the case.

'Why?' says Shaw.

'A simple reason,' I tell her. 'He didn't commit the crimes.'

There follows the clink of silverware laid on china, in unison, like the sound of a well-trained chain gang breaking rock. Suddenly, eight eyes are on me, boring in.

'You're not serious?' Cayhill shakes his head. There's a lot of scoffing going on around the table, like a choir chiming in for the chorus, looks of disbelief on their faces. Even Emil has been drafted for this part.

'I'll tell you,' he says, 'I don't agree with this. It's not the conclusion of my office,' he says, 'my people. They see a definite link. It's the state. I never thought it was a good idea to get too close to that place.'

That place he is talking about is the state crime lab, and

Kay Sellig. It is an easy cop out to blame her.

'Mr Madriani.' It is left to Janice Shaw to be the voice of reason.

'Paul,' she says. 'Do you mind if I call you Paul?'

'It's my name,' I say.

She smiles broad and benign.

'Paul. You'll have to excuse us, but this comes as a bit of a surprise,' she says. 'You've knocked the wind out of us. The newspapers . . . One can only expect irresponsible speculation from the newspapers. But we in government, we must be more diligent, more responsible. How can you be so sure that this man didn't kill Professor Scofield and his wife?'

'*Former* wife,' I say.

'Whatever,' she says, brushing this aside like it is just one more nettlesome little detail.

'It would be improper for me to discuss the substance of the evidence,' I tell them.

I give Emil a look. He shies away, breaking more bread, anything to busy himself.

'You will have to trust me on this,' I say. 'Forensic experts are confident on this point. Iganovich did not kill the Scofields.'

Shaw looks down the table, a troubled expression. This is not going entirely as she'd expected.

She tries again. 'You have to understand that we have a *big* problem here.' All the emphasis on the 'b'.

'Since these murders started we've been a community living on the edge,' she says. 'The citizens in my city have armed themselves to the teeth. They're afraid to go to bed, afraid to walk on the streets at night, afraid of their own shadows. A month ago I came home from a late-night meeting and my own husband nearly shot me in our living room.'

Lost opportunities, I think.

I can imagine that this has put a dent in life in their little town. A clerk of the court once described Davenport as 'Camelot on bicycles'.

Shaw keeps picking at it. 'When this man was captured, well, we figured it was all over. Sure, there'd be a trial, some headlines, but the worst was behind us.

'If you take to the airwaves tomorrow,' she says, 'tell the public there's another killer still out there, still stalking them, well.' She nods with emphasis like the point is made. 'We're going to have major problems, a fatal lack of confidence in public safety.'

'Lack of confidence, hell,' says Cayhill, 'we'll have a god damned panic.'

Shaw and Cayhill have broken from the script, shredded their little charade, the revelation that they know about the news conference, the substance of my intended announcement. It is the problem with deceptions, they require eternal maintenance.

'Well, obviously Emil has told you about the planned news conference,' I say.

'I heard about it elsewhere,' says Shaw, a half-assed attempt to cover for him.

'No matter,' I say. 'It was not intended to be a secret. You are the elected leaders of your community. You should know.'

I get a look from Emil, like 'damned right'.

'I'm not interested in causing hysteria. But to continue

to pretend that the focus of our investigation for the Scofield murders is on Iganovich is to play with lightning,' I tell them.

'How so?' says Cayhill, 'What's wrong with it? Is the defendant going to object?'

'Let's ignore the trifling matter of justice for the moment and discuss only the practical,' I say.

Smiles from Shaw and Cayhill. They like this.

'Aren't we taking some chances if we sit on this, ignore the evidence of a second killer?'

'What do you mean?' says Cayhill.

'What if this phantom, this second killer, what if he or she, or they murder again? What then?' Suddenly there's a perplexed look on Emil's face. He has not considered this possibility.

'Who among you,' I say, 'wants to tell the family of the victims, that we had every good reason to suspect the existence of another killer, but that we conspired to suppress this information, in the interests of public calm?'

Silence around the table. I pause several seconds waiting for volunteers. No takers.

'Let me ask you a question,' says Shaw. 'Do you have another suspect in the Scofield murders?'

'No. Not yet.'

She looks at Emil to see if maybe he has somebody in mind. Johnson shakes his head.

'Then I agree with George,' she says. 'We should not go public, not yet. What do you think, Don?' She looks at Esterhauss.

They're beginning to sound like this is a council meeting,

as if with a quorum and a quick second, the item will be history.

Esterhauss has a troubled look, like a politician in deep squish. He can't make up his mind.

'We can't weather any more trouble, Don.' She looks at him, intense, stern, trying to assemble a quick backbone and jam it up his ass.

'Well?' she says. Shaw is a combination of Little Nell and Lady Macbeth.

'I guess so,' says Esterhauss.

'Agreed,' she says. 'There will be no press conference.'

'Excuse me,' I say. 'But I don't recall asking for permission.'

I get an imperious look from Shaw.

'Let me make this as simple as I can for you.' She has suddenly turned to the darker side.

'So that there is no misunderstanding,' she says. 'We are empowered by our various bodies, the city council in my case, the board of supervisors in Don's, to instruct you not to discuss publicly the existence of another killer.'

'You've taken this up in public session?' I say.

'Of course not,' she says. 'We treated it as a matter of litigation in closed emergency session yesterday afternoon.'

'Then you violated the Open Meetings Act,' I say.

She looks at me and swallows.

'That exception, allowing closed meetings for items of litigation, applies only when the city or the county is a party to a law suit. It is not available for you to go behind closed doors to discuss the appropriate strategy in a murder trial, even if that were your role in the order of things, which it is not.'

I can see ire mixed with a lot of fear in her eyes, the realization that she has just owned up to a breach of the criminal statutes.

'Apart from any misdemeanor violations of the law,' I say, 'the last time I looked, the litigation of a capital case was not something for a committee of the city council or the board of supervisors. The tactics of trial, the charges to be brought, are matters for a public prosecutor,' I say. 'They are not points for political debate.'

Shaw gives me a stiff look, sorry that she's been so cordial.

'You were appointed by the board, sir,' she says. 'I would expect that you can be just as easily removed.'

'Nothing would please me more,' I tell her, 'than to withdraw, to leave you with this case, but unless you know something about the presiding judge of your court that I do not, that isn't going to happen.'

She still doesn't get it.

'What's he talking about?'

'We didn't make the formal appointment,' says Esterhauss. 'That's the way the local papers reported it. Technically, the appointment of Mr Madriani was made by Judge Ingel.'

'Certainly, if we made a recommendation to the court, he'd have to listen,' she says.

Clearly the lady has never met Derek Ingel.

'Remove me,' I say, 'and the Attorney General will be called in to replace me.'

This draws a sober look from Shaw and Cayhill.

'Of course, you could make your pitch to him,' I say. 'But the court's not going to remove a publicly appointed

prosecutor because you have some political problems.'
This last comment chills the conversation, just as our
meals arrive.

I pick gingerly through the pricey pink shell of my
lobster, as Janice Shaw sits next to me, choking down the
white breast of chicken Marsala, like maybe it is crow with
the feathers still on it.

Chapter Twenty-Three

The blast from our news conference earlier in the week, confirmation of a copy-cat in the Scofield cases, has now spent itself. It is no longer hocked as the lead on the evening news. It has moved to the inside pages of the morning paper, unless and until we have another similar murder.

Yesterday I took a hit, from, of all places, Jess Amara, Jeanette Scofield's brother. Under the guise of putting a face on it, like maybe he wants to patch things up, he told me maybe we got off on the wrong foot, apologized for his harsh words and manner at his sister's house that afternoon. Then in his own breathless style he hit me with the real reason for the call, his pitch, and questions as to why Iganovich is not being charged with his brother-in-law's murder.

'It's tough on my sister. My only interest in the case,' he assured me. 'While this thing remains unsolved, she is constantly forced to deal with it. I know you understand,' he said, more compassion in his voice than I can honestly credit him. 'The sooner she can close this chapter of her life and move on the better.'

I told him that if he or the City PD knew of any facts linking Iganovich to the Scofield murders, I would appreciate the information. This brought silence and an

abrupt end to our conversation, like who gives a shit about
the evidence? Even the grieving widow, it seems, wants the
Russian nailed, the case closed.

Beyond this I am still eating the full fury of the county's
politicians, none of whom will now talk to me. Claude tells
me that this includes Emil, though Johnson still does his
duty for me like a yeoman.

This morning we are gathered in the small law library in
Davenport, with the door closed, a sign hanging from the
doorknob on the outside, 'DO NOT DISTURB',
something no doubt copped by one of the office staff from
a motel on a county-paid trip.

The table is piled high with bound transcripts of grand
jury testimony, declarations of witnesses, a few treatises
and some code books.

Kay Sellig has dragged two sizable cardboard boxes to
this meeting. Sporting 'Marlboro' logos on the side, there
is an assortment of paper bags sticking up out of the open
tops of these cartons. The bags are crammed with items of
physical evidence, microscopic blow-ups, the cut ends of
plastic cord magnified seventy times, the tent stakes, some
of these still showing traces of dried blood on bright steel.
There is the bloodied rag, in hues of congealed brown,
stored in a clear plastic bag, looking as it did the day it was
discovered in Iganovich's van.

Sellig is now the custodian of these items, and a score of
others. She is responsible for the chain of custody
regarding all physical evidence in our case. Along with her
other duties as chief forensic expert, she will testify at trial
as to how each of these was found and tagged, the
procedure for storage to ensure production at trial.

Claude and Lenore Goya round out our group. It is the first of what will be many strategy sessions in the months ahead, leading up to trial.

'What do we hear?' I ask Goya.

'Unusually quiet on the defense front,' she says. 'But my sources tell me Chambers is busy at it.'

Lenore has had her ear to the ground over in Capital City. I have asked Harry Hinds to give her a little help. Though it is against his religion to assist any prosecutor, he made an exception after seeing Lenore. I think Harry is in love.

'What can we expect from Mr Chambers?' I ask her.

Before his suspension from the practice of law, Adrian Chambers had earned the title among the local bar as the 'dean of delay'. According to Goya he has not lost his touch.

'It's shaping up as a battle on two fronts,' she says. 'The first looks like a full-blown psych-eval. He probably figures that's good for at least a year,' she tells us.

Psychological evaluation is a standard procedure in high profile violent criminal cases.

According to Lenore, Chambers has been holding forth with anyone of the mental therapy persuasion who will talk to him, mostly psychiatrists and psychologists, people with sufficient credentials to qualify as persuasive experts with a judge.

'He's shopping opinions,' she says. 'Last week he even tried Forrest Hunter.'

Claude laughs. 'He must be desperate.'

'That's how we found out what he was doing,' she says. Forrest Hunter is the psychiatrist of choice among district attorneys north of the Tehachapies. I have never known him to testify for a criminal defendant. He is a prosecution witness of the first order, capable under oath of telling a jury of firemen that Nero was sane.

'What do you think,' says Claude, 'an insanity plea?'

She shakes her head. 'Word is, he's hoping for a long stretch of evaluation, maybe some treatment on the theory that Iganovich is incompetent to stand trial, unable to assist in his own defense. If he can make out a case to the judge, the competency hearing alone could last longer than most trials.'

Goya is right. It is not much of a reach to imagine Chambers selling this theory to the trial judge, who to date has not yet been named.

Under the due process clause, it is a cardinal rule that one who is not mentally competent at the time of trial cannot be convicted or punished for his crime. This does not go to the issue of the defendant's sanity at the time of the crimes, but rather whether he is mentally present for the trial.

'You think he could make out a case?' says Claude.

'Expert opinions on the state of the human mind are for rent,' I tell him.

'We might be able to blunt the argument,' says Lenore.

I look at her.

'We could stipulate to a short-term period of evaluation in an institution, a state hospital,' she says.

This would avoid a protracted hearing on competence. Chambers wouldn't like it, but a judge faced with the alternatives is likely to accept this lesser of two evils.

'We cut him off at the knees,' she says. 'Ninety days for

evaluation instead of a year for hearing and, if he wins, treatment.'

I agree that this could work to avoid considerable delay. We make notes to start assembling our own psychiatric experts. Chambers has knocked Hunter out of the box by talking to him, made him unavailable to us for reasons of conflict, the upside of tipping his hand. This was probably part of his plan.

Sellig says that the DA's Association has a long list of expert psychiatric witnesses, people whose opinions are generally safe, and available to the state.

'You say he's dragging his feet with two arguments. What's the other?' I ask.

'Change of venue,' says Goya.

This we have anticipated from the start. Based on the adverse pretrial publicity, it is a safe bet that Chambers will try to have the trial moved from Davenport to some other county in the state where his client conceivably can receive a more fair trial.

Ordinarily this would be a dead-bang winner. Except that in this case publicity has been so pervasive that there is not a county in the state that has not been deluged in the news of these crimes, bathed daily by a sobering emersion in the graphic details of these murders.

We have sampled public opinion in the seven counties of comparable demographics and size to Davenport, the most likely candidates for a change of venue.

According to Lenore, in four of these, if we send the defendant for trial, we can ship the cyanide at the same time. These are places where voters eyed Ronald Reagan suspiciously for his permissive views, and where gun control is defined as a steady hand.

It is the paradox of the Putah Creek crimes, that Iganovich chose to kill in an otherwise rural county which ordinarily would harbor similar provincial attitudes of hang-tree justice, except that in Davenport there is the leavening effect of a major university.

'In the other three counties,' says Goya, 'it's a pull.' She means that there is no real difference in the views of the electorate in those counties. From the raw data, Chambers could not expect to get an appreciably better result if the case were tried in any of these, rather than Davenport.

'He may still try,' I say, 'if for no other reason than to stall. We should firm up our data, put it in a form ready to present to the court when he makes his move.'

Goya agrees. She makes a quick note.

We turn our attention to Sellig and her cardboard boxes.

I'm looking at one of the enlarged photos of the cut cross-sections of cord as they make their rounds through our group. They are a little fuzzy, black-and-whites without much contrast. I tell Kay this.

'We could go for some higher resolution, color,' says Sellig, 'but I would have to send the evidence to a commercial lab for processing.'

Goya and I discuss it. She says she thinks it will be critical that the jurors see for themselves the extrusion pattern on the inside of the cord. For this, clear enlargements that we can prop on an easel will be vital. It is the concensus that we shoot for higher quality, processed photos from a commercial lab.

Kay takes us on a quick tour of the evidence. A strong case she believes, but still one built on circumstance.

'The key is the van,' she says. 'All of the incriminating evidence that we have was found in a vehicle registered to the defendant. That is the soft underbelly of our case,' she says. 'Remove these items from possession by the defendant, and our case evaporates.'

'Then that's where Chambers will go,' I say.

'He will come up with some artful explanations,' says Claude.

The most obvious of these is the broken window. Chambers will no doubt argue that the incriminating evidence was tossed into the vehicle by whoever broke the glass, after the van was abandoned by Iganovich. I point this out.

'Do we know the window was broken in the garage?' says Goya. 'Maybe it was broken someplace else, earlier.'

Sellig shakes her head. 'We found minute traces of glass fragments on the concrete beneath the side door of the van. Reconstruction indicates it was broken in the garage. Most of the glass was on the inside of the vehicle. So it was broken from outside.'

'Were there traces of glass under the cord and stakes?' says Claude.

The point here is whether the spray of safety glass from the broken window was all on top of the coiled cord and stakes, or underneath them. If glass was found only on top of the objects it would mean that they were in the vehicle already, when the glass was broken. Iganovich could not wiggle out.

'We looked,' she says. 'It's inconclusive. The items were too far from the window to get a sufficient spraying of glass particles to know.'

295

Claude makes a face like it was a good thought anyway.

'There's another possibility,' says Goya. 'Maybe Iganovich broke the window himself to provide a later explanation for the cord and stakes inside.'

This doesn't wash with Sellig. 'Easier just to get rid of the stuff,' she says. 'If he was thinking about it, would he have dumped it?' She shakes her head. 'No. I think he just didn't see the stuff as incriminating.'

'Even the bloody rag?' says Lenore.

'Probably an oversight,' says Sellig. 'He may have been in a hurry when he dumped the van.'

Claude tells us that the broken window offers more complications.

'Our investigators,' he says, 'have identified two other vehicles in the same garage during the same period with insurance claims filed by the owners for broken windows.'

'Vandals?' I say.

He nods like this is a likely explanation. 'Probably kids,' he says.

'Anything missing from the other vehicles?' I ask him.

He shrugs his shoulders. 'I don't know.'

'Check it out,' I tell him.

'Why?'

'If there's personal property missing from the other cars, it means it wasn't pure vandalism. Whoever broke the windows was looking for valuables inside. When they got to the van, if they did the van, they would have looked inside.'

He looks at me and suddenly it registers. 'Maybe they saw the cord and the stakes.'

I give him a smile. It's the longest of shots, finding

juveniles who smash the windows of cars for whatever they can find inside. Still cases have turned on more perilous leads.

It is my turn to report. At noon today I had lunch with Ravi Sahdalgi, the Pakistani graduate student from our grand jury. Over salads at a restaurant not far from the university, I picked his brain on the quality of our evidence, and in particular whether Chambers, if given the chance, could confuse a good jury with the evidence in the Scofield murders.

'His testimony was good.' This is how Sahdalgi characterized the evidence presented by Harold Thornton, our psychologist and expert on the theory of criminal profiles. But Sahdalgi said the jury did not totally buy into his theories.

I wonder what he would say if I'd dumped the medical evidence from the autopsy on them? I am confident that had they received the information that the Scofields were killed elsewhere with a knife rather than the stakes, they would see distinctions galore between these cases.

Gesturing with his hands, as if to assure me that it was nothing that I had done in the presentation of the case, Sahdalgi told me that the similar circumstances of the murders was too much for most of the jurors to overlook. 'It is too easy to purchase rope, the clothes line cord, and the stakes. The fact that different ones were used was not particularly persuasive,' he told me.

'And the other things; the missing eye of the Scofield woman, the supposition that the killer knew her.' He made a face like this did not wash with the jury, too much of a psychic reach. In all, Sahdalgi let me down easy, but the message was clear. Had I brought charges against Iganovich for the Scofield murders, the discrepancies in those cases would not have troubled the grand jury greatly. They would have returned indictments in those cases as well.

It causes me to wonder if maybe I've made a mistake in failing to charge the Russian with the Scofield killings. It is, after all, possible even in light of the medical evidence, that the Russian is responsible for the Scofields. These victims were older, perhaps more wary than the others. Maybe it was necessary for Iganovich to use a knife first, and to follow the ritual of the stakes after they were dead?

Goya gives me a perplexed look. 'I thought Thornton's testimony was solid,' she says.

It's the problem with trying to predict the whims of a jury, nine guesses in ten will be wrong.

'Maybe we should charge him,' says Claude, 'with the Scofields.' Emil would love it. Claude doesn't say this, but the message is clear.

I look at Sellig. She would like to wade in, to argue the opposite view. But lately I sense that on this call she is prepared to defer to the local authorities. She is the penultimate professional; having given us her best rendition of the evidence, the decision now rests with me.

I weigh it only for a moment, Claude looking at me all the while. He is politic enough to enjoy the thought of carrying a pleasant message to a superior.

'We still have a problem,' I say. 'We can't be sure that Iganovich was available for the Scofield murders.'

Lenore nods. 'We don't know if he was still here — or up in Canada when they were killed. If we charge him and

Chambers produces hard evidence of an alibi, it could taint the charges on the other four. Play to his theory of defense,' she says.

We all sit, mulling this in silence for a moment.

'It makes the witness up in the trees that much bigger.' Claude finally breaks the reverie.

'Any leads?' I'm asking Claude about this shadowy figure in the trees.

He makes a face. Shakes his head. 'We're still looking. Ran a trace on the spotting scope,' he says. 'Six thousand of that model sold nationwide last year. We checked the serial number with the manufacturer. Nothing. Whoever bought it never registered for warranty protection.'

Another dead end.

I'm back to Goya. 'How long do you think we have before trial?'

'At a minimum,' she says, 'six months.'

I relax a little.

'Chambers can delay any trial at least that long, nine if he really tries,' she says. Enough time for us to chase down the open ends of our investigation, perhaps to find the man in the trees, the figure who is now shaping up as a prime witness.

Stress tortures the human mind in a thousand untold ways. For me during periods of anxiety, sleep becomes difficult. In recent years, in the throes of a trial or some other exacting event, I have turned increasingly to over-the-counter medications as a refuge from insomnia. Under the arresting spell of these elixirs, nothing, not the pounding hoofbeats of the horsemen and their apocalypse, can rouse me.

Tonight, the incessant ringing in my ears brings me to a state of semi-conscious stupor. Then I realize that this sound is the phone. I feel weight on my body. Nikki has reached across me and taken the receiver from the phone on my bedside stand. In my dream-like state I hear silence as she listens, then her voice.

'Who is this? Who are you?'

Then a return to quiet, the peace of silence. I slip back again, into the abyss, the sleep of the innocent.

I feel the sharp point of bone in my back. The light is on. I fight the grip of the medication. Focus my eyes with some effort at the clock in the radio next to me on the stand. It is three-forty in the morning.

'Who the hell is calling at this hour?' I find speech difficult, a little slurred.

I roll over, try to shake the cobwebs. Nikki is still holding the receiver, but it is away from her ear. She is kneeling up on the mattress, the blankets and sheets pushed to the foot of the bed. I can hear the hum of an unbroken dial tone from the receiver in her hand. Whoever it was has hung up.

'Who was it?' I say.

'They didn't leave a name. It was for you,' she says, 'but they wouldn't wait.'

'Yeah.' I'm rolling over, yawning, covering my mouth with the back of one hand, like let's talk about it in the morning.

Nikki's bolt upright staring at me, like I should be more curious.

'What did they want?'

'They left a message.'

'Yes?' I'm fighting to keep my eyes open.

'The man on the phone says that if you know what's good for your family, your wife and your daughter,' she says, 'you'll charge the Russian with the Scofield murders.'

'Damn it.' I say this under my breath. It has started. The crank phone calls, the crackpots, who seem always to follow the high profile cases. From time to time, in my practice, we have had to change our home number, unlisted as it is, twice in the same month. So relentless are some in this army of the unhinged.

'Oh, come over here,' I smile, reach out to put my arm around Nikki's shoulder, to give her a hug, an attempt to comfort, to lull her back to sleep.

She pulls away from me, fear in her eyes.

'He told me that Sarah — he used her *name* — he told me that Sarah was real pretty.' She's talking about the voice on the phone again.

'He said she was lucky we could afford the private tuition — at the Westchester School,' she says. Nikki is looking at me, her gaze a mixture of pain and contempt, an expression, in my wife, reserved only for acts of betrayal.

'They know where Sarah goes to school.' She looks at me, an expression so cold it would fracture tempered steel.

'You did this to us,' she says. 'To help a friend who was apparently more important than your own family.'

Chapter Twenty-Four

This morning I'm picking little bits of lost sleep from the corner of my eye, yawning. After Nikki's fear turned to fury last night, because of our mystery phone caller, I never got back to the sheets, but spent the night on the lumpy couch in the living room. It was my only refuge. Nikki would not leave it alone. Three times with me on the verge of sleep, she got into it again, until I finally left the bed.

For the moment I have other problems. Claude is in my office giving me the latest on Jeanette Scofield.

'Maybe she felt it was her obligation to moves his things out of the office,' I say. 'Maybe the school needed the space.'

'Sure,' he says, 'two days after the funeral? With hubby still warm?' Claude's face is a cynic's mask. 'The lady must have a driven house-cleaning ethic,' he says. Claude's nailed me this morning in my office, early, on his way to work. And he is not happy.

Dusalt has been rummaging around the university looking for anything that might hone into a lead on the witness in the trees. In his travels he has discovered that Jeanette Scofield cleared some documents and books out of Abbott Scofield's campus office the day before police searched the place. He was not told this during his several

303

questionings of the widow. And, like a good cop, he is now suspicious.

He tells me that according to people who work in the building, Jeanette and Jess Amara carted boxes of books and papers out of the office and loaded them into two cars in the parking lot. 'One of them was a city police unit,' he says.

He is convinced that this is something more than just compulsive neatness.

'Have you talked to her?' I ask. 'Maybe she still has the stuff.'

'You bet. I beat a path to her door when I found out,' he says. 'She has a shit-load of text books on birds, all musty, and stacked in her garage in boxes. She told me I could take anything I wanted.'

I make a face, as if to say 'see, no foul'.

'But all the papers,' he says, 'Scofield's files, his memos and letters, they all got trashed.' He looks at me from under arched eyebrows. 'Courtesy of an incinerator, in the basement of city hall.' He motions toward my office window in the direction of the large brick building across the square.

Neat and orderly as they are, it seems brother Jess doesn't mind polluting the air. Any hints as to identity of the prime witness that Abbott Scofield might have committed to written memoranda, hunches he might have had, are now wafting on the winds.

'Did she have an explanation?'

'Overflowing with them,' he says. 'More stories than Dickens. She says she didn't think the papers were important. She says she had no place to store them. She

304

says it hurt too much to go through them, so her brother took care of them all. Touching and sensitive guy that he is.' Claude's expression is one of calculated disbelief.

'Are there any back-up files?' I'm thinking specifically about computers. Maybe the documents were done on a word processor. If so, back-up disks of the material might exist.

He shakes his head. 'The steno pool used by Scofield, in the department,' he says. 'Just our luck. It used old Selectrics.' These are IBM typewriters, one step up from stone tablets.

'If the faculty wanted copies, they had to order them made themselves,' he says, 'at the central copy center, where I'm told the machines didn't work half the time.' It seems the funds for new equipment in the department somehow found their way into rosewood paneling for the chancellor's office and the silver service he and his wife use for entertaining.

'I'm told any copies Scofield might have made would have been stored in his office files. The ones that were burned. Circle-jerk city,' he says. This is how Claude describes the merry chase he's been on at the University.

Then he smiles at me.

'But the bastards missed one,' he says. He pulls a folded piece of paper from his pocket, little slips stapled to one corner, and hands this to me.

It's a printed form with spaces and blanks, an application for travel expenses and per diem from the university. This one is made out in the name of Abbott Scofield but unsigned, and seeks $526.56 in expenses.

'Where did you get this?'

'It was in the steno pool for typing when Mrs Clean and the Tidy Bowl Man came in to do their deed,' he says. 'Seems Scofield took a recent trip.'

I look at the point of destination on the form: San Diego. The form is dated eight days before his death, for travel that took place a week before that. There is no purpose for this sojourn. That line on the form is blank.

I look at the stapled slips. One of them is a computer-generated receipt from a hotel, two nights lodging at two-hundred-and-twenty-five dollars a night, assorted beverages and movies. It seems not all the department's money went for polished rosewood and silver spoons.

Attached are what look like several restaurant receipts for meals, and a ticket stub, torn in half, from the San Diego Wild Animal Park.

'So, the man took a trip?' I say.

'Yeah. To a nice place,' he says. 'But he didn't go alone.'

He points with one finger to an entry on the hotel receipt. 'Double occupancy', it says.

'The good professor checked in with somebody else. They stayed in the same room,' he tells me.

'Maybe he went down with another faculty member, and they shared expenses? Not unheard of.'

'Maybe,' he says. 'But if so his friend wore a skirt.'

I look at him.

Another entry on the receipt, lost in the little dots of computer driven print: 'Rental — Woman's swmst.'

'I called the hotel,' he says. 'They rent swimsuits for the hot tub, for guests who forgot to pack 'em. Robes are gratis,' he says.

Claude winks at me. I can see where he is going. The thought that maybe a tryst on the side could be a motive for murder.

'What are you thinking?' I say.

'That maybe it was a two-fer.'

I give him a look like a question mark.

'A single hit for two targets,' he says, 'Karen and Abbott. Maybe they were getting it on again — and somebody wasn't happy about it.'

The law in this state requires a separate arraignment in superior court after indictments are handed down. Lenore and I are here in court this afternoon for this purpose, and to set a date for trial. Security in the courthouse is tighter than usual, additional armed officers downstairs at the entrance by the metal detector.

With only four judges, Emmet Fisher does triple duty in the superior court of this county. Besides the occasional trial, Fisher handles the master calendar where he sets trial dates, and juggles law and motion, the lawyer's battleground for the early scotching of evidence.

This afternoon Fisher is perched up high on the bench. He is tufted out in bulging black robes; his heavy eyebrows, like vagrant tumbleweeds, are trapped behind glasses with rims black as tire tubes. He has the appearance of some oversized predatory animal, not all that wise.

'What do you think about ninety days?' says Lenore.

'Sixty would be better, but three months will do,' I tell her.

We are talking about the expected pitch for psychological evaluation that Chambers is likely to make today, the big stall, to back the case down the calendar. Lenore will try to cut this off by offering up a set period for evaluation, rather than fighting over it. We are hoping that this may avoid a court order that could be open-ended as to time.

Fisher finishes with the two lawyers ahead of us on the calendar.

'Next case,' says Fisher.

The clerk swings around in her chair and hands him up a file.

Fisher reads: '*People v. Andre Iganovich*, case number 453287.'

There's some jostling in the front row as reporters elbow each other in the move for position. Like players under the hoop they are hustling to see who will get the best rebound on this story.

Goya and I take up our seats at the counsel table.

Iganovich is brought in. Wearing jail togs, manacled and chained at the waist, he stands off to one side of the courtroom, in the dock by the heavy steel door that leads to the holding cells. Chambers is leaning on the other side of the railing talking through an interpreter, into his client's ear, last minute explanations to the Russian as to what will happen here.

'Gentlemen.' The judge greets us. 'And lady,' he says. Fisher looks at Lenore. In his early sixties he is of the old school, where women at the bar are still perceived as a novelty. He is not sure how much chivalry should be shown here.

He scans the file. 'Here for arraignment,' he says. He asks for a statement of representations for the record.

'Paul Madriani, acting district attorney of Davenport County, and Lenore Goya of that office appearing for the people,' I say.

'Adrian Chambers representing the defendant, Andre Iganovich.'

Through an interpreter, the court has Iganovich identify himself for the record.

Fisher does not waste time here. He cuts to the substance of the charges, four counts of first-degree murder with special circumstances. He does a formal reading, which drones on for several minutes, mostly reading from bench books, filling in the blanks with the names of the victims, the dates of deaths, a recitation of the special circumstances that carry the death penalty.

He finishes, gives the Russian a grave look from high on the bench, an expression that transcends the language barrier.

'Mr Iganovich. Do you understand the charges?'

A brief interpretation.

'Da.'

'Yes.'

'Then, to the charge of first-degree murder in the death of Sharon Collins on the twenty-fourth of June of this year, how do you plead?'

Iganovich says something, unintelligible, to his interpreter. A brief conversation, a few words with Chambers.

Then: 'Not Guilty.'

They repeat this exercise three more times. Each time a plea of not guilty is entered.

'Very well,' says Fisher. 'Any early motions?'

If a pitch for psych-eval is to come, it will be now.

Lenore casts a quick glance at Chambers. I can feel her edging forward, inching her way up to get into it. Trial, even in the preliminaries, is a form of combat. Those involved always itch for the opening shots to be taken, the only cure for cotton mouth and butterflies.

Chambers is in his client's ear, talking with both hands.

He comes back out, looks at the bench. 'Your honor, we would request that the protective order on pretrial publicity entered by the municipal court be continued in effect,' he says, 'in these proceedings.'

Fisher smiles, obviously pleased that someone should take this responsible act. It avoids the judge having to impose it himself, turns the heat off with the papers. Chambers is earning early brownie points.

'Any objections, Mr Madriani?'

We, of course, have none. I tell the court this.

'Very well. There being no objection I will incorporate the order of the lower court as it is written,' says Fisher. He makes a note in the file. 'Anything else?' he says. He looks to Chambers first.

Goya nudges me with her thumb on my pant leg, as if to say, here it comes — the pitch to plumb the bottomless pit of the Russian's psyche, Chambers's vision of perpetual employment for subliminal set, the couch doctors.

'Mr Chambers?'

'Your honor, we would like to defer other motions until we have a trial date.' Adrian is busy again, talking to his client. Like a master chess-player, he is busy putting all the set pieces in proper order.

'Any objection, Mr Madriani, to returning to the matter

of motions after we have a trial date?'

'None, your honor.' Lenore will have to wait a little longer.

'Then I guess we're ready for a date.'

'How many days, gentlemen? How long do you estimate for trial?' says Fisher.

'Seven days for the state's case,' I say.

'Nine for defense,' says Chambers.

If he's true to form, Adrian will be scouring the streets for alibi witnesses. A legion of winos will no doubt benefit from witness fees to augment their welfare checks in the month of this trial. Such are the tactics of Adrian Chambers. Suspension from the practice, I would venture, has taught him only that the vice is not in doing the act, but in getting caught.

'With *voir dire*, and arguments, pretrial motions, we'd better make it twenty-five days,' says Fisher. 'Betty, can you give us some dates?' Fisher directs his clerk to open the big book while he poises with his pen to make notes on a form, a minute order that will be placed in the file, copies to the parties.

Betty Hamilton, Fisher's clerk, studies the massive book like some gray-haired angel gate-keeping at heaven's door.

'Do either party wish an early pretrial conference?' says Fisher.

'It might be a good idea,' says Chambers.

Fisher looks at me. 'No objection, your honor.'

He checks the little box on the form. This will give us a chance to lay out ground rules for the trial.

'Plea is entered,' Fisher's mumbling to himself,

checking the little boxes all in order. One-hundred-and-ten-thousand a year and he spends eighty per cent of his time X-ing little boxes. Good work if you can get it. 'The defendant waives time,' he's still mumbling. Another X in the box.

'No, your honor, we don't.'

'Emm?' Chambers has pulled Fisher from his reverie over the little form.

'The defendant does not waive time,' he says.

Fisher gives Adrian a look, like somehow the judge's hearing-aid has failed him. He taps his ear once to ensure that it hasn't fallen out.

I stand daunted, stunned. It takes several seconds before I can pull myself together enough to look over at Goya. Her jaw is slack.

'I don't think I heard that,' says Fisher.

'The defendant does *not* waive time.' Chambers repeats it a third time, clipping off the letters with his lips so that Fisher can read them from across the room.

'Counsel,' he says. 'This is a capital trial. Your client is on trial for his life. You're not telling this court you're prepared to go to trial in sixty days?'

'Your honor, I'm concerned about this,' I say.

'No more than the court,' says Fisher.

'That's exactly what I'm telling you, your honor. My client has a right to a speedy trial. He is demanding the right.'

'Does your client understand what you're doing? The risk he's taking?'

'He does.'

'I might like to hear that from him,' says Fisher. He's

motioning toward Iganovich, then grumbles at the translator to do his thing.

'Mr Iganovich,' says Fisher. 'Do you understand that this is a capital trial, that you could be executed, put to death, if you are convicted?'

He waits a few moments.

'Da.' A surly look from the Russian, who has no intention of being cowed by this old man.

'Yes.'

'And do you understand that your lawyer has just declined to waive your right to a speedy trial? This means that your trial must begin within sixty days of today's date. This is not much time to prepare for a complex trial. Your case could be compromised by the shortage of time.' Fisher waits a second for the interpreter to catch up, looking for signs of affect on the Russian's face. Nothing.

'You could find yourself at a severe disadvantage if proper preparation is not made for this trial. Do you understand this?'

Iganovich listens to the interpreter finish, then shrugs and makes a face, a wrinkled prune of disinterest.

'Da.' A few more words, unintelligible to the interpreter.

'Yes. I understand. What difference?' says the interpreter.

'The difference,' says the judge, 'could be the difference between life and death.'

Words by the interpreter. Another prune, and no verbal response.

'Does he understand that?'

A quick interpretation.

'He does.'

Angry resignation by the judge. 'Very well,' he says. 'Betty, what can we do in sixty days?' he says.

Pained expressions back up at the bench from the clerk. She's motioning, like it's impossible. I hear a little colloquy off the record between Betty and Fisher.

'Judge Ingel is scheduled for vacation. You're in trial, two cases.' More muffled words between the two, little bits and pieces. One of the other judges is assigned out of county on another matter. Judge Kerney is scheduled for surgery that cannot be postponed.

Fisher is perplexed, angry that he's been put in this position. He looks at Chambers as much as to say, 'fine, you want it, you got it.'

'Judge Ingel will just have to take the trial,' he says. 'He can reschedule his trip to Maui.'

I stand there in a blind stupor. Derek Ingel, the humorless fucking Prussian, his disposition soured by a trashed trip to more pleasant climes, is now to try this case. Nearly as bad as if I'd just been tossed back across the river to try the case in the venue of the Coconut in Capital City. I would prefer a ten-day junket to hell.

Chapter Twenty-Five

If one's actions can be said to speak, Adrian Chambers is the lord of liars, the master of misdirection.

His trip to see Forrest Hunter, the paragon of state shrinks, is now taking on the smell of a well-baited trap. The only ones psyched were us. He has led us down the daisy path of delay, setting all the decoys in motion, while he was whittling away on a mass of paper, a lawyer's blizzard of motions, and edging toward an early trial date.

'Son-of-a-bitch,' Lenore is swearing under her breath, in my office this morning, pawing through the pile of written motions, more pages than the *Internal Revenue Code*. There are motions to quash the indictment, a renewed motion for bail, motions to suppress evidence, and a motion for discovery, more extensive than the *Articles of Confederation*.

Chambers has now jammed us, pushed us into the most notable prosecution in this county's history, on short notice.

Not to be outdone, Derek Ingel has turned the screws down even harder. It seems he has no intention of rescheduling his vacation. Ingel sent us all little missives yesterday by fax. We now face trial in little more than three weeks. The trial will take no more than thirty days, says Ingel, complete with verdict, or we will deal with his wrath.

Apparently Ingel is not troubled by his earlier conversations with Acosta, the fact that the Coconut has leaned on him for a little extra justice in these cases.

'A certifiable asshole,' says Goya.

I wonder whether Lenore's talking about Chambers or Ingel. For the moment I can probably take my pick.

She's reading one of the discovery motions dumped on us by Adrian at the end of our court session with Fisher.

'He wants us to deliver the entire investigative file on the Scofield murders,' says Lenore. 'In his dreams. It's irrelevant. We'll quash it.' The fighting words of a pissed-off lawyer. Having killed it in her fantasies, she slaps the page down on the corner of my desk. Goya is both tired and angry. She is missing sleep from three nights running, prepping for an argument on psych-eval that never came.

She's into the next motion, reads for several seconds, agitated hissing under her breath.

'Pendajo,' she says. In the Catholic mission school of my early childhood, little Mexican children often used this word as a pejorative for others. I do not know its literal translation, but I know it is not good.

'His father's a *putah* in drag,' she says. Lenore's not talking about our case, but Adrian's ancestry. In moments of fatigue and stress, it seems her dark Latin temper takes hold. An edge of adolescent hardness slips from beneath the educated veneer. She looks at me to see if I have noticed.

I tell her to relax. 'Not the first time a lawyer's been had. It won't be the last.' She blames herself I think for being taken in by Chambers's sleight of hand with the shrinks.

I smile at her, a little encouragement. 'Face it. It was a smooth move.' I'm talking about Adrian's feigned strategy of delay that suckered us so well.

She fixes me with a piercing stare, olive eyes.

'About as smooth as a barbed-wire enema,' she says. Lenore is not magnanimous in defeat. Having made her the fool, I think Chambers has now joined Roland on her short-list, people with matching dolls, into whom I suspect she may be sticking pins at night.

'I should have seen it coming,' I tell her. I try to lighten her spirits by taking much of the blame myself. She shrugs this off and goes on reading the motions.

When Chambers jammed us on time for the preliminary hearing, I thought he was just testing our evidence, our ability to obtain a quick indictment. Since all that hung in the balance then was the perfecting of formal charges, there was little risk to his move, not much down-side. I did not see it, his play to shorten time, as some grand strategy.

Lenore tells me that she believes the defendant, Iganovich, will pay the price, that it was not a smart move to shoot for an early trial date, especially now that they have bought Ingel as the trial judge.

I'm not so sure she's right, but I don't say this. In measuring a case, I am told that Adrian is a quick read, like a cipher. A mind that is a vacuum for facts, he sifted these and made an early decision; that time was not on his side. In part this is dictated by the evidence of our case. It is all physical and circumstantial in nature, cut pieces of cord, metal stakes, and the location where they were found, a vehicle owned by the defendant. These you can touch, tangibles that will not die, or fade over time, like a witness or his memory.

The passage of time is only likely to make things worse

for them. It may bring the production of a witness, the vandal who smashed the window of the van, who may have seen the contents in the vehicle, who can testify that they were not placed there by some intervening third party.

Delay may find the Russian linked to the other murders in Oregon or down south.

With time may come the wallets and purses of the Davenport victims, their elusive documents of identification, and a trail that could lead back to Iganovich.

Then there is the riddle of the Scofield murders, a similar scenario with a different perpetrator, a difficulty for our case. In time this too may be solved. This crime, for which I suspect Adrian can produce a credible alibi for his client, if still unresolved at the time of trial, can be exploited, used to move shadows of doubt across the stage in his unfolding drama of defense.

In all this there is one certainty: Adrian Chambers is no fool. He has perceived, correctly, that in the trial of this cause, time is not his friend.

Pretrial motions are the first skirmish lines thrown out by lawyers in preparation for the full-blown battle of open trial. They are important because they set the groundwork for the conflict that follows. Lose a motion and you may find yourself stripped of vital evidence, doing combat hobbled on one leg, or missing an arm.

Today, Lenore and I are meeting in camera, behind closed doors, with Judge Fisher, out of the presence of glaring lights, and the press, and more important without the attendance of Adrian Chambers. Only the court clerk is here to take down our words.

This is what is known in the law as an ex-parte conference — Latin for 'single party' — a one-sided conversation with the judge, generally forbidden except in specific cases.

Fisher has agreed to hear all the pretrial motions in our case, a concession to Ingel.

'What's the problem here?' he says. 'This could be exculpatory evidence.'

Fisher's talking about the witness in the trees at the Scofield killings, our prime witness. Adrian has thrown a net over this information by the breadth of his discovery motion.

We are here without him today, courtesy of a crack in the law, an initiative passed by voters and generally considered the bane of the defense bar. It allows us to talk privately with the judge on the narrow issues of police informants and witnesses.

'It may be exculpatory, your honor, but we don't know. We have no idea as to the identity of this witness, or, for that matter, whether he or she, whoever they were, really saw anything.'

'It's part of an on-going investigation,' says Lenore. 'We shouldn't be compelled to disclose the information.'

We are double-teaming Fisher today, a last-ditch effort to keep Chambers away from this stuff, so that he cannot use it to confuse a jury.

'So, let me get this straight,' says Fisher. 'You're not arguing that the evidence this witness might offer is irrelevant?'

Lenore bites her lip. She's not ready to concede the point.

319

'We don't know whether it's relevant or not,' I say. 'We have no idea what they saw, or whether they saw anything.'

Fisher swivels in his big black tufted chair, head resting back, taking in the track lights on the ceiling while he thinks.

I don't give him too long.

'A defendant's not entitled to know the identity of an anonymous informant not known to the police,' I tell him. '*People v. Callen.*' I cite him the case.

'But this is not an anonymous informant,' he says. 'It's not just the identity of the witness that's in question, but whether the witness has any information relative to your case.'

'That's true,' I say.

'So you're asking me to mask from the defendant the very existence of this potential witness?'

'We are, your honor.'

He's shaking his head. 'No,' he says. 'That goes too far.'

I argue with him, tell him there are real risks here.

'There are circumstances surrounding the location of the witness — what he was doing at the scene — that will not only imperil the investigation,' I say, 'but perhaps put the life of this witness in jeopardy.'

Fisher looks at me.

'How could it endanger the witness?' he says.

'We have no idea who the killer or killers are,' I tell him. 'They therefore know considerably more than we do. How much they know, the motives for these murders, we have no idea.'

'And?' he says.

'By disclosing the specifics — the circumstances surrounding this potential witness in open court, what we believe was happening up in that blind — with these details the killer may be able to find our witness before we can.'

I watch as the consequences of this argument settle on Fisher. He is no longer shaking his head. Then he comes back.

'But the defendant here.' He's talking about Iganovich. 'He has a right to any evidence that could be viewed as exculpatory, anything that might be useful in proving his innocence. The law demands that he be given this. How can I withhold it?' he says.

'Iganovich is not charged with the Scofield murders,' says Lenore. 'So where is the relevance?' she says. Lenore cannot resist.

'Give me a break, counselor.' Fisher fixes her with a stare. 'It's not a quantum leap to argue that this other killer, whoever murdered the Scofields, is the Putah Creek killer; that the police have the wrong man in Mr Iganovich.' He flexes an eyebrow. 'If that's your pitch to the jury, a witness who may have seen this other killer becomes rather pivotal to your case, don't you think?' he says.

It is the thing I like best about Lenore. She does not cow easily.

She looks him in the eye. 'No, I don't,' she says. 'Until Mr Chambers can prove that the witness saw something,' she says, 'that he actually has evidence relevant even to those killings, until then,' she tells him, 'the identity of the party or parties in the tree, and all of the circumstances surrounding them, are irrelevant.'

This stops Fisher in his tracks. He makes a face like maybe she's right, a hook on which to hang some qualified order.

'Still, how can he prove the relevance of what this witness may or may not have seen, if you have a monopoly on all of the information?'

I sense that we have hit a high point in our argument, as much of a concession as we are going to get from Fisher. It is time to play Solomon, if necessary to offer up the division of the infant.

'We are searching for the witness. Every resource we have is on this case. I would propose a compromise,' I say. 'A qualified order, limiting what we are compelled to turn over to the defense on this one issue. Allow us to mask the information on the witness, the blind in the trees, until we have identified and sequestered this person, taken him into custody, and discovered what it is he has to say.'

Fisher makes a face, like close, but no cigar.

'We have to make some disclosure to the defense,' he says.

'Fine, we tell them there is a potential witness, but no details, none of the circumstances surrounding the witness, nothing that might be used to ferret out his identity.'

Fisher is silent, sitting, musing in his chair. Then slowly he nods, like maybe this is not a perfect solution, just the best we may be able to do for now. For the moment I think we have dodged a bullet.

Chapter Twenty-Six

I have spent the better part of a week on the phone, eating so much crow that I now spit feathers when I talk. These calls were placed to Herb Jacoby, the Crown Counsel in Canada. I have pleaded with him for cooperation, his help in producing one of the two security guards who arrested Iganovich.

Jacoby is not exactly the soul of benevolence these days, still nursing his anger over the abduction of the Russian. I have been applying apologies like a shaman's balm to his sovereign pride, assuring him repeatedly that my office, our government, had nothing to do with this escapade, that it was a private self-help venture of Kim Park.

In the scheme of things, Iganovich's statements regarding the abandoned van at the time of his arrest in Canada could be important to my case. I want this evidence available for trial. Chambers has thrown a net over it in one of his myriad motions to suppress.

This morning, Judge Fisher looks down at the defense table and Adrian Chambers.

'A lot of paper,' he says. He's talking about the small mountain of defense motions. 'I hope they're all necessary.'

'Every one of them, your honor.' This from Adrian.

'Emm.' Fisher is not convinced.

'Are we ready to proceed?' he says.

Nodding heads from both tables.

'Fine,' says Fisher. 'Let's get to it.'

Chambers's motions contain more redundancies than the fail-safe systems on the space shuttle, a lawyer's grab-bag of back-up arguments: there was no probable cause for the arrest; his client was not Mirandized, or given the Canadian equivalent, before he opened his mouth; the statements were coerced in violation of due process.

While a warrant for murder was issued for the Russian's arrest, he was originally detained in Canada on charges of shop-lifting. For this reason, the fact that the warrant did not match the charges of arrest, it is deemed to be a warrantless arrest. This means I have the burden of going forward, presenting my case first.

I outline the issues for the court. We will now argue on turf that I have created. I call my first witness.

Reginald Beckworth is the picture of a proper British constable, even though he is only private security. Precisely trimmed mustache and dark sideburns, a tweed wool suit and vest, he is better dressed than most lawyers and half of the judges in this courthouse. Eight years in corporate security, he is part of mid-management with the Hudson Bay Company, heading security for one of their larger stores.

The witness identifies Iganovich as the man he and his partner stopped on suspicions the day of the arrest.

'He made a good number of furtive gestures with his hands to the inside linings of his clothing,' says Beckworth.

'So you thought he might be concealing merchandise?'

'Objection, leading.' Chambers is on his feet.

'Let me rephrase,' I say. 'What did you conclude by these moves on the part of the defendant?'

'That he might be concealing merchandise,' says Beckworth.

'Thank you. Now tell me, during the time of these observations, who employed you? Who was paying your salary?'

'The Hudson Bay Company.'

'Have you ever been in the employ of any official police agency?'

'Twelve years with the Vancouver Police Department, but I retired,' he says, 'eight years ago.'

I want to get this out early, his prior police employment, so that it is not later exploited by Chambers. I open the issue like a book to the court so that it does not appear that we have anything to hide.

'So, at the time of this detention, when you stopped Mr Iganovich, you were solely in the employ of the Hudson Bay Company?'

'Correct.'

'I take it that this was true of your partner as well, that he was employed exclusively by the Hudson Bay Company?'

'That's correct. The company has its own in-house security, with its own training program.'

My object in this line of questioning is straightforward. To overcome Chambers's contention that these guards were acting as agents of the state, I must place them clearly in the private sphere, beyond the pale of any state action.

'At the time you stopped Mr Iganovich did you know

that there was a warrant for his arrest issued in this country?'

'No, I did not.'

'Did you have any reason to believe that he had committed any crime other than the suspected shop theft for which you sought to detain him?'

'No.'

'So, in your mind, when you stopped Mr Iganovich, this was a routine case of suspected shop theft and nothing more?'

'That's right.'

'So prior to turning the defendant over to the police following his assault on your partner and yourself, there was no police involvement whatever in his original detention and apprehension?'

'None.'

I have slammed this door shut, as tight as I can on this issue.

'Would you tell the court what happened when you first approached Mr Iganovich on the day in question?'

He gives a considered sigh. 'I thought he'd like to have killed us both,' says Beckworth.

'We had watched him for some time, both on a surveillance camera in the store as well as from close observation from two angles down on the main floor. It was his manner of dress that initially brought him to our attention,' he says.

'Shoddy?' I ask.

'Yes. It was that,' he says.

Looking at the dapper Beckworth I can believe that this might have caught his attention.

'But more than that,' he says. 'He was wearing a long overcoat, blousey, loose clothing underneath. The kind of thing we watch for.'

'So, there's a profile,' I say, 'for shoplifters?'

'Oh yes.' He says this with the conviction of a convert. 'Long coats for men. Large full skirts and oversized panty hose for women. Baggy warm-up suits have become the unisex favorite in the last few years. People will hide the stuff in places you wouldn't believe,' he says.

'I can imagine.' Visions of cavity searches for Walkman stereos flash before my eyes. The proctologist's worst nightmare.

'It's a much larger problem that most people imagine,' he says, talking about shoplifters.

'Your suspect was milling about a table of expensive silk scarves,' says Beckworth. 'We believed that he had palmed one of these.'

I stop him right there.

'What made you conclude that he had palmed the scarf?'

'One minute we saw it on the table, in his hand, and the next minute it seemed to disappear, into the inner folds of the suspect's clothing.'

'You saw this?'

'I did.'

'Thank you. Go on.'

'We approached the suspect. My partner barely had time to identify himself as store security, and we were into it with him, the three of us were on the floor, wrestling.'

'What did Mr Iganovich do?' I say.

'For starters, he kicked my partner. Tried for the crotch,

but missed. Took out his knee,' he says. 'The man is still off on disability,' he tells us. 'Before I could get there,' Beckworth explains that he was an aisle away, 'the suspect hit my partner with an electronic device you call a stun gun, twice on the arm. Completely incapacitated him.

'With the help of two patrons, we finally subdued him. He scratched my face, tore another fellow's jacket,' he says. 'Finally I managed to get a hold on him from behind, got the stun gun up behind his back where I could remove it from his hand.'

I show Beckworth a copy of his investigative report, the part that chronicles Iganovich's statements about the abandoned van. He identifies this entry as being written by himself.

'Was it during this time, while you were wrestling him to the ground, that Mr Iganovich made the statements referred to in your report?'

'Moments after,' he says, 'when we had him down on the floor. He seemed panicked, preoccupied by other things—'

'Objection. Move to strike.' Chambers is on his feet. 'That's pure speculation on the part of the witness,' he says, 'that the defendant was panicked or preoccupied.'

'Common experience?' I tell the court. It is one of the exceptions to opinion testimony offered by a non-expert.

Fisher looks at me like nice try.

These are subjective feelings, not physical manifestations of demeanor and I know it.

'Next you'll have the witness climbing into the defendant's head to tell us what he was thinking,' says Fisher.

I would if I could. Thoughts kept to myself.

'The objection is sustained, at least until Mr Beckworth shows me his ouija board.'

'What about the motion to strike?' asks Chambers.

The judge looks at him, like don't be greedy.

'Fine,' he says, looks at the court reporter. 'Strike it.'

A point for the other side. I move on.

'So when the defendant was on the floor being restrained, this was when he made the statements about his van?'

'That's correct.'

'In your capacity as a private security officer under the Canadian system, do you normally caution a suspect that anything he says may be taken down and used against him?'

'Not usually. We leave that for the police if it becomes necessary to involve them.'

'In this case did you make such an admonition to the defendant?'

'No.'

'Why not?'

'Well, as I said, it wasn't standard procedure. And in this case, even if we'd wanted to admonish him, there was no opportunity,' he says. 'The statements were made without any warning, during a physical altercation. We weren't questioning the man. We were trying to restrain him.'

'Would you call the defendant's statements as set forth in your report purely voluntary?'

'Objection.' Chambers is out of his seat again. 'The defendant had at least three men on his back, one of whom was twisting his arm off. The prosecution has a funny sense of what is voluntary.'

Fisher looks at him, a little puzzlement. 'Mr Chambers, are there grounds for your objection in there some place? Maybe I missed them,' he says.

'Leading question,' he says.

'Thank you. Overruled.'

One for two, Chambers sits down.

Beckworth sits there looking at me, not sure whether there is a question before him.

More than one case has been lost on appeal because a lawyer on pretrial motions lost track of his questions, became mired in objections, and forgot to return for a vital answer.

I ask the court reporter to read back my last question.

She fingers through the fan-folded little sheets from the stenograph machine, finds her place and reads:

'Mr Madriani,' she says. 'Would you call the defendant's statements as set forth in your report purely voluntary?'

I look at the witness.

'Absolutely,' says Beckworth. One more piece cobbled into place.

'Then from your testimony is it safe to characterize the statements, the admissions made by the defendant about his van at the time of his detention, as unsolicited and spontaneous?'

'Yes,' he says. 'That's a good description.'

I walk toward our counsel table. Goya is sitting there, checking off points on a yellow legal pad. We will confer before I release the witness to make sure that I haven't missed anything.

'Now, immediately after your altercation with the defendant, did you have any reason to believe that he was wanted for any crime other than the suspected shop theft?'

'No.'

'Even with such a violent reaction, you still had no reason to suspect that Mr Iganovich might have committed a more serious crime?'

'Not at all,' he says. 'Shop thefts all react differently,' he tells us. 'Some are retiring. They will simply stand there and empty their pockets. Carry on the most cordial conversation as they confess their crime. Women often cry, and some men. Then again, a few will pull a gun or a knife, and try to kill you. It's very much like a traffic stop,' he tells us, 'you're dealing with the unknown.'

'Have you ever been assaulted before while detaining a suspected shoplifter?'

'Several times,' he says, 'though this was clearly the most violent. If he'd been armed with deadly force, we would clearly have been in big trouble,' he adds. This last is gratuitous.

'Objection,' says Chambers. He's on his feet. 'The witness is speculating again.'

'Sustained,' says Fisher.

'Mr Beckworth, please just answer the questions.'

'Yes, your lordship.'

Fisher looks at him. He's been called a lot of things in his time, but never this.

After coming all this way Beckworth seems determined to stick a pike in the defendant. Half of the cops in this city, given the injuries meted out by Iganovich in this brawl, would sit in the witness box seething, overflowing with venom. This witness at least puts a polished face on it.

'You said earlier that your employer has its own training program for security personnel?'

'That's correct.'

'Did you take this training?'

'I did.'

'Did they teach you there how to deal with violent situations?'

'Usually to avoid them, wherever possible. It isn't worth the risk of injury to ourselves or a customer.'

'But in the course of your career as a police officer, and later in private security, were you taught the techniques, the holds and maneuvers that might be used in restraining a violent suspect?'

'Oh, yes.'

I move with the witness through a line of questions intended to remove the specter of some brawl on the floor, to lift this thing to a more professional level. Then I pop the clincher, the reason for this line.

'And did they teach you to use only that degree of force absolutely necessary to restrain the individual, and no more?'

This goes beyond leading. I am prepping him now and Chambers knows it. He sits up straight in his chair ready to object. But it's too late. The damage is done. He sits back, looking at me, a glare from the corner of his eye.

'Yes,' says Beckworth.

'Mr Beckworth, how would you characterize the amount of force used to restrain Mr Iganovich on the day in question?'

'Just the minimum,' he says. 'Only what was absolutely necessary to disarm him, to take him into custody,' he says.

Wonder of wonders.

Having drawn the desired legal conclusion, I take the witness on a tour of the less refined and lower martial arts. In three minutes Beckworth has verbally choreographed all of his moves that day, the holds used on Iganovich, in minute detail. It may bear little resemblance to fact, a symphony of recollections that sounds more like *Swan Lake* than the 'Thrilla in Manilla'. But it serves to lock a clean version of the events in the witness's psyche, a version the state can live with, one not likely to be tumbled and shaken too much on cross.

It is why, in a motion to suppress evidence, it is not always bad to shoulder the burden of going forward.

I confer with Lenore back at the table. Everything is crossed off her long list. I hand the witness over to Chambers.

He gets up from the table, maintains a polite distance, but stares directly at the witness before asking any questions. Then he speaks.

'Mr Beckworth. Did you have a chance to go over your testimony with Mr Madriani before appearing in court here today?'

'I did.'

'When was that?'

'Once yesterday. And earlier today before arriving in court.'

'Did you rehearse your answers with him?'

'I wouldn't call it a rehearsal,' says Beckworth.

'Well, did he tell you which questions were significant and which were not?'

'If you're asking me whether he coached me, told me what to say, the answer is no, he did not.'

Chambers smiles. Beckworth is a seasoned witness. Some who are not might have slipped and fallen badly here.

'Let's go back to the very beginning,' says Chambers. 'The first time you ever laid eyes on my client, Mr Iganovich. What was he doing?'

'He was walking in the aisles of our store, looking at various clothing items.'

'And you saw him picking these up and stuffing them into his pockets?'

'No.'

'Oh. Well then, you must have seen him grabbing handfuls of clothing and sticking them inside his coat, or down his trousers?'

'No.'

'Your honor, do we really need the sarcasm? Mr Chambers is aware that actual observation of theft is not necessary for probable cause to detain in a case of shoplifting. A good faith belief is all that is required.'

Actually I have no idea whether Chambers knows the law of shop-theft or probable cause. But I can now be certain that my witness does.

Chambers shoots me a look, like class is now out. Coaching the witness on my own time, on direct examination, is bad enough. He will not tolerate it here on cross. He complains to Fisher, more whining on court than John McEnroe.

Fisher's heard enough of this lawyers' cat fight. 'Get on with it,' he says. 'And, Mr Madriani, keep your comments to formal objections.'

'Thank you, your honor,' Chambers smiles at him. Then gives me a toothy grin like some four-year-old who's just peed in my sandbox.

'Mr Beckworth, exactly what was Mr Iganovich doing when you first saw him?'

'As I said he was walking between the aisles picking up some of the merchandise, looking at it, moving on.'

'That's all?'

'And making furtive gestures,' he says.

Chambers spins on him in front of the witness box.

'Ah, "and making furtive gestures". And what *were* these furtive gestures? Can you describe them?' he says.

'Moves to the inside of his coat with his hands, buttoning and unbuttoning his coat. That sort of thing,' says Beckworth. 'Idle movement with the hands. We are trained to watch for this.'

'Ah, I see. Furtive gestures,' says Chambers. He's nodding his head, slow, solemn motions.

'So, if I were in your store right now, and I buttoned my coat, that would be a furtive gesture?' he says.

'Could be.'

'And you would feel justified in approaching me, detaining me and searching me to see if I'd taken any merchandise?'

Beckworth rolls his eyes.

'No,' he says, 'I would not. It's a combination of things.'

'Ah, a combination,' says Chambers, finger to the nose,

335

like now we're finally getting somewhere.

'This combination, this is sort of like a formula?' says Chambers. 'Things you look for in detecting shop-theft?'

'If you like.'

Oh, he likes, putting words in the mouth of the witness.

'Excellent,' says Chambers, his voice filled with mock enthusiasm, like he's just found the Rosetta Stone.

'Then one part of this formula is the so-called furtive gesture?' says Chambers.

'It can be, yes.'

'Well, either it is or it isn't?'

'It depends on the circumstances,' says Beckworth.

A look from Chambers, like a hurt child.

'I thought we had a formula,' he says. 'Now you tell me it depends on the circumstances. How do we know whether the formula fits a suspect or not if it's always changing?' he says.

'I didn't say it's always changing.'

'Oh. Good,' says Chambers. 'For a minute there you had me worried.' This is Chambers's special talent, the thinly veiled derision of a witness, a kind of microwaved mockery that can fry sound judgment in the most sensible of witnesses, bring on a wave of anger and in time the witless responses that breed trouble for your case.

'Let's get the rest of this formula,' he says. 'You said earlier that the defendant was wearing a baggy coat. Is that part of the formula?'

Beckworth is beginning to regret that he's allowed Chambers to coin this term.

'It can be,' he says. 'Depends on the circumstances.'

'Oh, come on. Can't we have a formula that works?' says Chambers.

Beckworth does not answer this, but gives Chambers the look it deserves.

The lawyer moves on.

'Well, let me ask you. Did it look like Mr Iganovich was examining merchandise when you saw him?'

'He was. Yes.'

'So would you say that examining merchandise is also part of the formula?'

'If you say so.'

'Hey. It's not my formula. It's yours,' says Chambers. Big smile like he's just sold the Canadian a hunk-a-shit used car.

'What else?' he says.

'What do you mean?' says Beckworth.

'Well, you stopped and arrested the man. What else caused you to be suspicious? What was the rest of the formula?'

'Well,' Beckworth thinks for a moment. 'The way he examined the merchandise.'

'What was it about the way he examined the merchandise, exactly, that caused you to question him?'

'He would look at the merchandise, then he would look around, like he was looking to see if anyone was watching him.'

'Ah.' Chambers is nodding now like he's found the missing link. 'Looking sort of shifty-eyed?' he says.

'You could call it that.' Though from Beckworth's tone this would clearly not be his choice of words.

'Another part to the formula,' says Chambers.

'Shifty . . . eyes.' He says this slowly as he goes through the exercise of writing it on a piece of paper, something to be saved for posterity.

'Lemme see,' he says. 'So, we have, furtive gestures, a baggy coat, examining merchandise, and shifty eyes.' Chambers nods, makes a face like he's convinced. A little more derision.

'Anything else?' he says.

'No, that was it.'

'Oh, good. So, we have the formula.' Chambers holds his notes up for Fisher to see, then he smiles.

'Now, ultimately you stopped Mr Iganovich?'

'Yes. After he attacked us,' says Beckworth.

'We'll get to that later,' says Chambers. 'Exactly who attacked whom? For now, just answer my questions.' The smile is gone from his face.

'Ultimately, you searched Mr Iganovich, isn't that true?'

'Yes.'

'Well, how much did you find?' says Chambers.

'What do you mean?'

'How many items of store merchandise did you find on Mr Iganovich after you wrestled him to the ground – you and what, three other people? – and searched him?'

'We didn't find anything.'

'Excuse me?'

'We didn't find any merchandise on the suspect.'

A big mock sigh from Chambers, shoulders shrugging, hands out, palms up.

'What do you mean you didn't find anything? He did the furtive-gestures thing, didn't he?'

'Yes.'

'And a baggy coat. He was wearing the baggy coat?'

'Yes.'

'And shifty eyes. You said he had shifty eyes?'

Nothing from Beckworth.

'Well, did he or didn't he?'

'Yes.'

'That's your formula, isn't it?' Conveniently Chambers ignores the other item, that the Russian was fingering the scarf when Beckworth saw it disappear.

'Not *my* formula,' says Beckworth.

'I thought we had something here,' says Chambers. 'This formula,' he says. 'Are you telling me that after all this, after sweaten' blood, getting writer's cramp – look at my notes,' he says. He turns the paper toward the witness, a lot of unintelligible scribbling. 'Now you're telling me that this thing doesn't work after all – that your formula's worthless?'

'I never said it was a formula,' says Beckworth.

'Sure you did. Would you like me to have the court reporter read it back to you?'

'No.'

Chambers moves away from the witness, stands with one hand on his hip.

'And after all that, you didn't find anything on my client.'

'We found a silk scarf on the floor,' says Beckworth, 'near where we scuffled.'

'Ah. And the police charged Mr Iganovich with stealing this scarf?'

'No. They didn't.'

Mock shock from Chambers. 'No? Why not?'

'Insufficient evidence,' says Beckworth.

'In other words the scarf could have fallen off the table of merchandise while you and the others were beating on Mr Iganovich?'

'Objection.'

'Sustained. Mr Chambers.'

'Sorry, your honor. Slip of the tongue.'

A deep sigh from the witness. It will be a long day. Before it is over, Reginald Beckworth will be wondering where Adrian Chambers left his rubber hose and flood light.

Chapter Twenty-Seven

'Aw, your honor.' Hands in the air, arching back, Chambers is complaining to Judge Fisher. Then he stamps around on the floor like some six-year-old, slapping the thigh of his pant-leg. He's putting on a tantrum that seems to be more amusing to Fisher than disturbing.

'This was wrong,' he says. 'There's no basis, no basis at all.' Chambers is huffing and puffing below the bench, showing more aggravation than anger, playing on Fisher's sense of fairness, like some sacred trust has been violated. He's just been told about my earlier meeting with the judge, behind closed doors, my session to mask the evidence on the prime witness in the Scofield cases. Existence of a witness has not yet been mentioned. We can expect the eruption of Vesuvius with that.

'This is ex-parte communication,' he says. Something generally considered a high taboo in the law. 'Unethical as hell,' Chambers calls it.

To this, Fisher takes exception, a little personal privilege to shield his integrity. He cites the code section that permits this process for limited purposes.

'You're being notified now,' says Fisher. 'Everything was on the record,' he says. 'The transcript of our in-camera session is available for review, on appeal.'

'Good,' says Adrian. 'Then I would like a copy as soon as possible.'

'It will remain sealed until the appropriate time.'

'Not good enough,' says Chambers,

'It'll have to be,' says the judge. 'You don't like it, take an appeal.' Adrian knows this will not get him a glimpse of the transcript. Only the court on appeal would see it, to ensure that Fisher has not abused his discretion in going behind closed doors.

The judge is in no mood to tarry with Chambers. Two thirds of the motions filed by the defense bordered on the frivolous. In Fisher's view, he has now wasted four days hearing these.

Today has not been a winner for Adrian. After taking them under submission, the bulk of his motions have been denied by the court. The Russian's statements to the security guards as they wrestled on the floor of the department store have been ruled admissible for trial.

Chambers has also failed to exclude the stun gun, which pathologists may now link to the burn wounds on two of the victims, the first two college kids.

In all, Adrian is not happy. It is the lot of the defense lawyer confronted with mounting adverse evidence. I know the sinking feeling that he must be experiencing now, in the pit of his stomach. Having lost on these motions, for Chambers and Iganovich the start of trial will feel like the second half of a football game, with the home team down 21 – zip.

Fisher launches into a reading of the minute order from our closed session. Chambers is to get all our investigative and lab reports, everything we have on the Scofield murders with a single exception, he says.

'All information pertaining to any witness or witnesses to those crimes shall be withheld from discovery, treated as confidential and not disclosed to the public until such time as any and all witnesses are in police custody. At that time fair disclosure shall be made to the defense concerning any and all evidence provided by such witness.' He looks up. 'Is that clear?'

Chambers stands stone silent, staring up at the bench, his jaw slack, seemingly struck by this revelation. Several seconds pass, then a single question, nearly inaudible.

'There was a witness?' he says. Puzzlement like a mask on his face.

Iganovich has just heard the translation. He's trying to talk to his lawyer. Chambers isn't paying attention. Finally sees him, holds out a hand and tells him to sit down and be quiet. Chambers's frustration is now matched by his client's.

Fisher says that the court will not comment further on the matter, and admonishes the parties to exercise similar restraint. We are given copies of the order by the clerk. Chambers looks at his, reads it again carefully. He takes several seconds mentally to regroup, recover, like a prize-fighter staggered by a punch.

'Your honor,' he says. 'May we approach? A sidebar?'

Fisher waves us on.

Chambers, Goya and I huddle at the bench. Adrian's doing all the talking.

'This is the first I've heard, your honor, about a witness. Clearly the state must have known about this for some time?'

343

He gets nothing but stone faces from the rest of us huddled there. He can see he's getting nowhere like this.

'Well, of course, it's a major coup,' he says. 'Congratulations,' he tells me. He takes another tack like maybe with this witness we are now finally on the track of the true Putah Creek killer. This is all very cordial, though Adrian's face has the pallor of a sick man. Clearly we have caught him flat-footed on this.

Still, there is no question, he sees this as an opportunity for his case. The classic SODDI defense (Some Other Dude Did It) is always more persuasive with a jury when you can put a face to the deed. This is part of the reason why I have delayed in turning over information on the prime witness as long as I have.

When Chambers finds out what this witness knows, he will no doubt move as quickly as possible to construct it neatly into his case. He will sand off the rough edges of discrepancy regarding this witness, his testimony, and the Russian's version of defense. Knowing Adrian, he will apply a little lawyer's license, indulge the facts until the two stories slide together like a well-oiled drawer. The longer I can keep him from this information, the better.

'You can understand this comes as a major surprise, this witness,' Chambers says to Fisher.

One of the chief purposes of discovery, that exercise in the exchange of information between opposing sides before trial, is the avoidance of surprise. Chambers reminds us all of this, still beaming with cordiality and smiles.

'This information, your witness, will be critical to my case,' he says.

Then he looks me square on, a broad smile, the expression of some intimate. 'Of course, I understand,' he says. 'A disclosure of this kind, the identity of the witness, it would raise hell in the press.'

Chambers thinks we know who the witness is, just not where to find him. I leave him with illusions.

'You were wise,' he tells Fisher, 'to provide a protective order.'

The judge is all smiles, delighted by Chambers's demonstration of tolerance and understanding.

'Still,' he says, 'it would be appropriate to share what the state knows. I'm an officer of the court, with an obligation to protect the interests of my client.' He reminds us that we're all under a gag order.

Fisher doesn't bite. 'You'll get all the information as soon as we have the witness,' he says.

'It is a critical witness,' says Chambers. 'Until you can find him . . .' He stops in mid sentence, calms down and looks at me. 'I am assuming,' he says, 'that the witness is a male?' He stands there, a big-eyed question mark.

I offer him the social intercourse of a chimney brick. 'Never mind, not important,' he says. His inquiry dies.

'Mr Chambers, is there a point to this?' sighs Fisher.

Chambers shields one side of his mouth with a legal pad to keep his voice from carrying. He's giving sideways squints at the fourth estate in the front row.

'I wonder, your honor, if we could at least have some estimation as to how long before there will be some disclosure concerning this witness? How close are you,' he says, 'to finding this witness?' This last is stated in high confidence to me.

345

'It's a fair question,' says Fisher. 'Any idea, Mr Madriani?'

'We're looking, your honor. It has top priority in our investigation,' I say.

'But no estimate of time?' he says.

'No. Not yet.'

'There you have it, Mr Chambers.' Fisher looks at him. 'Maybe your client would like to reconsider the time frame for trial? The court would be willing to accommodate,' he says, 'if Mr Iganovich wishes to change his mind, to waive time. In light of this information.'

Chambers makes a face, almost an idle gesture, like maybe he already knows the answer.

'Would you let me confer?' he says.

'Certainly. Take your time.' Fisher is more than willing. Anything to get Iganovich to waive time for trial, to push it back a few months, to give Ingel the tawny rose-colored hues of a tropical tan and the disposition to match.

Adrian's off to the table, hunkered down with his client and the interpreter. A lot of talking and animation from the Russian, shrugging shoulders and perplexed expressions.

In less than a minute, Chambers returns. 'Can't get him to budge,' he says. 'He's adamant. He wants a speedy trial.'

'Maybe I should try?' says Fisher.

'No. No. That would be a mistake,' says Chambers. 'Let me work on him. I think if I push a little, he'll come around.'

This is all very interesting, our little cabal, the judge, prosecutor and Iganovich's own lawyer conspiring, a love

feast of reasonable lawyers, working to a common
purpose, to get the Russian to waive time.

'If I can get him to see the importance of this witness,'
says Chambers, 'it will make a difference.'

We leave it at that, return to our respective positions at
the counsel tables.

'Your honor, for the record,' says Chambers, 'I must
record my objection, perfect it for possible appeal. You do
understand?' He's talking about the failure to disclose all
the information about our witness. It is one thing to
understand the practical wisdom surrounding a court's
ruling, another to pass on possible grounds for a later
appeal.

Fisher nods.

Adrian outlines what he believes is an erroneous ruling
by the court, the failure to turn over what could be
exculpatory evidence. A major hindrance to the
defendant's investigation of his own case, he calls it.

This is all very polite, not the Adrian Chambers of old.
Just for the record, he says, ever solicitous of the court's
sensibilities. Then he finishes.

'Objection noted,' says Fisher, 'and overruled. For the
time being my order will stand.'

The judge is collecting his papers from the bench as if
he's about to adjourn.

'Is there any other business before the court?' he says.
Fisher sits like an auctioneer, gavel raised ready to pound.

'Oh, there is one more thing,' says Chambers.

'What's that?'

Adrian is shuffling through his briefcase looking for
something.

'I was going to hold off on this,' he says, 'but in light of this news, information on a witness . . .' He finds what he's looking for, a single sheet of letter-sized paper, typewritten on one side.

'I move at this time,' he says, 'that the state be ordered by this court to amend its indictment to charge my client with the Scofield murders . . .'

There are audible voices, murmurs from the front row of 'Whaddid he say?'

Fisher stares at Adrian as if the lawyer has suddenly lost his mind.

'Or, in the alternative,' says Chambers, 'that the state be barred forever from bringing any charges in those cases against Mr Iganovich.'

'What?' says Fisher. 'You're asking this court to order the prosecutor to charge your client with two more counts of murder?'

'Let me explain,' says Adrian.

'Mr Chambers,' says Fisher, 'you have more moods than the three faces of Eve.'

'There *is* authority, your honor.'

I'm out of my chair protesting. 'Mr Chambers had ample opportunity to notice this motion, to give us an opportunity to respond,' I say. 'The People object and ask the court to rule it out of order, as not being brought in a proper manner.'

'Good point,' says Fisher.

'Your honor, I would not be bringing this motion at this time, except for the information dropped on me here today that there is a witness to the Scofield murders. Mr Madriani has held charges in the Scofield cases in abeyance, refusing to commit himself as to whether he was going to charge my client or not. He's made public pronouncements that he's searching for another killer, a so-called copy cat. Now on the eve of trial, he tells us there's a mystery witness out there some-where. A witness who, if found, will testify to god knows what.'

Adrian makes a face, like what is he to do with all of this?

'I'm left to face the specter of a piecemeal prosecution. The state is free to try the first four murders against Mr Iganovich and if they fail, if we obtain an acquittal,' his voice goes up, a single finger held in the air for effect, 'then Mr Madriani can turn around and bring separate and new indictments against my client in the Scofield cases. He can change his mind about a copy-cat, say it was all a mistake, produce his secret witness who has suddenly shown him the light, and try again.'

Fisher looks at me only for the briefest second, wondering, I think, whether such a devious plot has crossed my mind.

'We should not be required to defend on a piecemeal basis,' says Chambers. 'Make no mistake,' he says. 'I'm not anxious to have my client charged with additional counts. But it is either that or the court must tell Mr Madriani that he may not bring these charges later.'

'On what authority?' says Fisher.

'*Kellett v. Superior Court*, your honor. As I read that case,' he says, 'Mr Madriani is compelled to consolidate all of his charges in a single prosecution.'

Adrian holds up the piece of paper, a citation to the

court opinion. 'Nineteen sixty-six case,' he says, 'and still good law.'

He passes the paper up to the judge. Fisher adjusts his glasses and reads. Several seconds pass. Then he arches an eyebrow and looks at me.

'Mr Madriani, have you read this case?'

'The name doesn't ring a bell, your honor.' Goya is scrambling behind me, fighting with a volume of the annotated *Penal Code*, the only resource book she has with her, looking to see if she can find a citation to the case, a veritable long-shot.

'Maybe you should read it. I think Mr Chambers may have a valid point.' He see-saws his head a little, like maybe he's about to make a ruling, some shot from the hip.

I cut him off. 'Your honor, we should have time to consider this. To prepare a response,' I say. 'At least to Sheppardize the case, to see if it has not been overturned by a later opinion, or limited to different facts.'

Fisher nods, aggravated that he is still not finished with these motions.

'Very well,' he says. Heavy sighs. 'Forty-eight hours,' he says. 'Two days. I will expect written points and authorities from each of you in two days. No more than five pages on this single issue, the facts in Kellett. Do you understand, Mr Chambers?'

Nods from Adrian.

Fisher looks at me. I give my assent.

'Don't try to stretch it,' says Fisher. 'This issue only.'

A solemn posture from Chambers, palm up like he's taking an oath of honesty.

'This issue alone,' he says.

'We're gonna eat it,' she says. 'It's settle law.' Lenore is talking about *Kellett v. Superior Court*. 'I've pulled everything on it, every case in which Kellett is cited. Even punched it up on Lexis.'

Lexis/Nexis is the lawyer's research tool for the computer literate, cases input to the system back to the 1940s: all the law you can handle in a nano-second.

We are back in my office, just before noon. Lenore has been up most of the night poring over the cases, researching Adrian's latest shot. This one appears to have bounced into us, below the waterline.

'It has not been overruled, or limited. In fact,' she tells me, 'Kellett was cited in a case last year that, if Chambers finds, he will argue is on all fours with the facts of our own — separate charges of first-degree murder.' She hands me computer printout sheets still joined at the perforated tops and bottoms, four pages.

'Read it and weep,' she says.

This is bad news. I had hoped for some crack through which we might slip.

'There's nothing we can use?' I ask her. We are obligated to provide points and authorities to an unhappy judge tomorrow.

She makes a face, like every good lawyer can always argue something — even if it's only the direction of the grain in the wood on the table in front of him.

'Chambers over-stepped himself, just a little,' she says. What she means is that he has stretched the legal authority of Kellett to the snapping point. I am not surprised with

351

Adrian. On matters of law, he has always been famous for this.

'There's no authority,' she says, 'for the court to order us to charge Iganovich with the Scofield killings. That's purely a matter of prosecutorial discretion. On that you call the shot alone,' she tells me. 'There are some cases on point in there.' She taps the computer sheets in my hand.

'At least we can nail his feet to the floor on that,' I say.

'The down-side is the case slams the door on your fingers if you fail to charge the Russian with the Scofield murders.'

What this means is that I must either charge Iganovich for the Scofield murders, or give him a free ride for life, irrespective of any evidence we may later discover linking him to those crimes; a lifetime pass for double murder. The city fathers will love it.

While Kay Sellig and my better judgment tell me that Iganovich did not do Abbott and Karen Scofield, the Kellett case forces me to fish or cut bait.

'Did you see this?' says Lenore. She's holding a copy of the morning *Times*, the only paper so far to get the story right. They've used a law grad as a reporter to cover this trial. This morning it's paid off. After research they have come to the same legal conclusions as Goya.

The rest of the pack have gotten it all wrong. They are reporting that the court is about to order me to charge Iganovich with these crimes, but that I am resisting. They leave it to the reader to decide whether it is simple incompetence or corruption that is my motivating force.

As I turn into my driveway this evening, coming home

from work, I see Nikki at the mail-box. Dressed up, with her purse in hand, apparently she's just beaten me home from some errand or other.

Sarah's outside the front door, waiting for her mother to come and open it with her key, when she sees me.

Before I can turn off the headlights, my daughter's at my car door clutching at the handle to open it. 'Daddy, Daddy.' The unbridled enthusiasm of a little child happy to see a parent; one of the only true touchstones of life.

I pick her up and listen as she tells me about her day, where they've been. Something about a puppet show and friends. At the age of five, for children of moderate affluence, life is nearly always good, it seems. Nikki and I have talked about this, whether we are spoiling Sarah.

Nikki has made her way back up the driveway. A peck on her cheek. 'How was your day?' I say.

'OK. And yours?'

'Fine,' I tell her. I don't get into it, the mess over Adrian's latest motion, the points and authorities, my continuing travails in the press. Nikki would not be sympathetic.

Lenore believes Chambers is pursuing his grand strategy in all this. Before I left the office we discussed it, his full court press to get me to charge his client with two more murders. If we succumb, Lenore believes Adrian will drop his alibi on us at trial, solid witnesses or irrefutable documents which can place Iganovich already in Canada on the day that the Scofields died. This would raise the specter of a shoddy investigation. So far we have not managed to come up with any solid information retracing the Russian's steps on his trip north.

This leaves me with a large dilemma, whether to charge him with Scofield or not. If I do, and there is another killer, for all intents I may give him a free pass. Except for conspirators and co-defendants acting in concert, juries don't like cases in which others have previously been charged with the same crime. It makes the system look too chancy.

'Home a little early tonight,' says Nikki. I look at my watch. She's right. It's only a little after eight. Darkness is coming earlier with each day now that we are edging toward Autumn.

Nikki's picking through the mail, separating hers and mine. Along with all the household chores, Nikki has now taken to paying the bills, another job that I no longer have time for. More of the load for Nikki to shoulder. The only thing she hands me is an envelope marked 'occupant'.

'I'm not sure you qualify,' she says. Only the slightest smile. We both know there is a broad band of truth here.

She keeps for herself a letter addressed to the two of us, no return address or stamp. This apparently has been put in our mailbox by a neighbor, or some business trying to beat the government out of postage.

There's another envelope. She looks at the return address.

'Jim and Mary,' she says. Suddenly a little lightness coming into her voice.

Jim and Mary Blaycock are former neighbors who moved back east last year, a job transfer. We have been missing them greatly, one of those relationships beginning to blossom when it was cut short. They have a little girl, Sarah's age, and a son a little older. The chemistry of the children at play was something special, that cemented the two families' close kinship.

Nikki peels the envelope and reads as I open the door and turn on the lights in the entry hall.

I get the news in the letter line by line from her. The kids have started back to school, Jim has been promoted, Mary's still looking for a job.

'They've invited us to go back for Christmas. Oh, that would be great,' says Nikki. 'Snow for the holidays. Good friends.'

I can hear in my mind the unstated − Something to look forward to besides this empty existence.

She starts to package the letter up again, like so much for dreams.

'We'll look at it,' I say.

She looks at me. 'Really?'

'I can try to clear my calendar. I think we can probably do it.'

Suddenly her face is more animated than I have seen it in months. She grabs me by both shoulders, letter crinkled in one hand, and plants a deep, passionate kiss on my lips, molding her body to mine. It is the first show of real affection I can recall since my decision to help Mario Feretti.

'I said we'd look at it.' I'm trying to temper this now, prevent too many rising expectations.

'Sure,' she says. 'Sarah, how would you like to go see Tim and Susie for Christmas?'

Sarah's all smiles. 'Oh, yes.' Little 'yippees', while she jumps around the table in the dining room.

'Aren't you gonna open yours?' Nikki's looking at the

letter marked 'occupant', in my hand.

'I think I'll save it for later,' I tell her. 'Something to balance the good news. What's for dinner?'

Sarah's already eaten, she tells me.

'How about I get a couple of steaks from the freezer, nuke 'em to thaw in the microwave and I'll broil them? Baked potatoes and a salad to round it out,' she says.

'A little wine to celebrate.' She holds up the letter like our trip is now an accomplished fact. My wife can be good at manipulation.

'Fine. I'm gonna change. Be out in a minute,' I tell her.

I drop my briefcase in the den on my way down the hall and find my casual clothes hanging on the hook in the closet where I left them last weekend. Lately I have been getting home so late in the evening that changing into something comfortable is a waste of time and energy.

I'm into a light sweater and a pair of Dockers when I hear something smash on the kitchen floor, a bowl or dish. Sounds like a million pieces. No swearing or commotion after this. Nikki must be in a good mood, I think.

A minute later I'm buckling my belt as I walk down the hall toward the kitchen. Nikki is seated at the table, a single light on over her head. The rest of the kitchen is in shadows. I look at the microwave. It's off. No steaks on the countertop. The broken dish, shattered in splinters, is on the floor. It is a hand-painted soup tureen, porcelain ladle and top, a gift from her parents that she has guarded with her life for ten years.

'Awe, Jeez. I'm sorry.' I'm looking at the bowl, little pieces all over the floor.

Nikki is not. Her head is bent low, over the table, resting

in her hands, elbows propped. For a moment I thinks she's crying. But when she looks up at me, it is not tears I see, but the abject face of fear, sheer and undisguised. This is something utterly alien to my wife's expression, a look I have not seen more than twice in our marriage, the first time when we were told that Sarah might have juvenile diabetes, a blood test, the results of which had been misread.

'What is it?' I say.

She is speechless, motioning with her hands. There spread before her on the table is an envelope, a single sheet of letter paper and a glossy photo. She says nothing, unable to speak like her jaw is wired shut, but pushes these toward me. I pick up the page and read.

Before I can make out the first word, I know that I should not have touched this paper. The cops will want to dust it for prints. The words, some letters, have each been individually pasted on the page, neatly clipped from newsprint, magazines and newspapers. The prose has all the elegance of a Western Union Telegram.

You FuCKing IVan LOVER
Charge THE russian OR Else

The note itself would be almost comic if it were not for the accompanying photograph. Someone has gone to considerable trouble to produce this. It is not the garden variety snapshot developed at your neighborhood Kodak dealer. This is a large glossy, five-by-seven inch, black and white, the kind not even processed by many commercial labs any longer. It has an artsy quality about it, shot

357

against a darkening gray sky that I suspect is early morning, with a familiar backdrop.

It's the playground at the Westchester – Sarah's school. There in the foreground with two other little children I can see Sarah playing on the bars. It is hard to tell how far away she is from the camera. If the photographer has not used a telephoto-lens, I would guess no more than ten feet.

I call Sarah. She's watching television in the front room. She comes into the kitchen. I show her the picture. Nikki's still sitting at the table, looking at me, silent.

'Sarah. Do you see this picture?'

A big nod. She knows something is wrong from the tone of my voice.

I stand her up on a chair so that she can see the photo lying on the table, without anyone touching it.

'Do you remember someone taking your picture at school? Here, while you were playing on the bars?'

She looks at me with an expression reserved for those times when she has been in trouble. Large round eyes, she shakes her head resolutely, like she is not responsible for this. She sees her mother, the face of fear. Now my daughter has joined my wife in wordless silence, intimidated by my interrogation, looking at me, wondering, I think, what is happening to her sheltered world.

Chapter Twenty-Eight

'Why didn't you tell us about the phone call?' Claude is more than a little perturbed with me, my failure to inform him about the earlier telephone threat.

He tells me this in muted tones, over salad and soup at the Lettuce Patch, a luncheon spot near the courthouse, for secretaries and other watchers of weight. Dusalt is on a diet, though I'm at a loss to understand why.

'I thought it was just a crank,' I tell him. 'Nikki took the call, so I didn't hear the words myself.' This is a point of some regret with me now, my initial reaction that perhaps Nikki had made more of the phone call that night than was warranted. I make a little bluster about prosecutors and threats. 'More common than rain in April, and mostly idle,' I say.

'You think this is idle?' Claude's examining the letter and the photograph, each of which I have encased in clear zip-lock bags, and delivered to him here over lunch.

'I don't know,' I say. 'Somebody went to a lot of trouble to scare the hell out of my family. Whoever did it has my full attention. In a word, even if it's a prank, I'd like to have their ass.' I must admit that my 'dago' is up, the flare of the Italian temper.

He smiles. 'You take this very personally.'

'You bet.'

'A little advice?' He's offering.

I listen.

'You are now personally involved. You should leave this to me.'

'That's why we're talking,' I say. 'Still, I don't like people jerking my family around.'

Claude passes a single hand over the table, as if to calm troubled waters.

'You are right to take this seriously.' He reminds me that in this state, threats against law enforcement officers and prosecutors are considered crimes, prosecutable even without overt moves to carry them out.

'How does your wife feel about all this?' he asks.

Nikki is now a basket case. She will not let go of Sarah, even to have her go as far as her room. I put a face on it, tell him simply that she is 'upset'.

He nods like he understands.

'Where is she, and your daughter? You didn't leave them home alone?'

'Not today. They're with friends, a guy who works nights, a retired cop and his wife. They live across town, in Capital City,' I say.

'Good.' He says it like at least on this point I have thought clearly. 'Give me the address and phone number,' he says.

I write down the information on a napkin and Claude excuses himself from the table, leaves me sitting there chewing on greens. He is gone for five minutes and when he returns I've hardly touched lunch; a measure of how tightly strung I am after the events of last evening and a sleepless night.

'I've made a phone call, across the river. Capital City Police,' he says. 'There's an unmarked unit on its way. They'll park outside the house and keep an eye,' he says, 'until we can make more permanent arrangements.'

'What kind of arrangements?'

'I would suggest,' he says, 'that you move your family out of town until the trial is over. To another location where they cannot be traced,' he says, 'just until then. To be safe.'

Great. Something that will only serve to heighten Nikki's already intense level of paranoia.

'Is that necessary?'

He looks at me.

'I mean my daughter has school; my wife has a job.'

'Somebody will have to talk to the school, and with your wife's employer, and hope they'll understand,' says Claude.

'How do I tell my wife?'

'Talk to her; explain,' he says. He doesn't know Nikki, or understand the tenuous nature of my marriage at this moment. But what is clear is that Claude sees this episode as more serious than I, something beyond a harmless and nutty asshole with scissors and glue.

I ask him if he does this every time a deputy DA gets a threatening piece of mail. If so, he would have little time for anything else.

He makes a face. 'We take precautions. They vary with the case.' He looks at the envelope through its plastic bag.

'This sender's not shy,' he says.

'You wouldn't expect some shrinking violet to do this?'

361

I say. 'I mean take pictures of my daughter and send us thinly veiled death threats.'

'You miss my point,' he says. 'I mean, the fact that it has no stamp, that the envelope was hand-delivered to your mail box.'

'Oh.'

Claude's talking about the boldness of the act, coming nearly to our front door. I'd not considered this point of near invasion until now. It is becoming clear to me that I am rattled, no longer focusing on significant details. It's what happens when you become personally involved. Like a lawyer representing himself, you tend to lose your edge.

He holds up the letter. 'And a nice touch,' he says.

'Emm?'

'The little hint of bigotry,' he says. Claude's referring to the description of Iganovich as 'Ivan'.

He smiles at this, like he's amused. He and I have never discussed social issues and I wonder whether this appeals to some darker side in Claude. Then I realize again I have missed his meaning.

'Makes it sound like the writer has a thing for immigrants,' he says. 'Maybe. But I think it's a lot of smoke.'

'What do you mean?'

'You really think Joe-six-pack reads enough to care how many counts are in an indictment? I mean Iganovich is already charged with four capital murders. After all, how many times can you execute a man?'

Claude thinks we either have the world's most scrupulous redneck here, or whoever delivered the letter and photo is pumping sunshine up our skirts.

'Then you think maybe this isn't serious?' I say.

'Oh no. I think it's very serious.' He says this with meaning. 'I think it's possible that whoever sent this,' he's tapping the plastic bags on the table, 'perhaps has killed, twice already.' He looks directly at me, engaging eyes. 'If so,' he says, 'they would not hesitate to do so again.'

The mind of the cop, always thinking motivation, studying the act for its calculated effect. Who would have a greater stake in seeing Iganovich charged with the Scofield murders than the person who actually killed them? I am beginning to think that Claude may be right. I want Nikki and Sarah out of town today.

'My turn,' he says. Claude picks up the check and drops a tip. We wend our way through the tables, past the booths, toward the register at the front door. Halfway there, Claude slows a little, leans back into my ear and whispers.

'Wouldn't you like to be a fly on the wall?' he says. He's gesturing with a hand, subtle, keeping the movement below his waist, as we walk, motioning toward one of the corner booths off in the distance. I'm in no mood for gossip. My mind is on other things, missing sleep. But I look. There at the table is Adrian Chambers, fitted out in a three piece suit, his face illuminated under the chin by candle-light, the visage of some evil genie. Next to him, with his back to me, is a head of silver-gray, nodding in animated conversation. As I focus, this has me doing a double-take, uncertain whether my eyes have deceived. But, as I look again, first impressions are confirmed. Sitting at the table with Adrian, indulging himself in boisterous conversation, is Roland Overroy, the two men laughing in synchronous harmony, no doubt, I suspect, at my expense.

Chapter Twenty-Nine

'I'll can him,' I say. 'Fire the son-of-a-bitch on the spot.' I'm talking about Overroy. I am back in the office, after lunch, storming around my desk, unable to sit and talk coherently, so palpable is the undirected energy driving my anger.

In light of the subject matter, the calming voice comes from an unexpected quarter. Lenore Goya is telling me to cool down. To think before I act. She's in one of the client chairs that I am now dancing behind.

'After all,' she says, 'they were only having lunch.'

'If you believe that,' I say, 'I'll leave a tooth under my pillow tonight.'

She smiles, gives me a look.

'So maybe they weren't just having lunch,' she says. 'How do you prove it?'

'It answers one question,' I say.

'What's that?'

'How all those little details got into the Johnson letter, Chambers's missive to the grand jury,' I tell her. I'm talking about the tire tracks on the dirt road, near where the Scofields were found. There is only one way Chambers could have known about that. If someone with information, on the inside of our investigation, told him. On the short-list of available candidates, people in positions of trust who might kick dirt on our case, leak information to the other side, Roland now has my vote.

'You think he would do that?' she says.

Does Howdy Doody have wooden balls? I think this, but do not say it.

Still, she reminds me that this is not a private law firm where I can fire an associate on mere suspicion, though, in Overroy's case, Lenore would clearly like to make an exception.

'In civil service,' she says, 'you get a hearing, and the burden is on the employer, to produce evidence of cause to terminate. Take a shot and miss and he will sue you on a dozen different theories of discrimination.'

She is, of course, right.

'So, what am I supposed to do, look the other way?'

'Seal him off from the case,' she says, 'like a Chinese Wall, so that he cannot do us more harm.'

In a small office, where everybody talks, this would be difficult.

Lenore is of the school that believes all is possible; if you give him enough rope . . . She would live with the hope that eventually Roland will do himself in, that the brass coating his balls and between his ears will in time end his career.

I am not so patient.

Before I can say more, Lenore drops some pages on my desk, three pieces stapled at the top.

'I don't want to add to your woe,' she says, 'but it ain't good.'

I read. It's a minute order from Judge Fisher, the results of our points and authorities on the Kellett case. This does not come as any great surprise. The court has ruled that unless we charge Iganovich with the Scofield murders before the jury retires to deliberate its verdict, that prevailing law would bar us from any further prosecution of the Russian for these crimes at a later date.

'He doesn't mince words,' I say.

Lenore shakes her head. 'Chambers has put us in a box,' she says, 'with no way out.'

She is right. If we have miscalculated. If Chambers has no alibi for his client on the date of the Scofield murders and if evidence later surfaces implicating the Russian in those crimes, I will be the biggest goat this county has ever seen.

Goya's about to open discussion on this again when the phone rings on my desk. It's Sharon at reception.

'Judge Ingel, line one for you,' she says.

I punch the button on the phone.

'Your honor,' I grit my teeth.

It's a feminine voice on the other end. 'The judge will be with you in a minute.' Ingel's clerk. I love the self-important people who do this, call you and leave you hanging on the phone listening to the hyperventilation of some underling.

Lenore is making questioning eyes at me, then reads my lips as I silently form two words: the Prussian.

No sooner is this done than I hear his voice on the phone.

'Mr Madriani,' he says. 'Are you busy?' His voice is stiff. No small talk here.

'I have time to talk,' I say.

'I wonder if you might have a few minutes to meet

with me, here at the courthouse?'

'Certainly. No problem. When?'

'Now.' He says like I should have read his mind.

'Something specific?' I ask.

'We'll talk when you get here,' he says and hangs up. I suspect that most telephone conversations with this man probably end this way, with the other party feeling that perhaps they are in trouble. It is how people like Derek Ingel assert their authority.

'What did he want?'

'Beats me,' I tell her. 'Command performance in chambers, now.' I grab my coat and head for the door.

'Probably wants you to waive opening argument so he can catch an extra luau.' She's talking about the judge's scheduled vacation; the force now driving our entire trial schedule.

When I arrive, Ingel's courtroom is dark, but the door is unlocked. A single shaft of light from the clerk's station back stage bathes the bench in an eerie glow. This place appears much larger, somehow more imposing and ominous in this half light. The double flags hanging on their stanchions, sharp brass spear-tipped points on these poles, and the state seal behind the judge's chair, up high, take on an imperial quality in the shadows, something from the reign of Tiberius, images of Roman legions, something, no doubt, Ingel would spare no effort to foster.

I introduce myself to his clerk. She remembers me from my last visit and asks me to take a seat while she calls the inner sanctum. I can hear voices behind the closed door, nothing intelligible, just the hum of human discourse. Apparently, the judge has been waylaid since his call to me, some business he must first finish. The intercom buzzes inside, voices die, the clerk announces me, and then as if through a hose: 'Tell him I'll be with him in a moment.'

I have often wondered why, with the confidences that are bared in such places, their builders construct them with the acoustical integrity of a paper-walled Nippon Summer palace.

'He'll be with you in a moment,' she says. I nod, smile at the redundancy, and listen as the voices again accelerate to speed, though the volume is now turned down.

I cool my heels looking at my watch, ten minutes go by. I read a magazine, wishing I'd brought some work with me from the office. When I look at my watch again I have been here twenty-five minutes. I'm into another article when the intercom buzzes on the clerk's desk.

'Yes, sir.' She hangs up.

'Mr Madriani, you can go in now.'

I straighten my tie and open the door.

Ingel is behind his desk, imperious and stiff, looking as ever himself, like a warmed-over cadaver. I had assumed his earlier audience was concluded, that his company had left by way of the door leading to the main hallway outside. But now I see Don Esterhauss, chairman of the supervisors, seated in one of the client chairs across from the judge. I turn to shut the door.

Nothing can prepare me for the juvenile rush I feel as I swing it closed and see the other faces. Seated on the couch, behind the door, at opposite ends are Adrian

Chambers and Roland Overroy, a reprise of their role over lunch, each of them looking at me, studying my response.

I stand there frozen in place, until this becomes awkward. The judge motions me to take a seat, the client chair that is left. When I don't move, he gets up and makes a charade of introductions, anything to ease the unpleasantness.

'I think you know Don Esterhauss,' he says.

'Yes,' I say, but I don't look at him.

Don's not quite sure whether he should get up to shake my hand, so he stays where he is, smiles and nods.

'And, of course, you know Mr Chambers, and Roland from your own staff.' I'm still looking at these two. He does not linger long on this. I think Ingel senses molten lava close under the surface with me.

'Sit down,' he says. He makes this no longer an invitation, but a command.

I settle into the chair, turn it a little sideways to keep my back away from the couch, as a feeling of foreboding washes over me.

Ingel engages in a little small talk, something to take the edge off, how law in a small town is more intimate, less formal than across the river. Soon he will be telling me that this excuses breaches of professional ethics. He knows he is walking on the thin edge here, that I could complain that his closed door discussions out of my presence are ex parte, a violation of the Code of Judicial Conduct. Called to answer, he would no doubt insist that Roland represented my office in this meeting, notwithstanding Overroy's lack of authority to do so. And he would win. My problems with Roland are an internal affair, an open office pissing contest, which the courts would no doubt tell me I am solely responsible to manage.

Ingel asks me if I would like some coffee. I decline.

'I hope I won't be here that long,' I say.

He gives me a sharp look.

'I've a lot of work to do,' I explain.

'Well, then we should get to it. We've been talking for a few minutes,' says Ingel, like this is news.

'Covering some ground,' he says. He's arranging a number of things on his desk, a paperweight, some files, finally he stops to toy with his coffee cup. He will not look me in the eye, but continues to talk.

'Roland,' he says, 'ran into Mr Chambers at a county bar function a few weeks back, introduced by a mutual acquaintance,' he explains.

My mind conjures images of Adam's encounter with the serpent, though clearly Roland is not so innocent.

He tells me that they had occasion to discuss what he refers to as just 'some things'. The judge presents all this to me as rather fortuitous. The good luck of a chance meeting.

'Birds of a feather,' I say.

Adrian stiffens. Ingel gives me a look.

'What did you say?'

'Nothing,' I tell him.

Ingel issues a pained expression and goes on.

'One thing led to another,' he says, 'and resulted in our discussion here today.'

'And what's that?' I ask.

'Emm?'

'Your discussion here today?'

Ingel knows that I can sense the subject matter. But I will force him to say it out loud.

'Well . . .' He looks at the couch and wonders, I think, if he shouldn't have one of these two carry this load from here. But there are no volunteers.

'Well, they started exploring some common ground,' he says. He gives me a quick sideways glance, then looks away before he finishes his thought. 'The Putah Creek cases,' he says. There it is out.

With this I come up out of my chair.

'No. No. Now sit down,' he says. 'I want you to hear this out. I know this is sensitive. I also know that you weren't told. Roland has informed me of this.'

'Then he's told you more than he has me. Maybe he can explain to me what he's doing discussing a case for which he has absolutely no responsibility, or authority,' I say.

Overroy starts to open his mouth, but Ingel cuts him off.

'I don't think that would be productive,' he says. 'Not now. For the time being,' he says, 'I think we can just say that he was operating under my auspices. To see if, maybe, we could bring this thing to a conclusion short of a long and costly trial,' says Ingel. 'Something that I think you would agree is in everyone's best interest.'

I am stunned by the duplicity and boldness of this, the brazen manner in which it is announced.

'I assured him, that you would take no reprisals for his actions in this regard.' Ingel's talking about Overroy, who now sits on the couch next to Chambers, his head seeming to float like shit in high cotton, an insolent grin planted on his face. Roland now sees himself beyond my reach, a diplomat on my turf, but with immunity. With this, there will be no end to his mischief.

'Roland,' says Ingel, 'and Mr Chambers have had several meetings, and with time running out on us, nearing trial,' he says, 'they have narrowed the issues. We thought maybe it was time to talk settlement, a possible plea.'

'If Mr Chambers wanted to talk plea bargains he should have approached me, not one of my deputies assigned to other cases.'

'Agreed,' says Ingel. 'It was not done entirely according to Hoyle, but then no one planned it,' he says.

He expects me to accept this. Assurances from on high.

'Since he's taken it upon himself to negotiate for my office without authority, all I can say is that I hope that Roland's been hard-nosed on behalf of the people,' I tell him.

'He's done a good job,' says Ingel.

Roland beams.

'Then can I assume that the defendant's ready to stipulate to the death penalty?'

'I told you,' Chambers is moving to get up. 'I warned you that this would be a waste of time. There's no talking to the man,' he says. 'Let's forget it.'

He's up off the couch, briefcase in hand, all the maneuvers of a well-drilled routine. If I were alone, this is where I would wait to see if he would actually leave, cross the threshold and slam the door, or whether he would continue to carp over my desk a litany about justice and the clogged courts.

As it is, we'll never know. Ingel pleads with him to sit down.

'We've come a long way,' he says. 'Let's not lose it now.'

He makes this sound as if there's already some done deal.

Grudging, looking at me cross-eyed, Chambers slowly settles back into the couch.

To all of this, Esterhauss is a silent audience. Lawyer talk and a lot of bile. I think he is intimidated, and more than a little embarrassed at what is shaping up to be the ugly marketplace of justice.

'Mr Madriani,' says Ingel. 'There's a great deal at stake here. I wouldn't want your ego to get in the way. You should consider very seriously the terms and conditions that have been discussed. I will expect you to.'

Chambers gives just the slightest perception of a smile.

The message is clear, the trial judge is demanding that, at a minimum, I entertain this offer, however absurd.

I have from the inception not seen this as a case susceptible to settlement by plea bargain. There are no minor players here, co-conspirators for whose testimony we might offer some deal. From what we know, Iganovich acted alone to commit multiple murder, calculated in separate acts, not something that lends itself to theories of mitigating circumstances. The hideous repetition leaves little middle ground. These crimes are not some blind act of passion, at least not in the way a normal mind could comprehend, that might justify anything less than the maximum penalty.

'It appears I'm a captive audience,' I tell Ingel.

He gives me a look that could scorch paper.

'Mr Overroy, maybe you or Mr Chambers . . .' He

motions them to fill me in on the details.

Overroy makes the move, his eyes not on me but Esterhauss. He sees this, no doubt, as the close in his pitch to replace Mario on a permanent basis. A prosecutor with his eye fixed firmly on the fiscal bottom line, someone the county fathers could embrace, pragmatic and politically malleable as plastic.

'It's straightforward,' he says, 'no mysteries. We've worked out a plea of guilty,' he says, 'to multiple counts of first-degree murder. Mr Chambers has already discussed this with his client, explained to him the risks of going to trial.'

This risk, of course, is a death sentence, something that Roland proposes to deal away. It is the only basis for a deal, and his only bargaining chit.

He's talking around me, trying to convince Ingel and Esterhauss of the wisdom of this move. He talks about the evidence, conversant, as if perhaps he's been rifling our files at night. To listen to Roland, the case for the state is at best a toss-up, a possible loser on the circumstantial evidence.

I cut him off before he can get deeply into details.

'If our case is so weak,' I say, 'why would you want to cop a plea?' I put this to Chambers.

'Maybe you should discuss that privately with your own deputy.' He's talking about Overroy and his assessment of our case.

'Why would I want to question the monkey, when I can talk to the organ grinder,' I say.

Mean slits from Roland, though Esterhauss laughs, unable to keep it in.

Overroy tries to ignore this, rolls with the punch and keeps going.

'Mr Iganovich has consented, generally, to the terms discussed,' he says.

'Is this true?' Ingel asks Chambers.

'More or less,' says Adrian.

'In return for what?' I ask. This forces Roland back to me.

Here he sucks a little of air, how to couch it without appearing to give away the store.

'A guarantee that the man will be put away forever,' he says, 'that society will be protected.'

'You mean that he will not be executed?' I say.

'Yes.'

Roland sits up a little, sticks out his chest.

'What we propose is an L-WOP,' he says. This is lawyer slang; shorthand for a term of 'life without possibility of parole'.

Before I can say a word, Overroy anticipates. 'We tell the community, the families of the victims that the defendant will spend his entire life behind bars, never to be released. In some ways, this is more punitive than death.'

I would like to see him sell this to Kim Park.

He minimizes the political fall-out, tortures the truth, a good day's work for Roland.

Life without possibility of parole is a euphemism in this state. As long as there are courts and judges to administer them, parole is always possible. The people sitting in this room know there is only one irrevocable sentence in the law.

'Forget the assurances of public safety,' I say, 'what's the legal basis for such a plea?'

Overroy looks at me doe-eyed.

'The codes, 'he says, 'it's in the codes.' He means that such a sentence is mentioned in the statutes, which, of course we all know. No doubt, if I handed him the books he would look in the index under 'L-WOP', such is Roland's depth of legal research.

I continue to look at him, like try again.

'Life without possibility of parole,' he says, 'is a recognized sentence. I'm sure of it,' though his voice is now quivering with questions. He still does not get it.

'He means,' says Chambers, 'how do you justify the sentence under the statutes.' Unlike Overroy, Adrian comprehends where I am going.

Under the law of this state in a capital case, a life term without possibility of parole is permissible only where mitigating circumstances outweigh other aggravating factors. It is a balancing test on the scales of justice.

I do not see much cause for compassion here. Four kids staked to the ground and brutally murdered is not exactly a prescription for clemency. I tell them this.

'Aggravation and mitigation are only factors to be considered by the jury in the penalty phase of a trial,' says Chambers. He means that this would be a plea bargain without trial.

'The court,' he says, 'has broader latitude. The parties can effect a settlement for tactical reasons, irrespective of the evidence.' He cites case law, *People v. West*. Adrian has clearly come prepared to this meeting.

I turn to Ingel. Time to put his toes in the flames.

'Are you prepared to condone this?' I say. 'To sanction a settlement on these terms?' In a felony, the court must approve any plea.

He dances around it, makes a few faces. He would prefer that I commit myself first, then ride on my coattails. After all, I will be long gone by the next election, when he would be free to blame any fall-out on me, like this deal was driven by a imprudent prosecutor who is now gone.

Before Ingel can speak, Chambers saves him.

'There are ample mitigating circumstances in this case, your honor, of which you should be aware. In the defendant's past.' He calls Iganovich's childhood a life of deprivation and abuse, which he says he can document.

Ingel smiles. The hook he needs to hang his hat.

'I think I can live with it,' says Ingel.

Of course, all of these things, the Russian's childhood, his early history, are matters which we cannot corroborate, not in the time available to us and in the chaos that is the Russian's homeland.

'Your honor, for the state it's a particularly good deal,' says Roland. 'The defendant has agreed,' he says, 'to enter a similar plea, guilty to murder in the first degree on the two other charges.'

Frosting on the cake. Overroy's talking about the Scofield murders, wiping the slate clean.

I cast a quick glance at Esterhauss and catch the glint in his eye. The prospect of a quick plea bargain that will bury everything in a single fell swoop, no trial, and end to the perpetual publicity. To Esterhauss and the other doyens of this county, this scenario must be a political wet dream.

I remind them all that the Scofield cases aren't even charged.

'So we get an indictment,' says Overroy. 'How difficult can it be?'

'We have multiple murders,' I say. 'Life without possibility,' I tell him, 'is ridiculous. Even if I wanted to, I could not in good conscience.

'And the Scofield thing,' I turn to Chambers. 'Your client is ready to enter a plea, to factually acknowledge that he committed these crimes, in open court?'

'He will enter a *West* plea,' he says, 'for tactical reasons.'

What he means is that Iganovich will not state in open court that he has committed these murders, but instead enter a plea for purposes of legal strategy. Decisional law, cases laid down by the courts of this state permit this, though I, for one, think it is bad public policy.

'Why is this so necessary?' I say. 'To join Scofield in a plea at all?'

I am concerned, that to charge these crimes to the Russian may result in the closure of a serious case without finding the real perpetrator.

Chambers explains that unless we wash the Scofield cases through this deal, he cannot go forward. It seems he has thought this through.

'Without a trial, *Kellett* would no longer apply,' he says. He's referring to the case which he cited in court to Fisher.

'Unless we include Scofield, what are we gaining?' he says. 'We enter a plea on the four college students and the state is still free to charge Mr Iganovich with Scofield. With pleas then entered to four counts of first degree murder, a conviction in Scofield brings the death penalty,' he says. 'Not a scenario I find helpful.'

As a tactical matter, Chambers is right. To eliminate any possibility that his client would face death, he must include a plea on the Scofield killings as part of the bargain. The Rubric's Cube of the law.

Overroy, ever helpful, suggests that we could confer immunity on the Russian for the Scofield murders.

The specter of this even causes Ingel to wince.

'No,' I say. 'I can't do it.'

'OK,' says Roland, 'no immunity. We charge him instead.'

Overroy it seems is still operating on another wavelength from the rest of us in this room.

'No. I mean no deal. No plea bargain,' I say.

Ingel is out of his chair, sallying forth around the desk, cajoling, telling me to look at the facts of the case, something which he himself has not done. He pitches me on the circumstantial loose ends, that I could lose it all in trial.

'I'll take my chances,' I say.

'On a multi-million dollar trial,' says Ingel. 'That's rich. That's generous.'

Now it is getting ugly. Soon he will kneel on my throat. The man is hearing the strings of Hawaiian guitars, feeling the warm sands of Waikiki under his ass.

There's a deep sigh from Chambers, like maybe he wanted this more than I know. Perhaps his defenses are not as sure as he makes out.

The judge starts to lean on me heavily, veiled threats that I will not be getting the benefit of any doubt in trial.

I wonder what has happened to Ingel's blood oath to Armando Acosta, the man at the judicial back-door — how he would explain a plea bargain that spares the killer of the Coconut's own niece?

Ingel is, no doubt, pressured by the county for this result. Faced with a decision between a colleague of the cloth and the vagaries of politics, he has apparently made his choice. He comes at me again, assures me that if I make even the slightest slip he will see that I carry the mark of it on my career for life.

'The courts in this part of the state,' he says, 'are a finite universe, a small world. A word of advice.' He pulls up close in my ear. 'Always make certain that you can sleep in your bed before you make it.'

I glance at Esterhauss, who chooses to look away. It seems this has all left a little taste with him.

Ingel has now moved to where he is standing behind my chair, boring a hole in the back of my head with his eyes.

I get up, turn to look at him.

'We can all thank God for little favors,' I say.

'What's that?' says the judge.

'That the founders saw benefit in a separation among the powers. If you don't mind,' I say, 'I'll bring the charges, and you can try them.'

He looks at me with an acid gaze.

With that I am out the door, closing it quietly behind me, listening to the receding din of voices, the wailing and gnashing of teeth.

Chapter Thirty

While I may be on the out with the city's power structure, at least today I have the admiring eye of Claude Dusalt. In the way that only happens in a small town, word has now filtered to the organs of law enforcement concerning my meeting with Ingel, the news that I've rejected a proposed plea bargain to spare the Russian's life.

'How did you find out so fast?' I ask him. 'I mean we didn't finish the meeting until late yesterday afternoon?'

'If the judge doesn't want things to get around,' he says, 'he shouldn't talk in front of his people.'

In Davenport County, the Sheriff's Office staffs the courts for security.

'Ingel's bailiff,' I say.

Claude won't say. But the answer is clear.

This news is probably all over the city by now. Dirt in the average cop shop travels faster than telepathy, and is generally more accurate than CNN.

'I thought such people took blood oaths,' I say, 'I mean, to work in the courts?' This is generally considered privileged duty.

'Working for Derek Ingel is not considered a choice assignment,' he tells me. 'My source drew the short straw.'

From the inception, Claude has been scrupulous in his dealings with me, tireless in his efforts to pursue every item of evidence I have requested. But there has also been a certain reserve in his attitude toward me, something more than the mere deference paid to a prosecutor. In his cop's eyes, I think, I was marked by the sign of Cain; after all I came from the criminal-defense side of the bar. Nothing was ever said, but in his eyes, the subtle gestures of conversation, Claude revealed doubts concerning my commitment, whether I would go the last mile in this case.

My meeting with Ingel and Chambers, telling the judge to put his deal where the sun don't shine, has put an end to Claude's qualms.

He sits behind the wheel of his unmarked police unit, doing nearly seventy, on the ribbon of highway that rolls from the foothills down toward Capital City and Davenport beyond.

This morning's errand was not one either of us much enjoyed. We have deposited Nikki and Sarah in what Claude now ridicules as our 'safe house', not his choice, but a compromise made necessary by Nikki's continuing anger.

This morning she was fingerprinted at the Sheriff's Department, a procedure required to eliminate her prints on the threatening letter, envelope and photo deposited in our mailbox. Still the cops found only one other set of latents when they dusted; my own, placed on the letter before I realized its contents.

Nikki feels violated, forced to be printed in the little room at the jail next to junkies and other collars waiting to be booked. She knows this is necessary, but still she wonders how and why she and Sarah have been ensnared in all of this. She is being forced to burn limited vacation time from her job until the trial is over. Her employer says he will carry her, off-salary, once all-paid leave is consumed. This was time she'd been saving for an extended vacation for the family. Now it will be gone.

Nikki has exacted a price for all of this. 'If I'm on vacation,' she told us, 'then I'm going to stay in a resort.' It is fortunate for me that my wife's sense of high living is a small bed-and-breakfast in the little town of Coloma; the place where Sutter found gold and started the stampede to this state that has never ended.

We spent an anniversary there three years ago. Now Nikki is held up there with Sarah and a pile of kindergarten workbooks, in a room with a brass bed, playing tutor to my daughter, at the Vineyard House. The building is a mammoth white pseudo-Victorian, dating from the nineteenth century, overgrown with wisteria and other clinging vines. It is said to be haunted by the ghost of a former owner, a man who suffered from dementia and was chained in the basement by his wife. This is a fate I fear for myself, if I do not put a quick end to this trial. Such is Nikki's growing sense of ire.

'I don't know about that place,' says Claude.

'They'll be fine,' I say. 'They're comfortable, and safe.'

'It's too public for me,' he says. 'A private house or an apartment would have been better.

'I've arranged periodic security,' he tells me. 'El Dorado County's sheriff will keep a car patrolling in the area.' In the next breath tells me that this is probably unnecessary.

Nikki is there, registered under an assumed name. We have paid cash for the room and I will be traveling to and from this place daily more than an hour's ride each way during the trial, so she will not be alone at night.

Claude tells me that this is probably all over-kill, needless precautions.

I look at him as if to say, 'Why the hell are we doing it then?'

'Still, a good investment in some peace of mind,' he says.

Then, without missing a beat, he slides something across the seat in my direction. This has come from under the flap of his coat near the seat-belt, like he's waiting for just the right moment to reveal it.

'I thought maybe you could use this,' he says. There's a disturbed look, a little chagrin on his face as he pushes this toward me.

As he removes his hand, I'm looking down at the lustrous blued-steel of a small revolver, wrapped in its tight leather holster.

'In the glove box,' he says, 'is a permit, so you can carry it concealed. Emil issued it last night.'

So much for peace of mind.

It's a truism that in the trial of any case, something will always go wrong, though usually it does not occur on the eve of opening argument as it has here. This maxim has now struck my own case, dead center and below the proverbial waterline.

The commercial photo lab hired by Kay Sellig to up-grade the quality of our photos to be put before the jury has misplaced a critical piece of evidence, a short length of cord used in one of the murders. Sellig has me on the phone, giving me this news.

'How in the hell?' I say.

'They are looking for it,' she says, 'turning the place upside down.' She's trying to calm me down. She tells me that they are confident they will find it.

'When?' I say.

'That's the big question,' she tells me.

'We have crystal clear, colored photos of all of the pieces,' she says. Apparently the lab lost the missing piece of plastic sheathing after their processing was finished.

I wonder aloud whether they could have thrown this out without thinking.

Sellig cannot be sure, but tells me she doesn't think this is the case. 'They knew what it was for,' she says. 'That it was important.'

'That didn't stop them from losing it.'

She is silent on the other end of the line. Sellig had advised against allowing the evidence out of our possession, but I pushed for better enlargements as this was the centerpiece of our case. I am now paying the price for not heeding her warning.

She tells me that she's about to leave for the lab, to talk to the owner, to help them look.

'If we can't find it,' she says, 'maybe the court would allow us to use the photos instead, as the best evidence,' she says.

This is not likely, I tell her. 'The defense has an absolute right to have the cord examined by its own experts. I wouldn't count on it,' I say.

Tomorrow morning, I start my case-in-chief, opening argument. We have spent the last two days selecting our jury, or rather the judge has. Ingel, true to his promise not to cut any slack, pressed us to the wall, finally insisting on doing the *voir dire* himself, posing questions we submitted in writing, at least the ones he thought appropriate. Judges in criminal cases are permitted to do this under an initiative adopted by voters a few years ago, though unlike Ingel, most still allow the lawyers to ask critical questions.

Chambers stomped up and down the courtroom railing about this, his exclusion from the jury selection process. He got nowhere, except perhaps the listing of another ground for appeal. That Ingel completed this task in two days was no mean feat, probably a record. In a capital case the jury must be 'death qualified', questions must be posed to assure that, if convicted as charged, the panel would have no qualms about imposing the death penalty.

The haste with which this process was completed, has turned it into a dry exercise. Neither Goya nor I have any real feel for this group, our panel of twelve jurors and six alternatives. I suspect that Chambers is equally blind, but no more so than one of the prospective jurors.

When the man with the white cane appeared in the box, I objected, told Ingel that a major portion of our case was demonstrative in nature, photos of evidence that required visual acuity on the part of the trier of fact. He hammered me down, citing a code section that does not permit the exclusion of a juror because of impaired sight. I was ultimately forced to burn a preemptory challenge to remove the man from the panel. With this Ingel smiled, as if to say now I could deal with the wrath of the sight-impaired lobby.

He knew, as well as I, that no reader could describe our photographic evidence to the juror without making the fundamental judgment for the juror, the question whether the pictures portrayed what they purported to or not.

I hold my breath and ask Sellig the critical legal question about the missing evidence, the piece of cord.

'Do you know which piece it is?' I say. 'The missing length of sheathing from the cord?'

The sections of clothes-line cord, sixteen in all, used on the victims, seventeen if you count the coiled length discovered in the Russian's van, are the critical links in our chain of evidence. Taken together, piece-by-piece they form a continuum connecting the four college victims with the coiled length of cord found in the vehicle. The question is, at what point this chain is now broken. This will tell me how many of the counts of murder may be in jeopardy if we cannot find the missing length.

Sellig is scrambling through her notes on the other end of the line, breathing heavily into the phone as she looks for the information. She has coded these pieces by number and letter, marking them for identification. It takes her several seconds to locate what she's looking for, the legend for this code.

'It looks like. Yes,' she says. 'It was Two-D.'

This means nothing to me.

She explains that four pieces of cord were used on each victim, two to tie off the ankles, and two more to bind the wrists. Each of these pieces have been lettered in sequence, A through D.

'The number assigned represents the order of the victims,' she says. 'This is from the second victim, the last section of cord used on that victim.'

'Julie Park,' I say.

'Yes.'

This means the evidentiary link is broken between Park and the third victim. Unless we can find the missing piece of cord, I could be compelled to dismiss the charges involving the murders of Julie Park and the first victim, her boyfriend Jonathan Snider. Without the cord, there is nothing linking them to Iganovich other than a similar MO in the commission of the crimes. Chambers who is keying on the Scofield murders and the similar fact pattern there would chew me up in such an argument.

I lean back in my chair, suck a lot of air, and look up at the tiny perforated holes in the ceiling. I wonder how I would ever garner the courage to break this news to Kim Park, and pray that it will not be necessary.

'Keep me posted,' I tell Sellig. 'Call me as soon as you talk to the people at the lab.' I hang up.

Lenore is waiting patiently to talk to me, sitting in one of the chairs across from my desk; she has tuned in to a portion of my phone conversation.

'They lost part of the rope?' she says.

I nod. 'We could be forced to dump the counts relating to the Julie Park and the Snider kid,' I say.

'Damn it.' Goya gives me a pained expression. Then she quickly picks up the broken pieces of this equation and puts a face on it, I think, for my benefit.

'I guess it could be worse,' she says. 'They could have lost the last piece.' She means the slender length of cord linking all the others to the coiled rope in the van. With this our entire case would have evaporated.

'We're not out of the woods,' I say. 'Our case may only be marginally better than none at all.'

'What do you mean?'

'I mean Chambers is already keying on the Scofield cases. If we're forced to dismiss the Park and Snider counts, we have only one set of murders to the jury.'

A look comes over her face as she sees where I'm going. There is nothing left to distinguish the second set of student killings from the Scofield crimes. In both cases the killer used consecutive sections of cord to tie down the couples, though the cord between cases doesn't match up. The metal stakes used in the second murders are a match, as are the stakes used on the Scofields. But in between these two crimes, again, the stakes are different.

'It makes it look as if the killer changed his tools with each set of murders,' she says.

'We can forget our expert on criminal profiling,' I tell her. 'Without Park and Snider we no longer have pattern crimes, just an isolated set of gruesome killings. And if Chambers can put his man in Canada at the time of the Scofield murders . . .' I let the thought trail off, the conclusion obvious. It is the trouble with a theory built entirely around circumstantial evidence: remove one of the critical pins holding it together and your case can fall apart.

Chapter Thirty-One

This morning, early before court, Lenore prepped with Lloyd Tolar, our first meeting with him face-to-face. The guy is harder to get a hold of than the Pope, but, apparently, a little more lascivious.

She tells me he is tall, gray-haired and distinguished, the kind of witness juries fall in love with. They went over his evidence, a cordial conversation of Y-incisions to the human body, from crotch to breast bone and, between the liver and spleen, he asked her out to lunch.

'Randy old goat,' she says.

Trying to get a hold of Tolar, I should have known. From what she tells me, I could have sent him Lenore's picture clipped to her business card and saved myself a dozen phone calls.

'He says it won't be necessary to put on the profile experts when he is finished laying out his evidence, so devastating will be his testimony,' she says.

It is easy to see where the young intern caught his arrogance, the kid in Tolar's office the day I went looking for him. It is a required course in medical school. But we don't argue with the good doctor. Lenore says he has enough gall that he speaks with the authority of a god, and possesses a résumé to match.

Today I am forced to confront our missing evidence, the

length of cord lost by our photo people.

I look over. The counsel table for the defense is crowded. Chambers and Iganovich form a sandwich with the interpreter squeezed between them. On the other side of the Russian is Bob Haselid, a last minute addition to the defense team.

Haselid is a young lawyer, a growing reputation as a comer in the bar. He will serve as Keenan Counsel, responsible for the penalty phase of the defense, to save the Russian's life if we convict and the jury finds special circumstances.

Before we begin, I have asked for a few minutes with Ingel and Adrian in private. The bailiff wags a finger at me, then buttonholes Chambers. He leads us both back behind the bench to huddle with the judge.

When we arrive, Ingel is busy picking fuzz off his robes, the sticky side of some scotch tape threaded between his fingers. The life of the busy judge.

He looks at me. 'What is it,' he says, 'some last-minute ground rules?'

'A problem,' I tell him.

He lays the black garment aside, on the edge of his desk.

'Some of our evidence has been misplaced,' I say.

I get a look, as if meanness is not far below the surface this morning.

'I'm told it's only temporary, that they will find it.' My effort to take a little of the edge off these tidings.

'What evidence?' Ingel's gaze is icy.

'A piece of the cord, from the first two murders, the outer plastic sheathing,' I say. In the next breath, before he can say more, I tell him that we have detailed photos, offer this bait to see if maybe he will bite.

'Photographs of evidence are not evidence,' he says, 'not in my court.' Unfortunately for me, Ingel, unlike the Coconut, has employed his copy of the *Evidence Code* for something more than a dense coaster for his coffee cup.

I get a quick tongue-lashing from him, admonitions that he warned me during discussions on settlement not to be looking for judicial dispensations. He questions me, in not too subtle ways, as to which of the charges are affected. He is no doubt probing to determine the effect of this mishap on the murder of Sharon Collins. Ingel does not want to tell Armando Acosta that he was forced by circumstance to dump charges in the murder of the Coconut's niece. When he sees Chambers beginning to take note of this line of questioning, Ingel drops it quickly.

'How did it happen?' he says.

'The commercial photo lab,' I say. 'They came in with their equipment to do some pictures. Apparently, they misplaced the evidence in processing the film.'

'Threw it out?' says Ingel.

'They tell me no,' I say, 'that that is unlikely, your honor.'

'The buck,' he says, 'for every fuck-up in your case stops with you, counselor.' He makes it sound like I'm giving excuses.

'They're confident they'll find it,' I say.

'Good for them,' says Ingel. 'In the meantime what are we supposed to do?'

Chambers smells advantage here, some unexpected boon. In a death case, chivalry is a stranger to the courtroom and defense attorneys, the good ones, give no quarter. He edges in close to the Prussian's desk.

'We'll oppose any motion for continuance,' he says. 'The defense is ready to proceed.' He reminds the judge that the defendant has not waived time.

There is more than a week left before the sixty-day period will run requiring a dismissal for failure to prosecute. But Ingel makes clear that he is not entertaining any motions to continue.

'We've picked our jury,' he says. 'I'm not about to let them sit around and chew on the facts of this case while the prosecutor looks for missing evidence.'

The less charitable might accuse the Prussian of hearing Hawaiian strings, but in point of fact he is right. There is nothing more dangerous than a restless jury once empaneled. Left to their own devices, there is no end of mischief they might get into; speculation about the case they are about to hear, suppositions on the evidence.

Most of the jurors have read news accounts of these murders, seen the white-sheeted bodies, the cleaned-up aftermath of these crimes on their television screens.

'We are ready to go,' says Ingel, 'and go we will, on this trial, this morning.'

'I'm not asking for a continuance,' I say, 'just some latitude.'

Ingel looks at me like he doesn't know the word.

My tactic in coming here is not deep. The continuum of cord is the common thread of evidence running through my case. It was presented to the grand jury and is highlighted in that transcript, which by now Chambers has read and dissected. That a piece of this is now missing, is not something likely to elude Adrian.

When he sees it he will make an immediate motion to dismiss the first two counts of murder, Julie Park and Jonathan Snider. Knowing the Prussian and his attitude toward me, I don't want him to make a snap judgment from the bench on this. So I raise it here in private, off the record, a rehearsal to help temper his judgment. I ask Ingel for some leeway, to hold off on any motion to dismiss until we have time to find the cord, to give me a little license in presenting my case until then.

He is noncommittal.

He reminds me of my opportunity to settle the case, the proffered plea bargain on six counts of murder. If he could, Ingel would order me to don sackcloth while he shovels ash on my head. For a moment, I think, maybe he would like to reopen negotiations, but suspects that Adrian, now sensing blood on the water, is not so keen. Instead he says nothing.

'How critical is this evidence?' he says. He wants a damage assessment on my case, here in front of Adrian, how the missing piece of cord fits in.

I give him the facts, but stop short of summing them up; that two counts of murder are now hanging perilously on a slender thread.

The sense of relief in his face when he discovers that the count on Sharon Collins is still intact is nearly palpable. He will not have to carry bad news to Acosta, at least not yet.

Adrian sees his opening. 'I move for dismissal,' he says, 'on Park and Snider, the first two counts, your honor.'

Ingel holds him off, palm outstretched.

'Is this the only evidence linking the defendant to these

397

crimes?' he asks. 'The missing piece of cord?'

I tell him it is not. 'The fact that we can link evidence in the defendant's van to the murders of the second two college students, this, together with the fact that all four killings involved a similar MO,' I say, 'provides a nexus to the defendant.'

'With a reach like that you should be the heavy-weight champ,' says Chambers. He means that I am stretching my case. He is right, but it is all that I have left for the moment.

'The pieces of cord in all four murders are of the same manufacture, as are the metal stakes,' I tell Ingel, this latter to add a little gloss.

'And could have been bought in ten thousand places by a million people,' says Adrian.

'A question of fact for the jury,' I tell Ingel.

The judge makes a face, like maybe. I have him thinking at least in the right direction.

Adrian is jumping all over his desk, pointing out that the Scofield murders also have a common MO, but that these have not been charged against his client. Instead, he says, the police have tacitly admitted that these crimes were committed by another perpetrator. 'It's the only thing so far that they got right,' he says.

He will be singing a different tune when I dump Tolar's medical evidence on him, the autopsy results showing the knife wounds and the fact that the Scofields were killed someplace else. Let him try to massage that and make it fit.

'Two days ago, you were ready to cop a plea in Scofield,' I tell him.

'That was tactical,' he says. He knows I cannot make

this argument or reveal any of the matters pertaining to settlement negotiations to the jury. Mention of such failed deals is taboo at trial, a policy rooted in the ancient maxim that the law favors settlement. If defendants knew their openers to cop a plea would be revealed to the jury, the time-honored practice of bargaining would die a quick, natural death.

Ingel finally looks up. He's had enough.

'We'll take this out on the record,' he says. If he gives me a break it is against his better judgment, but, one thing is clear, he will not spare me a good thrashing in the press. The papers and TV will have a field day, headlines and ten o'clock teasers about how the DA lost critical evidence.

With all of my problems, Adrian still has a single overweening difficulty with his case. He must explain how the coiled cord, the one now tied to the second two murders, and the metal stakes, came to be found in his client's vehicle. It is on this pivot point that his entire defense now turns.

For the moment, Ingel has rejected his motion to dismiss the Park and Snider murders. This was done out of the presence of the jury, to avoid tainting them with thoughts of evidence, the missing cord, which may or may not later be produced.

I can no longer look Kim Park square in the face as he sits in the audience and glares. I know that on the first break he will accost me in the hall, ask me how justice is possible in the face of such negligence.

To avoid Ingel's mounting hostility, I have clung to the inner-limits of restraint in my opening statement to the jury, a straight recitation of the evidence, the van, its registration, the incriminating items found in it.

'We will demonstrate, ladies and gentlemen, by expert testimony the sociopathic links among these four murders, the common methods employed, and the inner-workings of a sick and dangerous mind that will demonstrate beyond a shadow of doubt that the defendant, Andre Iganovich, committed all four murders and did so in a cold and calculating manner.'

I lay out the bloody rag found in the van which DNA testing now shows to have traces of blood not inconsistent with that of Sharon Collins and Rodney Slate. A few round eyes in the jury box.

I talk about the common manufacture of the cord, the fact that some pieces found at the second murder scene have been scientifically linked, a conclusive match, with the coiled length found in the Russian's vehicle. The measure of my loss, the missing piece of cord, is now underscored by the snapping of necks in the jury box with mention of this forensic connection. It is the touchstone of my case.

Here I concede the broken window of the vehicle, touch on this briefly so that it does not look as if I am running from this circumstance of fact.

I talk about the stun gun taken from Iganovich at his arrest, and the burn marks found on Julie Park and Rodney Snider, evidence that the medical examiner will talk about.

Ingel shows appearances of growing restive as I hit the final issue, the uncharged Scofield murders.

'The defense will no doubt,' I say, 'try to confuse you

with a third and final set of murders, the deaths of Abbott and Karen Scofield, which at this time, and based on the evidence in our possession, we believe are copy-cat crimes.'

I take the middle ground here, not entirely absolving Iganovich, but leaving a little wiggle room if evidence later develops, which might allow me, at the last moment before the close of my case, to amend and charge the Russian. Lenore is feeling particularly nervous on this. She wants to talk about something involving Scofield when we break for lunch today.

'The evidence,' I tell the jury, 'will demonstrate marked differences in the manner in which these crimes were carried out, which, at this time, and given the evidence available, lead us to believe that Andre Iganovich did not commit them.'

I use this to foster a picture of even-handed justice, the avoidance of over-zealous prosecution. But the fact is that I must touch on it to avoid giving the appearance that we are hiding from these unresolved questions, unsolved murders with a seemingly common perpetrator.

With this, I turn and take my place at the counsel table.

Chambers does not reserve his opening to the commencement of his case, instead he is on his feet, almost before the invitation from Ingel. He wants to neutralize early any major points I may have scored, and he wastes no time.

He hits on Scofield, the theme that the true murderer is out there, stalking, still at large, that his client is a defendant of convenience, an immigrant with limited language abilities, someone obvious to dislike, easy to convict.

Ingel stops him. 'You're making argument, Mr Chambers. Stick to the evidence of your case,' he says.

'Yes, sir,' he says. Adrian regroups.

'The evidence of this case,' he says, 'is entirely circumstantial. The fact is that my client would not be here today but for three pieces of evidence, a coil of cord, some metal tent-stakes, and a piece of cloth with human blood on it.

'This, and the inference,' he says, 'that found in his car they must therefore belong to Mr Iganovich. That, in a nutshell, is the state's case.

'On first blush,' he says, 'this may seem damning. But consider for a moment the rest of the evidence, the part that Mr Madriani did not emphasize, the part that he does not know.'

With this he turns and looks at me sitting at the table.

'The evidence will show,' he says, 'that, indeed, a window of this vehicle was broken as the prosecutor willingly admits. What he does not tell you,' he says, 'what he fails to disclose is the fact that this window was smashed completely out, leaving the vehicle open to anyone who chanced by. The van sat there in a public garage, open to any passer-by for a substantial period, for a number of days, before police came upon it, opened it, and found the seemingly incriminating evidence. This is the state of the evidence.

'The fact is, anyone could have deposited the evidence in that vehicle after it was parked.'

'You're arguing again,' says Ingel. 'Keep to the evidence, I don't want to tell you again,' he says.

'I was just getting to it, your honor, a critical piece of evidence.'

Ingel looks at him and nods as if to say, 'then do it'.

'For some time, police operated on the theory,' he says, 'that this window was broken by a vandal, a possible witness who may have looked inside, who may have noticed the presence,' he lingers for a moment, mental italic for the words that follow, '*or the absence*,' he says, 'of this critical evidence inside.

'They had reason to believe,' he says, 'that this was the case. Testimony from their own officers will reveal that this theory, in fact, was pursued, but to no effect. The police,' he says, 'on that stand,' he points to the witness box, 'will tell you this.'

I look at Lenore, like how could he know this.

She leans in my ear. 'Roland,' she whispers.

She is right, the tripping little fingers of Roland Overroy are all over this, revelations, no doubt, intended as a show of good faith to Adrian in their negotiations.

'But the police failed,' says Chambers, 'to find this critical witness. Perhaps they should have looked a little harder. For it is a failure that we have rectified.'

Lenore is leaning toward me to add something; when she hears this, she breaks off and looks instead at Adrian, his hands gripping the jury railing.

'We will present a witness,' he says, 'who will testify that he is responsible for breaking the window of this van, a man who has cut no deals with the prosecution for his testimony, who is willing to face the penalty for his crime.'

Like this is an assurance of credibility, a single misdemeanor count for vandalism.

'Our witness,' he says, 'will testify, under oath, that when this window was smashed, he intended to burglarize the vehicle, that he opened the doors and went inside. He will testify unequivocally that after entering the van he was disappointed. He will tell you that he found nothing of value to take, no radio or tape deck, no tools, nothing of significance.'

Adrian turns from the jury and looks directly at me. In the instant before he speaks I get a premonition of what is to follow. Then he drops the hammer.

'He will also tell you,' he says, 'here, under oath, that on the day he smashed the window there was no coiled cord, no tent stakes and no bloody rag in the defendant's vehicle.'

With this, all I get is Adrian's simpering smile.

Lenore and I are the picture of cool, sitting at the table, seeming indifference dripping from us, like perhaps the only thing on our minds is an early lunch.

Inside I am a hot caldron, steaming to get my hands on Chambers's witness list, buried in the pile of papers in front of me.

Adrian takes his seat. Ingel checks his watch.

'Too late,' he says, 'to call a witness. We'll take the luncheon recess now. Mr Madriani,' he looks down at me. 'You will be ready for your first witness when we convene,' he looks at his watch. 'At one-fifteen.'

'Yes, your honor.'

He admonishes the jury not to discuss the case, then smacks the gavel on its wooden base.

Chapter Thirty-Two

This noon Lenore and I order out for lunch from the office, sandwiches in brown bags from the greasy spoon a block away. While one of the secretaries is running for these, we are talking strategy, and poring over the list of Adrian's witnesses. Something that, by law, we are forced to exchange.

The artifice of his case at this point is beginning to emerge. The defense in a capital murder trial is always a variation on some age-old theme; in this case, that somebody else did it.

Adrian will put his own flourish on this old saw. Using the unsolved Scofield murders as a diversion, he starts with our own hypothesis that someone else did the Scofield crimes. That we agree on this premise gives his case a gloss of legitimacy.

From his witness list, the experts assembled, we can surmise the main point of attack, an all-out assault on the factual distinctions that set the Scofield killings apart from the other murders. If someone else did the Scofields, and if the differences in the MO between these crimes and the others appear illusory, Adrian is halfway home.

The flanking move is his secret vandal. A planned *coup de grâce* aimed at the head of our case. If credible, this witness can destroy the only link binding Iganovich to the incriminating evidence in the van.

Lenore and I study his list like some seer perusing tea leaves. There's a lot of misdirection here. Both sides have seeded these with deliberate distractions, an ocean of red herrings, people with whom they have rubbed shoulders during their investigation, but who have nothing meaningful to offer in the case. In this way it is easy to conceal the handful of actual witnesses, to put the other side to a great deal of work before trial.

For my part, Adrian now has the name of Julie Park's former hairdresser, and the guy who read the gas meter at her apartment building, this along with two dozen others whose only knowledge of the facts in these cases are what they've read in the papers or seen on the tube.

But one reaps what one sows. For the most part, studying Adrian's list is a barren exercise. It is a column of names and addresses, the bare minimum required by law. We are also entitled to any written reports of testimony prepared by witnesses. Adrian has kept all of this verbal.

In the frame for this trial we have had little time to check his witnesses, to send Claude and his minions to talk to many of these names, to winnow away the chaff. We are stabbing in the dark as to which of these people is Adrian's magic pellet, his mystery vandal. I'm scoping down the column of names with the point of my pen, an idle exercise until I hit one that sounds familiar.

'James Sloan.' I look at Goya. 'Any bells?'

She shakes her head.

I go down the balance of the sheet. Nothing.

I come back to Sloan. I'm wondering where I've heard this name. Something recent, in the last several weeks.

I pick up the phone, dial a number. A female voice answers.

'Ester, Paul Madriani across the street,' I say.

Ester Peoples is the docket clerk who handles filings for the criminal courts in the main lobby of the Davenport County Courthouse. I can hear her chewing on something. Another bureaucrat donating her lunch hour.

'Can you check a name for me, on the computer?'

'Sure. How far back?'

'A year,' I say.

I give her James Sloan, spelling the last name. I hear the clicking of keys. 'Which one do you want?' she says.

'More than one James Sloan?' I say.

'One guy,' she says, 'three convictions.'

'What for?'

'One count arson, reduced to malicious mischief, two counts vandalism . . .'

'Bingo,' I say. I get his social security number from Ester, thank her and punch the next line on the phone to call out again. This time I don't dial, but hit one of the self-dialing numbers up top. Claude does not answer, but on the third ring I hear the voice of Denny Henderson.

He tells me that Claude is on his way over to my office. Dusalt is my first witness this afternoon. We will prep with him only briefly before heading back to court.

'Denny. I want you to pull the most recent booking sheet on one James Sloan.' I read him the social security number and court file number from Ester.

'Right now?' he says.

'No, yesterday,' I say.

Some grumbling on the line then dead air. I hold for

what seems like ten minutes. Then he's back on the line.

'Got it,' he says.

'See if there's a mug photo,' I say.

Some shuffling on the other end. 'Charming,' he says.

'You got it?'

'Yeah.'

'Let me guess, a purple do, done up in spikes, pockmarks on the face like the bubbles in a sulfur pot?'

'You know the guy?' he says.

'In a manner,' I say.

The porcelain prince, I think. The men's john at the courthouse the day I ran into Adrian, the punk with his schlung caught in the mesh of his zipper, Chambers's erstwhile client.

It was the zippered jacket and weird hair. There was something incongruous in the name James Sloan when Chambers went through the charade of introducing us that day. This, it seems, has held the name like some computer batch file at the edges of my recall ever since.

'I want everything you've got on him, every arrest file, as soon as you can get it over here. Then I want you to go by the courthouse and get the dispositions, the court files on the charges.'

'They won't let me take the originals,' says Henderson.

'Then copy them.'

He counts up the arrests. 'It'll take all day,' he says.

'You got something better to do?' I tell him he can draw straws with Claude as to who gets this duty. He gives me a groan knowing already that he will come up short in this contest. Claude is in court. I hear a lot of grousing like he's about to hang up.

'And, Denny.'

'Yeah.'

'Run a current rap sheet on the guy. See if he has any felony convictions anywhere else.' We hang up.

'It would be nice,' I tell Lenore, 'if we could hang him out on a felony conviction.' This would be something with which to impeach his credibility before the jury. Convicted felons carry the scar for life.

'Then you know who it is?' says Lenore. 'Chambers's witness.'

'If I know Adrian,' I say.

'But how did he find the guy when we couldn't?'

'You're assuming,' I say, 'that he did.'

She gives me a look.

'Adrian's famous for producing witnesses of convenience,' I tell her, 'better at curing the blind spots in his case than a faith healer.'

Watching Adrian in court over the years I have learned that the margin of victory is too often measured by the preponderance of perjury emitted by his witnesses, a stench like a good dose of mustard gas from the stand.

She looks at me wide-eyed, that any lawyer, an officer of the court, would do this knowingly, as a matter of course. For all of her street-smarts and barrio background, if you scratch the hard surface of Lenore, underneath you will find a romantic.

'If Adrian Chambers ate nails,' I tell her, 'he would pass cork screws. He does not simply torture the truth, he is more devious.'

Because I have seen it before, I can predict Adrian's tactic with some confidence.

'When we put Claude on the stand,' I tell her, 'to lay the foundation for the evidence of our investigation, Adrian will ask him about our theories on the vandal who broke the window, our futile efforts to find this witness. Thanks to Roland,' I say, 'he will build his defense by fulfilling our own prophesies, and modifying the message. In his version, the witness broke the window but can attest that none of the evidence was inside. It is Adrian's ethic, any means to defeat the perfidious powers of the state.'

There's a knock on my door.

'Come in.'

It's Claude. He's got a number of files under his arm, folders containing police reports and other business documents compiled during the course of our investigations. He will use these on the stand to refresh his memory in case any details are hazy.

'Ready to do it?' I say.

He makes a face like no big deal.

'Something for you,' he says. He hands me a slip of paper pulled from one of the files under his arm, a lab report from the State Department of Justice.

'Present from Kay Sellig,' he says.

I read, but it means nothing to me.

'Her people analyzed the paper and clippings that made up the note delivered to your house.' Claude's talking about the threat delivered with the photo of Sarah.

'Whoever did it got a little sloppy,' he tells us. 'One of the word groups clipped out and pasted to the note contained a trademark symbol and a small piece of a logo in one corner. Microscopic,' he says. 'But we got lucky. A lab assistant recognized the snippet of logo.'

I look at him, like how was this possible?

'The guy has seen the publication a lot,' he says. 'It's off the title page, the cover sheet to a publication produced for law enforcement agencies. The *State Criminal Law Reporter*,' says Claude.

I know this publication. Cop shops around the state use it to keep abreast of the latest court decisions in the areas of arrest, and the search and seizure of evidence. I am a subscriber myself, as are a growing legion of lawyers practicing in the field.

'Any ideas?' I say.

Claude wrinkles an eyebrow, like he has his own theories. 'We might want to check to see if the Davenport police subscribe to this thing,' he says. I know what he is thinking; Jess Amara.

'Do it.'

We change gears for the moment, as we are running out of time. I warn him about Adrian's likely tactic on cross: that he will fish for details on our theory that a vandal may have broken the window of the van, that thanks to the loose tongue of Roland, this now plays a part in the defense case.

He uses a few expletives to describe Overroy. But then he tells me that Roland may have problems of his own. One of the investigators Claude has assigned to Sellig to help her search for the missing piece of cord has talked to the photographer who was processing the stuff the day it disappeared.

'The guy tells us there was somebody hanging around in your library the day they were doing the job, shooting the cord. He was interested in cameras, talking up a hobby,

411

fingering all of their lenses. They got to talken',' says Claude. 'Then this guy leaves and an hour later when they go to close up shop they notices that the cord is gone.'

'Let me guess,' I say. 'Roland.'

'Suddenly he's a regular shutterbug,' says Dusalt.

This would not surprise me. Embittered by my rejection of his brokered settlement offer, it would be like Roland to take a half-measure, not the cord that links all of the murders to the Russian, just some of them. Spread a little pain, sit back and watch.

We will probably find the missing cord the day before the close of our case when I will have to crawl on my knees to Ingel pleading.

Claude looks at Goya. 'Did you tell him?' he says.

'Not yet.'

I look at them. 'What now?'

It is what Lenore has been waiting to talk to me about. She and Claude have been paring down Adrian's witness list for two days now, searching for the anticipated alibi, the person or persons who could testify to place Iganovich in Canada at the time of the Scofield murders. If we amend to charge his client, he will want this witness available. Even if we don't charge he may use the witness, pour water on our case to erode the factual discrepancies between the murders, and then show that his client was out of town for the last one.

'There's nobody that fits the bill,' she tells me.

We go over the list. Lenore is operating on the theory that any likely witness would be a resident of Canada, someone who saw him up there and who could testify as to the date. The list contains not a single Canadian address.

'What about ticketing agents in this country? Could be a local name who sold him the ticket and would remember him.'

She shakes her head. 'We checked that. And something more,' she says. 'Some weeks ago Claude checked with the airlines. They just got back to him yesterday. The flights out of Capital City to Canada, there are four each day. One of the flight attendants on an Air Canada flight thinks she remembers seeing somebody who looked like Iganovich. From a picture,' she says.

'Well then that's it,' I say.

'The problem is,' says Claude, 'when the lady checked her flight schedule, the particular flight in question left Capital City the day *after* the Scofield murders. She'd been off on maternity leave until that date.'

This sets like molten lead in my veins. A moment of dazed silence. We have been operating from the beginning on the belief that Iganovich could produce an absolute alibi for his whereabouts on the day the Scofields were killed, that he was a thousand miles away. Now, on the opening day of trial, Claude and Lenore are telling me that this assumption may be wrong. Our theory in Scofield is beginning to settle in deep squish, grounded on the touchy-feelie surmises of the shrinks, their prognostications and profiles for the serial mind. The fact that the Russian was available in town at the time of the murders, is, in my book, worth more than a thousand Rorschach tests and psych-evals.

'It may explain,' says Lenore, 'why Chambers was so willing to cop a plea on the Scofield counts. Maybe he knows his client did 'em,' she says.

'Damn it,' I say. I'm up out of my chair, pacing behind the desk. 'Why is this information just coming in now?' I say.

'Took a while to find the flight attendant. She was out of town. Stays in Capital City on a rotating basis only once every three weeks.' Claude's got a list of excuses. 'Besides,' he says, 'she's equivocal. She *thinks* it's him. Not absolutely certain.'

'Still,' I say, 'we should have talked to her sooner.'

'Maybe we should charge him.' Lenore's getting nervous.

I look at Claude. 'What kind of a witness would your flight attendant make?'

'You want me to be honest.'

'Brutally,' I tell him.

'Not solid enough to put on the stand,' he says. 'Chambers would have her for lunch, "maybe it's him, maybe it's not".' He makes a gesture, some body English for '*comme-ci, comme-ça*'.

I'm leaning over the desk, looking down at the two of them.

'You can be sure if we charge him, Adrian will pull another witness from his hat,' I say, 'some ten-time loser who will testify that he put Iganovich on the plane, kissed him on both cheeks and strapped him in his seat two days before the Scofields bought it.' Silence falls on our little group like a dark cloud. Given the evidence, I would rather have Chambers's side of this case at this moment.

'How much leeway will Ingel give to amend?' asks Lenore. She's talking about an amendment to add the Scofield charges against Iganovich.

414

'Maybe to the close of our case in chief. Not beyond that,' I say. 'Maybe not even that far. It would depend on the evidence. We'd have to have something hot.'

'A percipient witness,' she says, 'somebody who saw the Scofields go down, with their own eyes.'

We both look at Claude. He knows what we're thinking. The prime witness in the trees.

'Give me a lead and I'll chase it,' he says.

'What have you got on him so far?'

'The spotting scope. Couldn't trace it to the point of purchase, no usable prints, just one smudged, looked like a thumb,' he says. 'Same result with the climbing gear, too common to trace. According to the information from Rattigan at the Center for Birds of Prey, their best guess is that the witness was a poacher, using an owl to kill peregrine falcons, adults and chicks. He figures this was done so whoever it was could work under cover of darkness, with no noisy gun shots to rouse the neighbors. Why they were killing the birds, Rattigan has no idea. He says he could understand if they were taking 'em alive. The birds, apparently, have some value. In good condition, Rattigan says, a mature peregrine is worth in the neighborhood of fifty thousand.'

'Dollars?' I say.

He nods. 'We're in the wrong business. From the bits and pieces,' he says, 'bones and feathers we found up in the blind and on the ground, whoever was in those trees that night killed a cool half million on the wing.'

But from what Claude is telling me, in terms of our search for a witness, it all adds up to zero.

'Something I want you to check,' I tell Claude. 'Have

one of your guys do a title search, over at the county recorder's office, on the property where the Scofields were killed. I'd like to know who owns it.'

Claude makes a note. 'Why?' he says.

'Just a hunch,' I say. 'Maybe we've been working from the wrong end on this.'

Claude looks at me.

'Maybe we should be working backward from the other end, from the Scofields on the ground back the other way,' I say. 'What do we have there?'

'Mice and pellets used to feed the birds, at least according to Rattigan,' says Claude. 'Reams of working papers, unfortunately destroyed by Jeanette Scofield and Amara. And the travel claim I gave you. That's it. Not much.'

I spin around in my chair, paw through a pile of items on the credenza behind me and come up with a single manilla folder. I put it on the desk and open it. Inside is the travel claim made out for Abbott Scofield, but never signed, and the attached receipts. I pick through these. The hotel bill and restaurant receipts. When Lenore looks at me I'm holding the two torn tickets, the ones reading San Diego Wild Animal Park.

'The zoo?' I say.

She makes a face, like search me.

I pull out the *Triple-A Tour Guide*, something Mario left in the bottom drawer of his desk. I look in the front, under San Diego, for attractions. Nothing. I look under Other Points of Interest.

'San Diego Wild Animal Park – see Escondido.'

I thumb back to the E's. There it is, right under the

Lawrence Welk Resort Theatre.

I read to Lenore and Claude:

San Diego Wild Animal Park embraces eighteen hundred acres about five miles east of I-fifteen, exit Rancho Parkway. More than twenty-five-hundred animals, including elephants, tigers, rhinos, zebras, and giraffes roam over expanses of land that simulate Africa and Asia.

Visitors can view the reserve on a fifty-minute monorail ride or from lookout points along a one-and-three-quarter mile hiking trail. Animal and bird—

I stop in mid-sentence.

— bird shows are presented daily in Nairobi Village . . .

My voice trails off. I look at Claude.

'You want me to get an airline ticket to San Diego?' he says.

Claude is stuck here to testify.

'Henderson, on the next plane out,' I say. Something no doubt more to Denny's liking than copying the reams that comprise James Sloan's criminal history.

Claude Dusalt makes an impressive witness on the stand. Even I am a bit surprised by the bearing he brings to this. Claude has one of those faces, craggy and benign, something aristocratic in that slender, jagged nose, the piercing emerald eyes. He has dressed for the occasion, his best gray pin-stripe three-piece. No power suit for this man. He will let his position as chief of detectives speak for itself.

He may be a little frazzled. It was a rush getting here from my office. Claude wanted to connect with the San Diego PD before Henderson's trip south, a little diplomatic courtesy, and to coordinate in case Denny required assistance. We nearly ran the entire way here to avoid being late.

I lead him through his résumé: thirty years on the force, more than a hundred homicide investigations to his credit, his own estimate. He is here to lay the groundwork for our case.

Behind me, I am competing with the constant hum of human conversation, the undertone of the interpreter in Iganovich's ear, calling the play by play to the defendant.

We take the murders in chronological order, Julie Park and Jonathan Snider first. Claude tells the jury that he was on the scene in less than an hour after the bodies were discovered, that he took charge to seal off the immediate area along the Putah Creek, and personally supervised the collection of physical evidence at the site.

'Did you oversee the taking of any photographs at the scene, by other officers?' I ask.

'I did.'

I move to the counsel table where Goya has these waiting for me. She hands me a file folder. Inside are three separate sets of photographs, one for the judge. I give these to the bailiff to deliver. A second set goes to Chambers, which I drop on his table, and the third I hand to Claude on the witness stand. I take my time allowing

Ingel and Chambers to examine these, waiting for the screaming and gnashing of teeth from Adrian.

These photos are nothing if not inflammatory. Several full body shots of the victims staked out on the ground are likely to leave the jury wishing it had skipped lunch.

Chambers fingers through them, dropping each face down on the table after examining it. But he says nothing. Instead when he's finished he looks at me standing in front of the witness box. The lack of expression in his face forms a veritable green light to go ahead.

This surprises me, but I'm beginning to understand his strategy here. Why bellow about the evidence, the gruesome nature of these crimes, if the premise of your case is that your client did not do them?

The first rule of courtroom combat: don't complain unless it serves your ends. A lot of whining about these photographs, quibbling over the angles, may leave the jury with the impression that Adrian is trying to mitigate unpardonable crimes.

Instead, he will distance the Russian from these acts. He will no doubt shower empathy on the victims' families in his closing argument and administer a sound hiding to the police and prosecution for failing to find the true perpetrator of these horrid deeds.

Claude makes quick work of the photographs, identifying each as having been taken at the scene. I have them marked for identification and make a motion to put them into evidence.

Ingel looks at Chambers.

'No objection?' The judge seems a little incredulous, but Adrian waives him off.

'I'll reserve judgment on the photographs until I have seen them all,' says Ingel. He wants a single motion for the photos in all four murders after he has seen the lot.

We repeat the exercise for the photos of Sharon Collins and Rodney Slate. I note Ingel looking hard at the Collins girl, Acosta's niece, as we go over this shot.

'Is it necessary,' he says, 'that we have such graphic pictures?'

What I had not expected, objections from the bench.

'There were brutal crimes committed here,' I tell him. 'It's appropriate that we do something to document that fact,' I say.

'Still,' he says, 'we should be sensitive to the survivors.' He paws through the photos to find the one of the Collins girl. 'This one,' he says, 'is particularly bad.' Then he looks at me to see if I've noticed. 'And several of these others.' He reaches back into the stack of shots he has already reviewed up on the bench. 'I think some of these we can do without.'

Though it is rarely used, the court has the power, on its own motion, to limit evidence which is highly prejudicial in a case. Ingel cites the section of law here and begins winnowing out my photographs, a little cover for the one shot he really wants to exclude, the naked frontal photo of Sharon Collins. He is shameless in his pandering to the delicate sensibilities of Armando Acosta. The clan of the black robe.

I am objecting from below the bench, but to no avail. With a quick slap of his gavel Ingel overrules my objection, and like that sanitizes the visual image of four grisly murders before this jury. He passes on the balance of the photos and lets them go to the jury.

I look over at Chambers, a Cheshire grin painted across his face. The court has done a good day's work for him, without his even entering the fray.

I take Claude through the details of the crimes. He explains what he saw when he arrived at each of the murder scenes, how the victims were tied with plastic-coated cord to metal stakes driven into the ground, and how a fifth stake was driven through the abdomen of each victim. He steers away from details, like the extrusion marks on the plastic coating. We will leave that for Kay Sellig and hope that we can find the missing piece of insulation before she testifies.

Claude is leading off for other later witnesses: the campus cop and tow-truck operator, who first opened the van and found the evidence, and Sellig, who will hit clean-up for us.

When this is done in detail, I turn my attention to the one last item.

'Lieutenant Dusalt,' I say, 'was there another set of murders, similar in respects to the college students killed here, which you also investigated about this same time?'

'There was,' he says. 'The murder of Abbott Scofield, a member of the university faculty, and his former wife Karen Scofield.'

I cannot afford to leave this for Chambers to take up for the first time in his case in chief. To avoid the similarities of these murders would be to leave the impression with the jury that we have something to hide.

'Lieutenant, can you tell the jury, at the time that the Scofield victims were first discovered, did your

421

investigation initially operate on the theory that these crimes, the Scofield murders, and the four student victims, were part of a series of crimes committed by a common perpetrator?'

'We did. That was our theory, initially,' he says.

'But as your investigation proceeded facts came to light which caused you to alter that theory, is that correct?'

'It is.'

'Objection,' Chambers is up. 'Leading the witness,' he says.

'Maybe if you would place your question in that form,' says Ingel. He sustains the objection.

I rephrase. 'Did you alter your theory as to a single perpetrator in all of these crimes?'

'Yes.'

'And why did you do that?'

'Because certain facts came to light during our investigation which caused us to suspect that this was not the case. That there was more than one killer at work here.'

'Can you tell the jury what those factors were?'

'There were several discrepancies with the Scofield murders that did not square with the others. The age of the victims for one thing. They were older than the college-aged students taken in the first four murders. The method of killing was somewhat different,' he says.

'Also,' he says, 'there was considerable facial disfigurement on one of the Scofield victims, Karen Scofield, a practice that was not followed in the murders of any of the other victims.'

He could reach for more, the blind in the trees, the dead

birds at the site, the inkling that these have something to do with the Scofield crimes. But Claude is conservative. We have decided to stay away from these things for the time being.

'And what did you conclude, based upon these differences?'

'That there was a second killer, working independently, who was responsible for killing the Scofields. A copy-cat killer,' he says. 'Someone who apparently had followed the details of the first four murders sufficiently to mimic them closely, but not precisely.'

'In your years in law enforcement have you ever experienced, or heard of such a so-called copy-cat crime?'

'It's not unheard of,' he says. 'I've never investigated one before, but I know of cases.'

'And at the present time, the officers investigating the Scofield murders, are they continuing to operate on the belief that another killer, not Mr Iganovich, is responsible for the Scofield crimes?'

'They are,' he says, 'unless and until we receive other evidence, other information that may cause us to change our minds.'

Claude and I have carefully gone over this, some middle ground giving us enough wiggle room to charge the Russian if the evidence turns up, if we can find our prime witness. I take my chair, turn Claude over to Chambers.

Adrian is slow, deliberate in his movements toward the witness.

'May I approach?' he says, asking permission of Ingel to walk up to Claude on the stand. Adrian's holding photographs in his hand.

'You may,' says Ingel.

'Lieutenant Dusalt. I'm going to show you some photographs and ask you if you can identify these.' He hands three eight-by-ten glossies to Claude. About the same time Bob Haselid, Adrian's Keenan Counsel, delivers a set to the judge and drops another on me. These are investigative photographs of the Scofield murder scene, subpoenaed from our files by Adrian during discovery. He has everything but pictures of the bird blind, which is still under wraps of Judge Fisher's modified discovery order, at least until we can find the witness.

'Do you recognize these photographs?' says Adrian.

Claude studies them, turns them over to examine the evidence stamp on the back. 'They're taken by our department,' he says.

'The Davenport County Sheriff's Department?'

'Yes.'

'And what do they depict? What are these pictures of?'

'They are various angle shots of the victims, Karen and Abbott Scofield and the murder scene.'

'Did you direct the taking of these photographs?'

'I did.'

'You have the other photographs there, next to you.' Adrian's pointing to the shots I have already put into evidence, what is left of my legion of photographs.

He reaches in and grabs one of these. 'This is a good one,' he says. He holds it up from a distance to show the judge and me. It's a close-up of a hand, a fist clenched in the agonies of death, flesh the color of blued steel. This is blood trapped, coagulated at the extremity by the confines of the cord, tightly coiled around the wrist.

'What is this photograph?'

Claude looks at it, reads the label on the back side. 'That's the right hand of Jonathan Snider.'

'Good. Now look at this photograph.'

Claude takes the second shot from Chambers, again reading the label on the back. He looks at the lawyer.

'Can you identify that photograph, Lieutenant?'

'It's the right hand of the victim Abbott Scofield.'

'Looking at the two photographs side-by-side, can you tell me,' says Adrian, 'is there any difference in the way the rope is tied around the wrist of each of the victims?'

'No, a common loop,' says Claude.

'And the knot used to tie the cord, any difference between the two knots?'

'Not that I'm aware of.'

'Well, you're the investigating officer, if there was a difference in the knots you'd be aware of it, wouldn't you?'

'I suppose.'

'Well, is there a difference?'

'No, it's a common knot. If I were to tie ten knots, I'd probably tie nine like that myself.'

'But there's no difference?' says Adrian, coming back to the point at hand.

'No. There's no difference.'

'Besides the knots and the way the victims were tied off on the ground, was there any difference in the position of the victims on the ground as between the college students and the Scofield victims?'

Claude thinks for a moment. 'No appreciable difference.'

'Was there any difference?'

'No.' A grudging admission.

'The metal stake that was used to kill each of the six victims, the students and the Scofields, was there any difference in the positioning of this stake in the bodies, generally?'

'Objection. The witness is not a medical expert.' I'm up trying to give Claude a little close cover.

'I'm not asking for medical expertise,' says Chambers. He turns on me. 'I assume the witness knows the difference between the head on the human anatomy, and the abdomen. Were all of the stakes driven into the abdomen in generally the same location, at roughly the same angle?'

'The witness may answer,' says Ingel.

Chambers smiles at me, tight, intense.

'Yes.' No more from Claude but the bare essentials.

He takes Claude over the falls on the arrangement of clothing, in an arc over the heads of all six victims, and draws a quick concession that there was no marked difference in the arrangement of these items in the Scofield cases from the others.

Chambers moves away from the stand, a few steps.

'Now, the facial disfigurement,' he says. 'You make a big thing of the facial disfigurement of Karen Scofield.'

'I guess I'm funny that way,' says Claude. 'To me, tearing an eye from the head of a human being is a big thing.'

Ingel looks at him sharply, but says nothing.

'You know what I mean,' says Chambers. 'Is it really that significant in terms of distinguishing one of these killings from the others?'

'According to some people,' says Claude. 'The

psychiatrists and psychologists who study such things.'

'Oh, so then you're relying on the advice of others in this.'

'Yes.'

'So you yourself wouldn't know whether such facial disfigurement is significant, a basis to distinguish these crimes?'

'Not really.'

Adrian seems happy with this.

'And, of course,' he says, 'if the facial disfigurement were incidental to the crime, an unintended consequence of other violence, it might take on less significance, perhaps no significance at all?'

'What do you mean?'

'Isn't it possible that this injury could have happened during the physical altercation prior to death, perhaps when the victim was being initially attacked or restrained, that it was not specifically intended?'

'I don't know.'

'Well, surely, lieutenant, during your years as a law enforcement officer you've seen injuries arising from assaults, physical altercations between people? Haven't you ever seen an injury to the eye occasioned during such an altercation?'

'I suppose,' he says.

'And if a perpetrator of a crime attacked six separate people assaulting each of them, and in one case he just happened to injure an eye, perhaps take an eye out during the altercation, would you attribute any particular significance to that?'

'I don't know.'

'If it was unintended?' he says. 'I mean, if you knew it was unintended, you wouldn't go running off and assume that because of the eye injury, that this crime necessarily was committed by a different perpetrator?'

'Not if I knew it was an unintended injury.'

'Then it would really be insignificant, wouldn't it?'

'Yes. I suppose.'

'Lieutenant Dusalt, do you know whether the loss of Karen Scofield's eye was intentional or unintentional?'

Claude looks at me.

'I'm going to object to that,' I say. 'Calls for medical expertise.'

'No. No,' says Chambers. 'I'm not asking him for any opinion on his part. I want to know whether he has any facts, knows of any information from whatever source, that would inform him as to whether the eye of Karen Schofield was removed intentionally or was the result of some unintentional act?'

'The witness will answer the question,' says Ingel.

'I don't know.'

'So you do not know whether it was the result of an intentional act?'

'No.'

'So you do not know whether it's really significant or not, do you?'

The many faces of pain from Claude on the stand. It is the problem with logic; how it has a way of coming around and biting you in the butt.

'Well?' say Chambers.

'No,' says Claude. 'I don't know for certain whether it's significant.'

'Well, we can disregard that then, can't we?'

Nothing but stone silence and deadly looks from Claude.

Like pulling a set of rear molars, Adrian has dragged him this far.

'Let's talk,' he says, 'about the cord used to tie the victims and the metal stakes. Let's take the cord first,' he says. Adrian looks at me as he says this.

'This is pretty common stuff isn't it? I mean you or I could go out and purchase a similar type of cord in a dozen different stores in this town today if we wanted to, couldn't we?'

'I haven't counted the stores that sell it.'

'But it's not just sold in one store?'

'No.'

'This is what we commonly refer to as clothes-line cord isn't it?'

'I've heard it called that.'

'It's made up of interior filaments and covered with a white plastic sheathing?'

'Yes.

'And the metal tent stakes, these were common metal stakes, L-shaped, with a point at one end; what I would find if I went into a store that sold hiking gear, back-packing equipment?'

'I suppose.'

'Now you testified,' says Adrian, 'that one of the factors that caused you to change your theory that it was a single common murderer who killed all of the victims, including the Scofields, was the fact that different cord and stakes were used in the Scofield case from the other murders?'

'That's correct.'

'How did these differ?'

'They were made by different manufacturers.'

'And you could tell this when you looked at them?'

'No. I was advised by our lab.'

Adrian gives him a questioning look.

'The State Crime Lab,' says Claude.

I could object on grounds of hearsay, but what is coming in here is doing us no harm. It will only serve to reinforce what Sellig will tell the jury later.

'So the cord used in the student murders was all made by the same company, and the same is true about the stakes. Whereas the cord used to tie down the Scofield victims was made by another manufacturer, as were the stakes?'

'That's correct.'

'There was nothing else, no other characteristic other than the point of manufacture that served to distinguish these items one from the other?'

Claude looks at me, a dilemma. He would, of course, like to tell the jury that all of the pieces of cord used in the student murders came from a common length, the balance of which was found in the defendant's van, but he has a problem. Without the missing piece we cannot say this.

I'm out of my chair. 'Your honor, may we approach the bench?'

Ingel waves us on.

Adrian and I huddle with the judge.

Ingel is being scrupulous here. He cannot allow the state to put testimony on the record concerning evidence we may not be able to produce. Adrian, of course knows this, and has struck early to force the issue, to exploit this weakness in our case.

'Your honor, Mr Chambers knows we have not had time to find the missing piece of cord. He knows there is a common link for all of these pieces. He's trying to put the issue before the jury before we can locate it.'

Chambers looks at me. 'You lost the cord,' he says.

I ignore him, appeal to the judge. 'But the witness can't answer the question truthfully,' I say.

Ingel puts a little pressure on Chambers, subtle hints that maybe he could withdraw this line of questioning, reserve it for a later witness, perhaps Sellig.

'It's a fair question,' says Adrian. 'Nothing improper,' he says. 'It is one thing to ask the court to give some leeway, another to ask me to lay down and roll over.'

Ingel looks at me. 'Does your witness have the missing piece of cord?'

'You know he doesn't, your honor.'

'Then the truthful answer to the question is no.' He cuts me off before I can say more, puts an end to the little sidebar. We retreat.

Chambers has the question read to the witness by the court reporter.

Claude sits composed in the box. While we have been talking he has been thinking.

'The answer to your questions is yes,' he says, 'there was another characteristic difference in these items,' he says.

Ingel nearly tears his head off, turning to look at the witness, ready to come out of his chair at the mention of the cord.

'The metal stakes,' says Claude, 'the ones used to kill

the students, were each sharpened to a point, probably on a grinding wheel. The ones used to kill the Scofields were not.'

Adrian looks at him, dead in the eyes.

'I was thinking about the cord,' he says. 'Were there any other differences, other than the common manufacturer, that would distinguish the cord in the student cases, from the Scofield cord?'

Claude bites his lip.

'Answer the question,' says Ingel.

'Not at this time,' he says.

'Yes or no?' says Adrian. 'Where there any other—'

'No.'

'Thank you.'

Chambers moves away from the witness stand, takes a few seconds to regroup, and then comes back at Claude.

'Now, Lieutenant Dusalt, isn't it possible under the circumstances that you describe that a single killer could have murdered all six of the victims in question, the students as well as the Scofields, and simply used different cord and metal stakes for the last two murders, the Scofields?'

'Possible,' he says.

'I mean these items are readily available to anyone who wants to purchase them at a number of stores, are they not?'

'Yes.'

'And if you did purchase them, there's no absolute assurance that they would be of the same manufacture as the original cord and stakes used in the first four murders is there?'

'I suppose not.'

'As long as we're supposing,' says Adrian, 'let's suppose that whoever killed the students discarded his supply of cord and stakes after the second set of murders. Threw them away,' he says, 'maybe dumped them in a trash can, or, better yet, tossed them through an open window of a vehicle in a public garage, some stranger's vehicle to get rid of them,' he says. 'Suppose this had happened. Wouldn't it be necessary for this person to obtain other cord and stakes?'

I'm about to come up and object when Claude answers.

'Unless he had access to the vehicle where they were dumped,' says Claude. 'Then I would think he would go back and get them.'

'Oh, but let's suppose that he didn't have access, to such a vehicle. Then he'd have to get new cord, new stakes wouldn't he?'

'Objection, calls for speculation on the part of the witness.'

'Sustained.'

Claude does not answer. He does not have to. The picture painted by Adrian for the jury is clear, bold and blunt, all the finesse of a crayon wielded by a child. Still it is effective, like any good defense, simple and consistent.

'Lieutenant Dusalt, you talked earlier about the defendant's van, found in the public garage on the university campus. You're aware that at the time the van was discovered by authorities that a rear window on the passenger side of that vehicle was broken, smashed out?'

'I am.'

'During the course of your investigation did you, your

department, or the prosecutor form any theories as to how that window came to be broken?'

It is the problem when you follow a lead, search for evidence and come up empty. This is now pointed out to the jury.

'For a while we thought that perhaps the window had been broken as an act of random vandalism.' Claude does his best to make this sound as if we abandoned this theory. It doesn't work.

'Did you conduct an investigation on the basis of that theory? Did you search for such a vandal?'

'We did.'

'And were you successful in finding that person, the person responsible for breaking the window of the van?'

'No.'

'I have nothing further of this witness,' he says.

From beyond the interpreter I can see a big smile, broken pickets and a lot of yellow to the gums, Andre Iganovich looking my way.

I look over at Lenore, at the sinking feeling written on the wrinkles of her brow. Many more days like this and Adrian will not need much for his case-in-chief. A few carefully crafted lies could break our back.

Chapter Thirty-Three

We are minutes from the start of this morning's session, Lenore and I, busy at counsel table arranging the documents, and items of physical evidence needed for today's witness, Dr Lloyd Tolar, our pathologist. He is outside in the hall, sequestered from the courtroom, going over his notes. We have decided that Lenore will take this witness on the stand. She may possess powers of persuasion and suggestion with this witness, which I lack. At trial you learn to use every advantage.

Lenore is oblivious to the defense lawyers, the interpreter and Andre Iganovich at the other table. She is focused on the task at hand. The only one who pays much attention to us is the Russian, from whom we draw unremitting icy stares. It seems he has not picked up on the proper etiquette for these proceedings, the quiet and polite contempt that passes for professionalism among adversaries in court. He seems not to fathom, why in these moments when we are here alone in the courtroom, his representatives do not cross the gulf between tables and bludgeon us.

The guards are outside in the hall, by the rear entrance, two bulls who look as if they would rather eat iron than pump it.

Claude comes into the empty courtroom and through

the railing. Today he will join us at the counsel table. Under the law of this state each side has a right to designate a chief investigator to join them, somebody who can whisper in your ear, critical little details of the case at opportune times.

This morning he appears agitated, slides into the empty chair next to me and tells me he has some news.

'A couple of items,' he says. This is all done in low tones, under his breath.

First he has checked with the Davenport Police Department. It seems the department subscribes to the *Criminal Law Reporter*, the publication clipped to make the threatening letter sent to my house. He tells me they throw out old editions as they are updated, a ready source for the print used in the note.

'Guess where they keep them, the old editions?' he says.

'Tell me.'

'In the basement at City Hall,' he says. 'The same place our friend Jess Amara burned all of Scofield's old notes.'

Clearly, his suspicions are heightened.

'But that's not all,' he says. Claude is leaning into my ear now so that even Lenore does not hear what comes next.

'The title search,' he says, 'the one you asked for on the property where we found the Scofield bodies. It's not done, but some interesting information.'

The owner, who they have yet to identify, because of what appear to be a series of bogus strawman transfers, was bankrolled by foreign money, he tells me.

'A bank in Tokyo,' says Claude. 'A consortium of Japanese investors.' With this I get heavily arched eyebrows from Claude. Jess Amara's little sideline business, the Asian trading company.

I had not pursued this earlier, but it is a curious point. The bodies of the four students were staked out on public land, open and unfenced. But the Scofields were killed on private property, fenced, if you could call it that, and posted against trespassers. It struck me that perhaps the Scofield killer had used this property because it was familiar. Maybe it was a place where he could feel comfortable, where he knew he would not be disturbed.

Claude asks me what I want to do about all this.

I tell him to finish the title search, to get the results to me as soon as possible.

'Should I put a tail on him?' He's talking about Amara.

'He'd know it in a minute,' I say, 'and lose them in two.'

Claude ponders this for a moment then concludes that I am right. He may not respect the man, but suspects, as do I, that he is competent at his job and would know if he were being followed.

Claude tells me they should have all the information from the title search by the end of the day, first thing in the morning at the latest.

Dr Lloyd Tolar has the portent of a troublesome witness for Adrian. His opinions will be grounded in harder science than the seeming whimsy of the psychiatrists and their theories of criminal profiles. The physician examined the bodies of each of the victims, explored their wounds. Before the missing piece of the cord, I would have gauged Tolar as my next strongest witness behind Sellig. With the turn of events, unless Kay can find the missing cord, he may now be the summit of my case.

This morning, Lenore has him up on the stand. Tall and imposing, piercing blue eyes and a continence like some feted Solon inside the beltway, his eminence, he sits on the stand like the patriarch of medicine.

'Dr Tolar, you are the medical examiner for Davenport County, is that correct?'

'I am.'

'You are also on the teaching faculty of the medical school at the university here in Davenport?'

'That's correct.'

'And what do you teach?'

'Several courses,' he says, 'but I hold the chair in medical pathology and am board certified in forensic pathology.'

All the while he is giving Lenore enchanted looks. Tolar never takes his eyes off of her, the form-fitted blue suit and ruffled blouse, her feline moves below the bench.

Lenore is meeting him with a dark Mediterranean look, a brooding expression that fails to engage his ardent interest.

'Tell the jury,' she says, 'what forensic pathology is.'

Goya moves to the jury railing and leans on a distant corner, out of the way, an effort to take herself out of the picture, to create at least the illusion that the witness is talking to the jury.

'Pathology is the study of human diseases,' says Tolar, 'abnormal changes in body tissues or functions caused by disease.

'Forensic pathology is generally concerned with sudden,

unexpected or violent death,' he says.

'So you teach in the field as well as perform the duties of a forensic pathologist for this county?'

'That's correct.'

'What are your credentials in this field?'

'I've brought a copy of my curriculum vitae,' he says.

He holds this up, a résumé thicker than this city's phone directory.

Tolar has taught at three different medical schools in this country, is board certified in two specialties, is licensed to practice medicine in this state as well as two others, and belongs to a dozen professional societies and associations. Beyond this he has authored volumes of scholarly articles in the field of pathology, the most recent appearing four months ago in the *New England Journal of Medicine*. He is nearly breathless, and three inches higher in his chair when he finishes touting this background. The male ego at work.

Lenore moves smoothly through the common elements of these murders.

Tolar explains that he served as ME responding to the murder sites and performed all of the autopsies, on the four college students as well as the Scofields.

I notice, as we edge toward the details of death, that Kim Park and his wife leave the courtroom. This is apparently too much for them. Two of the other parents stopped coming after the second day of trial, though they now send surrogates, an uncle and a cousin. Only Jess Amara and Jeanette Scofield, of the immediate families, are here in the courtroom at this moment.

'Then, doctor, you personally performed the autopsies

on Julie Park and Jonathan Snider, Sharon Collins and Rodney Slate?'

'That's correct.'

'Can you tell us the date that those autopsies were done?'

He's looking down at something on his lap, I suspect copies of the autopsy reports. He gives Lenore the dates.

'And you also performed the autopsies on Abbott and Karen Scofield?'

'Yes.'

Lenore is moving back toward the counsel table when she thinks of something.

'Probably not significant,' she says, 'but were you acquainted with Dr Scofield?'

'I know that he taught at the university. We may have met a few times at faculty functions. I knew who he was. The university is a big place,' he says, 'forty-six-thousand students, twelve-hundred faculty.'

'On the Scofield post mortems do you recall the date that those were performed?'

He looks down in his lap.

Suddenly Chambers is on his feet. 'If the witness is reading something, we'd like to know what it is.'

'Dr Tolar, are you reading something?' says Lenore. 'Notes?'

'Yes,' he says, 'my notes.' He holds these up above the railing that surrounds the witness box for all to see. 'And a copy of the autopsy report in the Scofield matter.'

'Are these notes that you took yourself, close to the time of the autopsies?'

'Yes, they are.'

'And the autopsy report on the Scofields, is it something that you prepared, at or near the time that you performed the autopsy?'

'It is.'

'And do you have independent recollection of these events, the autopsies, the dates that you performed them?'

'I do.'

'So these documents merely help to refresh your recollection of the events, the details, is that correct?'

'Precisely,' he says.

Lenore looks at Chambers. He sits down.

She repeats her initial question. Tolar says he did the Scofield autopsies both on the same date, July twelfth, this year.

Lenore is moving steadily toward the object of her pursuit, the revelation, not fleshed out in the reports, but attested to here by Tolar, that the Scofields were killed someplace else, a major departure from the Putah Creek MO, something that will cause Adrian major grief in his quest to show that another common killer did them all.

Right now, as I look over, Adrian is busy talking to co-counsel, he and Haselid in heated dialogue, some problem or other. For co-counsel, they seem not to get along. Then anyone working with Chambers is likely to have a difficult time. Haselid is no doubt straining to hold up his own ethical skirts, clear of the mud from Adrian's witnesses hunting. I can imagine that this is no mean feat. The rising chorus of whispers finally overtakes Ingel's concentration.

The judge interrupts the testimony. 'Mr Chambers. I'd like the jury to be able to hear,' he says.

Adrian looks up at him. I sense that there is

441

disagreement between the two lawyers on some matter of strategy with this witness.

'Your honor,' says Chambers, 'we'd like to *voir dire* this witness, as to his qualifications,' he says, 'his expertise.'

Lenore looks at me, a little funny, like what does he want, the dean of Johns Hopkins? This is not some country quack.

Still, Adrian has an absolute right here, to challenge the qualifications of the witness, his professional pedigree. To do this, he is entitled to break into our direct examination and question the witness on this limited issue.

Goya shrugs her shoulders, like good luck, but she doesn't sit down, instead she leans against the jury railing out of the way. This should not take long.

Adrian's out from behind his table.

'Doctor, you say that you performed the autopsies on all of the victims, the four students as well as Abbott and Karen Scofield. Is that correct?'

'Yes.'

'And as to the Scofields, you said that you performed these autopsies on July twelfth. Is that correct?'

A face from the physician. 'Yes.'

I look over at Lenore. She is thinking what I am: what does this have to do with qualifications?

I give her a signal, a little shift with my shoulder, a psychic nudge.

'Your honor, we agreed to *voir dire*, not cross examination. Counsel's not talking about the witness's qualifications.'

Ingel looks down. 'How about it, Mr Chambers?'

'If you'll allow me, your honor, a couple more questions

you will see that this line of inquiry goes directly to this witness's competence to testify on issues before this court.'

Ingel makes a face. 'A couple more questions,' he says 'but make 'em quick, and keep 'em on point.'

'You say the Scofield autopsies were performed on July twelfth, that is correct?'

Tolar looks at the report again. 'That's right.'

Adrian moves toward his counsel table, picks up a couple of documents but keeps his distance from the doctor.

'And you did these, the Scofields?' he says.

I can see a little bead of sweat begin its journey from Tolar's temple down one cheek, but no change of expression.

'I did the Scofield autopsies, that's right,' he says.

'That's because you have a contract with the county, isn't it, to perform all post-mortem examinations referred by law enforcement agencies in this county?'

'That's right.'

'And you are contracted to perform these examinations, these autopsies yourself, isn't that correct?'

'Right.'

'You don't have another licensed physician working with you to service this contract, do you?'

'No.'

'It's just yourself, assisted periodically by some of your students, whom you supervise. Is that correct?' Adrian knows that it is. He has a copy of the county contract for pathology services in his hand.

'That's right.'

'Well then, doctor, can you tell this court how it was

possible for you to have performed the autopsies on Abbott and Karen Scofield on July twelfth of this year, between the hours of oh-eight-hundred and sixteen-hundred, when during that time on that date, you were in Los Angeles speaking before a seminar of the American Medical Association – a seminar on forensic sciences?'

Like the air has left my lungs, I feel light-headed. I know that at this moment I sit at counsel table with the most witless expression painted on my face for the jury to see, but I cannot help myself. I have visions. The last stop in the sieve that is my case is collapsing. We are going down like a colander in dishwater.

'You must have your dates wrong,' says Tolar.

'The date of the autopsy?' says Adrian.

'Objection.' Lenore is faster than I. She is away from the railing, steaming toward the center of the courtroom, a cruiser trying to draw fire, laying down smoke.

'This has nothing to do with the witness's qualifications,' she says. 'He's a physician licensed in this state, qualified to comment and give opinion on the medical reports in this case.'

This ignores, of course, the fact that the witness is halfway to being caught in a dozen lies.

'It has everything to do with his competence to testify as a percipient witness to an autopsy which he did not perform,' says Chambers. 'Which he did not even observe.'

Ingel is giving Tolar sharp looks, the kind reserved for the smell of perjury.

'I'll allow counsel to go on,' he says. 'A few more questions.'

Lenore looks at me, one of those expressions that pleads for fate to intervene, a quick earthquake, the rumble of Mount St Helen's, anything.

'Dr Tolar, isn't it true that on July twelfth, the date of the Scofield autopsy, you were in fact in Los Angeles, three hundred miles away, attending a seminar of the American Medical Association.'

'I attended a seminar,' he says, 'I don't know the date.'

'Well, let me refresh your recollection.' Adrian approaches the witness box. He hands Tolar one of the documents from the counsel table. 'Do you recognize that signature?' Chambers points with his pen. 'Right there.'

Nothing from Tolar, but he brings his eyes up to look at Lenore. It is this expression, the shallow, ineffective attempt to control his panic, the bobbing adam's apple, like an epileptic yo-yo, that for the first time confirms that we are now in deep squish.

'Do you recognize the signature, doctor?'

'It looks like mine,' he says.

'And the date on the form?'

'July twelve,' says Tolar.

'The same date as the Scofield autopsies?'

'Yes.'

'Isn't that the attendance sheet for the seminar in Los Angeles?'

'They must have misdated it,' says Tolar.

'Doctor, I have the tapes of the autopsy performed on Abbott and Karen Scofield,' says Adrian. 'Do you want me to bring them in and play them for the jury? Do you want them to hear the voice, the name of the medical intern who performed these autopsies?' Adrian looks at him, then turns his head to the jury, looking at them square-on for emphasis and effect. Adrian is good at this, maximizing the effect of the blow.

'Your name,' he says, 'your voice, doctor, are notable by their absence from those tapes,' says Chambers.

Silence from the doctor.

'OK,' says Tolar. 'I may have forgotten. I do a lot of autopsies,' he says.

'Forgotten?' says Adrian. 'Forgotten whether you performed an autopsy? You have the report there in your hand. You've read it. You apparently know the details, and now you tell us that you forget that somebody else, one of your students, unlicensed in medicine, unsupervised under the terms of your contract, did this autopsy. That this student,' Adrian makes the word sound like it should have four letters, 'that some student wrote the report. His opinions, his conclusions.' Chambers's voice bellows in the courtroom like an angry god.

Ingel slaps his gavel. 'Enough,' he says. 'We will take a recess. I will have counsel back in my chambers.'

'So what did you know and when did you know it?' Ingel is in my face. I am in the hot seat directly across from him in chambers. Lenore may have taken the witness, but it is my ass in the flames.

'Believe me, your honor, we had no idea. The county's own medical examiner. The man has testified in hundreds of trial, an experienced expert witness. How could we know that he would do such a thing?'

I tell him that we prepped him in detail, went over his testimony carefully, that he never gave any hint, any clue, that someone else might have performed the Scofield autopsies.

'He signed the report,' I say.

'He signs all the reports,' snaps Ingel. 'You could have checked the autopsy tapes,' he says. 'It seems somebody had the presence of mind to do that.' He looks over, the slightest of smiles, a psychic kudos for Adrian.

Chambers sits next to Haselid on the couch in the corner, one leg draped loosely over the other. Strangely he does not seem to be enjoying this as much as I would have thought. He fidgets nervously, like he's uncomfortable to be here. Maybe the bad blood is beginning to sour in his own veins, though I doubt this would stop him producing tainted testimony, if it served an end.

'You're batting a thousand.' Ingel is seething over his desk. 'So far, you've managed to lose a vital piece of evidence, and trotted a lying son-of-a-bitch up onto the stand in my courtroom.'

He ignores that this lying son-of-a-bitch has been there, on a regular and repeated basis before, that the county may now have scores of tainted convictions. When this news gets out, the filing counter at the Court of Appeals will look like a gasoline line during an oil embargo.

'What's in store for us tomorrow?' says Ingel. He's looking at me, intense, unremitting. 'Perhaps doctored evidence?' he says. He leaves me sitting there with nothing that I can say.

Goya jumps in the void. 'The problem goes to the weight,' she says. Lenore means that Tolar's testimony should not be stricken, that the jury should be allowed to hear what he has to say, to weigh it for themselves,

447

considering his misconduct on the bench.

'He is still an expert,' she says. 'He can comment on the autopsy report, his conclusions and opinions from reading the document.'

'Not likely,' says Ingel. 'Not in my court. If he wants to talk about the four kids, that's fine. Unless we find out he didn't do those,' he says. He looks over at Chambers to see if Adrian has any contribution on this point. The lawyer shrugs his shoulders, an expression like maybe he should take the time to look.

'As to the Scofields, you can forget it,' Ingel says.

Adrian unfolds his legs and edges closer to the front of the couch, like maybe he thinks this meeting is over. Then he pipes in.

'Your honor, we'd like to renew our motion,' he says, 'to dismiss the first two counts.' It is like Adrian to seize the advantage in a moment of crisis, to capitalize on Ingel's anger. Though, in his position, seeing the chance for a quick end, I would no doubt do the same.

The judge looks at him: drowning for the moment in his own wrath, he has trouble focusing on the change of subject.

'The lost piece of cord,' says Adrian. 'We'd like to renew our motion at this time to dismiss the first two counts.'

'Not now.' Ingel brushes him off with the back of his hand, too busy chewing on my ass to be bothered with distractions. In a strange way I have been saved by the seething fury that now grips the Prussian, his eyes fixed on me. He dismisses the others, tells me to stay put. I am in for a tongue-lashing from hell.

* * *

'The biggest goddamned owl I ever saw.' This is how Denny Henderson over the telephone describes the great horned owl at the San Diego Wild Animal Park. 'A wing-span like a B-fifty-two,' he says.

It is just after one in the afternoon. I am still smarting from the verbal battery administered by Ingel in our private meeting. He has threatened to bring me up on charges before the state bar, suborning perjury of a witness, notwithstanding that he has no evidence to support this charge, not the slightest inkling that I knew about Tolar's lies. Within an hour, I'm sure that his lecture will be the talk of the courthouse, chewed on by judges and their clerks. Such is the grapevine that grows in these places.

After kicking my ass, the judge adjourned early. I can imagine the phone call he is having with Coconut across the river. Between the two of them, they no doubt are planning my future.

Lenore and I have a meeting with Ingel and Chambers at four, to go over jury instructions. This is a little premature, but Ingel has made it clear that nothing at the end of this trial is going to delay his vacation. Once the jury gets the case they'd better move quickly, or they're in for a trip. I have visions of the panel, flowered leis around their necks, cracking coconuts and fingering poi during deliberations.

Claude is in my office. We are on the speaker phone. Denny has managed to find his way to this place, the Wild Animal Park in San Diego. He has spent the entire morning dogging the bird show, talking to the staff, the

449

trainers at work, before he keyed on one guy. He is now at the San Diego PD.

'He doesn't work there anymore,' he says. 'Used to. His name is Cleo Coltrane,' he tells us. 'They canned him last year. Wanna know why?'

'Tell us,' says Claude. Dusalt is in no mood for twenty questions. He sees his case twirling down the tubes.

'He's got a record, two federal convictions,' says Denny. He reads us a section number from the US Codes which he says comes off a rap sheet on the man Coltrane.

'What the hell's that?' says Claude.

'Violations of the Endangered Species Act,' says Henderson.

'He worked at the park part-time, until the first conviction,' says Denny.

'He killed birds?' I say.

'No. In the two cases they nailed him on, he was caught taking rare birds from the wild, trapping them alive.'

Close enough, I think. All the pieces are falling into place. Scofield had somehow gotten a lead on this guy, and traced him back to San Diego and his place of employment. It is probably not a large fraternity, the people who deal in endangered species.

'Do they know where he is?' I say.

'Sure. Right now he sitting in a cell down the hall.' Denny sounds cocky as hell. I can picture him with his feet on somebody's desk, drinking coffee from a borrowed mug.

'You arrested him?'

This concerns me. We have no legal authority to hold this man. It would take a subpoena issued by a superior court judge, coupled with some unwillingness on the part of the witness to comply, before we could lawfully take him into custody, even as a material witness, for his own protection.

'Didn't have to,' says Denny. 'This guy was made to order,' he says. 'Seems there was an outstanding warrant on a traffic violation. The cops down here are real nice, real cooperative.' What he means is any excuse to roust a necessary witness.

'Have you questioned him?' I ask.

'That's the bad part. He denies knowing anything. The guy'd make a good mason,' says Denny. 'He builds a real solid stone wall. Can't get him to budge.'

I can imagine that with two prior federal convictions, Mr Coltrane is not anxious to volunteer information about more. What he was doing in the blind that night could probably get him accommodations at one of the federal country clubs for at least a few years.

But, right now, I'm more interested in how I'm going to get him transported north, where Claude and I can maybe work our magic on him, a subtle psychic rubber-hose.

I tell Denny to stay put, that I will call him back. I place a call to the District Attorney in San Diego. He is out but I draw his chief deputy. I introduce myself. There's some bowing and scraping here, the deputy extending professional courtesy, unaware that I'm not really elected in this county. I let him live with illusions. I am on my hands and knees over the phone, the desperate suppliant. In five minutes I have walked him through our dilemma. He agrees to help, to serve a witness subpoena on our behalf. He will do it immediately if I can fax him a captioned copy along with a copy of the complaint in our case. I hang up, tell one of the secretaries what to do, and I call Denny back.

'Where's your guy?' I ask him.

'Still cooling his heels down the hall.'

'Can you bring him in there so I can talk to him?'

'Sure.'

There's a lot of noise on the other end, shuffling of feet, doors being opened and closed. Three minutes later the speaker phone is back on and I'm introduced to Cleo Coltrane.

'Mr Coltrane?'

Some dead air, like maybe the guy doesn't recognize his own name.

'Yeah.' A surly voice, standard fare in this trade.

'My name is Paul Madriani, Mr Coltrane. I'm the District Attorney of Davenport County. At the present time a witness subpoena is being received down there in San Diego to be served on you.'

Silence from the other end, some coughing in the background.

'Do you understand what I'm saying?'

'Umm, umm.' I can visualize tight lips, like perhaps I have said the words that will give this man quick amnesia.

'We have reason to believe, Mr Coltrane, that your life may be in danger, because of what you saw along the Putah Creek up here that night. You don't have to answer any questions,' I say. 'But I think you know what I'm talking about.'

Nothing but dead air on the line.

He is not likely to say things on the phone to me, which he would not reveal to Denny and others who are there, who he can see, offering warm smiles and empty promises. This is just as good. Without specific confirmation that this is our prime witness, I need not comply as yet with Judge Fisher's discovery order, to disclose the identity of this witness to Adrian and company. At this point Coltrane is merely a lead, though I can feel in my bones that he is more.

'Are you there?'

'Yeah.' More wary this time.

'I understand that you are being held on an outstanding traffic warrant. That's not a serious charge, as you know,' I say. 'Still, it could cost you some money, maybe some jail time. I'm in a position to help you.' The prosecutor as Good Samaritan.

'I would be willing to talk to the District Attorney down there to request that those charges be dropped, dismissed, if you will voluntarily travel north with my officer, under the subpoena, to talk to me. Now, I can't guarantee that the DA down there will do this, but I think he will. I can get a firm commitment before you leave. Do you understand?'

'Yeah.'

'Now, you don't have to say anything when you get here, just listen,' I say. 'I think you should be aware of what physical danger you face. You are not under arrest. I want to make that clear. We simply want to talk to you. Are you willing to do this?'

'Ah, let me ask ya a question,' he says. 'You gonna put me in jail up there?'

He should worry more about bright lights and sleep deprivation.

'No. We will fly you up here at our expense, a round-trip ticket, and put you up in a hotel.' I don't tell him that he may be batching with Denny and a dozen other cops down the hall. Right now I have only one goal, to get him in my physical clutches. He can watch Jekyll turn to Hyde after he gets here.

'All I want to do is talk to you,' I say, like the spider to the fly.

Silence. He is weighing his options.

'If you don't come voluntarily, we will simply wait until your current problems down there are over and then we will have to serve our subpoena. Then if you don't come, we'll have to arrest you,' I tell him. I don't explain that by that time the ship will have sailed, my case against Andre Iganovich will be history.

'Sounds like I have no choice,' he says.

'You do,' I say. 'You can either come the easy way or the hard way.'

'I guess,' he says, 'I'll come up there.'

'Good,' I say. 'They're gonna put you back in the cell now, just for a few minutes while we make all the arrangements. I look forward to meeting with you.'

'Sure,' he says, his tone dripping with cynicism.

I let him go and Denny is back on the line. I hear the door close, probably behind Coltrane on his way to the cell. Denny's snickering, a high-pitched giggle. 'You should sell shoes,' he says, 'suede loafers.' A lot of cackling from the other cops.

I give Denny a few quick instructions. There's one final

afternoon flight from San Diego to Capital City. Denny's not sure he can make it. If he doesn't, he says it will be tomorrow morning before he can get Coltrane up here for questioning. I tell him to do the best he can, to keep us posted, and then hang up.

'You think it's him?' says Claude.

'Don't you?'

He nods. 'Doesn't even ask why somebody would want to kill him. Isn't that the first thing you'd ask if somebody told you your life was in danger and you didn't know why?'

'You caught that, too,' I say. 'When he gets up here we can test him. There are a few things to play with. Details only the man in the blind would know.'

Claude heads out to make travel arrangements for Henderson and get some sleep. It is sure to be a long night.

As the door closes to my office I am left alone for the first time since arriving at the office this morning, left to consider the options available to me, my back to the wall.

With Tolar imploding on the stand this morning, I have no choice but to play the long odds. I can no longer sit back and finesse the issue of the copy-cat killer. I must know before I go further whether Andre Iganovich is the Scofield murderer. Cleo Coltrane is my last chance to salvage this case, my reputation and, perhaps, my career.

It is a hunch, the longest of shots, but one based on the dissolute nature of Adrian Chambers, that the Russian's Canadian alibi, Adrian's coveted ace which to date he has managed to conceal from us, is cooked up.

I start to believe that I have been wrong from the inception, that there is no copy-cat, that for whatever reason Iganovich used a knife on the Scofields, killed them someplace else and brought them to the river. When I know the truth, I will know the reason. If Cleo Coltrane can identify Iganovich as the killer on the creek that night, then this prime witness will be my poison pill, something I can use to put down Chambers's case, his theory of defense, like a rabid dog.

I pick up the phone to call Nikki at the bed-and-breakfast. The man at the front desk answers.

'Laura Warren,' I say. It is the name we have registered Nikki under.

'Ms Warren has stepped out,' he tells me, 'with her daughter.'

'Where did they go?'

'I don't know. They left several hours ago.'

'Have her call her husband when she gets back,' I tell him. I give him the number, and wonder where Nikki would go, left in a country village with no mall or shops, where they roll in the sidewalks at dusk.

Chapter Thirty-Four

I hear tapping on the glass, my office door, a figure through the translucence on which Mario's name is still stenciled in gold letters, reversed like an image in a mirror.

'Come in.'

A dense expression invades my face as I see who it is.

'You got a minute?' It's Adrian Chambers, a wrinkled suit, collar-button open, the knot on his tie four inches down.

I look at him, wonder what he's doing here. I suppose he can read this thought on my face.

'Dusalt told me you might be here,' he says. 'I ran into him in the parking lot at the PD twenty minutes ago. Headin' someplace.'

Claude's running late for the airport. Denny in a cold sweat caught the afternoon flight. Dusalt should have picked him up, and his surly cargo, at the airport ten minutes ago.

'I'm working on jury instructions,' I tell him. What he should be doing. We have a meeting in an hour.

He rolls his eyes. 'The son-of-a-bitch is obsessive, isn't he?' he says. He's talking about Ingel and his penchant for early jury instructions.

'You got a couple of minutes?' he says. 'I'd like to talk.'

I look at my watch. 'Not much time,' I say. I'm trying to get rid of him.

I am glad that Claude is not bringing Coltrane back here. A chance meeting with Adrian and our case might suddenly take a turn for the worse, though this is hard to imagine. Chambers has the olfactory senses of a blood hound. A meeting with someone, Coltrane, he's not seen before, in the middle of our case and he would smell weighty consequence all over the man.

'It'll just take a second,' he says.

I give him a look of annoyance, as if to say 'if we must'.

'Come in.'

He drops his briefcase, reaches in his pocket and comes out with a pack of cigarettes. He offers me one. I decline. Adrian looks tired and drawn. Out of practice for five years, and older, I think, maybe he's forgotten the sapping mental and physical strain that is a major felony trial. On the nether side of fifty, I am told, you begin to see this as the work of the young, like thirty-year-olds dragging their haunches across Astroturf in the NFL.

I motion to one of the client chairs. He sits.

'What is it?'

'I've been hearing things,' he says. 'Talk.' He lights up. There's the flare of spent tobacco from the tip. He's talking, choppy words, as he strips little pieces of the raw unburnt stuff, using his teeth and one finger, from the tip of his tongue.

'It's a small town. The bar's a tight group, whether here or in Capital City,' he says. There is no real direct eye-contact here. Instead he is looking around the office, at the pictures on the wall, the windows, anything but me. He is a map of simmering indifference, Adrian's image of cool.

'Word is, that you believe I took this case as some kind of vendetta, that it's personal, between you and me.' He is not smiling as he says this, not that I much care.

'I hear that you've been saying that I took this case for one reason, to break your back.' Now he looks at me, for the first time I get the force of full eye-contact.

I have said this to a few people, Claude and Harry, one or two others, intimates who I trusted to keep a confidence. Now I feel like a fool, betrayed by my own predilection to talk, not because my assumption is wrong, but because it is coming back to me in my own words.

I smile at him, nearly laugh. 'Well, Adrian, you gotta admit there's no love lost,' I say.

'We've had our differences,' he says. That he can call five years without a license to practice law 'a difference' is a measure of Adrian's powers of reduction.

'So what do you want?' I say. I'm growing restive with this conversation.

'I thought it was time that we cleared the air,' he says. 'I wanted you to know that for my part this is no vendetta. I did not take this case because you're involved. You're not that important to me. I am not that obsessive.'

'This sounds like a conversation you should be having with your analyst,' I tell him. For Adrian this is a major disrobing of the soul, an unnatural act for the lawyer as renegade.

'Fine,' he says, 'you wanna keep the bad blood flowing, then it's on you, not me. Don't go telling people that I'm engaged in some crusade of vengeance, when it's you who won't let it go.'

This stops me in my tracks for a moment, this man who I despise sitting before me analyzing my thoughts — not because he is doing it, but because he is so right. I will not let it go.

'I took no personal pleasure,' he says, 'in what happened today.' He's talking about the disemboweling of Dr Tolar. 'I did what I had to, advocated for my client. You forget I've been sand-bagged myself.' Adrian is talking about his bout with perjury, the fable-as-evidence that got him disbarred.

Then it hits me, like a thunder bolt. He's putting me in his own shoes. He thinks I knew Tolar would lie when I put him up. He talks, and it becomes clear that this is his basis for *détente*. In Adrian's mind, we now have something in common, his image of me as the fallen angel.

I look at him, about to toss him from the office.

'Ingel threatened to go to the bar, didn't he? Fucking judges,' he says. 'A robe and a pension for life and they forget what it is to scrape for a living.'

Before I can say anything, he's telling me how he found out about Tolar and his failure to perform the Scofield autopsies. Curiosity silences me, bottles my anger for the moment.

'A lotta luck,' he says. 'Another client, a civil matter.' He's smiling at his good fortune.

'The kid works as a lab tech over at the medical school. Word gets around,' he says. 'Tolar's a schmuck. A six-figure income and tenure, he figures the world owes him based on his IQ.'

Adrian looks. No ash tray. He taps the ash on the carpet and steps on it with his foot.

'Once I found out, the evidence was easy to get,' he says. 'How often do you listen to tapes of an autopsy prepping for a case? What lawyer has time? But there were nuggets in there I did not expect.'

It is like Adrian, talking to my placid, painted smile, a discussion of worthless confidences, trading on secrets no longer of value, shopping for a little goodwill.

Then he says: 'I will tell you that the knife wounds, the fact that they died somewhere else, came as a real surprise.'

Adrian's talking about the Scofields. He must have thought an oracle had intervened to send him copies of the Scofield autopsy tapes. These no doubt filled in all the blanks. Cryptic references to 'sharp-edged lacerations at the point of entry wounds', these in the written reports, on tape became stab wounds caused by a knife before introduction of the metal stakes. Naked, unembellished observations in the written report about the limited volume of blood at the scene, on tape seemingly grew conclusions; that the Scofields were killed elsewhere and moved to the creek.

That we finessed some of these findings and conclusions to keep him in the dark is a nuance Adrian can appreciate. 'All's fair,' he says.

'Glad you feel that way. Now, as I've said, I've got some work to do.'

'That's only part of what I came to talk to you about. I'm looking at things. The jury is not exactly what we would have hoped for. From our side, Ingel's *voir dire*,' he's talking about the judge's questioning of prospective jurors, 'left a lot to be desired. And you,' he says, 'your case is flying like some wounded duck.'

'Thank you for the appraisal, but I'll wait for the jury's verdict if you don't mind.'

He puts up a hand and smiles. 'No offense,' he says. 'It's what happens in trials. Things we can't control.'

Given his creative approach to evidence I'm surprised that Adrian would concede the possibility.

'I know,' he says, 'there could be some rocky places for our side from here to the end. The stuff in the van, the broken window – who knows what a jury will make of it all? That's why I'm here. My client is nervous. He's dreaming about death at night.'

He does not make clear whether these visions are of the Russian's own demise or of some bloody bodies on the Putah Creek.

'You understand,' he says, 'that I don't necessarily agree with this. But he wants me to take one more shot, to get the charges reduced.'

I can't help myself. 'You wanna plead?' I am more than a little surprised that, given the state of our case, that he would even broach the subject at this point.

His look at me is almost whimsical.

'Not the same deal, you understand. Your case is not what it was when we started. Major holes in your theory,' he says. 'It's why I'm not sure this is a good idea.'

Then it hits me. This man indeed does have crystal balls. Somehow he knows. Someplace he has heard. The leaks continue. Someone has told him that we have the prime witness. The confirmation. At this moment, Adrian Chambers may not know his name, but in his heart of hearts, he knows that Cleo Coltrane will finger his client for the murder of Abbott and Karen Scofield.

'Why so generous?' I say. 'It would seem to cut against the grain of nature.'

He makes a face, like these things can happen.

'Second degree, terms to run concurrent, fifteen to life,' he says. 'Same deal, we package 'em all. The six,' he says. 'No loose ends.'

'And he'd be out in nine,' I say.

Adrian gestures with one hand, a little swivel at the wrist, like whatever happens.

'It's a certain result for both of us,' he says. 'The judge, I think, will go for it.'

He is probably right, Ingel at this moment is not exactly a well of confidence overflowing with faith in my abilities. With Acosta no doubt heckling him from the wings, the Prussian might do anything at this point to avoid an acquittal, or worse, a dismissal of the case by his own hand, for lack of evidence.

Adrian studies my expression like a rug merchant looking for a sale.

Before I can answer, the phone rings, the back-line, the one not available to the general public.

'A second,' I say, telling Adrian to be patient.

He waves me on with his cigaretted hand, like go ahead.

I reach over and grab the receiver. It's Claude.

'Guess who's looking for you?' he says.

'Yeah?'

'Adrian.'

'I know.'

'He's there. You can't talk?'

'Right. Where are you?' I ask.

'We got a problem,' he says.

'No Denny,' I say. I'm watching what I say in front of Adrian.

'No, he's here all right, with Coltrane.'

I can hear the hum of human traffic and a PA system in the background. Claude's at the airport.

'Problem is Coltrane won't talk to anybody but you. He says he made the deal with you. If you're not here, he wants to see a lawyer.'

This is a major problem for us. If Cleo Coltrane gets legal counsel, the first advice he will receive is to say nothing. It will take a week, maybe a month, to negotiate the ticket with a lawyer, concessions on the federal charges.

I give a deep sigh. Ingel will kill me. Probably issue a bench warrant for my arrest, but I will have to send Lenore in my stead to talk about jury instructions at four o'clock.

'I'll be there,' I tell Claude. 'Tell him I'll be there.' I take down the information from Claude, on the little calendar, the one propped up this way so Chambers can't see. I write 'Coltrane' across from the time. Claude estimates four fifteen. I will have to make myself scarce so Ingel can't find me.

'Where?' I ask Claude.

'Interrogation Room Four, ground floor of the jail,' he says.

I write this down next to Coltrane's name.

'What's Chambers after?' says Claude.

'Not now,' I say. 'We can talk later. See you in a few minutes.'

Claude hangs up.

I look at Adrian again, seated in the chair, seemingly aloof, like he's doing me some favor, indifferent as he plumbs my being for some answer, a sure result against the vagaries of a jury.

'A problem?' he says.

'Nothing I can't handle.'

He smiles.

'No deal,' I tell him.

Suddenly his leg is off the other, beady little slits for eyes.

'Why not? Your case is in the shit can,' he says.

'Like I said, Adrian, I'd rather take my chances with a jury.'

There are a lot of expletives here, Adrian's voice running the range to the soprano. I can see the shadowed forms of secretaries outside my door standing idly, listening to this tirade overflow in my office.

He finishes, his face flushed.

I look at him. 'Nothing personal, Adrian.' This seems to send him ballistic.

'Fine. It's your funeral,' he says. 'See you in court.'

He slams the door going out nearly breaking the glass.

I pick up the phone and hit the intercom button.

Lenore answers after one ring. Before she can say anything I start.

'Listen, I've got a problem. You're gonna have to take the meeting with Ingel and Adrian alone.'

We are standing in a dimly lit little room, not much larger than a closet, Claude and I, looking through a one-way mirror into an interrogation room at the county jail. For

465

the moment it is empty. Denny Henderson is bringing Coltrane up now.

I've told Claude about Adrian's eleventh-hour deal. His suspicious mind is like my own. He believes that Adrian is anxious to cut a quick deal, before this witness can bury his case, place Iganovich at the scene of the Scofield murders and end Chambers's hopes of fixing doubt in the jury's mind. How he got news of the witness neither of us can guess. 'Maybe the man's clairvoyant,' says Claude.

I make a face. With Adrian, one never knows.

Denny taps on the door to our cubicle as he passes by, the signal that Coltrane is here, to keep our voices down.

I am holding the evening paper, the afternoon edition from Capital City. I pulled it from a rack on the way over here. It is already ablaze with unflattering headlines; the debacle with Tolar on the stand. On the front page is a three-column picture, Iganovich a beaming smile, flanked by his two lawyers. This was taken by one enterprising photographer who slipped into the courtroom in the seconds following adjournment, after Ingel left the bench and before the deputies hauled the Russian back to his cell.

Just then the door to the interrogation room opens. A man enters followed by Denny.

'Sit down there,' says Henderson. He points to a chair behind the steel table bolted to the floor, then leaves the room.

Noise, the shuffling of shoes on linoleum over concrete is piped in through the tinny little speaker screwed to the wall above our heads.

Cleo Coltrane has one of those faces that defies estimations of age. He is medium height, a complexion like chewed rawhide and a body to match, wiry and a little bow-legged in worn jeans and cowboy boots. Shots of disheveled dirty blond hair rise from a wild cowlick on the back of his head like the crown on lady liberty..

His shirt is a size too big, with imitation pearl snap buttons and a lot of stitching. It hangs on his upper frame looking like a flag in dead air. For all of the wary voice over the phone, his appearance here, in this bleak room under harsh light, has a certain frontier innocence about it, the artless countenance of the common man.

Seated at the end of a small table, he looks around at nothing in particular, though he glances several times hard-eyed at the mirror where we stand, like he suspects that maybe someone is back here.

A second later, Henderson joins us in the cubicle. Off a hot plane, no shower since yesterday, I am glad that I will not be staying in here with Denny.

'Wish us luck,' I say. Henderson will watch from here keeping notes of anything we might miss. It would not do to have too many people crowding around Coltrane if we want him to talk.

Dusalt and I head out. Seconds, later, we enter the interrogation room.

Coltrane is out of his chair, up on his feet as we enter. He is gangly, some nervous gestures with his hands, like he doesn't know what to do with them. I get a kind of shy smile one might see from a stranger on the Montana prairie.

'Mr Coltrane,' I say. 'I'm Paul Madriani. We spoke on the phone.'

'Oh, yeah,' he says. A guileless grin. He shakes my

hand, a grip like a warmed and raspy vice. But there is no
venom or animus apparent in the man. If he suffers from
anxiety, it dances to the tune of a different drummer, not
the rhythm I was beating to him over the phone.

I introduce Claude. Dusalt gives him his best cop's look,
a death mask of menace, a nod and no handshake.

'Sit down,' I tell him. 'Go ahead. Relax. We just want to
talk for a while. Cup of coffee?' I say.

'Sure.'

'Cream and sugar?'

'Just sugar,' he says.

Claude does the duty, tells the guard outside to relay the
message to bring some coffee.

'You wanna smoke? Go ahead,' I say.

He shakes his head.

Claude and I remain standing, Dusalt with his back
leaning against the wall behind me as I do the talking.

'Mr Coltrane, we've been looking for you for a long
time.'

He points with his finger to his chest, like surely you
don't mean me.

'Yes,' I say. 'You. We didn't know your name. But
we've been looking for you. As I'm sure, by now, you're
aware, we have had a series of murders in this county,
brutal crimes that have taken the lives of four college
students, a distinguished member of the university faculty
and his former wife. We are currently in trial on some of
those charges. And we believe we have the killer.'

He looks at me with sheepish eyes.

'We also believe that you witnessed two of these
murders, or at least saw the bodies being staked out on the

ground, from a blind in the trees along the Putah Creek?'

He's shaking his head. 'No,' he says. 'Not me. Musta been somebody else.'

I look at him, a benign smile, the kind I reserve for Sarah when she tells me the dirty little handprints by the light switch in the kitchen are not hers.

'It's what I told you over the phone,' I say. 'Whoever did this. Whoever committed these murders, particularly the last one, pretty soon, that person is going to know there was a witness. He's going to be looking for you the same way we were. It would be best, a whole lot better for you, if we catch up with him, before he catches up with you.'

I can see Coltrane's adam's apple take a deep bob with this thought. He has been in trouble before, but the expression in his eyes makes me think that this is the deepest it has ever gotten.

'Can I chew?' he says.

I look at him.

He scoots forward in the chair and tugs a little round canister from his hind pants pocket. He looks like he's going to offer me some.

I wave him off with one hand and glance at Claude. He's rolling his eyes as if to say 'we got a real winner here'.

'We know what you were involved in,' I tell him. 'We know about the falcons, we have physical evidence. You might say we've almost become experts on birds of prey in the last few months.'

'That so?' he says. 'What was I involved in?'

'We know,' I say, 'that in the past, you've possessed and trained great horned owls. They tell us, the people who

469

know about such things, that this bird is a natural enemy of the peregrine falcon. A lot of these falcons were killed near the site of the last murder.'

He looks at me but says nothing.

'We've found feathers belonging to a great horned owl in the bird blind. The one up in the trees,' I say.

The first art of interrogation; to make him think we know a lot more than we do.

'We know you have a record,' Claude chimes in. 'Federal violations on which you did time. We are not interested in those,' he says. 'We are interested in murder.'

'I didn't murder nobody,' says Coltrane, calm, collected. He's packing what looks like black tar between his cheek and gum, a wad the size of a walnut.

Claude makes a face, like maybe he doesn't believe him.

'Listen, am I under arrest?' he says.

'No. No. I told you, you're not under arrest.' My biggest fear now is that he will get smart, and either ask to leave or demand to see an attorney if we say no.

'But you think I did some crime?'

I make a face. 'Maybe. We don't enforce the federal law here,' I say. 'That's for the federal government to do. Now, we could help them out, give them some of our evidence, and see what they want to do with it.'

For the first time he chooses to look the other way, not at me.

'There's a lotta horned owls,' he says.

'I wouldn't know,' I tell him. 'All I know is that the folks down in San Diego, the Wild Animal Park; they say you own one. What's his name again?'

He looks at me, but doesn't volunteer.

I look at Claude.

'Harvey,' says Dusalt.

'Harvey.' I pause for a second. 'Like the rabbit.' The people where he worked told us this is how he came up with the name. 'You picked the name?' I say.

He nods.

Harvey is now in the hands of animal control down in San Diego. He was found on property outside of town rented by Coltrane, where he kept two horses, near a trailer in which he lived. The authorities took the animals to protect them while their owner was otherwise detained. In reality, they are waiting for nature to take its course, for the bird to drop a few of its feathers in the cage where they have it confined. They cannot pluck these without a search warrant. But evidence dropped into their hands by the forces of nature; that is something else.

The coffee arrives. Coltrane stirs a little sugar into the cup while we watch him. We pass the time, idle chitchat to put him back on an even keel. I drop the rolled newspaper, which I am still carrying, onto the table in front of him.

'Had time to see the paper today?' I ask him.

He shakes his head. 'Go ahead and read,' I say. 'Lieutenant Dusalt and I have something we have to discuss, outside,' I say. 'We'll be back in a couple of minutes.'

Claude and I step outside and close the door.

'He listens well,' says Claude. 'Problem is he doesn't talk much.'

'A good listener is usually thinking about something else,' I say. 'In this case, I think Mr Coltrane is thinking about the jam he's in.'

Claude and I are doing a quick two-step around the corner to the little observation cubicle where Denny is waiting. We step inside and close the door.

Coltrane's still sitting at the table, reading.

'What's he doing?' says Claude.

'Like he's starved for news,' says Henderson. 'The story at the top of page one.'

'Has he looked at the picture?' I ask.

'He keeps going back to it,' he says. 'A little reading, then back to the picture.'

I see him do this as Denny's talking.

We give him a few minutes. He's searching for the jump on the story, the inside pages. The man should take remedial reading lessons. Sarah could teach him speed. Three times he closes the paper, turns away from the inside pages, to look at the picture on page one, and then goes back to the inside. Finally, we give him enough time. He's out of his chair walking around, stretching his legs.

'Let's not let him get too relaxed,' says Claude. We head back in.

Back inside we have a little more idle chitchat. I tell him about a woman in my office, a good-looker, a lawyer named Lenore.

'Must be nice for you,' he says.

'Ms Goya used to work for the United States Attorney's Office in Southern California.'

He stops smiling, like maybe he's not interested in meeting any of her old friends from the office. It is how progress is made, little threats, some more subtle than others.

He's back in his chair now.

Claude takes the lead this time, a no-frills approach to questioning, like an inquisition on the cheap.

'You can stash the cowboy homilies act,' says Dusalt. 'I lost interest when Will Rogers died.'

Their eyes lock on each other. Coltrane doesn't appear particularly concerned.

'We got your spotting scope.' Claude is leaning across the table now into Cleo's face. 'The one you left behind up in the blind, remember? We've been running traces on it,' he says. 'Not very many made like that. Pretty expensive,' he says, 'for a cheap fuck, like you.'

If this is getting to him it doesn't show.

Claude raises his voice a notch, a few more expletives. Then he comes back down to a more normal tone.

'Tight jeans you got there,' he says. 'A good lush.'

Coltrane looks at him, not certain whether he should be offended.

'Ever see what people in prison for a few years can do to loosen up a pair of tight buns like that?' says Claude. 'They're real adept at it. And they seem to enjoy their work.'

Coltrane chews on the lump in his cheek, unmoved, like they'd have to catch him first.

'Six people are dead and you're busy covering for their killer. You can jack these good people around,' says Claude, looking at me, 'but I'll see to it that your ass is put in the federal slammer so fast you won't believe it,' he says. 'Now I wanna know what you saw, and I wanna know it now.'

Coltrane looks down at the newspaper, something to

divert his eyes from Claude, a silent variation on the word 'no'.

Dusalt sweeps the paper off the table with the back of his hand, sending it sailing halfway across the room.

Coltrane stiffens, pushes back his chair, away from Claude as far as he can get, rigid like a head-case subjected to shock therapy. He can't be sure how far Claude will go. His eyes come to me again, a sign that we have bonded. He would much rather talk to me than Claude. With me he gets coffee with sugar.

'The scope,' says Claude, 'we got a fingerprint off the scope.' This is a lie of misdirection. We did get a print, smudged and unusable.

'We're waiting for yours to be sent up by wire now,' he says. In fact, this can be done instantaneously by computer link now, a fact that Coltrane probably doesn't know, and intended to make him sweat.

Claude tells him if he cuts a deal now before we match the prints it will go easier, we will help him with the federal violations, put in a good word that he cooperated.

This does not seem to move the man much. He shows the kind of confidence that grows when you know you wore gloves. I have suspected from the beginning that with only a single smudged thumbprint on the scope that maybe this belongs to the evidence tech, the one sent up to flop around on the perch the day I first met Claude.

Dusalt tries a few more pitches, variations on the common theme. Each of them fails to move Coltrane. Dusalt's powers of persuasion exhausted, Coltrane has taken Claude's worse punch and is still psychologically on his feet.

Claude gives me a little glance, like maybe he should get a rubber hose. We take a break. Coltrane wants to hit the head. We send him with a guard.

Outside in the hall we cluster near an open window at the fire escape for some fresh air, Denny, Dusalt and I.

I've tried to reach Nikki up in Coloma three times in the last two hours. She has still not returned. I am beginning to get worried.

'Any ideas?' I ask Claude.

He is rung out.

The sun is down much earlier these days. I can see dusk closing on the horizon, through the wire mesh. One would wonder what good the fire escape would be, sealed off like this.

I look at my watch, a quarter-to seven. Lenore should be deep into it with Ingel and Chambers by now, trench warfare over terms of the jury charge, in Ingel's chambers at the courthouse. With the details to cover, this could go on until well after nine.

'What do you want to do?' says Claude. He wants to know how late I want to go.

'A while longer,' I say. 'Then we'll give it a rest. Put him up in a hotel and go at it tomorrow, after court,' I say.

'Sooner or later,' says Claude, 'he's gonna want it to stop. Ask to go free or to see a lawyer.'

'I'll show him a lawyer,' I say. 'Somebody at the US Justice Department.' The message is clear. Cleo Coltrane is not leaving this town unless he tells us what he knows.

In the distance, I hear the click of heels on terrazzo, coming this way. A second later Betty, one of the senior secretaries from the office, comes wheeling around the corner.

'Mr Madriani. We've been looking all over for you.'

'What is it?'

'Judge Ingel's called from the courthouse. He was quite insistent, wanted to know why you weren't at the meeting. He was very angry,' she says. This is how Betty describes the Prussian.

I can imagine. 'How did you find me?' I say. I have specifically avoided telling anyone where I was. I had a feeling this would happen.

'It wasn't easy,' she says. A little exasperation. 'He wanted to talk to a lawyer. The judge,' she says.

'Let me guess?' I say. 'Roland.'

She nods. 'He took the call, and a lot of abuse from the judge.' She says this, like I should be grateful to Roland.

'What did Overroy tell him?'

'He looked in your office, saw the note and told the judge you were over here meeting with someone named Coltrane.'

Mental expletives fill my brain. Ingel will no doubt repeat this to Chambers while venting his spleen in his office. Adrian is not stupid. I have missed a command performance at the courthouse to talk to somebody at the county jail. My missing witness. Adrian will be ranting about Fisher's discovery order, my failure to disclose that we now have our prime witness. I can feel another hiding coming from the judge, and Adrian helping me off with my shirt. After my having shafted his settlement offer, he will no doubt take glee in this one.

I'm shaking my head, wishing I were up with Nikki at

this moment, breathing mountain air, anywhere but here.

'They did seem angry,' says Betty.

'They?'

'Mr Chambers called five minutes ago, a few minutes after the judge. He said the bailiff and clerk had left to go home, but that the courtroom door would be left open for you.'

I raise an eyebrow. Adrian's taking charge. He is probably walking all over Lenore by now, jamming instructions down her throat. If I don't get there soon, he'll be wearing Ingel's black robes.

'They expect you to be there,' she says.

'Wonderful.' I roll my eyes, thank Betty and tell her to go home. Why kill the messenger?

'Get him back in here,' I tell Claude. I'm talking about Coltrane. 'Pull him off the john if you have to.'

One more shot then I'm going to have to go over to the court. Maybe I can bring them a present, a little hard evidence identifying the Scofield killer. It may be my only chance to mollify the Prussian.

Inside, Coltrane looks at me, like it must be my turn again.

'Cleo. Can I call you Cleo?' I ask.

He nods.

I'm holding a large manilla folder in my hand as I approach him. From this I pull an eight-by-ten color glossy photo and slide it on the table in front of Coltrane.

'Do you know this woman?' I say.

He looks hard, at the dead head of Karen Scofield, then swallows. The brown hues of congealed blood and the empty eye-socket stare back at him from the table.

He shakes his head.

'You didn't know her, but you've seen her before, haven't you, Cleo? On the creek that night?'

'No,' he says. 'I've never seen her.'

'These marks.' I point with a finger to her brow and cheek. 'You know how they were made, don't you, Cleo?'

He shakes his head.

It is something that has burdened this case from the beginning, the profile experts and their theories of facial disfigurement, the violence to Karen Scofield's face, the missing eye. It had troubled me for weeks, until yesterday when it finally struck me in the quiet of my office, in the dead of evening, working alone, the pincer marks, the deep wounds on the brow and cheek of Karen Scofield.

'Let me tell you how they happened,' I say. 'They were made by the talons of a large bird,' I tell him. 'A bird of prey. They were made by your bird, Cleo. They were made by Harvey.'

He's shaking his head, his eyes closed, all the motions of denial, but not a word is passing from his lips.

This morning I had Claude wire a copy of this photo to William Rattigan at the World Center for Birds of Prey. He has told me what none of the shrinks or pathologists could: that Karen Scofield's eye was not removed by the killer at all, but was gouged from her head by the razor-sharp talons of a giant bird of prey.

I give him a moment, the photo lying on the table before him.

'It's been a long day.' I soften my voice. 'And I'm getting a little tired. So I'm going to tell you what's going to happen to you. And you can believe that this is gospel.'

There is no sense in drawing this out any longer.

'Have you ever heard,' I say, 'of DNA?'

'I've heard of it,' he says.

'It has to do with genetics,' I tell him. 'Chromosomes, the basic building blocks of life that make each of us different. You have different chromosomes than I do, different from Lieutenant Dusalt here.'

Coltrane looks at Claude and, I think, is pleased by this thought.

'Your chromosomes are specific to you,' I say, 'and they can be traced from hair and blood — even your saliva,' I tell him.

He stops chewing for the moment. Dense thoughts. Did he spit up in the perch? From the look in his eye, he cannot be sure.

'With a little of your saliva, and a drop of your blood we would be able to determine whether these each came from you, to the exclusion of nearly everyone else on earth,' I say.

As I say this I am reaching into my pant pocket.

He looks at me wondering, I think, whether I'm about to produce something sharp, a needle for blood.

Instead, when my hand comes out it's holding a single small feather, delicate and gossamer under the florid lights, which I pinch from its point between finger and thumb, and twirl in a slow revolution.

'Cleo, we can get the blood later,' I say, 'because Harvey has chromosomes too.'

From the look in his eye one can tell that my words, the soft drama of the quill, something from a pigeon in the plaza on my way over here, has struck a deep responsive

chord with Cleo, like the impact of a laser-guided bomb —
he and Harvey are trapped: birds of a feather.

He is swallowing a lot of air now. Looks to me, then to
Claude.

'You can do that?' he says. He's talking about DNA.

'We can do that,' I say. 'And, if we have to, you are
going down for the hard fall.' There's an edge to my voice
now. I'm tired of screwing around.

His adam's apple is going up and down, dunking like a
doughnut, his eyes making the rounds in this room, to
Claude, then back to me.

'The minimum, they tell me, for what you've done is
three years,' I say. 'The parole board will not look kindly
on the fact that you refused to help us catch a killer.

'Cleo,' I lean down into his face, 'you can believe me
when I tell you that if you don't help us, you will do more
than three years.' My tone carries the authority of Yahweh
carving the Commandments on tablets of stone.

He looks big round eyes at me. A time for silent
thought. Seconds go by as Coltrane weighs this. He is
teetering on the verge. His jaw slacks a little.

Just then the door behind me opens. I turn.

It's Denny Henderson.

If looks could kill, Henderson would need the services of
an undertaker at this moment.

Coltrane's trance is broken, the momentum stopped.

I look back to Henderson. 'What the hell is it?'

'I thought you'd want to see this,' he says. He hands me
a slip of paper. I look at it. A name or other written on
what looks like the torn corner of yellow page from a
phone book.

'What's this?'

'The name of the property owner. Along the Putah Creek,' he says. 'Where the doer did the Scofields.'

I look down at the ragged-edged little corner in my hand, the note handed to me by Denny.

The cold acid of alarm spreads through me an instant before full comprehension. It was there before me all the time. I can feel the blood drain from my face, settle like lead in the pit of my stomach, more fear here than anger. I look up at Claude.

'What is it?' he says.

I crumple the note in my hand, reach over and grab Coltrane by the collar of his shirt. It is pure adrenaline that hoists him out of the chair, throws him with his back against the table. A pained expression as the corner catches a kidney, the small of his back.

'Tell me about the man on the creek,' I say. 'Now.' I make this single word sound as if it has a dozen W's.

Coltrane is bug-eyed. This is a whole new side of me he has never seen.

Claude and Denny are on me from behind grabbing my arms, trying to keep them from Cleo's throat. It is the thing about an adrenaline rush. It would take an army at this moment.

Cleo is gasping struggling with his hands. Nodding like if I'll let him, he'll talk.

'OK,' he says. 'Get offa me. I'll tell you. Tell . . .' he says. Cleo's face is flushed. His body shaking as I finally loosen my grip.

Self-conscious, I straighten his collar a little, pat the front of his shirt, help him back down into his seat. Claude

481

and Denny slowly ease their grip on me, but stay close, in case I should suffer a relapse.

I move around them, pick up the newspaper, which Claude scattered to the floor earlier in our session. I lay this on the table before Coltrane, front page up and slap my palm hard on the picture.

'Now identify the man you saw on the Putah Creek that night,' I say, 'the one with the two bodies on the ground?'

He flinches once, then stops. He looks up at me one last time, the futile thought written in his eyes that maybe in this last moment I will lift this cup from his lips. He sees the answer carved in my unremitting gaze as I fix my eyes on the picture before him.

Then in the most deliberate of moves, quick and sure, Cleo Coltrane points with a gnarled outstretched index finger, to a single image, a face burned into the newsprint on the table before him.

In this instant of revelation wild thoughts flood my mind, images of flashing metal stakes driven through soft flesh, the hellish visage that was the end of Abbott and Karen Scofield — the night they were murdered by Adrian Chambers.

Chapter Thirty-Five

As the three of us cross the city plaza there is but a single thought running through our minds. It is repeated on our tongues in all the myriad forms that make up nervous banter; whether Adrian Chambers has any idea that we know.

'Maybe Ingel didn't say anything.' This is Claude's happy thought for the day. He is hoping that maybe the judge has kept his mouth shut, not carped and complained after calling my office that I was meeting with someone named Coltrane at the jail. Claude knows, as I do, that Coltrane's name could be the password to violence.

We are jogging across the square, around the fountain. Denny is falling behind.

If Ingel kept quiet, the three of them may still be sitting there, idly arguing about the sophistry of jury instructions.

'How would Chambers recognize Coltrane's name?' says Denny.

Henderson's still running a half-step behind, literally and figuratively.

'Who do you think hired Cleo?' My words come out in little half-breaths.

'Chambers?' says Denny.

'Right.'

It was Henderson's little scrap of paper, the note

scribbled on the corner torn from the yellow pages, that gave me the answer. The owner of the property along the Putah Creek, where the Scofields were found, was A.C. Associates, Adrian's firm, his little empire of limited partnerships. It was on the business card Chambers gave me that first day, when I ran into him with Harry by the jail in Capital City.

Coltrane has already told us that he was hired over the phone, paid in cash through the mail, that he never met his employer on the Putah Creek job, did not know his name. Like star-crossed lovers, their paths met not by design, but chance, the happenstance that is a single gravel access road on isolated land near a river, a road which each man used for his own purposes.

As we race up the courthouse steps my mind is on Lenore. I try to calm myself with assurances that Adrian is, after all, a lawyer. There would be no purpose to more violence. But then I am dealing with Adrian Chambers. And he has already killed twice.

Claude placed two phone calls before we left the jail; the first to Ingel's courtroom, an attempt to warn the judge. There was no answer. This is not unusual after hours. The second call went to the County SWAT unit. It will be a while before they can assemble, maybe a half hour. The guys who make it up come from all ends of the county.

When I reach the front door to the courthouse I find it is locked. I shade the glass with one hand. A dim light is on back near the county clerk's office but no guard, no marshal on duty. Or maybe he's busy making his rounds.

'Come on.' I'm down the steps heading for the garage in the back. The door in the basement, the one leading to the library, will be open, the lawyer's entrance for after-hours research.

By this time Henderson is falling out badly, a half-block behind us by the time we reach the rear of the building and the underground. I don't break stride, but am through the door inside and heading down the hall for the freight elevator, Claude right on my heals.

We get inside. I look. No sign of Henderson. We can't wait. I push the button for the fourth floor and the heavy grated door comes down.

A minute later, Claude and I are outside the large double doors to Department Four. The courtroom is pitch dark, but through the tall slots in these doors, bullet-proof acrylic, I can see lights on in the back, at the clerk's station near the judge's chambers. I listen for voices, but with three inches of oak and steel between me and the inner room, I can hear nothing.

I reach up and tug on the heavy handle of the door, just a little. It opens an inch. Still no sound.

'They probably have the door to the judge's office closed,' I tell him.

'Probably,' says Claude. He is fishing at the bottom of his pant leg for something wrapped around his ankle. He hands this to me. It's a small semi-automatic pistol, something he carries for back-up.

'The safety's here,' he says. He whispers.

I shake my head, hand it back to him.

'I'd shoot myself.'

He makes a face, like he doesn't believe this.

'Or somebody else,' I say.

'That's the idea,' he says.

'No. You keep it. Besides, we don't even know if there's anything wrong in there.'

Claude looks at me, something he reserves for fools.

'Listen, they're expecting me. The phone call. Why don't I just do the lawyerly thing: go inside and take a look. You can watch from the door. If I hear voices talking back there, when I get up past the bench, I'll give you the high sign. You come inside and wait in the hall back there.' I point to a place lost in shadows just below the bench.

'Then what?' he say.

'I'll go into the chambers and listen. Believe me,' I say, 'you can hear what's going on back there without going inside. I've done it.'

'Yeah.' He's waiting for the rest of the plan.

'If they're talking about jury instructions I'll waltz in, give the judge some happy horse-shit. Tell him that fire trucks are downstairs, that there's smoke coming out of the basement and they want everybody out of the building. When they're filing out you take Chambers,' I say.

He looks at me, an old-world expression, sagging wrinkles around the nose, like this sounds as good as anything.

He drops the little pistol in his jacket pocket and comes up with something bigger from under his coat. A blue steel thing with a muzzle like field artillery.

Crouching outside, I reach up and pull the door handle again. I rise to full height and step inside, into the dark little foyer, a four-by-four section that opens onto the courtroom itself. I check the door behind me to make sure that it has not somehow locked on me. I look into the courtroom. The bench at the far end is completely lost in shadows. Only vague outlines and the brass tips on the flags can be seen. There's not a sign of movement. A steady shaft of bright light comes from the hall off to the left of the bench, leading to the clerk's station in the back. Still no sound of voices, only the constant hum of central air, little grids in the high ceiling.

I move silently down the center aisle toward the railing in the bar. When I get to this I use two fingers like flesh forceps to open one side of the swinging gate, step through and quietly close it behind me.

I turn and look. I can see Claude watching me through the slot in the door, the glint of lights, in the hall outside, off the barrel of his gun. Someone else has joined him, a hulking figure several feet behind, hovering over his shoulder. Denny, no doubt, catching up.

I've now made my way along the side of the bench, to the steps leading to the judge's chair. In the dim light I can see the two spear-tipped flags and the judge's chair, which, at this moment, has its high back swung around facing me. I try to focus my eyes in the darkness.

There is something bizarre about the chair, a curious deformity like some tumor growing on its back side. The leather in the center, up high, has taken on a large distorted bulge.

I have seen enough to know that it is time for Claude to join me here in this room. I turn to the door, to the twin slots at the rear of the room. I look. Claude is gone. There's no one there. I watch for a moment to see if maybe he's just moved away, perhaps shifted position. Nothing.

My eyes are back on the chair, high on the bench. I look. No shadows of movement, no voices from back stage.

Quietly, I slip off my loafers and in stocking feet climb the wooden steps of the bench. At the top, I reach out with one hand, toward the back of the chair, and give it a gentle push.

Like a carousel it spins slowly on its axis, until, in the half-light from behind I make out the form of a man, his features distorted, propped in the chair. His eyes are wide ovals, jaw hanging, mouth open. Dressed as he is in black robes, the river of blood merges with dark cloth and disappears into the folds. Imbedded in his chest is one of the sharpened metal stakes taken from the evidence cart down in the courtroom. Derek Ingel isn't going on vacation.

I am frozen in place, my feet seemingly cemented to the floor. I cannot move. For several seconds I remain, my gaze glued on the Prussian's dead face.

Then a noise. I'm drawn from this reverie of horror by the slightest of sounds, a metallic click at the back of the room. I look. No one. Claude is still not there. Then it settles on me. The noise. Someone has pushed the button that locks the doors from the inside.

Department Four is the criminal court in this building. It has the highest level of security of any courtroom, bullet-proof doors that can be electronically locked from two points; the bailiff's station below the bench, and back stage, another switch near the clerk's desk. Once locked, these doors can only be opened with the bailiff's key inserted in the lock on the door.

I am now sealed in this room, with death. My mind turns to Lenore, somewhere in the back. I am pining for Claude's little pistol, outside in the hall. Where the hell is he?

In the darkness off the bench, with blood dripping down the steps, I have the presence of mind, or, perhaps, just the foolishness of habit, to find my shoes.

I make my way to the evidence cart a few feet away. I look. Of the metal stakes, pointed pieces of angle-iron fourteen-inches long used in the student murders, four had been ground to a razor-sharp tip before being driven through the bodies of the victims. Only two now remain on the cart. Another is accounted for in Ingel. I grab one that remains.

Hugging the wall I move down the corridor toward the private offices in the back. Here the light is bright, the full intensity, a ceiling of fluorescence. At the door to the clerk's station I edge one eye around the frame and peek in. The room is empty. On the desk I see a ring of keys, large like something a jailer might use. There are four keys on this. My guess is that one of these will open the security locks on the front door. So carefully laid are these, in the center of the desk, I look, and wonder, if this is not bait.

To the left is the door to the judge's chambers, it is half open, the lights inside are on. But from this angle I cannot see in. I would have to move inside, beyond the clerk's desk, for a clear line of sight.

To my right, and a little behind me is another door, closed this time. This leads to the private corridor that links the back of each courtroom on this floor. Out of bounds to the general public, this corridor is for use by the judges and their staffs, to communicate and pass papers. It is sealed by steel doors at each end of the building where the corridor would otherwise join the public hallways outside. The judges only, I am told, know the little button combination that allows them to enter this sanctum, the private corridor, beyond the steel doors.

I study the clerk's station, places where Adrian could conceal himself if he is waiting for me. There are few. My guess is he is in the judge's chambers.

I make my way around the door, the metal stake in my right hand, pointed up and out should I need it.

Now I can see through the doorway into Ingel's office, the desk and the chair behind it.

Then I see her, in the distance, Lenore lying on the couch, against the far wall of the office, her back to me. She appears to be bound hand and foot, white cord. Adrian has made good use of our evidence cart. Everything he needed.

As I pass the clerk's desk my peripheral vision goes wide, taking in both sides of the room, low behind the desk, in the corner beyond the filing cabinet, anywhere Adrian could hide. I grab the keys off the desk. Despite my efforts these jingle a bit as I pick them up.

I edge my way toward Ingel's office. I check the opening, the crack by the hinges. There's no one behind the door. As I do this I hold the stake poised in one hand in case he should rush. By now Adrian surely knows I am here. I would think he might have made his way out the back door, a clean escape, except for the click of the lock out front. Someone had to do that.

He is here, and I know it. To say this is anything but personal is, at this point, to ignore reality. I was right about one thing. His words this afternoon in my office, his final futile attempt at settlement, was indeed a conversation more appropriate to Adrian's analyst.

Through the door I can see Lenore more clearly now. I cannot tell from this distance whether there is the rise of respiration from her body. I look for blood. Then I see it. A mass, congealed hues of brown, on the white of her blouse, near her neck. I stand, still, staring at this. With the volume of blood I can see, she cannot be alive. I stand there stunned, angry, feeling the rise of hormones that drove me to rip Coltrane from his chair in the little room at the jail. I can feel it in my fists, out to the tips of my ears, like molten lead driving rage to the top of my head. I stare at the motionless body of Lenore Goya coiled on the couch, her knees drawn up, her arms twisted and tied behind her.

If Adrian Chambers is in this room, only one of us will come out alive.

I push the door slowly, allowing it to swing open. As it makes its slow arc toward the wall, I step through the threshold.

Nothing.

The room is empty. I look. The leg-well to the desk. It is the only place anyone could hide. The door hits the stop on the wall with a gentle thud, and suddenly there's movement. On the couch, Lenore has struggled to turn her head. Quickly I move toward the couch, reach her body and feel the warmth of her arm, the confirmation that she is still alive. Then I see it. The cloth with dried blood. Chambers has used the bloody towel from the evidence cart, the one found in the Russian's van, as a gag on Lenore. I untie this from the back of her head.

'Where he is?' I say.

Breathless. 'I don't know,' she gasps. 'He went off

behind me somewhere and I lost him, the sound of his footsteps out the door.'

I fight with the cord on her wrists. It takes several seconds to undo. She rolls over and sits up. Together we work on the piece around her ankles. This is heavily knotted. Finally I use the scissors from the desk to cut it. So much for evidence.

'Let's get the hell out of here.' I pull her to her feet and we head out the door, past the clerk's station and into the corridor leading to the courtroom. My eyes have trouble with the darkness, adjusting from the bright light.

I hear noise. Someone is pulling on the doors out front, jiggling the lock. Then I see him, through the tall slits in the front door, Denny Henderson, and another cop dressed in black garb, an automatic rifle in his hand. They are both pulling on the door, rattling, as much as you can, a three-hundred-pound door in its frame.

Denny is waving at me, pounding on the door, motioning, trying to yell, to say something through the door. I cup a hand to my ear and shrug, a sign that I cannot make this out.

I take one step, and in my left shoulder, a searing pain, heat like sheet lightning, spreads through my upper body. I am dazed, look down and there, protruding from my suit coat, is three inches of cold steel, angle-iron honed to a fine point. My knees buckle, as nausea racks my body. With my gaze still on it I watch this point disappear, backed out through my body like a boat leaving its berth.

I turn and lash blindly behind me. I miss. But I see Chambers, his dark silhouette back-lit in the corridor behind us.

'Run,' I tell Lenore. I am between her and Adrian. But he pushes me aside, and Lenore isn't fast enough. He grabs her by one arm, raises the stake.

Before he can bring it down, I lash at his face with my own steel, tearing the flesh in a jagged arc on his cheek. I hear him cry out. Instead of stabbing Lenore he punches her square in the jaw with his fist, sending her reeling backward against the bench.

He turns on me, strikes out and punches a hole in the wall near my head. He pulls it out and brings the metal down on my head like a club, sending me to the floor. I lie there in a heap, crawling, clawing at the wall to get up, the feel of warm liquid oozing from my body, my feet sliding in my own blood.

Adrian turns on Lenore. She is back up, climbing the stairs to the bench, her only avenue of escape. She is to the top step when he grabs her ankle, rips the spiked heel from her foot and sends her careening into the flag. She kicks him with her other foot, and Adrian is driven backward within range. Getting dizzy, going dark, I lash out at his leg, ripping through his pants, driving the point feebly into one thigh. It is not deep, but it gets his attention.

Chambers turns on me. Rising up over me, a hulking, brooding figure, his eyes glazed like some rabid dog. The blue serge of his suit-coat lifting with the rise of his shoulders, he brings the metal stake, gripped in both hands, arms extended over his head, the vision of a high priest doing sacrifice to the gods. And suddenly through the seam of his shirt, like the shaft of an arrow, the razor-sharp tip of a spear, comes six inches through the wall of Adrian's chest. He is suspended in air, frozen in place by

493

the shock. In an instant there is the gurgling sound of blood as it rushes to fill his lungs, an expression almost quizzical, as if somehow he has seen beyond the veil. Then Adrian Chambers collapses in a heap on the floor. The partially furled flag, wrapped around its stanchion, protrudes from his back.

Beyond him, her feet spread for leverage, blood on her chin, Lenore stands, looking down at the lifeless body on the floor. In the white of her eyes, the cut of her jaw, is not the slightest hint of pity or remorse. The vision burned in my mind as my eyes go dark, is of fire and wind, sparks on the air, the burnished image of some ancient goddess of war.

Epilogue

It has now been five months. The Russian's case has ended in a mistrial, poisoned by the devious plotting and double dealing of his lawyer.

Today my shoulder is a brooding ache. I have learned with this thing there are good days and bad, a lasting memento from Adrian Chambers. The doctors tell me that in time, and with therapy, I will fully recover.

Through all of this, the last months of pain, Nikki has been good to me, putting aside the danger that I had unwittingly exposed us to. It seems the reason I could not reach her by phone that afternoon up at the inn in Coloma was that Nikki had carted Sarah off to a movie in Placerville. She had hired a cab for the twenty-mile drive there and back. I now have the bill to prove it. In the weeks after coming home from the hospital she spent time nursing me; draining my wound and packing it. We have talked long hours, about life and the value of love. In the end, I have learned that among all of her qualities, Nikki is, first and foremost, forgiving. Today she waits for me in the car outside.

As I pass through the reception area Jane Rhodes greets me with a smile. The mood in this place seems lighter. I suspect that this is in part a reflection of my own delight in passing the torch to another. I am no longer district attorney of Davenport County.

As I head for the door a man in white overalls is busy scraping gold letters from the mottled glass, the final vestige of Mario falling in chips to the floor.

I will need some help packing boxes to the car. For this, a couple of the people from the office have offered.

Bits and pieces of the story are still coming out. I was three days in the hospital before I discovered what happened to Claude outside in the hall that night. He ended up with a massive concussion and was out on leave for nearly a month. The impression left on his head matched precisely a heavy marble gavel, a paperweight from Ingel's desk. It seems the image I saw in the shadows that night crouching behind Claude was not Denny Henderson at all, but Adrian.

The police have traced his steps from the few items dropped in his travels. After killing Ingel, and tying Lenore on the couch, Chambers exited the courtroom by way of the locked corridor in the rear. By propping open a door that led to the main hall, he was able to come up on Claude from behind and return to the courtroom by the same route. The rest is history.

To this scheme, Adrian brought his tireless efforts at settlement. It is why he demanded a package deal to plead his client out to all six of the murders — the Scofields as well as the four students. It was a quick dirty deal designed to solve all his problems. When his first attempt at settlement failed, he resorted to other less genteel methods: the photo of Sarah at play and the note threatening her life. The cops have now traced the water mark on the note paper used for this pasted-up missive to similar sheets found in Adrian's desk drawer. They have also found old editions of the *Criminal Law Reporter*, the print type used in part of that message.

It seems that Adrian had managed to place himself heavily in debt, real estate deals gone sour in his time before reinstatement to the practice of law. This was the result of declining land values and Adrian's high living. I have now seen the offices of A.C. Associates in a high rise across the river in Capital City, more tony than the Pope's private john and with nearly as much art. He had spawned a considerable Ponzi scheme to keep himself afloat, stealing money from later investors to pay off early claims. The bean counters, a small army of accountants, are now trying to determine the full extent of these losses and the ensuing fraud. My own count stopped when they reached twelve-million dollars. I am told that figure may well double before they are finished.

Adrian was under the gun. With time running out, he had a deal from developers on the Putah Creek property, a sale with the potential to pull himself even. And then came the birds.

The peregrine falcons first came to Adrian's attention when a farmer in the area noticed them killing his pigeons. The man complained to Chambers, this according to the man's wife who is now a grieving widow. A month after talking to Chambers the farmer died in an accident, mysteriously crushed under the tires of his tractor and cut to ribbons by the sharp metal discs it was pulling through a field. The cops are now looking into this accident. We will probably never know whether Adrian had a hand in it.

A few questions and a little research and Adrian soon

understood the peril. Any development of the property would require an environmental impact report, a document longer than the Bible, and filled nearly as much with the story of creation. When government agencies discovered from this report the presence of endangered species on the land, Adrian could kiss his sale goodbye. The state would force a major set-aside of the land as natural habitat, severely restricting its development and value. Unable to account for vast sums of money stolen from investors Chambers would soon be looking at another stint in prison, this one much longer than the last.

Enter Cleo Coltrane. When the Scofields discovered the birds were dying in droves, the victims of some natural predator, they were closing in on Cleo and would soon be onto Adrian. Chambers, strapped for cash, struggling to capitalize on the only thing he owned of any value, was forced to rid himself of another problem. What were two more deaths, more or less? By now he had the cover of the Putah Creek murders. There was no need for further unexplained accidents like the one that claimed the farmer.

I should have seen it, the endless attempts to fold the Scofield murders into the plea bargain for the others. Chambers was confident that once a court passed judgement on Andre Iganovich for all of the murders the cops would close the case on the Scofields. No jury would ever convict another suspect, when the Russian was already doing time on these crimes. To Adrian, it was not a question of justice, but efficiency. He knew that Iganovich had done the first four. He was a natural for the Scofields.

As for the Russian, police in Oregon and Orange County have now closed the loop in the unsolved murders there.

They have found physical evidence linking Iganovich to those killings. With time and the help of the State Department we have discovered a long and lurid trail of littered bodies and unsolved murders, at least twelve in three countries in Eastern Europe, places where Andre Iganovich traveled and lived while he was waiting for his US visa. That this man could so easily become a security guard says reams about this industry.

We have also found the missing piece of cord in our own case. Like serendipity, it turned up, still in its marked plastic evidence bag, lying in plain view on the floor in the library nearly at the site where the photographers were processing it the day it disappeared. It was found the day after Chambers drove the stake through my shoulder. It seems Roland was seen doing research at the stacks in this room moments before a secretary found the missing evidence. I am told he has a meeting with one of Claude's deputies this afternoon to explain this.

Adrian, it seems, during that last meeting in my office, told the truth about one thing. His part in the Putah Creek cases was not personal, not part of some vendetta. As Jacoby in Canada had noted, Adrian had nearly beat the defendant to the northern border, so anxious was he to pick up the defense of the Putah Creek killer, whoever he was, when he was caught. He must have scoured the papers, kept his ear to the ground with the cops for days. He was no glory hunter seeking publicity. Adrian had other fish to fry. He had a desperate need to steer the defense to his own ends.

I take the last framed item from the wall, a certificate of appreciation from the doyens of this county, something hatched by Emil, a sheepish last gesture, and hung on the wall in my absence. As I drop this in the box, a shadow fills the door behind me. I turn. It is Lenore Goya.

In the battle for our lives, it seems that Lenore has captured the public's imagination. Papers throughout the state, across the country, have covered the story. It seems justice was never served so well in Derek Ingel's court as it was by Lenore at the point of pike.

In a face-saving gesture, the county fathers have offered her Mario's old job. But I think they are too late. Lenore is now awash in better offers, including one from the governor to fill Derek Ingel's old seat on the bench. Somehow I cannot see Lenore in black robes. I think she would find this tedious.

'How are you?' she says.

'Good. You?' The bruise on her cheek and chin have long since healed.

She smiles like it couldn't be better.

'You just missed Roland,' she says. 'He got the better boxes.'

Overroy has been cleaning out his office as well. He has taken the hint and grabbed the golden handshake, retired while he can. Roland's stocks have been dipping lately with the powers that be in this county. Besides the unanswered questions about the missing evidence, his part in Adrian's settlement offers are raising eyebrows in high places, the fact that he was so badly and so publicly duped. That the county leaders would have taken the deals, groveled in the dirt for them, is now forgotten.

'Who's doing Iganovich?' I say.

'The Attorney General,' she tells me. 'We thought it was

best.' According to Lenore, she will not be around long enough to handle this prosecution.

She tells me that among the things she is looking at is a supervising position with the prosecutor's office in Capital County.

'Maybe I will see you,' she says, 'across the gulf between counsel tables sometime.'

'Maybe.' I smile. I put out my good hand to shake. She steps close, near my ear, and plants a single soft kiss at the nape of my neck, a squeeze, and she is out the door, down the hall.

As I make my way down the gray stone steps toward the plaza and the car beyond, I can see the Sierras a hundred miles away, their outline sharp against an imposing and impossibly blue sky. On the air is a bitter chill as December approaches.

I turn and look toward the west, toward the plowed fields where dust devils form on the zephyr. In the distance I can hear a whistle, faint and shrill, a sound primordial, like the screech of a wild raptor on the wing. I stop, turn, and listen. It is a tone crystalline, clear and unquestionable. It is the wind screaming through the Canyons of the Putah Creek.